Varina

ALSO BY CHARLES FRAZIER

Nightwoods

Thirteen Moons

Cold Mountain

Varina

A Novel

Charles Frazier

An Imprint of HarperCollinsPublishers

VARINA. Copyright © 2018 by 3 Crows Corporation. All rights reserved. Printed in the United States of America. No part of this book may be used or reproduced in any manner whatsoever without written permission except in the case of brief quotations embodied in critical articles and reviews. For information address HarperCollins Publishers, 195 Broadway, New York, NY 10007.

HarperCollins books may be purchased for educational, business, or sales promotional use. For information please e-mail the Special Markets Department at SPsales@harpercollins.com.

FIRST HARPERLUXE EDITION

ISBN: 978-0-06-240601-9

HarperLuxe™ is a trademark of HarperCollins Publishers.

Library of Congress Cataloging-in-Publication Data is available upon request.

18 19 20 21 22 ID/LSC 10 9 8 7 6 5 4 3 2 1

For Nancy Olson
1941–2016

Varina

First Sunday

The Blue Book

Saratoga Springs, 1906

If he is the boy in the blue book, where to start? He can't expect to recognize her after four decades, and he certainly doesn't expect her to recognize him. The last time they saw each other he would have been no more than six.

Firm memory of childhood eludes him until about eight years old, and before that it's mostly whispers of sound and images flashing like photographs. A dead boy lying on the ground, a grand house, a tall woman with black hair and a soothing voice.

A year ago, walking down a street in Albany, he heard a dozen syllables of someone singing "Alouette" through an open second-story window. The song twitched a strong nerve of memory from the deep past—a ribbon of road stretching forward, a swath of starry sky visible between tops of pine trees, a thin paring of moon, a brown-eyed mother hugging him close and pointing out the patterns of constellations, telling their names and stories. Entrained with those hazy memories came a surging feeling something like love.

First Sunday of August, early afternoon, James Blake walks through the heavy front doors of The Retreat carrying a marbled journal and a book bound in dark blue nubby cloth, bristling with torn newspaper place-marks. He wears his best gray suit, a club-collar shirt bleached perfect white, a striped black-and-gray waistcoat, a coral silk tie knotted loose. Three steps inside the door he removes his hat—a new boater—and walks purposefully to the front desk like he belongs there. The desk clerk looks him over and then pauses long enough to make sure Blake becomes aware that his shade of skin has been noted. The clerk—maybe fifty, thinning hair combed straight back, teeth marks intact—finally says, May I help?

Blake hands him a small envelope. Says, Could you deliver this to a guest? Mrs. Davis.

The clerk pats the envelope down onto his desktop without taking his eyes off Blake. He turns his palms up and says, She's expecting you?

—I doubt it.

—You're not here to interview her for some publication?

—No.

The clerk rings for a bellboy and then says, You might be more comfortable waiting outside. Turn left and there are benches. We'll notify you if Mrs. Davis is available.

—Here in front of the fireplace will be better. So I'll see her when she arrives.

The lobby of The Retreat matches every detail of public rooms in tasteful modern resort hotels designed in the Arts & Crafts style—Limbert furniture, Voysey rugs, Roycroft lighting. Except, faint and far down one of the long corridors, James thinks he hears someone scream.

He shifts uncomfortably in the strict angles of an oak and leather settle facing the massive stone hearth. Broad windows and French doors look out across a green and blue landscape—fields, woods, valleys, hills. A few people scattered around the great room read books and flap papers from Boston and New York and Philadelphia. In a corner, a tousled young blond woman sits bowed in concentration at the piano trying to play "Sunflower Slow Drag." It keeps getting away from her until she gives up and plays it half-speed.

Over the big hearth, a sentiment cuts deep into the massive keystone, lettered like a Gothic forgery on a famous man's grave marker. It reads WHAT LIES BEHIND US AND WHAT LIES BEFORE US ARE TINY MATTERS COMPARED TO WHAT LIES WITHIN US. ~ EMERSON.

James stands and traces each letter with his forefinger, as if writing the sentence for the first time. It works to establish balance—like perfectly equal pinches of sand in each cup of a set of scales—and then he draws a deep breath and blows it all away. He touches each junction of that grand E and tries to reckon what state of guilt and dread about time past and time future Emerson proposed to comfort.

James sits again and thumbs through his blue book until he comes to a chapter toward the end that he has read and reread and underscored in pencil to the point that every line appears profound. Margins congest with question marks and checks and exclamations. If he's right and the boy described in the book is him, this is all he knows of his origin. No living relatives, recently a widower, no links to the past until six months ago when a title on a bookstore shelf drew him—*First Days Among the Contrabands*. He had reached for it thinking it would be a mystery.

An elderly woman enters the great room from one of the corridors. She resembles later photographs of Queen Victoria—much taller, but with similar gravity and tiredness dragging from behind. Same hairstyle. Her dress a sheen of eggplant. She walks by the piano player and palms the small of her back to correct her posture.

James doesn't recognize the woman, but he makes an assumption and stands.

At the chair beside the settle, V stops and says, Mister Blake? I don't recollect your name, but I'm curious.

—Yes, ma'am. Thank you for seeing me. I'll be brief. What I wanted to speak to you about concerns the war.

She had started to sit, but now remains standing.

—Please. I'm long since exhausted with that insane war and don't need to re-dream a nightmare.

V turns to walk away but then turns back, angry. She tells him how uninterested she is in the past, except people keep trying to clench its fist around her throat. Whatever old story he needs to tell, she's heard a thousand of them—all the tales of waste and loss. And heaps of guilt too, for failing to find a bloodless way to end ownership of people—choosing a bloodbath instead. Since then, South and North have been busy constructing new memories and new histories, fictions fighting to become facts.

—If you haven't noticed, she says, we're a furious nation, and war drums beat in our chest. Our leaders proclaim better than they negotiate. The only bright spot is, the right side won. My only advice is to be where you are now—don't look back. Otherwise, good luck and good day, sir.

—My apologies, Mrs. Davis. I saw in the Albany paper that you were here, and I wanted to see you and ask about this book and about the children. I don't recall all the names, but I remember Joe.

—What could you possibly know about Joe?

—I remember sitting with the others, trying to wake him up.

V pauses and then says, I don't know what you're after, but I've dealt with confidence artists for decades. Or else you're just recalling the funeral. Thousands attended.

—Not the funeral. I remember him lying on the pavement. And I remember him that night, upstairs. So still on the big bed with candles and flowers all around. He'd gotten smaller and very white, and his lips were a color I'd never seen. He looked like himself, but changed. It terrified me. I remember people coming and going late in the night. Every lamp and candle in the house lit and all the windows open and curtains blowing out.

V says, I'm lost.

She works at remembrance, looks harder at Blake's broad forehead, brown skin, curling hair graying at the temples. She tries to cast back four decades to the war. When she arrived, who was there in that huddle of people on the cobbles beneath the balcony of the house stupidly called the Confederate White House?

She had been down by the river making an appearance at a celebration—a mass of people welcoming a boatload of men and women returned through prisoner exchange from Northern detention. A brass band played "Home, Sweet Home." The kind of event where V's every move was watched side-eyed by those hoping for a gossip-worthy moment. She stood near her carriage and chatted with Mary Chesnut, who had been circulating through the crowd birdlike in her brief, bright attentions—snapping up bits of language, facial expressions, details of wardrobe, witty comments, stupid comments, moments of human grace and foolishness—every detail of observation to be entered into her journal at day's end.

A man, a stranger, walked up and stood close like trying to eavesdrop on their conversation. Then low and breathy, looking oddly off to the side, he said, Little Joe has gotten himself killed.

V turned to her driver, and trying not to scream said, Get me home now.

A fast rattling dash—the driver popping his whip above the horses, their shoes striking sparks off the cobbles—and she found a crowd arranged in concentric arcs below the balcony at the high end of the house. Gawkers stood at the fringes, then a few neighbors and their servants, and then Ellen and the children ringed tight around Joe. He had recently turned five and had fallen twenty feet and lay completely broken on the cobblestones. Ellen bent over trying to hug the live children and to ease them away from Joe. But when she saw V, Ellen collapsed onto her knees and buried her face in her hands.

The children—Maggie and Jeffy and Billy and Jimmie—sat on the pavers saying Joe's name and trying to nudge him out of sleep. Joe lay on his side, and his limbs formed strange angles. A puddle of blood the size of a saucer thickened beneath his head. Maggie held Joe's hand and the three boys kept touching his shoulder. Joe and Jimmie were close to the same age and often shared clothes.

—Missus V, Ellen said. He was playing and fell between the railings. Must have.

With her face all scared and confused, Ellen looked so young.

V remembers trying to kneel beside Joe, how pregnant she was at the time, how heavy and awkward. She remembers looking at him and touching his face and feeling numb. And then slipping sideways from her knees onto her hip, a hard jolt against the cobbles. And then the new baby began flailing inside her.

V holds her right hand out toward James Blake, pushes at him like gesturing *Stop*. Then she presses her left palm against the fingertips and bends the right hand back toward her wrist. She presses hard, but ninety degrees is her limit.

She says, Show me.

James Blake bends his hand until the fingernails almost fold against the top of his forearm. An inch gap.

—Lately, I can't go all the way back, he says.

—You're Jimmie Limber.

—I don't remember that name, but I believe the Jimmie in this book is me.

He holds out the bristling blue book.

V won't take it. She reaches two fingers and touches the inside of his wrist as if testing his pulse, his materiality.

—I don't need a book to know you, she says. I've believed for years that all my boys were long gone, crossed over. I've thought of it as my diminishing circle of boys pinching to a black point, like the period at the end of a sentence. But here you are.

—I hardly know anything about my life then, he says.

—Sit down and I'll tell you what I remember.

Fugitive

1865

Things fell apart slowly before they fell apart fast. Late March—Friday night before Richmond burned—V fled the false White House and the capital city. That afternoon she and Ellen Barnes packed in a rush, knowing they might never be back. Billy and Jimmie went back and forth from V to Ellen, touching their arms or hips for reassurance. Ellen always kept her hair parted in the middle and oiled, pulled back tight against her scalp. But that day, long curling strands escaped, and she kept sweeping them back from her face.

—Don't fret, Jimmie Limber, Ellen said. Just a little jaunt south. Billy's been on one before, so ask him about it.

Ellen took an apple out of her apron pocket and held it in both hands to get the boys' attention. Then with hardly any effort or sense of motion, she snapped it perfectly in half and handed the pieces to the boys, and they went on their way laughing and studying the apple halves as if the secret to Ellen's magic might reveal itself.

When the packing was done, Jeff took V aside and gave her a departure present. A purse pistol, slight and pretty, almost an art object suited for display in a museum.

—Do you know how to load and aim and fire? he said.

—I didn't grow up in Mississippi for nothing.

He said that if the country fell, she should take the children to Florida and find passage to Havana. Then he told V to keep the little pistol with her at all times, and if Federals tried to violate her, she should shoot herself. Or if she couldn't do that, at least fire it in their direction to make them kill her.

He gave her what money he could gather, and she had been building her own hoard of running money from selling furnishings and china and crystal. Her carriage horses had been seized for the army, and Jeff said he couldn't allow her to take food beyond a few pounds of flour and grits and dried beans. Wouldn't be fair. But he didn't at all believe Richmond or the nation faced doom. This alarm would be like all the others. Two weeks from now, she would be coming back. General Lee would find a way.

Except V knew it wasn't like the other alarms because he hadn't gifted her a suicide pistol before now.

A couple of weeks later, vagrants traveled southwest down springtime Carolina roads, red mud and pale leaves on the poplar trees only big as the tip of your little finger, a green haze at the tree line. They fled like a band of Gypsies—a ragged little caravan of saddle horses and wagons with hay and horse feed and a sort of kitchen wagon and another for baggage. Two left-over battlefield ambulances for those not a-saddle. The band comprised a white woman, a black woman, five children, and a dwindling supply of white men—which V called Noah's animals, because as soon as they realized the war was truly lost, they began departing two by two.

Worse yet, the core of fugitives traveled under rumors of possible Federal warrants—including hanging charges, such as treason. If true, the price on their heads would be a mighty cash fortune in a time of destitution.

V had with her a scant bit of hard money and a bale or two of government bills. A single chicken, though, cost fistfuls of that nearly worthless paper. One-dollar bills—with her friend Clement Clay's graven image on the front—were useless except to wad by the dozens and light cookfires.

Wherever the fugitives traveled, rumor followed that their little caravan comprised the Treasure Train, the last hoard of gold and silver from the Rebel treasury, wagons heaped with millions in bullion instead of weary, scared children threatening to go croupy and feverish at every moment.

In delusion, bounty hunters surely rode hard behind, faces dark in the shadows of deep hat brims, daylight striking nothing but jawbones and chin grizzle, dirty necks, and once-white shirt collars banded with extrusions of their own amber grease. Below that, wool coats black as skillets, muddy tall boots, and bay horses foaming yellow sweat.

And yet, all along the way, the woods-edge spooled by lined with redbud blooming pink and dogwood blooming white, bearing the holy cross of the Savior. The nail wounds hammered into his hands printed on every blossom, reproduced in their billions through the

Southern woods and even blooming hopefully in the yards of homes recently burned down to middens of shiny black charcoal by the Northern army.

Their immediate goal? Escape to La Florida. Tierra Florida. Floridaland. A raw frontier with Spanish moss hanging ghostly and parasitic from granddaddy live oaks. Black mold streaked gray limestone Spanish forts from parapet to white sandy ground and algae-green moat. Alligators, bears, lions, and purple snakes nine feet long roamed the swamps and jungles and scrublands. But only a scattering of people, and those reputed to be more unreasonably lawless and corrupt and predatory than anything you'd find even deep in Texas.

V penciled a thought on the endpaper of *Northanger Abbey*: *The frontier is no place for those who can't afford to run.*

A rough stretch of road woke the children. The ambulance banged through rocks the size of pullets and potholes deep enough with red water to drown a shoat. The driver sawed at the reins, working the tired mules, trying to avoid the worst of it. But there was only so much he could do. All day the wagon went heading and pitching from mudhole to mudhole, and now the night gathered so dark you hardly saw the mules' haunches right in front of you.

Over the course of the journey, the children had become like weary sailors long out on the foam, able to sleep through all but the stormiest nights. But now, back in the bed of the ambulance, inside the cave of dirty beige canvas arched tight over bent oak-splint ribs, the children rose from their patchwork quilts all together and began fretting and whimpering. Winnie, though, just cried in place, being not even a year old. Every one of them suddenly needed easement.

V had been riding along for two hours, jostling dreamlike under a tiny taste of opium, feeling like the world had collapsed to rubble around her—an appropriate feeling, because it had. Not the best of times to have to budget medicine, though she had enough Dover's powder to last a month if she took it by the conservative directions on the label. But doing it that way, V felt little effect, not nearly enough to faze her anxiety, to loosen the tight knot her diaphragm and stomach had become even when she slept. So in reality she had only a few days' supply left. Which would have been desperate but for the promise of seeing Mary Chesnut in Abbeville, South Carolina, soon. Maybe more a hope than a promise, but surely even in an apocalypse one wonderful fact must remain unchanged, that Mary flitted through the world with morphine aplenty and used it freely to combat whatever new hell life threw at her day by day. Influenza, nausea, deaths of loved ones, loneliness, headache, boredom. She claimed it also aided in the reading of novels.

And Mary would probably have something much better than Dover's, which was not even close to pharmaceutical quality. She called Dover's housewife morphine, because along with opium it contained fillers like ipecacuanha, which in doses too small to cause vomiting induces sweating, thought to be good for women of fiery temperament. And also potassium sulfate, a laxative. So, a little morphine, a good sweat, and a bowel movement—the cure for everything that ails you.

V waited, but after a time the children still hadn't settled. Fretting became weeping. Jeffy called her name. And when you're called you answer, one way or the other.

V chose yes. She climbed back to the bed and knelt and lit a little brass-and-glass candle lantern. She gathered the children to her, hugging each of them separately and then all together like an enormous stinky bouquet. She held baby Winnie in her lap and began teaching the older children a song—"Alouette"—making a game of it, finding a correspondence between the bucking and swaying of the ambulance and the tub-thumping, foot-stomping rhythm of the song, the accumulating repetitions. *Je te plumerai la tête.*

They played along happily for a while, in a language they didn't know, singing a song of cheerful butchery. All the details of plucking the lovely skylark's feathers and pulling off its beak and legs and wings, its eyes and head. They all shuffled a little dance for a few moments of joy, shouting not words but sounds, their thin shoulders and angular arms and grubby hands expressing music in jagged movement.

And then they fell back happy and breathing hard onto the quilts. Soon they fell asleep, except for Jimmie Limber, who lay looking up at candle shadows on the arched canvas. He murmured the doubled three-beat chorus, dropping high to low—*Et la tête, et la tête, et les yeux, et les yeux.* Over and over.

V kissed him and said, Sleep, little man.

—Got us a long night? Jimmie Limber said.

—We need it to be, V said. If we're going to make it to Havana.

She kissed his forehead again and blew out the candle and climbed back over the wagon seat.

Delrey shifted the reins to one hand and lifted his hat and set it on his lap and scratched the crown of his head. He said, We really going all night?

—Camp at dawn off in the woods. Become noctur-
nal as possums, V said.

==

—**Wait, James** Blake says. Before you go on, I'm all
confused about children. I'm not even imagining this
right, much less remembering.

—Seven often seemed like a lot of children to me
too, V says.

—But I just remember Joe. And a boy around my
age and possibly an older girl.

—You're conflating Jeffy and Billy. You would have
been halfway between them in age. And Maggie was
enough older she would have largely ignored you little
boys. But this will be easier on paper. Hand me your
notebook and pencil.

James turns to a fresh page and watches as V draws
dashes and lines and writes dates and names and
place-names. She numbers the names and strikes lines
through two of them and swoops a pair of brackets and
hands back the open notebook.

—Attend, please, she says. And then she talks James
through the list of names, explaining a family tree.
Says, Samuel there, top of the chart, number one? Born
in Washington?

—Yes. With a line through his name.

—Meaning that when your memory begins, Samuel had been gone ten years. You never knew him. And then Maggie? Number two, also born in Washington. Not struck through, so still alive when your memory begins and the only one alive now. Then Jeffy, born in Washington with no line through his name, so still alive when you came to us, though he passed away more than twenty-five years ago of yellow fever. And now skip down to number six, Billy—also born in Washington and with no line, though he died in Memphis a few years after the war. Diphtheria. Now go back to numbers four and five. Four is Joe, born in Washington, and you're there bracketed with him because you two were the same age. I have Richmond after your name with a question mark, because I assume that's where you were born but don't know for sure. And then finally, number seven, Winnie. Born in Richmond right after Joe died and a crying lap-baby when we ran south. She died nearly eight years ago.

V says, The point I'm making is that Joe's death is your memory's year zero—spring, 1864.

She reaches to his notebook and turns back the page corner and says, For future reference.

—Did one of the boys have black hair and a cannon? James asks.

—See, conflation. Billy was the only child with my dark hair, and Jeffy had a miniature cannon. The neighbors complained constantly that he was knocking chunks of plaster off their walls. It shot iron balls the size of big marbles, and the black powder sent up clouds of smoke. It's a wonder he didn't kill somebody. Ellen was the only one who could wrangle the bunch of you, which is why I moved her up from the kitchen to the nursery. She could soothe you all to sleep at night and reason with you during the day to make you mind her. At most, if she was really mad, she would snatch you boys up by your collars onto your tiptoes to get your attention. I was never good at reasoning with children. I either gave hugs and kisses or impatient swats on the bottom.

James looks at his notebook and says, It's so much, seeing all these names together. So many children passed on. I can't imagine.

—Yes, I still sometimes hear those slow drumbeats, V says. Dirt clods striking small coffin lids muffled with straw. I grieved, of course. When Samuel died, I couldn't leave the house for two or three months. But he was my first and only child then. Later, deaths fell differently because living children need so much from you, and you can't indulge yourself and collapse into grief. Like with Joe—six weeks later Winnie arrived.

Unless you're just worthless, you get up and put on the black dress and keep going.

V tells James how her children had died, scattered from New York to Washington to Richmond to Memphis, but had been dug up and dragged to Richmond to surround their father's monument. And of course Jeff was dug up from New Orleans and dragged there too. Even before he was dead yet, businessmen and governments from Georgia and Kentucky and Mississippi and Virginia tried to offer her deals for possession of the body when the time came. Bragging how they would make his obelisk taller and grander than Washington's. And that's not even factoring the money they offered her to seal the deal. But a hill in Hollywood Cemetery above the James River seemed the right choice, seasoned with the irony that she hated Richmond because it was where they met their apocalypse. And because Joe already waited by himself down the green hill.

Soon, she will be hauled there too, not that she cares one way or the other about graves. She imagines a little flat paving stone the dimensions of a shoe-box lid without even a name—just WIFE & MOTHER and a bracket of dates. Every sunny day, the shadow of his tall statue will cross over her like the gnomon of a sundial, like a blade.

—One thing I am sure of, though, V says to James. I'll never return to Richmond until it's feetfirst in a box.

———

Jimmie Limber came to the back of the wagon seat and reached to put a hand on V's arm. Not a word, just a touch—at which, she helped him climb over and sat him next to her and pulled him against her by his bony shoulder.

She said, Jimmie, do you need something?

—Nope. Can't sleep.

—Cold?

—Nope.

—Not scared, are you?

—I don't scare.

—Of course not, V said.

—Just want to watch the road.

Delrey said, I hope you can see it better than I can, Jimmie. We've run off into the pines three times already tonight. The mules can't tell woods and cornfields from road much better than I can.

—I see real good, Jimmie said.

—Well, V said.

—Yes, ma'am. Real well.

He watched down the road awhile and then said, Mighty dark to travel.

V said, We're deep in the world here, Jimmie.

He sat with her arm draped across his shoulders. If she tried to hug him too long he squirmed, but sometimes he rested his head against her, breathing deep but always awake and watching.

—I believe the road's about to bear left, he'd say. Long straightaway coming after a creek crossing. Might be a burned-out house after that. I can smell it.

He predicted little better than Delrey or the mules or V did, which is to say about like blind chance. But he tried hard.

Jimmie said, How far is it we're going?

V said, A hundred miles, and then a hundred miles more. Who knows how many times after that? Maybe a boat trip somewhere along the way. You boys will enjoy that.

—Keep going till we stop?

—Can you do that, Jimmie?

He thought about it a long time and then said, I'll try it.

V said, If you'll watch out for me, I'll watch out for you.

He stuck out his hand to shake on the deal. Little clammy palm.

V shook and then said, A kiss on the cheek too.

He turned his head and angled his cheek for a kiss.

She said, No, I meant you kiss me.

She turned her cheek, and he made a quick peck.

An hour before dawn started showing in the sky, Jimmie Limber faded away to sleep and V held him against her with both arms awhile for her own benefit and then lifted him back to the fragrant tick mattress and patchwork quilts with the others. Under the canvas, their bedding cast an odor of overripe fruit, though they'd had no fruit for weeks, unless you counted half-rotted winter squash.

V dissolved pinches of Dover's into a metal cup with a splash of red wine. She wanted to time it so the opium rose in her with the dawn. Both coming on in gradations of blue and gray like a bruise swelling above the pines.

La Florida. V sat on the wagon bench and looked down the road like it might appear around the next bend. Her mind kept circling back to when she was seventeen—two decades ago—wondering how she got from there to here. Thinking how all the lesser increments of time between then and now—years, months, days, hours, moments—drained constantly into the black sump where time resides after it's been used up, whether used well or squandered.

A part of her believed this one moment—Carolina woods, a wagonload of children, lights of heaven blazing on a clear spring night—was sufficient. An eternity in itself. A perfect instant if you erased guilt of the past and dread of the future. One key lay in not weighing the many impending threats and losses against grand past moments left behind, diminishing by the mile. Just breathe night air, listen to owls hoot, and be happy while it lasts. The dead are dead. Be happy for a wagonload of live children.

Glory aplenty through those past couple of decades, though. Several presidents—mostly dead now—thinking she was awfully pretty and smart and witty. That first stretch of time in Washington, she'd been eighteen, new wife of shiny new congressman Jeff, and thrilled to go to parties at the Polk White House and write her mother comic letters about how everyone dressed and how short and inconsequential Polk looked.

Another time, during her second era in Washington—so V was midtwenties and wife of the secretary of war—President Pierce walked alone from the real White House in a whirling snowstorm and knocked at the door and came in frosted top to bottom. He wore a heavy blue wool coat, military style with tall collars standing up to the tops of his ears. He lacked a hat, and his hair—usually a wavy voluminous mess—drooped slick and wet against the sides of his skull like the ears of a spaniel fresh from the water. He had been drinking as usual and stood in the foyer taking his coat off, apologizing for the puddle of snowmelt around his boots.

His pretext for the visit had been to ask about her health. A rumor ran around town that she had fallen fatally bronchial. Which was totally untrue, and he knew it. But he was lonely and wanted to sit by a friendly fire for an hour and have a few more drinks and talk to people who liked him and had read all the same books he had read plus plenty more.

That president and his wife—just before making the trip from New Hampshire to Washington for the inaugural ceremony—had been broken irreparably by witnessing their young boy, their last living child, run down beneath the engine of a train. The bloody horror of that violent meeting between massive mechanical steam-powered force and a small biologic body—a thin bag of skin over meat and organs and nerves and brittle bones—required no embellishment. They rushed to the boy, who lay like he was asleep, and then they took his cap off, and the top of his head was unspeakable. That instant left its image of loss stamped on their faces and on their souls forever, and not even the highest office in the land could erase or even partially reimburse them.

As Pierce waded haltingly into the swamp of absolute politics that slavery created, his wife, Jane, chose to stay upstairs in the White House, trying to learn the skill of invisibility. People—meaning the press up and down the country and all those newspaper readers who believe everything they see in print—entertained themselves spreading gossip that she was insane, a crazy woman holed up in the attic. Famous women wild in their minds—even very quietly and privately—sell newspapers.

And of course the gossip was completely untrue in regard to Jane's insanity. During a state dinner or a party or a dance—whatever they called it that night—V ventured upstairs sleuthing. And what she found was a smart, sad woman, deeply sane, tiny inside her big dress, face the color of a bleached bedsheet except around the eyes and cheekbones where it yellowed to old ivory. V discovered that Jane stayed upstairs because she had more serious and encompassing thoughts and emotions than could be contained in a White House gathering. She sat in a parlor surrounded by books, reading fairly desperately for pertinent helpful passages that might make sense of her broken life.

She coughed sometimes into a handkerchief and, not looking at it, carefully folded the cloth without revealing what V later knew would have been a bright smear of lung blood. They talked about books, of course. V recommended a couple of her favorite Greeks, and Jane asked for justification, the basis of her recommendation. V said that in her opinion, when the old Greek writers committed to cutting, they drove bone-deep with the first stroke. She suggested translations other than the current popular ones. Subtle matters like how they handled onomatopoeia, which the Greeks spewed all over the page.

Thereafter when V called at the White House, Jane never sent down a servant with a polite excuse. Sometimes they sat by the fire and had tea and talked between long intervals of silence. V learned that if she needed to fill the air with the sound of her own voice, she would never know what Jane thought about anything. Ask a question and then wait a quarter of a minute for an answer, an interval filled with thought. When Jane asked difficult questions in regard to Sophocles, V tried to answer with substance, having the advantage of reading the texts in their original language with help from a lexicon, though at the time she lacked sufficient experience of loss to understand them fully.

On days when Jane looked especially drained, eyes

puffy, V's attempts to rouse her failed—just the chatter a young woman imagines to be engaging for a woman whose children had all died. On those visits, V looked Jane in the eyes and kissed her on both cheeks and said, See you soon.

Every visit—last thing, V's hand on the doorknob—Jane always said, Thank you, dear girl, for remembering me. Much later, after the deaths of her own children, V believed she went just as far away from life as Jane, except that all of her didn't stay gone forever.

Then in four years came the inevitable next election. The wonderful drunk president didn't exactly lose the vote, because he was not even renominated by his own party. So, shortly, a new president was elected. And the thing about becoming president is that you don't just get your predecessor's job, you also get his house. V went to the White House to see if she could help pack or do anything whatsoever helpful. Jane kissed her and held her hand as they walked around, trying to make moving decisions. Jane looked at the sitting room upstairs and said, It is all beyond my knowledge.

The next president entered office in deep mourning too. In his case every day marked the loss of . . . what? A roommate? An old friend? The friend's name was King. Back when he and Buchanan were both members of the House they had lived together ten years in

Brown's Hotel as roommates. Under unusual circumstances King became vice president to Pierce for a few weeks and swore his oath of office in Havana and then died almost immediately afterward.

Back in the Brown's Hotel days—before King was vice president and long before Buchanan was president—Andrew Jackson—a brutal piece of work even if you were trying to be complimentary—liked to call the pair Miss Nancy and Aunt Fancy. Every piece of correspondence between Buchanan and King was burned after King's death.

Buchanan never married. A pretty and very shrewd and sharp-eyed niece—who didn't particularly approve of V—served as hostess, arranging state dinners and gracefully whispering in her uncle's ear the names of people in the receiving line he might have misremembered. She was expert at diverting the attention of unwelcome or tiring guests, as if she were dealing with a parade of fussy toddlers. Some newspaper writer, not knowing what to call her, since she wasn't the president's wife, made up the term First Lady, and it stuck.

Old Buchanan and V eventually became true friends without reference to her husband—then a senator. Or to her age—still shy of thirty. They were the kind of friends who gave each other bedroom slippers for Christmas. The sharper her tongue, the more he delighted in it. He was a lovely, lonely old bachelor, and V was so often at her best with older men. When he lay dying he sent for her, and she sat on the edge of his bed to say good-bye. His hair sprung greasy from his temples, white peaks and gray valleys. He held her hand and patted its smooth back with his old crepey palm and tried to console her.

—I'll miss you so much, he said.

—Then don't go, V said.

—Not my choice. Just don't forget me.

She snorted with laughter and said, Idiotic to imagine that's possible.

He gripped her hand, pressed her fingers into a fist and pulled it to his pleated lips and kissed the smooth dusky skin of her handback and then kissed the row of knuckles and the pale fingernails curled against the palm, and then he opened her hand flat and kissed the cup of her palm three times, like a spell in a fairy story.

—My dear, he said.

—You old fool, she said.

V jostled along on the wagon bench, wondering what to make of that past when her only future had become a muddy ribbon of road unspooling ahead with agonizing slowness and little ones confused and scared. All of them fugitives. Her husband—wherever he was—the chief fugitive, still pretending they weren't defeated, crushed, broken. The letters from him that reached her before the railroads quit working were sweet and deluded, as if everything wasn't lost and gone forever.

She opened *Northanger Abbey* again and jotted: *Head full of sorrows, heart full of dreams. How to maintain the latter as life progresses? How not to let the first cancel the second?*

A mile farther down the road she thought, You can mire yourself in the past, but you can't change a damn thing in that lost world. Nothing to do but sit on the wagon bench beside Delrey and stare forward into the distance. Or go lie stunned, dozing under piles of quilts in the back of the ambulance with the children, who shape themselves and the world around them anew moment by moment and always need baths and smell musty and sweet and alive.

=

James holds the blue book out toward her, spine forward, gold letters on blue cloth. *First Days Among the Contrabands.*

He says, This book, it's the reason I'm here. Miss Botume, the author, went from Boston down to the Sea Islands off South Carolina in the middle of the war—

occupied territory—to teach freed slaves. A brave act. She was young, full of ideas about making the world better. She would have been in danger if Confederates had retaken the islands. For legal reasons, the Federal government called all those people who'd been freed from slavery contraband, seized property, spoils of war. The book tells her experiences there, teaching those people reading and arithmetic and all sorts of other things previously kept secret from most of them. How to look at a clock and tell time, how to look at a coin and judge its value. She took care of me for a while. I wonder if I might read you a passage—see if it squares with your memory.

He opens the book to one of his markers and holds it for V to read the chapter title. *Jimmie.* Then, fast and urgent, he reads aloud: *An officer on board brought with him this small colored boy, sent by Mrs. Davis to General Saxton. She also sent a note by the boy, written with pencil on the blank leaf of a book. I quote from memory. She said:—"I send this boy to you, General Saxton, and beg you to take good care of him." His mother was a free colored woman in Richmond. She died when he was an infant, leaving him to the care of a friend, who was cruel and neglectful of him. One day Mrs. Davis and her children went to the house and found this woman beating the little fellow, who was then only two years old. So she took him home with her, intending to find a good place for him. But he was so bright and playful, her own children were unwilling to give him up. Then she decided to keep him until he was old enough to learn a trade. "That was five years ago, and he has shared our fortunes and misfortunes until the present time. But we can do nothing more for him. I send him to you, General Saxton, as you were a friend of our earlier and better times. You will find him affectionate and tractable. I beg you to be kind to him." This was the gist of her note.*

James looks up and waits.

V reaches her hand. Says, Might I look directly at the page?

She studies it and then says, *Gist.* It's an old French word. Means, to lie.

V runs her finger across several lines of text and then says, Your Miss Botume's fabricating my statements and using quotation marks to cover her tracks. Slapping memory and supposition together decades after the fact. Inventing her own history, which we all do. But to be truthful, I don't know exactly what I might have written in that moment. I was desperate. They were going to take you away. But I do know she has dates and times and ages all wrong. If I'd had you with me for five years, that would go back to when I lived in Washington. Also, I didn't know your mother. I was going down the street and saw you being beaten and took you with me. And as for the future, it felt too uncertain to bother thinking about planning a trade for you or anyone else.

All V finds indisputable is the last bit of the passage: *Jefferson Davis was captured at Irwinville, Georgia, May 10, 1865. He had with him his family, his Postmaster General Reagan, his Private Secretary Harrison.*

With angry resentment V points out Miss Botume's omission of the bare fact that long before Jefferson and his worn-down gang of hard-shell Rebels caught up with them, V and the children—including Jimmie— had made it almost to the Georgia-Florida line.

—It was a long and dangerous journey, she says, and we survived day by day, and I'm proud of that. Jeff arrived just in time—a few hours—to get everybody captured by the Federals. I will always maintain that if he had left us on our own, we could have made it to Havana—mainly because I wanted to escape and he didn't.

V raises a forefinger to signal a pause and then looks toward a bank of tall windows and studies the view of valleys and ridges. James sits within himself and waits. He mostly looks at the cold fireplace and the Emerson.

Her face is pale, and she begins taking deep, deliberate breaths.

When she resumes talking she finds a different voice, windless and quiet and gentle. She starts at the beginning of what she knows. How midway in the war, she found him on the streets of Richmond, a skinny, tiny boy taking a hard beating from a big drunk woman swinging a stick of kindling. The woman putting her shoulder into it, practically knocking him down with every blow. But he kept trying to stand up and bear it. V thought the woman was his mother, but when V stepped out of the carriage and went to stop her, the woman said he was a stray, hanging around too long begging food she didn't have to spare. He was filthy, and V lifted him by the armpits into the carriage and took him home. The only name he would say was Jimmie. The boys recognized him from the Hill Cats Gang but didn't know his full name, or wouldn't say it. Down his back he had cuts and bruises, some fresh, some scabbed, some scarred. He was double-jointed, and when he was nervous and uncertain he folded one hand backward and then the other. So Maggie started calling him Jimmie Limber, and soon the other children and V and Ellen did too.

—But on Sundays, V says, when you dressed up for

church, you wanted to be called James Brooks. Maybe that was your real name or maybe you made it up. At the end of the war, when they parted you from us, that's the name I wrote when I begged General Saxton to take care of you.

—I always wondered whether my name is real or if I made it up. I guess that question will never be answered. But my real question is simple. Why did you pick me up? James asks.

—I don't know. I just did it. You were so small.

—It must have been more complicated than that.

—Maybe so, but I can't explain it.

—**You mentioned** the Hill Cats Gang? James says.

—Little boys roaming streets and alleys and backyards of downtown Richmond. Women in the big houses criticized me for letting my children run wild, but it was good for you. And those women from the old Virginia families had little else to do but gossip and judge. The Hill Cats were enemies of the Butcher Cats from down toward Shockoe Bottom. Sometimes the older boys actually fought each other, but you little ones just threw pebbles and crab apples and yelled high-pitched threats. Police picked up a couple of Hill Cats once and hauled them into the Mayor's Court charged with throwing rocks at the Spotswood Hotel, but they argued innocence, since it was pieces of coal they threw, not rocks—and they won their case. Things got bad enough after a battle the papers said involved as many as a hundred boys—which probably meant thirty—that Jeff walked down the hill one day to make peace between the gangs. He argued to the Butcher Cats that both gangs were neighbors, separated by only a few blocks, and that they had much in common and should get to know each other, should play together whether it was down in the Bottom or up on the Hill. He explained that it was in everyone's best interests to stop fighting and like each other. When he was done talking, the leader of the Butcher Cats—probably a boy of ten—told Jeff what a fine gentleman he was, but said that it was impossible that they would ever like the Hill Cats. And equally impossible they would ever stop fighting.

When Jeff came puffing back up the hill and told V of his failure, she said it felt like 1860 all over again.

—**But could** we go back to the simplest parts of Miss Botume's memoir? James asks. Was I bright and playful, affectionate and tractable?

—Tractable? My God, no. You were spirited and independent. And of course careful and wary when you were uncertain. You had to have been to survive living stray during the shortages of the war. When you felt safe you were certainly affectionate, but you didn't give it away. It had to be earned. And that's what first made me love you. But in writing to my old friend General Saxton begging him to take care of you, I wasn't about to get into nuances. After all, he and my husband were on different sides. And as for whether you were bright, look at yourself now. My question is, what have you done with your brightness over the decades?

—I've been a teacher, James says. I've taught hundreds of children and adults reading and writing and arithmetic. Back when I started, a lot of my students were former slaves. It seemed like so many of them learned written language and understood the fundamental relationships of numbers almost overnight. They inhaled it like they'd been drowning and suddenly lifted their heads into the air. All they wanted was more.

—When you began classes with our tutor, you learned to read in a month, maybe less. You raced along, impatient to get to the next word, to the next line of text. Forward was your direction. So teaching must be a satisfying profession for you.

—It is. But the difference between a little boy learning to read in the president's mansion and a woman of fifty who'd been denied it by law for much of her lifetime is large.

—Yes, you're right. And teaching is truly a noble profession. Little money in it, though. I say that noticing your expensive footwear in particular.

Blake tips his right foot at an angle to get a profile view as if he hasn't noticed what handsome gusseted chisel-toe boots he wears. They shine like a mirror reflecting the night sky.

He says, I get a discount. My wife's family owns clothes stores, a good business. In New York they've just moved from San Juan Hill to Harlem, and in Philadelphia they've been on South Street for twenty years.

—I'd like to meet her.

—Julie died almost two years ago. Consumption. But she was lucky, I guess. That translucent stage some people pass through lasted a long time for her, and when it faded she finished quickly without the worst of the hemorrhaging. Being close with her family has helped me through it, and maybe I've helped them some. They were generous before, and they're still generous now and keep telling me I'm part of the family forever. They want me to join the business.

—I'm very sorry for your loss, V says.

She pauses and says, Maybe you should listen to them.

—Teaching is what I do best, not manage a store or keep books or write advertising copy. I'm grateful to them, but I think I'm going to keep doing my job.

—Do you have children?

—No, ma'am.

—So you're totally free to move forward in life un-encumbered, without needing to compound with your pride for the material interests of your family.

—I don't follow.

—I don't either. Never have, no matter how I parse the diction and grammar—whether *compound* is noun or verb—I'm still puzzled. After the war, Jeff wrote it in a letter, *I have compounded with my pride for the material interest of my family, and am ready to go on to the end as may best promote their happiness.* He's of course trying to blame me and the children for his fall. Guilt and pride nearly burnt our marriage down to the foundation.

V tells James that Jeff's letter arrived at her dingy apartment in London during a long separation after the war, much of the time with the entire width of the Atlantic between them. Those oddly constructed words and clauses and phrases were how he informed V he had taken a job beneath him in order to support his family. His great sacrifice was to lower himself and become president of an insurance company after being president of a country—or a failed rebellion or whatever label would be correct. The company covered the Southeast, Baltimore to Houston. Many of his former

generals—also broke—tried to make money writing
memoirs, struggled to make themselves sit alone at
a desk every day and conjure their version of history
constructed from the weightless tools of words and uncertain memory. And with a very uncertain payday at
the end of the job. So they were eager to earn a steady
salary in a more direct and concrete way as insurance
salesmen and regional managers and that sort of thing.
Go back to giving orders. V believes that General Hood
was one of Jeff's insurance salesmen. Hood lost the use
of an arm at Gettysburg, and afterward it just drooped
there at his side. And then a leg got taken off at Chicka-
mauga, four inches below the hip. The doctor who did
the sawing—as they hauled Hood away—put the leg
alongside him in the ambulance, assuming he would
die and would want it in the casket. But Hood didn't
die. He came to Richmond and healed. He was barely
over thirty, a tall, slim martyr with a long sad face
made longer by his tangled beard. Mary Chesnut always said he looked like Don Quixote or a crazed Cru-
sader fighting for crown and cross. He was shy with
women, but battle lit him up wild as a Viking. Young
Richmond ladies found him irresistible. But ever since
the early days of the war, he had been under the spell
of Mary Chesnut's good friend Buck Preston, who was
beautiful and a genius at inflicting love. Hood gave a

blockade-runner leaving for Europe a brief shopping list for Paris. Two cork legs, best quality. One diamond ring. When he presented the ring to Buck Preston, she declined his proposal. People accused her of being so shallow that she wouldn't marry him because he had one leg. Buck fired back that she wouldn't marry Hood if he had six legs. After the war he found a woman other than Buck to marry, and in ten years they had eleven children, quite a few of which were twins. Then the yellow fever that killed half of New Orleans killed Hood and his wife the same day, leaving those orphans behind.

—All that happened? James says. None of it? Some of it?

—All. But I got distracted from what I wanted to say to Jeff about compounding with his pride. I wrote back and told him that bad choices lead to bad consequences, like discussing misbehavior with a child. But he never accepted being wrong and never apologized for taking down our family. Or eleven states full of families. He and his older brother Joseph were alike in that. A shared trait. Never apologize for anything. Plow ahead always believing you're in the right.

—Go back, James says. You lived in London?

London

March 1874

The short stack of china stood only five dinner plates tall, each one chipped at the edges and crazed on the pink floral faces. Three soup bowls, five teacups, but only two saucers. Glassware—just four stems—cloudy as an old man's eye. Bed and table linens and towels worn by time to an indeterminate color, like a teaspoon of coal dust in a pint of heavy cream—the color of dirty soles and also the color of the plaster walls. The tiny fireplace might have been adequate for roasting a single sparrow over a fistful of twigs.

V pulled open a cupboard drawer and found a sprinkling of mouse droppings. The oblong black nubs moved like suddenly magnetized iron filings or swirled tea leaves until they settled and found their pattern on the drawer bottom. Prophetic, but not subtly so. Just another message from the gods about diminishing expectations.

The landlady—blade slim, and a nose so long and sharp she had to angle her head to see around it like a pelican—noted the drawer contents and rather than being apologetic or embarrassed or making a joke, she swelled with antagonism. Ready to start flapping with both long bony hands if V objected.

V walked to one of the parlor windows and looked up to the gray March sky and down into a narrow cobbled street. Good indirect light for reading. The three flights of stairs would improve her health. If she leaned at just the right angle, she could see a thin slice of St. Paul's dome. All in all not completely squalorous, but leaning toward.

V said, I'll take it.

She moved in the next afternoon. Her things—all her holdings—fit in two travel-scarred steamer trunks with arched lids. She wiped out the mousey cupboard drawers and placed her books in stacks of five around the sitting room and bumped the comfortable chair a few feet nearer the window. Then she walked down the street. Within four blocks she found shops to buy books and periodicals and bread and cheese and fruit and wine and glassine packets of morphine and small brown bottles of laudanum. She came back loaded with purchases and filled one of the clouded glasses with cheap Bordeaux and a few drops of tincture. She looked out the window, tracking the gradations of gray that marked sunset.

Well past forty, fortunes lost, alone in London. She still received a few invitations to posh parties but always declined because she no longer owned the correct clothes. The last time she accepted had been nearly a year before, a luncheon with the rebel princess Louise at Kensington Palace, though the minute V stepped out of the carriage she felt too shabby to be there and vowed to stop pretending, to accept that lives rarely have plots, but sometimes they find shape. And that hers fell and rose and fell so often that she imagined drawing its graph and ending up with a crosscut saw blade.

V sat very still, soaking in the coal smoke, fog, rattle and thump of carriage wheels and horses' hooves, the shuffle of feet and murmur of talk below the windows. Why would she ever want to go home? Home had ceased to be. She had acquired and shed four or five houses filled with fine furniture, paintings, decor in Mississippi, Washington, and Richmond. But now those names represented only the vast category of things that come and go. Impermanence.

Richmond never resembled home. During the war years, living in the president's mansion, which V preferred to call the Gray House, every day brought its own crisis—life lived to the sounds of blaring bugles and alarm bells. From a cold, gray ocean away, that past blurred. V remembered clear days, observation balloons of the Northern army hovering to the east of the city like great malignant bulbs hanging high in the sky out of reach of the guns. At night the multitudes of Northern campfires lit undersides of clouds hazy amber. During periods of fighting, the sound of artillery rattled windows, even in the Capitol itself. One such day the senators spent most of their time debating how many newspapers should be delivered to their desks, how often spittoons ought to be emptied. The war—sold to the people as a collective fantasy—became daily reality, a constant condition of life—death and strange days stretching from the present instant to the farthest horizon you could imagine or even dream until at some point of weariness, war rests quiet in the mind.

Sometimes, looking back, she wanted to claim—as Euripides and Stesichorus did of Helen—that she had nothing to do with the destruction and tragedy of war, that an eidolon took her place. Their radical variant of history proposed that the true Helen sat out the brutal messy years of the Trojan War in Egypt. V would have preferred London. Let her phantom deal with Richmond, its fall and the desperate flight south, let its blank mind deal with prison and the guilt of the war and the waste and cost and loss for everyone. One late night or early morning toward the end of the war she said as much to Mary Chesnut. Mary held her stem carefully between thumb and forefinger and lifted her glass to the ribbon of yellow-and-blue lamp flame. She studied and adjusted the dark liquid, establishing plumb and level. Mary sipped and said, The Trojan War wasn't fought over a woman. Or are you still as romantic as ever?

Being on the wrong side of history carries consequences. V lives that truth every day. If you've done terrible things, lived a terrible way, profited from pain in the face of history's power to judge, then guilt and loss accrue. Redemption becomes an abstract idea receding before you. Even if your sin—like dirt farmers in Sherman's path—had been simply to live in the wrong place, you suffered. Didn't matter whether you owned slaves or which way you voted or how good your intentions had been. Or how bad. You might suffer as much as the family of a great plantation, which was maybe not completely just. But if you were the family with a great plantation, you had it coming. Those were times that required choosing a side—and then, sooner or later, history asks, which side were you on?

The first sound of a culture collapsing from its highest steeples starts as a whisper, a sigh. The rattle of windows in their frames. Nobody listens until it thunders, when its structure—all the massive weight held in air as by a magician's trick depending on sleight of hand, misdirection of attention—collapses to its foundational sins. And after the steeples have fallen, warred-over landscapes lie burned and salted as thoroughly as Troy after the Greeks sailed home. Nothing left but frail and temporary and untrustworthy memory to image what stood before. Even near the end, many in the capital and elsewhere remained unsure whether they were engaged in a grand experiment or a pathetically inept confidence game, projecting boundaries of a new and uncertain country onto the landscape. North and South like grotesque reflections of one another in a carnival mirror.

Sad and stupid. And yet . . . what?

That London evening, sitting in the armchair with

the stain where many heads had rested, V felt not at all happy, but calmer. Irresistible gravity settling her into place. How lovely to live alone without the constant pull against attention, the strong outgoing tide dragging concentration away. Husband an ocean away and the children happy in school—the boys in America and the girls across the Channel learning French.

V began writing a letter. She first thought to spill out pages of recollections and resentments, tracing how their lives had year by year ramified beyond prediction or even the prophecy of nightmare, moving like a river in reverse, flowing from the mainstream out into so many branches that not a drop made it down to the sea. How they had lived rootless, homeless as fugitives until they became actual fugitives with an entire nation in pursuit. But instead she wrote:

Dearest Jeff,
Of course I live to serve you & children. All loved
& missed beyond excess—goes without saying. But
still, to be alone in this beautiful dirty old city after
the calamity of the past years, and feeling nothing
but a lift from letting go the faded glories. Letting
go youth & desire & hope. Yet to sense a possible
future rather than only a lurking ending—that
thing with the weight of a great black riverboat and

its stern-wheel beating like a scythe & the added force of a booming Mississippi current that bore down on us for years and finally swept us under. So, right now, I wish you every day a happy day & good appetite, warm feet, good friends & everything but forgetfulness. I do not think I would have longed for, or used, the water of Lethe. Memory is truly possession sometimes. Stay away from me until autumn & then see if we may feel we have a future together.

Devotedly, your wife,

V

=

V scans a pair of pages in James's blue book and says, My name in print always arrests my eye. Listen to this: *A little mulatto boy had been sent to General Saxton by Mrs. Jefferson Davis, and now the question came up, what was the best thing to do with him. He was about seven years old, but small for his age; was a very light mulatto, with brown curly hair, thin lips, and a defiant nose. When brought before us he looked around suspiciously and fearlessly. When Mrs. Saxton called him he walked calmly up to her; but when I held out my hand to him he folded his arms and stood still, straight as an*

arrow, with his head thrown back, without meeting my
friendly advances. It was comical to see the cool indif-
ference of this tiny scrap of humanity.

V stops and says, Scrap of humanity? Where did she
come up with that? Dragged it out of nowhere. You
were an intense little boy and more than covered the
ground you stood on. And you were not small for your
age, and you were not seven. And also, I didn't send
you away. I did the best I could in a horrible moment.
I'd kept you with me all the way from Richmond, every
mile. We were being held on board the *William P.*
Clyde at Hilton Head, prisoners not knowing which
prison awaited us.

She describes to James the *Tuscarora* lying alongside the *Clyde* with big guns aimed to blow them out
of the water in case the prisoners commandeered the
ship. The prisoners included V and the children and
sick, skeletal Jeff and Vice President Stephens, who
weighed ninety pounds and looked like a mummified
child and was called the Pale Star of Georgia by some
of the papers. Also Clement and Virginia Clay. Clement
had been both a U.S. senator and a Confederate senator. Late in the war Jeff sent him on a spy mission to
Canada. He came back looking like a hollow-cheeked
killer, face like an axe blade and greasy hair to his
shoulders, not at all like his plump, young face on the

one-dollar bill. And of course Burton Harrison was a prisoner, Jeff's private secretary through most of the war and V's friend, companion, ally.

They'd mostly taken different paths from Richmond to being prisoners on the *Clyde*. Jeff had stayed in Richmond until hours before the city burned, and then he escaped by railway with the cabinet to Danville and then Greensboro where they set up government in people's parlors. From there Jeff traveled on horseback through the Carolinas and Georgia, plotting most of the way how he could prolong the war. Burton, though, had stuck with V from Richmond all through the horrible flight south trying to get to Cuba. Horses and wagons, camping in tents or in the wagon-beds if it was raining too hard to set up camp. Sometimes sleeping in abandoned buildings or wayside churches.

—After they captured us, V tells James, they hauled us back north through Georgia and then east to the coast. They paraded us through jeering crowds in Macon and Augusta and Savannah. At the last minute before the ship departed, they pulled you away. The children and Ellen and I were screaming and crying, leaning over the rails of the *Clyde*. Ellen and I tried to convince them that you were her child because you were both about the same color, but they wrestled you onto a skiff. You fought and tried to jump into the water. Virginia Clay was crying too, and she tossed coins from her purse down into the skiff. I remember at some point Jeffy fell to his knees and held his cap over his face, not wanting to see what was happening.

I begged them to send you to General Saxton in Charleston. In Washington before the war he often dined with us. One night when it seemed that war was the only course our politicians—including my husband—had left open, I joked with Rufus Saxton that if he came to Mississippi leading an invading army, I would vow to see that his grave was kept clean. I believed he would honor that old friendship and take care of you. There was a young Northern officer there who hated me and would have tossed you out by the roadside just to punish me. I had to keep you out of his hands and did all I could in that moment. Otherwise, I pictured you wandering through the chaos starving and alone, put in more danger by being with me.

James Blake says, I only remember boats, gray water, and blue sky. Silver coins flashing and tinkling in the air and splashing in the water.

V says, A hundred thousand tragedies played out in the spring of 1865. We'd bet everything on anger and angry ideas, and we lost. Lee once wrote Jeff a letter—during a particularly nasty little moment of decision—in which he advised against action that he feared would bring down the reproach of our consciences and posterity's judgment. But by then, it was too late to apply Lee's advice more widely because we were in the middle of trying to pull apart a country to protect the wealth of slave owners. There was no going back. Bad, angry decisions left behind a huge cost in life and suffering for the entire nation. And utter loss of wealth for the South. But not for the North. Plenty made fortunes off the war. Give a real Yankee one little dried pea and three thimbles and he can buy groceries. Give him a boxful of cheap, shiny pocketknives and pistols to trade and he will turn it into a career. But give him a war, and he'll make a fortune to last centuries. It's not something they learn. They're saturated in it from birth. End result—we lose everything and they create thousands of new millionaires.

—Bitter feelings still, ma'am?

—No. The people who beat you get to take you apart however they wish.

—Certainly sounds bitter.

—It's reality. We lost. I've lived in New York City for more than fifteen years and it's been good for me. I've made much of my living writing for the papers and have learned a great deal there. And in London too. It does your mind good to talk to people different from you. Especially instructive in regard to opinions about owning people and trying to kill a country. I've come to accept that our debt may stretch to one of those generational Bible curses. Unto the seventh son of the seventh son. Born on the seventh hour of the seventh day.

—I don't believe that's from the Bible.

—I'm sure it's in there somewhere, V says. Seven is a powerful number.

James says, In South Carolina—the Sea Islands the year after the war—I announced that Mr. Davis was a fine man, and the black children I was in school with fought me, backed me up against a wall. And then before long I was in a northern school with nothing but white children—Massachusetts—and when I said Jefferson Davis was a fine man, they called me every derogatory racial name they knew and fought me. It's all here in Miss Botume's book.

—I'm certain you stood up and fought back. You were a strong-minded child. But I'm sharing personal memories with you, and all you're doing is telling me things from a book. So please tell me something you remember that's not from the book.

James pauses and then says, Pictures mostly. Steep steps and high ceilings. A big room with the other children. Tall windows looking down to a lawn. A fierce red rocking horse bouncing in a frame with four big metal springs, and I pinched my hand in a spring and bled. I picture children sitting on a staircase, looking down through balusters to a party with people wearing black and white clothes, listening to music—a piano and a violin. An enormous green field, all of us running and spinning and blue sky whirling. Another time, a room and a fire, loud flashes of lightning, people yelling, babies crying.

—Yes, V says. Every bit of that.

—The day you fled Richmond, some might have kissed me good-bye and sent me on my way. Back to being a stray.

—Maybe so, but I held on to you until I realized keeping you with me was worse for you than letting you go.

—That long trip south, James says. I wish I remembered more of it.

—Oh, I'll tell you everything you want to know. Write a book if you feel like it. Everybody seems to be inventing their own history and finding a publisher. Just don't write a tiresome biography—they all end the same way. But it's getting late, and since Albany is so nearby, we might reconvene to talk more next Sunday.

—Of course.

—Come about noon. I'll arrange lunch here, or maybe we'll picnic at the races. I like to see the little jockeys in their silk clothes and the green grass and white fences and big trees. But mostly I love looking at the horses beforehand more than the race itself. I rode well when I was young and can see things in their eyes and facial expressions and deportment that tell me how they feel about running that day. Sometimes I just know it's their day, a feeling not like a wave raging and breaking but a smooth swell almost ready to curl over. I bet a few dollars at a time and win more than I lose. I pay for my entertainment.

As James stands to leave, V says, When I was younger, I might have dreamed your arrival beforehand like I did that place where we were all captured. Every feature of south Georgia landscape exact—the road, a swale down to a creek, pine trees, fallow fields. Even the placement of the tents on either side of the road. But that gift or curse left me soon after the war. I still have vivid dreams, but now they never correspond with reality.

Second Sunday

Saratoga Springs

The Saratoga railway station pulses with race-day foot traffic, the energy of hope funneling people out the doors and toward the track. James Blake, blue book in hand, weaves his way to a clear space at the end of the platform. That scream down the hall of The Retreat repeats in his head. He's tried all week to decode the tone, whether it arose from some specific marital fight or from general anger, anguish, fear, frustration with life.

He raises a finger to a redcap porter and asks the man about The Retreat. What kind of place? Surely just what it appeared, an exclusive resort hotel?

The redcap is about fifty, not tall but big shouldered from shifting baggage all day for thirty years. Brass buttons shined bright down the breast of his uniform jacket. He is darker than James by several degrees.

He studies James carefully and says, Looking to take a room?

—No.

—Good. You're not close enough to passing to test them. Sundown's probably their borderline. Like little towns bragging no black man ever spent the night there and lived to tell it. Except polite about it. Plenty welcome during daylight hours to build roads, lay brick, plow gardens, clean houses, swing nine-pound hammers.

James says, Last Sunday, about this time, they let me sit in the lobby. But they made sure I knew it was grudging. I'll be back for the six-thirty-five to Albany. I just need to know what the place is.

—Hotel. People stay there because it's nice. The view and the food and the service. But they've got doctors. Guests can get treatments.

—Treatments for what?

—I couldn't tell you what ailments those people come down with. Tired of living, mainly. Must get dreary having nothing useful to do.

James laughs and says, Thank you, sir. You've set me straight.

He reaches out a coin, and the man pinches it out of habit but then lets go. He says, Save that for The Retreat. Might need it.

The Ophelia in the guests' upcoming production of *Hamlet*—a woman of twenty or so named Laura—stops by V's room. She doesn't knock but opens the door and drifts right in without a word. She wears a thin nightgown and light shawl and goes barefoot though the day is coming toward midmorning. Her hair, a beautiful blond tousle, holds light from the window in an aura around her face.

She is the youngest daughter from a cigarette-paper fortune, and her skin stretches over her bones pale and thin as the diaphanous rectangles that pay for therapy to ease her only two defects—which are that she sometimes seems to be hearing conversations different from the ones actually taking place, and that she sometimes becomes excessively demonstrative in her attraction to men.

She comes to V's chair and without a word climbs into her lap and wraps her arms around V's neck and rests her head on V's chest. She draws a long deep breath and hums a bit of "Sunflower Slow Drag," her fingers twitching to press imaginary keys. Soon she falls asleep. Her bony body relaxes and settles deep against V. Her skinny feet hang almost to the floor. V brushes her lips against the mass of blond hair and tries to shape her mind still as a mud puddle on a windless day. Tries to sit and wait quiet inside her head until the particulates settle to the dirty bottom and the water becomes clear as glass. But no matter how much she instructs her thoughts toward stillness, they circle, loop, and repeat, churning against themselves, whitewater climbing and spraying over rocks already passed.

When V returns to New York she plans to seek instruction on this topic from a Yogi or some other Eastern mystic. The city is full of them lately. Or maybe she'll find a piano teacher to remind her how to play, and she'll sit doodling repetitive minor key largos for a couple of hours a day to shape her mind in a helpful calm direction.

Laura wakes after perhaps half an hour and looks up. Her eyes are hazel with striae dark as walnut.

She says, Did you come to me, or did I come to you?

Her voice vibrates with a thin hoarse crack.

—The latter, V says.

—Has breakfast been served?

—Some time ago. Luncheon will be in a couple of hours.

—Oh, good. I could nap longer.

Laura breathes deep, one cycle through her mouth and two through her nose, and then she's gone again. V reaches to her wrist and presses her middle finger into the tangle of bone and gristle to find a heartbeat. The girl throbs at long intervals. V tries to number the beats saying one Mississippi, two Mississippi. She gets thirty beats a minute, which doesn't seem right. Not even possible. V worries the girl will die in her arms, and she doesn't need another gone child.

Laura smells like cut rye grass and ripe pears and a pillowcase needing washing. The skin of her cheeks is poreless and white as a piece of everyday china. She weighs nothing, rests against V like a goose down pillow. Laura doesn't remind V of her own children in the least, but she does call back youth. Like holding a pale version of her own young self.

V leans to Laura's ear and breathes, fainter than a whisper, an arrangement of three words. *Be well, get well.* She says it over and over like a prayer, a chant, an old mystic rhythm that if repeated long enough works magic.

At some point, V may have fallen asleep too. Or at least into a daze, watching the patterns of light through the window—a vertical rectangle of landscape, shades of green and blue, ridgeline and sky. The changes of light through the day happen in such slow rhythms that you have to pay strict attention to follow the melody.

At least she doesn't get bored, wishing she could reach ten feet to the nearest book. Each ticking minute tingles with life. Sheltering this sad girl, her shallow breaths and slow heart, abandoned by her family to the questionable authority of the self-satisfied alienists and mesmerists and semidoctors at The Retreat. Laura is lonely, alone, isolate. V keeps breathing the spell, *Be well, get well.*

Laura shifts her legs a bit, and the bottoms of her feet present themselves. Ivory, amber, and coal dust. Her shanks glow tight along the shinbone, a blond shimmer of fine hair down the slack muscle of the calf. V holds this body with its reluctant spark of life inside, compassed by such a frail container of skin, all its messy fluids and mysterious greasy dark organs held within a membrane hardly more substantive than a soap bubble. Touch it gently and it pops. Gone to nothing.

V says, It feels like rain. So next week for the races?

—Whatever you think, Mrs. Davis.

—Could we talk to each other without missus and ma'am? We have such a short time together, and manners only slow us down.

—What should I call you, then?

—You be James and I'll be Varina.

—I don't think I can do that.

—Yes, you can. If we hadn't been separated back then, what would we be calling each other now?

—I don't know.

—Neither do I. But if we'd reached Havana, we might be sitting under palm trees beside the Caribbean, talking in Spanish—your pretty children calling me *Abuela*. So for today, let's try James and Varina. If others come around listening in, snooping for gossip, we can go back to mister and missus for a minute. We could exaggerate the way we say it and laugh about it later. Booker T. Washington and I made all the newspapers just sitting together talking for an hour or two in a hotel lobby in New York City trying to discuss education, except people kept hovering, eavesdropping, and at some point we both started laughing.

—All right, Varina, James says. I have a question. Is this a hotel or a hospital?

She sweeps her hand to encompass the sun terrace and says, Look around, James. Guests fashionably dressed, nearly as fashionably as you. Nobody wearing a straitjacket. Just having drinks and food in the afternoon. Correct me if I am wrong, but it looks like a hotel.

—Except, last week I thought I heard someone scream.

—Words fail, V says. To live is to rant.

She announces the idea as if she had composed it and honed it down over time and rehearsed her delivery, meaning for it to be carved directly underneath Emerson's attempt to reconcile guilt and fear. Or perhaps she meant to scratch it with a nail on a smaller stone off to the side, a sort of marginal annotation.

Then she laughs and says, James, people like to gossip about The Retreat. All it amounts to is that therapies are offered. It's the fashion.

She runs down possibilities. Hydrotherapy, just a fancy name for a very hot or very cold bath. Physiotherapy, nothing but relaxing massages, taking walks and carriage rides, a bowling alley in the basement, badminton on the lawn for those still able to jump around, and recent talk of converting cow pastures into golf links. Mechanotherapy, a roomful of ugly exercise machines, but always a line of ladies waiting for the vibrating Zander apparatus. Electrotherapy, though, causes her to lower her voice. She barely breathes how way back in the basement they're playing around with a dark speculation of Benjamin Franklin's about the possible benefits of passing strong electric shock through the human head. Franklin took a jolt hard enough to rob him of consciousness, and when he came to he felt unusually fine. He theorized amnesia relieves melancholia. Which makes complete sense, because memory is so often to blame for it. Who couldn't use their load of time and history lightened?

She explains how the hotel even makes putting on a short play therapeutic. Dramatotherapy. Says that she and some other guests are doing an abbreviated *Hamlet* soon, and a man who makes moving pictures is coming from New York to film it so that they can look at it later and laugh at themselves.

—In Richmond during the war, V says, Mary Chesnut and I put on after-dinner comic theatricals and made famous people like Jeb Stuart—the great plumed hero straight off the battlefield—claim a role and join in. He loved it. Always demanded the silliest part and played for laughs. So did Judah Benjamin, the attorney general or secretary of state or secretary of war or whatever job he held that week in the improvised government. Jeff, of course, headed to bed or his office before the fun started. And fun—not therapy—was all we claimed for our evening entertainment. A chance to laugh.

—I don't remember any of that, James says.

—Well, V says cheerfully, I'm sure you children sneaked downstairs to watch a time or two. It wasn't all formal dress and serious music. But my main point is, we're volunteers at The Retreat. We choose our therapies from printed lists exactly like the menus in the dining room. Most of us want to lose a few pounds or to drink less so that we don't have to stop drinking altogether. Some want to become a little less fearful and a little more brave, less despondent and more hopeful. As for me, I want any improvement I can get, but I'll settle for cutting back on the powders and tinctures. Not stop, just moderate. Interesting for the first time since I was thirteen to have a doctor helping me ease up on opiates instead of recommending more. But if I keep living to my eighty-fifth birthday, I plan to start taking them as freely as Mary Chesnut.

—**What do** you want to get away from?

—Saratoga isn't the wilderness, James. I'm not running. I did plenty of that the first half of my life. I spent a day with a newspaper writer a few weeks ago. The article they published said I was old but still liked to keep up with new books, and to play cards, and go to the races. If I wanted to run away, why would I talk to a reporter?

—I mean personally. One thing you'd put behind you forever if you could.

—Take a wild guess.

—The war and all the things surrounding it.

—There. Asked and answered.

V leans and lifts the shaggy book from the table. She riffles pages. Bookmarks flutter.

—I imagine you'd like to get back to this. Compare Miss Botume's imagination against mine? Try to construct your own memory?

—Yes. I'd like to know about you and Mr. Davis. Particularly him letting me stay there, living in the same big room with his children, joining them with their tutor, learning to read. Me living like that in the presidential mansion of the Confederate States of America seems . . . James pauses, searches for the words, and finally says dryly, Of a low order of probability.

V smiles and says, You can take your tongue out of your cheek. However unlikely, it did happen. He went to the courthouse himself to get papers verifying you were free. We had photographs of all the children taken not long after you came. Maybe they still exist—I hope so. You're in them, standing plump-cheeked wearing a little striped suit. I don't know why he didn't object to you being there—maybe because he didn't have the energy to fight the war and me at the same time. To be able to live together we learned to pick our battles.

—Really, in blunt terms, my question is simple. If I'd been darker would he have let you keep me? Would he have picked that battle?

—Again, I don't think you need me to answer that question.

—What about you? Would you have stopped my beating and taken me home? Included me in the family pictures? Taken me with you fleeing Richmond?

—Fleeing America, to be precise.

—Would you have done it?

—Truth?

James nods.

—I don't know, V says. I hope so.

—Did we leave Richmond on a train? The other day I thought I remembered sleeping on a wood bench in a passenger car.

—Not bare wood, but a bad trip from the start, V says. At least I had my little suicide pistol to comfort me.

Falling Apart

March 1865

At the station a stub of train waited—a locomotive with a wood car, baggage car, and one old un-painted passenger car fitted with red velvet upholstery worn silvery bald in patches. V and Ellen and the chil-dren settled in. The Trenholm girls—beautiful daugh-ters of the secretary of the treasury, one of the richest men in America before the war—arrived like they were embarking on a pleasure cruise. The only men were Burton Harrison, Jefferson's secretary, and James Morgan, an officer—both in their twenties. Morgan had been yanked out of the trenches of Petersburg for this mission because Jefferson—still sometimes a romantic—knew love brewed between Morgan and one of the Trenholm girls and didn't want him to be among the last to die. Burton had accompanied V on all her emergency flights from Richmond—as protector, assistant, substitute husband—and they had long since become tight friends.

For the children V and Ellen made pallets of quilts on the floor between the rows of seats. Maggie and Billy and Jeffy and Jimmie lay down and pulled covers to their eyebrows. Jefferson came aboard and kissed cheeks and made assurances. Wished Morgan and the Trenholm girls bon voyage. He took Burton with him onto the platform, and they talked pretty urgently.

V sat next to Ellen and took her hand and said, You don't have to go with me. If it's better for you to stay here, then stay.

Ellen sat a long time looking down at the floor before saying, There's not anything here for me. And you can't handle all the children by yourself.

—Coming with me could get very bad.

—Bad here too with no money and food scarce till crops start growing. And besides, if it does get bad the children will need us both.

Somewhere in the night, only an hour or two below Petersburg, the locomotive broke down. No explosion of steam or clash of metal. They coasted quietly to a stop in dark woods and then sat through dawn and sunset and another dawn before finally rolling again. Four days in all to cover fewer than three hundred miles to Charlotte, during which time the provisional nation crumbled and many people died. Sherman's army still raged north after the burning of Columbia and no one knew what civilian target they would destroy next.

Word of V's arrival in Charlotte preceded them, and an angry, howling mob waited at the station—people already beaten in war and now standing at a cliff edge with nowhere to go but down. Among them, deserters and draftees and relatives of the pointlessly dead. Manners collapsed into rage. They saw V through the car window and began reviling. They shouted curses largely aimed at her husband, but since he wasn't present to absorb them, she would have to do. Burton convinced V and Ellen and the children to move away from the windows and huddle with the Trenholm girls in a corner, where they kept their courage up by making exaggerated shocked expressions at each angry vulgarity. V pulled her little weapon out and then realized the ammunition was packed away in a trunk, since she hadn't anticipated needing to kill herself in Charlotte.

Burton and Morgan had just a pistol and a sword between them. They stood inside the door to the car, and when a few brave mobsters climbed the steps, Burton showed his pistol and said, No.

If ten men had decided to board the car and do whatever their rage told them to do once inside, they could have stormed the door and succeeded, losing only two or three men. But no one wanted to go first. They backed off and shouted a few minutes more about killing Jeff Davis and the whole bunch of rich slave owners their friends and family had died for. Soon they lost interest and drifted away.

Burton went door-to-door through Charlotte looking for lodging at hotels and private homes, but everyone feared retribution, whether from their own angry people or from Sherman if he swept through killing and burning—the same people would have treated V like the queen of England twelve months before. Burton finally found a man named Weil who said he would be glad to offer shelter. The Trenholm girls and Morgan were moving on, the train set to take them as far down the line as it could toward their house in upstate South Carolina, the Charleston house being out of the question because of Sherman. One of the girls said, Come join us. We'll have a house party till they burn us out. Drink all the best wine to keep the Yankees from getting it.

Burton escorted V and Ellen and the children

through the angry streets of Charlotte to Mr. Weil's house. In the following days they stayed hidden away, though Burton went out once gathering scraps of news and rumor—the fall of Richmond, the flight of the government, Lee handing his sword to Grant at Appomattox.

==

—I still have that little pistol, V says. I keep it in my jewelry box.

—I can't imagine, whatever the danger, sending Julie away like that. If it was bad enough to give her a pistol to kill herself with, it would have been bad enough for me to walk away from everything else and try to take her someplace safe.

—Our situation was more complicated, V says. Jeff being president of a rebel country.

—Yes, but all that was over. How many days after we left Richmond did he go?

—I don't know. Three or four?

—And he didn't catch up with us for how long?

—Going on two months. And again, it's a point of pride that we could probably have made it to Cuba if he hadn't caught up with us.

James says, I told you last week about defending

him against black children in South Carolina and white children in Massachusetts and both groups of them fighting me. But all I remember of him is a slim, older white man in a suit. He was much older than you, and I've been wondering how you came together.

—It was briers and hurricanes right from the start, V says.

Hurricane & Brierfield

1842

She grew up outside Natchez in an old-fashioned house called The Briers. A house, not a plantation. No fields, no cotton. It sat on a few acres of high bluff overlooking the Mississippi. The ground sloped east to a dry bayou a hundred feet deep, its sides covered with pines and live oaks, and magnolia trees. To the west, deep yellow clay bluffs caved to the river below. The proportions of the house felt right—oversize windows and broad shady galleries across the front and back— but it was largely the river that made it beautiful.

Growing up, she witnessed every day all the dirty business of cotton and slaves, all the criminality and culture of the new country passing in miniature below her on the big brown river. Everything that floated—dugout canoes, and vast timber rafts, and every kind of john-boat, flatboat, keelboat, and barge, all the way to giant white paddle wheel steamboats—coasted down-current or struggled up.

Nights when she was young, looking down from the lawn of The Briers, steamboats passed below her lit up like Christmas. They trailed faint sounds of music and the distant grinding and churning of their great paddle wheels. She stood barefoot in the damp grass and watched their unreal passage below her, as if Venus had shifted its orbit and swooped by, a luminous world of its own, here and gone in minutes, leaving the blank space of wide river even quieter and darker than before.

At least once a month from twelve onward, dreams rode her nights. Prophetic, horrific, beautiful, mysterious. She never claimed they came true. Others did that, and during the Washington and Richmond years, she became famous for them. Most of them were no more important than anyone's dreams, but her spooky dreams, the scary ones, sometimes reappeared in the real world in large and small ways.

Twenty years before it happened, she dreamed the balcony and the cobbles and the house where little Joe fell to his death. She dreamed the whole bloody war long before it erupted. It was an epic nightmare that lasted until dawn. She was in Washington at the time, the wife of a freshman congressman, still in her teens and childless, delighted to be invited to parties at the White House and happy that Jeff's cotton plantation down on the Mississippi provided heaps of money. But she still remembers being yanked out of sleep by the horror of the war dream and getting up and squatting over the porcelain chamber pot in the dark and going back to sleep and the dream catching right back up. All the destruction and blood and punishment. Fallen heroes, victories and defeats, great acts of courage and cowardice. Battlefields muddy with blood, cotton fields full of slaves working ankle-deep in blood, whipping posts like red fountains, and all around a hurricane tide of red waves crashing over everyone. It was biblical in the sense that the Bible is a bloody red book. Even her beloved Greeks, back in the long dizziness of time, were nearly as bad—except for Sappho and a few other outliers. Otherwise, all dripping red down the green and blue globe.

At breakfast the next morning, her first words of the day were, About ninety-nine percent of the time, we're more awful than any animal you can name. But, in that final decimal, we're so beautiful.

Jeff said, You look tired. Bad dreams again?

The Briers did not belong to V's father. He leased it. The same thing with the few house slaves. WB Howell's theories of financial management were simple—why tie money to property when he could invest it in ill-conceived business schemes? WB was the youngest son of an eight-term New Jersey governor back when they held elections every year, and his money came mostly from inheritance and marriage to V's mother and from her very comfortable Mississippi family. Almost none of WB's money came from successful speculation, and none whatsoever came from actual work.

At age twenty, WB recognized that his pathways to success might not be so wide open in New Jersey or New York as he had grown up expecting. Older brothers stood in his way, and family politics tended unfavorably. After little more than a flicker of thought, he decided the likeliest place to realize his full potential was the American Southwest. Mississippi, Louisiana. Some town on the big river where he couldn't help but be the smartest man around. A place still whiffing the last tinge of lawless frontier. And Natchez—being to his understanding the fanciest town all the way from New Orleans to the frozen North where the great brown river arose—he chose it for home.

Sadly, contrary to WB's hopes, he was not the

smartest man in Natchez. In fact, those rubes picked his carcass clean. After marrying well—with a dowry of several thousand acres of land and nearly a hundred slaves, which he fairly quickly sold to raise investment cash—he spent nearly twenty years losing everything in countless failed business schemes. And then, after milking dry every teat he could pull in terms of borrowing, he found his world boiled down to one ugly frank reality. His southern adventure had broken him.

Back when she was thirteen—her family at the edge of bankruptcy—V's father had bet enough money to buy a small farm on a shooting match—a bet that always rested in her mind as the representative scene from that epoch of loss.

She pictured a muddle of wealthy, ignorant gentlemen, drunk and armed with rifles, in a raw patch of new-cleared ground, their horses and slaves shaded at the edge of the woods. A big lone pine tree sported a bull's-eye target nailed to its alligator-hide bark. Then WB, who would have been drinking heavily, stepped up to test his skill as a marksman. Or—since he had never in his life been able to hit the side of a cow barn from a hundred feet—to test his belief in the possibility of a miraculous light shining itself on him like a beam of Jacob's ladder.

When he came home he'd not only lost his money, but also misplaced his hat and tie. Red mud rose calf-high on his riding boots. He was reeling drunk, tacking wall-to-wall down the center hall of the house, grabbing unsuccessfully for a handhold on the shallow chair rail atop the wainscoting. Drunk had become a common gambit of his. But it had lost all effectiveness in their household except with V's mother, who always acted as if he'd unexpectedly suffered a mild stroke. And oh her joy a couple of afternoons later when he arose from his stupor, his recovery complete.

Unlike WB, V's grandfather believed in ownership. He had numerous slaves in New Jersey before, during, and after his governorship. The mansion depended on slaves as much as most every governor's residence in the country back then. Slaves accomplished everything from construction to maintenance, from cooking and cleaning to growing the kitchen gardens and emptying the chamber pots, all the way to wet nurses offering their weary nipples to somebody else's babies so that other mothers could get on with their lives. Some years later, V read Frederick Douglass's claim that he had seen the cotton fields of Mississippi and the pits of Yankee slave markets and considered their horrors about equal. So some version of that horror was how

WB grew up. And another version was how V grew up. How everyone grew up then, one way or the other, whichever side of the skin line you chanced to be born on. Children don't judge their own lives. Normal for them is what's laid before them day by day. Judgment comes later.

At sixteen—other than overwhelming scorn and rage—what power do you control? For the pimply boys V knew, it was guns and their prospects for inheritance. Girls had their bodies and minds. That age, you make choices and don't always know you're making them. Some don't matter, but a surprisingly large lot of them haunt forever. Each choice shuts off whole worlds that might have been.

The novels V liked at sixteen—and loved in a different way later—were the ones where young women exist at that precise thrilling hinge of time, the making of a dreadful, possibly fatal, choice. Who to marry, who to reject, which path to take? Whether to choose that plump, dullard heir to a vast estate or the handsome woodcutter living in a charming forest cottage. The moment forces decision. Wait, and risk choices disappearing forever. Make up your addled young mind too soon and afterward—unless you are a true and total rebel—your way forward in life narrows down to the dimensions of a railroad tunnel. Or, a better and more modern simile, to the horrific pinching aperture of a camera shutter, metal plates wrapping onto themselves, constricting, until the mechanism quickly opens and then closes for good with the snap of a trap, fixing you in a moment you'll regret to the grave.

Whether you pick well or poorly, the act of choosing carries grief. Leaves you wondering, years later, what life might have been had you chosen differently. You're living happy and comfortable as can be, mother of the placid heir's dull children, but still wondering about the higher pitch of romance that beautiful woodcutter offered. Or even wishing you'd simply paused, taken a long, deep breath. Not allowed the personal moment and the pattern of your family and your stupid culture to shove you two-handed from behind, forcing you to stumble unbalanced into the future.

Many years later, now that choices matter less, V has finally learned that sitting calm within herself and waiting is often the best choice. And even when it's not, those around you become uncomfortable because they think you are wise.

There's a photograph of V and Jeff on their honeymoon. They pose in a photographer's New Orleans studio after stopping along the way downriver from

Natchez to visit the grave of his first wife—what a lovely spot to be buried, pastel light filtering through live oaks drooping Spanish moss, prickly palmettos and cypress, and a stretch of opaque brown alligator swamp. In the photo the newlyweds look chilly and weary and very much separate, almost as if two different photographs had been grafted together. He avoids the camera. His eye-line slants stage left, an off-putting sense of evasion when frozen in time. His right eye shows white all around the iris. He poses stiff, impatient, his thin face an arrangement of angles, his right hand resting on his hip with the arm cocked strangely. A pale cravat grips his thin neck tight as a noose drawn up to his chin. The photograph magnifies the difference in their ages. He looks ancient beside her, grim and bloodless and predatory, caved cheeks and raptor nose. A few years later—in a political speech concerning the Wilmot Proviso—Jeff used the simile of a vampire lulling the victim he will soon destroy. Except in the flash of the photographer's ignited powder, V does not look lulled. She stares directly into the lens and appears angry and tired and more than a little smug.

This is all by way of prologue to the betrothal. Except, how to keep memory from rolling back to the months before that several-way transaction was struck between the Davises and the Howells that V fell into naive as Candide, with nothing but love and ambition burning in her young heart? Back before she realized everybody was racing for money and fame and power.

These days, she tries to be gentle with her young self. Her thinking must have been jangled and chaotic as a handful of steel ball bearings thrown onto the skin of a timpani in the middle of a performance. She keeps wanting to double back and re-dream the big river of her youth. Standing late at night barefoot in the damp lawn looking down on the campfires of the flatboats, the windows of little farms on the far bank glowing like pinpoints of yellow light for an hour or two after dark and then one by one going black. Re-dream the grand houses and parties in Natchez before her father's fall. Awkward fourteen-year-olds dancing on a Saturday night to a ragged quartet of piano, violin, cornet, and violoncello. Middle-size boys with overlapping front teeth and blemishes sweeping winglike from nose bridge across both cheeks almost to the ears. Black men in white jackets carrying silver trays of canapés—oysters and Gulf shrimp, terrapin minced with cucumber—everything perched on a crouton with a fat red pearl of pepper sauce at the center. The younger boys wiped out those big trays of food like a storm of locust. The fifteen-year-old boys carried flat pewter flasks of whiskey in their breast pockets and made a great show of sipping surreptitiously.

Memory filters all that sort of material through a slight haze of morphine, which back in her youth her doctors said V needed only a few days monthly and before important dances. So in memory all the pastel dresses and the boys' dark suits and white shirts trail smears of color behind them as they move about the dance floor, a watercolor blurred across wet paper by dragging a wide brush. A yellow parquet floor's jagged pattern vibrates in her mind. Many of the other girls lived a similar reality, their doctors believing the same orthodoxy in regard to the magical properties of opiates in managing females.

During a waltz an earnest young man—sweaty face and gloveless palms—pressed his urgent right hand so low on the small of her back that *back* isn't the precise word. And after the waltz drifted to a close and the couples parted, a girlfriend stepped up to whisper in V's ear that a dark replica of the boy's damp hand printed itself onto the peach silk of her dress in an indelicate place. Knowing that on a muggy May night in Natchez—air so wet catfish could survive in it—a sweat mark would never dry, like being stamped with the Puritan red letter except comic.

V remembers the details of that night to the extent

that she could still hum most of the tunes the band played, inhale the scent of lavender and sweat from the whispering girlfriend, the musty pomade of the urgent dance partner. She loves every instant of it. Sometimes, after a long series of nightmares, at bedtime she breathes deep and twists the lamp wick and tells herself to shut out the doom dreams that roar like hurricane winds and instead dream that night of awkward youth and dancing, when an ardent palm print on her bottom was her greatest imaginable problem.

The Great Divide—rivers change direction and you're stuck following one flow or the other from then on. That was the trip to Davis Bend. Out of The Briers, into The Hurricane.

In early fall of the year, at the dinner table, V's father announced that a very attractive and generous invitation had arrived for her. She would be traveling upriver to the plantation of Joseph Davis, a lawyer and planter and former partner of WB's in a rare successful investment. The Hurricane occupied a several-thousand-acre hunk of land in a big C-shaped meander of the Mississippi that people had started calling Davis Bend. She was to go up at the beginning of December and stay through Christmas and into the New Year, two months at least. Maybe more. Home by Valentine's Day at the latest. Her tutor, Winchester, would escort her there and then return to Natchez, leaving her in the care of the Davis women, a wife and some indeterminate number of daughters. At which point, her relationship with Winchester—at least as student and teacher—would end. WB suggested V should look upon the trip as a holiday—new places, new people. Important for her to make an impression. Also Joseph had a younger brother who was developing an adjoining plantation called Brierfield, and she would certainly meet him during the visit. Etc., etc. WB even raised his glass in a toast, as if something happy were being celebrated.

V raised her glass right back and said, How welcome. A worthy substitute for the debutante ball next spring, for which I won't be tapped. So, let's all drink to wonderful new opportunities no longer available in Natchez or Vicksburg or New Orleans. Here's to my new life among a band of wilderness strangers.

She delivered her lines with every grain of mighty sarcasm an unhappy teen can summon.

Winchester graduated from Princeton, which swung weight even in Mississippi. But it swung the other way too. He had passed the bar and started a struggling law practice but also knew all about Greek and Latin literature and philosophy and history, which some of WB's more suspect business friends felt served a similar function to sprinkling colored sugar on cake icing.

People became more indulgent after Winchester's inheritance. He suddenly owned better than two thousand very fine acres fronting on the Mississippi over on the Louisiana side. Except, immediately upon possession, Winchester began letting most of the fields return to their previous junglous state. He kept only a couple hundred in cotton—figuring that was all the cash he needed to live on—plus another ten in food crops.

When asked by his peers why he ran his plantation as he did—whether he meant something by it or not, whether there was a particular theme to his strange choices—he raised his arms before him and flippered both hands impatiently and said the word *slaves* with a tone of ambiguous annoyance. Some fellow planters agreed that slaves required constant attention and that for every good worker you also had to support a half-dozen children and a useless granny or two. Others agreed that as an institution, slavery's time had passed, its golden age behind it, though the Bible and the Constitution of the United States confirmed its holy justice. Others worried Winchester had gone north to school and had lost all his common sense and had abandoned belief in slavery altogether.

Then one mighty day, after months of thought on the topic, Winchester freed all his enslaved workers. He handed them their papers and shooed them on their way. Then he began hiring workers the way Yankees did, cheap and by the carefully measured hour. But, unlike Yankees, he paid everyone the same wages—remnant Choctaw and freed blacks got the same as whites. He hired back many of his previous slaves under the new economics. For those who wanted to live in his housing, he started charging rent. And when it came to food and clothing, he left everybody to manage for themselves. Winchester lived alone and ate mostly bean stews, grits and greens, and other such simple bowl meals that he cooked for himself.

He suffered under the judgment of his fellow rich planters who claimed he had gone crazy. He answered that he had seen the future of capitalism, and believed that if they fully understood it, the planters would embrace it like a favorite New Orleans whore.

V was seven the year Winchester got bored with farming and sold his land and moved in with the Howells under some arrangement with WB that she, even now, doesn't understand fully, but has celebrated nearly every day of her life when an electric spark of memory delivers a reminder that Winchester valued her far beyond what WB—or anyone else—ever did.

Winchester hadn't arrived with any intention of being her tutor. He lived out in one of the back cottages at The Briers with his books. He had an office in town and was just a struggling lawyer and not the judge in black robes he later became. He took supper at the family table, but otherwise they saw little of him.

A couple of months after his arrival, though, he volunteered to tutor V and would not accept a penny in pay. Maybe he felt the need to reimburse WB for room and board, or maybe he saw something in V worth his time and interest. She remembers one detail from their first day together as student and teacher. V had recently asked her mother what her odd name meant, where it came from. Her mother said, Your father came up with it. I guess he thought it sounded exotic. V asked Winchester the same question, what her name meant. He said, It comes from the Greeks. A variant of Barbara. It means foreigner. Barbarian. Onomatopoeia. They thought outsider languages sounded like baa, baa, baa, vaa, vaa, vaa. Grunts and chatter. From about that time, Winchester was V's only teacher and she was his only student—excepting a miserable few months at a school for hateful rich girls in Philadelphia ruled by a despot V ever after called Madame X. WB sent her there believing it would be a grand experience for her. The girls mocked her accent, laughed about her skin color, her height, her seriousness in discussing the fine points of translation. Said to her face that she was so frontier, so unpolished. After only one quarter, much to V's joy, Madame X sent her home.

All those years together, V thought of Winchester as elderly. Old Winchester. But looking back and doing the sums, he wasn't much past thirty when she met him. He hadn't married when he arrived at The Briers and never did.

V couldn't decide whether her father tried to be kind or cruel when he asked Winchester to escort her upriver to Davis Bend. Maybe WB thought the break would be easier on her if it was clean and quick and final. Or maybe he wanted to send her the message that at seventeen she was old enough to make her own way, that he had cut her loose, shoved her into a world where the contractual nature of marriage was stronger than novels had led her to expect.

Starting right then, and continuing through the rest of his life, she dropped addressing Winchester by any name but Dear Heart.

Right about here, cynics might need reassurance. Male tutors and piano teachers and art instructors hold dim reputations in regard to their behavior toward young female students. Yet as V has said many times over the years—hand to Holy Book—the only touches passing between them all those years, all those thousands of hours alone in the dim silent library and out in the little one-room schoolhouse on the back lawn, were occasional pats on the back of her hand, taps on each temple from his slim forefingers to encourage her to think harder rather than give up when some complex twist of language and thought from Aristotle or Plato or Heraclitus rose like a high gray stone wall between her and the distant brilliant past. Except for that last day at Davis Landing.

Despite living all her life with the wide brown flow of the Mississippi as the overwhelming geography of her world—the Pikes Peak and Mont Blanc—V had never traveled on a grand riverboat. So as she and Winchester boarded the *Magnolia* in Natchez, she was fairly overwhelmed by the scale of the thing. The big stern-wheel vessel—all its grinding and ratchety mechanisms of boilers and cranks and struts and gears and wheels and paddles—pulsed with kinetic power.

V worried about her clothes. Appropriate dress is so easy for men. They mostly want to wear uniforms, so their choices are strict and almost nonexistent. Winchester wore a black suit and a white shirt, and he could have gone to a funeral, a wedding, a baptism, or to testify in a court of law. But V had troubled herself for weeks coming up with a traveling outfit that would place her in the public eye as she wanted to be placed. Slightly more overdressed than underdressed and not looking like a frumpy governess on the way to a first job, but not like a little idiotic curly-haired belle either. She wanted to costume herself for a role that she wasn't sure existed.

Her compartment felt glamorous, though it was not. The whole space of her cabin measured six by nine with only enough floor space to stand and change clothes. A louvered door opened onto the outside boiler deck, and a solid door opened into the central salon. Her bunk, braced by metal rods, hung like a shelf from the wall. She turned back a wedge of coverlet to reveal perfectly white linen, but when she mashed her hand down, the mattress was only a thin, dense mat of kapok compressed by the weight of a thousand bodies. A tiny wax-blistered bedside shelf served as nightstand, with a single candle to read by. The energy of the big boat pulsed through the floors and walls and felt dangerous—which it was, given the many hundreds of passengers who had died on the river from boiler explosions.

———

After dinner—served at long tables in the salon—V and Winchester walked circles around the boiler deck and down the stairs to the main deck and all the way up to the hurricane deck where they stood at the rails and watched a muted early December sunset over Louisiana. A crescent moon and a bright planet or two stood in the deep sky above the horizon. She rested a hand on his forearm as they walked, but they couldn't find a topic for conversation sustainable beyond three exchanges. When the sky went fully dark, Winchester stopped as they passed her door. He said, We need to say good night.

V said, I thought we might take blankets and sit in the deck chairs and talk until dawn.

—I'm afraid not tonight, Winchester said.

—Then what other night?

—Not this one, dear.

V's baggage hunched on the dock. She stood at the rail of the *Magnolia* and looked down at them and was already slightly embarrassed that all her clothes and toiletries and books for the journey fit into only two arch top trunks.

After the settled, monied beauty of Natchez—pink azaleas and purple bougainvillea and white columns—

Davis Landing looked like bleeding-raw nothing, a vast expanse of brown water merged into a viscous mud landscape churned to slop by horses and oxen and wagon wheels. A stub of gray wood dock reached forty feet into the river. The weathered posts rotted half-a-foot deep into the rings of the cut tops, and deck boards curled upward against their nails at both ends like heathens raising their arms in praise of the sun. The riverboat floated self-contained, visiting for a brief moment, whiter and more powerful and more important than the muddy landscape and utterly transient.

A great many black men hefted large heavy things on and off the boat.

Winchester already waited on the dock alongside the trunks. Seeing him from the deck, V thought he looked like a preacher standing at the pulpit ready to begin a ceremony.

She walked down the lowered stage to the dock and stood close beside him. She said, Who gives this girl?

Winchester shook his head and smiled a grim smile. He looked tired.

A slim black man—V's age, wearing creased brown pants and a very white shirt—walked onto the dock and said, Miss Howell?

—Yes?

—I'll take you to Hurricane, miss. Be a while getting there, with the road and all.

—Just a few moments, V said.

As the unloading and reloading of the boat finished, she and Winchester stood together and looked away from the river into the country. The only visible structure stood at the tree line, a big shed roofed with old silvery shakes. It leaned off plumb, shadowed by tall pines. A sloppy wet one-track road stretched inland and disappeared in a curve between the woods and the shed and a fallow cotton field.

V said, I thought you were spending a night or two here and then taking a down boat?

—No, Winchester said. That's not possible.

—Of course it's possible. In fact I understood it was planned.

—Not possible for me. I'm sorry. I'll go on up to Vicksburg and find a boat back down to Natchez in a few days.

Winchester awkwardly kissed her hand. And then he reached his arms around her and held her in a long embrace like a man gripping his own life, trying to keep from being pulled below the opaque surface of the river and dragged to the Gulf by the weight of high muddy water. And then he gripped her shoulders at their bony points and pushed her out to arm's length and looked her level in the eyes. She and Winchester had become the same height a year before.

V looked back at him. She noticed a few threads of gray hairs at his temples.

Winchester said, Don't.

He shook his head, as if he had more to say, but he didn't finish. He kissed her on the forehead and on each cheek and then on the lips. And then he turned and walked up the stage to the boat.

V watched him until he was gone. Wondering, don't what?

Don't forget to write? Don't stop reading Homer? Don't ever forget me? Don't leave me? The instant passed so fast, and when that happens, it goes for good and all you have is a slow lifetime to speculate on revisions. Except time flows one way and drags us with it no matter how hard we paddle upstream.

Looking back, how much older was Winchester than the older man she married?

The slim black man sat in a flatbed wagon waiting—not a carriage but a wagon you might haul hay in. He was handsome and wore a pointed goatee that lengthened his face. His eyes were pale green and distant, a veil between himself and the world. V climbed in and sat on the bench beside the driver while her trunks were loaded. The *Magnolia*'s big paddle wheel began churning against the current.

The horses stood sunken in mud to the pasterns, and when the driver slapped the reins they took their first steps with loud sounds of suction.

When they reached the woods-edge, V said, This is strange territory.

All the warning the man could give was to turn his head her way and look her a glancing blow and say, Deep in the world round here, miss.

—Tell me your name, she said.

—Benjamin Montgomery.

They rolled past cotton fields and cornfields, ragged and brutalized, the rubble of stems and stalks and branches, all the biologic rot of the off-season. For a while, the driver hummed a weary delta pattern of notes, five of them, over and over.

V said, Benjamin, is it a nice house, The Hurricane?

—Better than most.

—I've met Mr. Joseph Davis before, back when I was a girl. But not his wife and children.

—All young ladies around the place, ma'am—about your same age.

—Really? And Mrs. Davis?

—The same too.

—Mysterious, V said.

—Ma'am?

—Mother and daughters all the same age. Unusual at least.

—They call each other all by their first names without saying Mama and Daddy and Sister.

—Yes? Like none of them are related?

Benjamin shrugged his shoulders.

Then the flurry of arrival, the greetings, all the strangeness of somebody else's house. The smells of people and food. All the figuring out of your bedroom, your baggage, the delicacy of how they handle chamber pots. Except that chamber pots didn't factor because, amazingly, each of the three floors had a toilet flushed with rainwater from a cistern down in the basement and a tank on the roof.

A strange table that evening—Old Joseph and his gathering of four young women, five counting V. They dined by the dim light of big silver candelabras with half the tapers burned down to useless stubs. Supper was perfunctory, almost a snack. Slices of cold salty ham, a white bowl of boiled potatoes, a small bowl of yesterday's greens, a cruet of cider vinegar, a straw basket of biscuits, and a small clump of butter slumping on a saucer.

Eliza, the young wife, said, You've come a day before I expected, so tomorrow night will be better. She cracked a smile to reveal tiny white teeth set in very pink gums.

—This is the third of the month, isn't it? V said, confused and ready to apologize for her presence.

—Oh, I wouldn't know, the wife said. I just expected you a day later than this one is all.

As Benjamin had said, Joseph's wife and his eldest daughter and V all looked much the same age. The two other daughters looked to be about thirteen, and both seemed like strange girls exiled to that lonely river bend without strong memories of anywhere else.

A servant poured alcohol only for Joseph, and he took just the one glass of brown whiskey, though he drank it out of a Champagne coupe poured brimful. He sat among them like their weary grandfather, nearly bald and hollow-cheeked and wealthy and shabby, the dome of his head pinkish gray. Big windows stood full open, and faint sounds of frogs and bugs and reptiles pulsed from the total black night outside. Mosquitoes and moths flew in and out the windows, and some of them immolated themselves in the candle flames, flashing and sizzling like tiny fireworks. The butter-colored plaster walls lay blank, without any blemish of framed art. For long stretches, little conversation occurred—sounds of people chewing and silverware on china.

At some point, like flinging a baited hook into a fished-out pond, more to test casting skills than in hope of catching something, V said, Mr. Davis, your peninsula of land, your Bend, is an interesting plot of geography.

—I suppose.

V cast again, Was it cleared when you arrived or did you hack it out of green wilderness? And, how did you and your girls come to move here from Natchez?

She expected a boring story of business opportunity, a shrewd real estate purchase, fertile soil, rising cotton prices, maybe something about favorable slave prices way out here in the wilderness.

But Old Joe clashed his fork down on his plate. The girls around the table looked down at their food.

He said very hot, What have you heard? Are they still gossiping about me in Natchez?

—No, sir, V said quickly. Not that I've heard.

After a long silence, Joseph finally answered V's question about the land. He said, It took a long time, scraping the jungle to bare dirt and burning all the bushes and vines and trees and digging up and burning the stumps to make the land ready for planting cotton.

Eliza said, I wasn't here then, but it must have been a challenge for the labor force.

—How many acres? V asked.

—Round it to eight thousand, Joseph said. Above all, though, The Hurricane is an experiment. Have you heard of Robert Owen, the Welshman? His famous utopian social philosophies?

—I know the name and little more, V said. His theme is social justice, isn't it?

—One of them. Democratic socialism is the heart of the matter. A few years ago I met him on a long stagecoach ride west out of Pittsburgh. He was on a speaking tour, explaining the utopian community he intended to build in Indiana. He had owned a factory town in Scotland and developed ideas about fairness between capital and labor. Interestingly, the other passenger was Mister Dickens's illustrator, Cruikshank, and all I remember him saying was how every country's artists depict Jesus with their own features. Owen and I, though, talked without stop for ten hours, and I've since read every word of his writings available on this side of the Atlantic. Very interesting, his notions concerning the relationship between labor and capital. His sense of a utopian manufacturing community of equity and fairness and justice. That day was transformative for me. I'm trying to apply his ideas here.

The older daughter pushed a little sweet pickle around her plate in boredom, and the younger girls whispered and bumped elbows and smothered laughs based on some derisive, isolate humor shared by just the two of them.

Eliza said, An example of Joseph's innovations is, slave court happens second Thursday of every month, and he rarely involves himself in decisions of crime and punishment unless the sentence is too harsh. And there's also a health clinic. A doctor comes monthly and inspects the force. And you'll see their church tomorrow. The slave preachers swap Sundays. Baptist and Methodist. And we're organizing the older women to take care of the babies so that the young mothers can get back to work.

—I like to think of The Hurricane as a community, Joseph said. A sort of campus.

V said, So, if I'm following the thread, your experiment is to test whether Mr. Owen's thoughts on labor and capital ownership can be applied under a slave economy?

—The real issue isn't *whether*. It's *how*. The details shouldn't concern you.

V—accustomed to arguing every detail concerning art and music and philosophy and history with Winchester—said, But the ideas interest me. Surely the difference between slave workers and paid workers is too enormous for the experiment to succeed?

Joseph, testy, said, Obviously it will require adaptations. Owen's insistence on educating workers beyond the needs of their task would be foolish. And the improvement of wages he advocates isn't applicable. But as my brother and I have discussed many times, the economic institution we operate under—the bondman model—solves one of the great problems of industrial capitalism, the conflict between capital and labor. And the value of labor itself. Under an Owenism adapted for the South, labor and capital become one and the same. Labor *is* capital and has a clear market value.

V paused a moment in disbelief and then said, I suppose the real issue is simply whether anything remains of Owen's philosophy after all the adaptations for slavery are made?

Joseph shook his head, sighed a deep sigh, and stood and excused himself, saying, We retire early here. Some of us rise early as well.

He walked to the door and turned back and said, Miss Howell, I worry that the pains your father has taken to educate you will result in little but finding himself with a wit on his hands.

———————

V couldn't sleep. Insects and frogs fell silent. The house made sounds, and the night lay too still to mask them with wind in the trees. A faint two-beat rhythm vibrated all the way from the basement—slaves working the pumps that forced water into the rooftop tank to flush The Hurricane's amazing toilets.

She turned the day over and over, penciling thoughts in a notebook. She tried to reconstruct every comment she had made at dinner and couldn't come up with even the feeblest attempt at wit.

Mostly, though, V wrote down thoughts of Winchester's tenderness leaving her there with the Davises, all their noses sharp and hooked as cheap hawkbill knives, parting the air as they moved through the world with hollow cheeks and ashy, distant eyes. She valued Winchester's tenderness and his kiss partly because at fourteen she had suffered under a violent crush for at least a month. And every time she flung herself at him he backed away so gracefully, so sweetly, that she never felt unduly shamed by her behavior. She wondered if she had been insensitive to him on the upriver trip—overly taken with the glory of the riverboat, the color of gaslight on gold and burgundy wallpaper and carpet. The tiny private sleeping rooms and the power of the great paddle wheel churning muddy water all night provoking intense, condensed dreams of great significance. And above all, the sheer sensation of travel, being suddenly in motion after so long static on her bluff-top looking down on the river.

She immediately began writing a letter of apology to Winchester.

A half hour later—three quick knuckle raps on V's door long past the time for that sort of thing. She pulled a dressing gown over her nightgown and opened the door a crack. The oldest daughter, with the questionable name of Florida, bumped right in uninvited, barefoot and wearing just the ultimate layer of thin, ivory night-gear, like she had draped herself in a sheet of linen bandaging. Her dark hair fell loose below her shoulders and her face shaped itself like all the Davises', narrow and predatory. Florida carried two slim books and an almost-full bottle of red wine. Her gray eyes looked straight at V.

She said, I may be wrong, but I think we could be good friends.

—Well, V said. How do you propose finding out?

—Let's read our favorite poems to each other, Florida said.

—Of course. I'll choose a few from the books I have

with me, and we can read together on the porch after breakfast.

Florida jabbed her books out at V—two stabs—and said, I meant tonight. Now.

Then she paused and looked down at her feet and flexed her long toes.

She said, I apologize. Was that pushy? It's so lonely sometimes, and then you came sweeping in and I got excited. And Old Joe gets touchy about Natchez and wagging tongues, and he only likes to hear opinions that agree with his. I worried everything had gone wrong from the start. And then I saw the light under your door. But we can talk in the morning.

—Now would be perfect, V said. This minute. I feel so strange, and I don't know why I'm here.

—We don't know why you're here either, Florida said, very brightly. But we have theories. In a few days, I might tell you some of our secrets.

—No, V said. If we're going to be friends, tell one right now.

Florida thought two beats and then said, This one's not about you, but it's the biggest secret here and nobody but Old Joe knows the whole truth of it, and maybe he doesn't either, really. It's that not a one of us has a birth certificate. No record of parentage, married or not. Like orphans. Nothing on paper to mark Old

Joe's trail. Not a single footprint. And I'm guessing you probably did hear plenty in Natchez about our complications.

Florida told how they had left town under a cackle of rumor and slur. Oldest daughter a thin crescent of new moon older than the teen wife. Three daughters not from the same mother and no corresponding certificates of marriage or death or, heaven forbid, divorce.

—Doesn't clarify anything that all of us look alike. Far as I'm concerned, people in Natchez can call us all bastards and leave it at that. Maybe we entered the world in the Delta or some Louisiana swamp where they do things different. Old Joe tells Eliza she is his first wife, but who knows? None of us have even vague memories of mothers. And about all Joe wants out of any of us, including Eliza, is to leave him alone. He's never cared if we knew whether the earth was flat or not as long as we could at minimum read and write. But he doesn't stop us when we educate ourselves out of his books. Which are about four-fifths boring law books, so I hope one of your trunks is full of literature. How's that for a start?

V said, Must have been quite the steamboat trip up from Natchez that first time.

Florida laughed and said, So you're really saying no

wonder Old Joe looks like he's seventy when he's really fifty-five.

—Really?

—What he claims.

V said, But he must be your father, yes?

Florida said, The rule here is, no assumptions. We don't spend time wondering if Old Joe is our natural daddy and how many mothers are involved. And we sure don't ask. You saw how he gets. But yes, he's my father. Whoever my mother was, she made him believe I was his. I don't know facts, and probably there aren't any to know. Whatever crazy thing people want to believe, that's what they call it, a fact. I do know that however hard you try, you can't see inside the tangle of somebody else's love—or whatever uglier word applies—not deep enough to make sense of it. Whoever my mother was, she either died right after I was born or else ran off. Old Joe didn't run, and that counts. And if I'm not his daughter by blood, maybe it counts even more.

Florida paused and said, Now, you tell one.

V said, Well, I've been in love with my tutor for years. And at your dock today, he kissed me on the lips.

—Ha, Florida said. If we had a tutor, all four of us would be climbing over each other's backs to kiss him. I mean a real secret.

—All right, V said. But I'll warn you nothing is as boring as other people's dreams and finances. I think I'm here because of my father's money troubles and his old friendship with Joseph. Everybody's mad at my father in Natchez.

—Now there you go, Florida said. That's a start.

So V told Florida what she knew. About how her father thought he was much better with money than he really was, how he invested like a gambler, always sure his luck was about to turn. Except it never did. How they went from a rich round of parties at the grand houses of Natchez to being stricken from everybody's invitation list due to WB's owing money to half the wealthy men in Natchez after talking them into various failing schemes and partnerships and outright loans. How they would have gone under except for distant family buying their best paintings and a pair of really fine carriage horses and other valuable objects those aunts and uncles had their eyes on for some time. Except afterward, those relatives started acting like they owned her family because they finally got what they wanted at a bargain price.

—Gone under, Florida said. That's a drowning metaphor, and death by water is said to be a bad way to go.

—The only wisdom my father has ever passed along

to me was, Borrow all you can when interest rates are low and use other people's money to invest, V said.

She went on talking, telling Florida that the main part of WB's mess that struck home at fifteen and sixteen was that invitations to the better dances and parties dwindled to nothing, all those social occasions where advantageous matches between young people were negotiated. Very quickly—without anyone having to say a word—she understood that she had become not the least bit advantageous. She had nothing but herself as dowry. And that fundamental offering was not really in demand. Too tall, too dark, too slim, too educated, too opinionated. Also prone to moods. And yet, until now, her family had traveled only within the highest levels of Natchez society, so no handsome, honest planter with a thousand acres but no pretensions—poorly educated but smart and teachable—would have dared approach her, even if willing to overlook all her liabilities.

—Information to think on, Florida said. Old Joe's always figuring his next move. Twiddling his fingers over a fan of cards, which one to pull from his hand and throw down. Maybe a knave of hearts.

The fourth morning of the visit, V and Florida sat in rockers on the lower front gallery talking favorite nov-

els. The younger girls sat under a tree in the yard playing a game of cards that sometimes involved throwing
them all in the air.

Florida said, I have to be so careful with novels. Important to pace myself with them. I love words more
than anything or anybody, but my mind is a feather
in the wind. So I mostly read poems. A novel drains
me entirely. More than one a month and I start getting
dark under the eyes. After *Nick of the Woods,* I didn't
sleep for a week.

Florida had been V's refuge from the challenges of
conversing with equally dour Old Joseph and young
Eliza. Sometimes, rarely, when an old man—gray
and bald and paunchy and blotchy—marries a much
younger woman, he becomes younger too, like having
her at his side equals a draft of black Gypsy potion or
crystal water from Ponce de León's magic fountain.
That's what old men want desperately to believe. With
Joseph and Eliza, it went the opposite way, as it gener-
ally does—Joseph kept *being* old and Eliza *became* old.
Though she was barely V's elder—and thus her age
still ended in *teen* for the next couple of months—Eliza
acted like an awful granny who had turned grim rather
than feisty with age. V's opinion was, give me an old
wrinkled woman with a blistering tongue any day to
a young beaten dog hump-shouldered by the fireside

hoping for death to grant release. To Eliza's credit, though, she could still rally to give V the bright, jealous side-eye when she looked particularly pretty at the dinner table.

So V said to Florida, Why would a girl Eliza's age marry her grandfather?

Florida laughed and said, To be fair, we don't know for certain that Old Joe's her grandfather.

V blushed, but one of the benefits of being brownish is that often nobody notices.

V said, I apologize. That's not what I meant. It was an expression. You hear all kinds of rumors around Natchez, some of them about my own family. Hardly any with a particle of truth.

Florida patted her arm and said, Easy down, girl. We're past that now. I don't know about you, but there's probably plenty of truth in what they say about us.

V said, One way or the other, I guess we're both outlaws. Fled to the wilderness, or driven to it.

Florida said, Let's kiss on that, like blood brothers.

Florida leaned and pecked V on the cheek. And then when V leaned to peck her back, Florida turned her face and kissed V on the mouth.

And then V was certain Florida saw the blush.

Florida laughed and said, Oh, you're gonna take a lot of breaking in. But while you cool off, I'll go back to your question about Eliza and Joe. The answer's easy. Some women feel like, if they've got to marry they want to marry the biggest, strongest, richest bear in the woods. Even if that bear's old and grumpy and shaggy and stinks, he's your big bear. He's won a lot of battles to be where he is, and he's not going down easy. Eliza's that kind of woman. And I'm not criticizing. I haven't figured out which kind of woman I am. Maybe that kind.

V sat quiet within her seventeen-year-old self, thinking about the handsome woodcutter.

—**The man** who drove me from the river, Benjamin Montgomery. I see him all over the place. One minute he's here in the house coming in and out of the library and the office, then he's on horseback studying the fields, then around the barns checking inventory of hay and feed. Always busy, always writing notes in a little book.

—Yes?

—Well, what is his job?

—A little bit of everything. Mostly, Ben stays busy making himself indispensable.

Florida explained how some while back, Joseph bought Ben out of Virginia, just across the Potomac from Washington. He arrived in Mississippi knowing how to read and write, and he was especially good with numbers. Then before long Ben began drawing architectural plans for outbuildings with compasses and rulers and squares. He learned how to survey land in no time—all that complicated business of rods and chains and that strange device on its tripod. But before all that, Ben hadn't been at the Bend much over a month when he ran. He was caught in Vicksburg trying to pass as free, looking for a job on a northbound riverboat. When he got hauled back to Davis Bend, Joseph didn't whip him. They had a meeting in the office, just the two of them, and the way they both tell it, Joseph asked Ben to name the source of his displeasure. Ben said he preferred the city life.

—Oh, please, V said. My experience may be limited, but I won't believe just anything. That is not the way it goes.

—I'm not making this up. They worked out some compromise between them. Soon Benjamin was married to a pretty girl named Edella and was keeping the books for all Joseph's holdings and running the plantation store—eventually with a cut of the profits. He has free run of Joseph's library and collects books of his own. Gets paid cash for some of his work, and uses some of his money to buy Edella's time back from Joseph—so she can stay home and care for their new baby. He's made himself so necessary to the running of The Hurricane that Joseph's recently taken out a fat insurance policy on his life. Joseph can leave for any stretch of time and Ben runs the whole place, and writes reports and asks permission for big expenditures but decides the smaller ones himself.

—You're making all this up.

—Am not. This place is strange aplenty.

V first saw Uncle Jeff riding through the front gates of The Hurricane on a thoroughbred, a chestnut mare, her coat gleaming when the sun hit. He was a fine horseman—perfect equitation, straight relaxed posture in the saddle—though she saw he was showing off, using a lot of leg urging the mare forward and at the same time using the reins to hold her back, collecting her energy and releasing it, trying to make her look harder to ride than she was. But still, he looked beautiful on a horse. Even during the war when he was tired and sick and half blind, he rode for hours almost daily.

V guessed he was about her mother's age—late thirties—and was surprised he could still maintain so athletic an aspect. Once he set foot on the ground, though, he lost something and became just a slim, middle-size man. She noticed right away his stacked boot heels lifting him an inch higher than reality and wondered what that might say about him, whether he was a fop or had a streak of bantam rooster in him.

The more she saw as he handed the reins to a bond-man and walked to the house, the real issue wasn't really his height. It was his slightness, how finespun his bones must be. Later—bad times during the war and worse times after—he didn't eat much and wouldn't have gone a hundred twenty even after one of Mary Chesnut's feasts, when oysters and turkeys and ducks and doves and bowls of fresh vegetables cooked shiny in pork fat appeared magically out of the scarcity of war. But that first moment she saw him, he carried a little more muscle, say one-forty.

Just before Jeff walked within earshot, Florida said, very dry and ironic, Your Romantic poet arrives. Then she raised her voice so that Jeff could hear her say, Oh, look! He's out of mourning at last.

V turned to Florida in confusion, and Florida laughed at the confusion she intended to create.

Then to Jeff, Florida said, Good Lord, brighten up. You're here to meet a pretty girl, not be the subject for a hanging. Cousin Jeffy, darling, I keep trying to tell you how to avoid that preying viper melancholy. It's sim-ple. Follow my six commandments. Cherish ambition. Cherish pride. Don't mope. Dismiss the past, because it's gone for good. Do not defer pleasure whenever and wherever it rears its smiling face. Run from excitement to excitement until the clock winds down. But you can't seem to learn any but the second commandment. You're the damned slowest student in the class.

Jeff glanced at V as Florida talked, and then he climbed the steps and removed his flat-brimmed hat and kissed Florida's cheeks. All smiles and manners—he welcomed V with a quick touch of hands. His hair lay mashed all around by the hatband, and he ran his fingers through it. He wore an unusual cravat, brighter and puffier and more patterned than the current fashion, a sort of peachy color, and it wrapped his neck almost to his sharp jawline. He wore not a hint of black.

Florida swept her hand toward another rocker and said, Join us, Cousin. Since that's why you saddled your best horse and rode all this way.

—Uncle, he said.

Florida, acting for just the audience of V and Jeff, said, That always sounds so strange, calling you Uncle, since my daddy is more like your daddy than your brother. I've decided from now on we're going to ignore our ridiculous family tree. Too much complication. Girls so young and Old Joe so old. And you're tending in that direction too if we don't do something about it. I plan to young you up. As relationships go, *Uncle* sounds old and imposes a distance and protocol, sets limits that *Cousin* doesn't. Way out here in the jungle, I understand cousins even marry now and then. So no arguments, no witness testimony. I've adjudicated the matter. We're all of us cousins except Old Daddy Joe.

V laughed at Florida, and Jeff looked at V, uncomfortable and embarrassed and a little angry.

He recovered and said, Miss Howell, by now you've probably learned that anything Cousin Florida says is suspect.

And then to Florida he said, Where is Old Joe? I have a business matter.

—Of course you do. He's in the office, but you know that. He lives there. Why don't you show V our steam-powered cotton gin. She's only been shown it twice since she got here.

Jeff shook his head and kept walking. After he passed through the front door, Florida turned to look at V.

All it took was a lift of eyebrow on V's part and Florida started spilling a story.

She told how Jeff's first little wife, Knoxie, remained close in his heart long after her death, her loss haunting him to the extent that he had lived in almost hermitic seclusion for nearly a decade. How in the early days of mourning—after Jeff and Pemberton went to Havana to sketch and read and recover from her loss and Jeff got arrested as a spy by the Cubans because he sketched too many fortifications—he and Pemberton had lived like savages out on Brierfield, going a month at a time without sticking their heads out of their hole—living in nearly identical log cabins they built themselves. It was just Jeff and Pemberton and a few slaves. Jeff would turn up his sleeves and clear land all day like he didn't care if he worked himself to death or anybody else either. Florida said that Jeff and Pemberton had been together since before West Point, and after graduation—because Jeff's grades were poor and a few of the faculty wrote scathing letters of evaluation—they found themselves stationed way up in the northwest wilderness. Nothing but dark fir forests and cold rivers, and frontier forts. Stockades of palings with the bark left on, the top ends sharpened to points with axes, like rows of upright primitive pencils. Otherwise just bears and wolves and Indians and British and French moving south out of Canada. Then before long Knoxie and Jeff fell in love. Her daddy, Zachary Taylor, was the officer in charge of the fort and didn't want his daughter to marry a soldier, or at least didn't want her to marry Cousin Jeff. So Jeff quit the army. They ran off and got married with none of her people there, and headed down the river on their honeymoon. Before they made it to New Orleans, they both got sick, and she died but he did not. That song "The Fairy Bells"—she was singing it when she died in his arms. At least that was the story. And he'd been wearing some degree of mourning ever since—seven years—until today.

A few days later, Jeff invited V to ride with him and have a look at Brierfield. The Hurricane's horse barn was two dozen stalls at least, filled with beautiful Kentucky thoroughbreds. V walked to the barn in what she had always worn riding since she started at five or six, a split skirt for sitting astride. She rode well due to lessons and lots of lonely hours along the bluffs of the Mississippi, jumping gullies and fallen trees.

Jeff looked at her with some concern. He said, We'll need to retack. I've had a sidesaddle ready for you on a reliable gelding, very calm.

V walked down the barn aisle and saw a bay mare looking white-eyed out of the stall. V held out the back of her hand and the horse leaned her velvet nose and took a deep breath and relaxed her ears, though she kept tossing her head and then made one quick spin in the stall and came back to breathe V's hand.

V said, Her, please.

They rode out to Brierfield side by side, sometimes at a walk and sometimes racing along past stretches of woods and big empty fields and pastures and smaller fields of cool weather crops—greens and root vegetables mostly. During the walking, they talked about the personalities of horses and about his house. The nearer they came to Brierfield the more Jeff apologized for his miscalculations in the design. He aspired to equal his namesake in every regard, and this was only his first attempt as architect.

When they arrived, V saw that he was right to apologize. The house was no Monticello. Just a plastered cat-and-clay construction without even a real chimney of stone or brick, just more cat-and-clay. The house lacked a gallery and made do with an awkwardly proportioned stoop sheltering the front door. The windows sat high on the walls and very small.

A black man, middle-aged, met them in the yard and held V's mare as she dismounted. He stood a couple of inches taller than Jeff, nearly as slim, and he wore about the same clothes Jeff did, except a little more worn. And a fine Panama hat frazzled at the front edge of the brim. Long fingers with big joints. Unless he was being addressed, his eyes looked into the middle distance like a hunter with a gun in his hands waiting.

Jeff said, Thank you, Pemberton. I'm going to show Miss Howell around and then we'll go back to The Hurricane shortly, so no need to untack. Just water and a little hay to keep them busy. Then come find us. If

Miss Howell has questions about what we've done here and what we plan to do, I might need your help explaining.

As Pemberton led the horses away, V couldn't stop looking at him. She had expected him to be some deep friend from West Point, a fellow newly minted lieutenant up on the northern frontier—half of a special pairing that human males make in late adolescence and sometimes have a hard time giving up.

Instead, Jeff owned Pemberton, held title to him. Legal papers.

V said, So, how long . . . ?

Jeff said, Since I was fourteen.

Walking inside the house jolted the senses. The main room stretched long and dark, like a grand hallway. The little dim windows with the sills very high felt even odder from inside, like something to shoot arrows at attackers from, except you'd need a tall ladder to do it. Scant furniture hovered around cavernous fireplaces at either end of the long room, and no paintings marred the high walls. Dimensions warped and distorted, the geometry strange and lacking correspondence to human scale. All it needed was for the walls to stand out of parallel with each other and the floors to slope at several angles to make the place truly crazy.

V walked twice around the room trying to think of something to say. She settled in front of one of the giant fireplaces. She could almost walk into it. A fire hardly bigger around than the lid to a stewpot smoked in one corner like an afterthought.

She finally said, Well, this looks like it was built in Queen Elizabeth's time, to roast a sheep whole.

A woman came out from the kitchen and asked if they would like tea or coffee.

They took their coffee outside in chairs under a big live oak to the side of the house. In a few minutes, Pemberton came carrying a cup of tea and without a word sat down with them, which seemed unusual to V.

V said, I hear you were up in the north woods?

Pemberton said, A long time ago, miss.

Jeff said, Pemberton and I—for a lark—made the first known overland passage from Prairie du Chien to Chicago.

—Mainly to get away from that muddy fort for a while, Pemberton said.

The three of them walked out past the kitchen gardens and the cow barn and horse barn, all scaled smaller than at The Hurricane because Brierfield only encompassed a thousand acres. Jeff and Pemberton explained that they still had plans to clear a couple hundred more acres for cotton someday but didn't want to lose all the woods.

Pemberton said, This place didn't get its name for nothing. First time we saw it, this place was a tangle. Plenty of cutting and burning—plenty of brush piles and log piles. Smoke in the air for years.

Jeff said, You remember that day we let the burn pile get out of hand?

Pemberton laughed and said, We nearly burned the world down.

Pemberton pointed nearby—a couple of hundred feet—and told how, as they cleared for the house site, they piled brush and pines and root ends of hardwoods to the size of a biggish cow barn. Said they'd let the pile dry for the months it took to build the house and then doused it with not much coal oil at four points of the compass and struck fire. The pile sizzled for a few minutes trying to find its voice, and then it went up with a great roaring suck of air that lifted the hat off Jeff's head and spun it high in the sky and then pulled it into the flames that stood taller than the tops of the biggest trees. The hat burned in one quick fizz. Before long, the wind carried the fire into the living woods. The pines caught first and the needles burned fast with a sound like tearing paper and flashed great sparks, and soon the woods were burning down and black smoke rose at a steep pitch toward heaven.

—God or chance, one saved the house, Pemberton said. The wind faced square around and shoved the fire back over black land it had just crossed. It soon burned out to smoke and embers.

He looked at Jeff and said, I'll never forget the look on your face when your hat flew off.

Jeff laughed and said, Maybe short judgment on both our parts in regard to the wind and closeness of the burn pile to the new house and the woods.

V and Jeff took a roundabout path back to The Hurricane, often at a gallop, daring each other to jump ditches and fences and downed tree trunks. And then, both of them still flushed and breathing hard from the wild ride, Jeff tried to kiss her in the barn aisle. The light was dim and brown except where high western windows cast angling yellow beams. Dust of hay drifted in the beams and hovered and disappeared into darkness.

The strange light flattered Jeff, made him look dramatic as an actor on a stage. He leaned into her, and she only had to touch his shoulder with a finger to ease him back.

That night V wrote to her mother:

I do not know whether this Jeff Davis is young or old. He looks both at times. But he must be old. I hear he is only two years younger than you are. He seems remarkable, but of uncertain temper. He takes for granted that everybody agrees with him when he expresses an opinion, which offends me. Yet he has a sweet voice and a winning manner of asserting himself. He is the kind of person who would rescue you from a mad dog at any risk, but then insist on stoical indifference to the fright afterward.

Love from Your daughter in exile,

V

What she didn't describe to her mother was that she found him very handsome in a lean, bony way. And he was bookish—adored words whether on the page or delivered in oratory. Out at Brierfield she had noticed stacks of books on a table by a leather chair. He had told her that what he wanted at sixteen was to study law so that he would have time to write. Told her that in another world he might have had a happy life as a small-town lawyer scribbling poetry and history in his office when he should have been dealing with real estate contracts or petty lawsuits. But when Jeff was fourteen, Joseph began calling upon connections among the wealthy men of the state, and eventually West Point began the arc of Jeff's destiny. And as he emerged from his long mourning—which in itself seemed romantic to seventeen-year-old V—he had become interested in politics, especially writing and delivering speeches. He was thinking about running for public office someday—by which V assumed he meant on a local or state level. She wrote the words *The Briers* and *Brierfield* over and over in her notebook, wondering if there might be some interconnection, some motif worth noting. An affinity or a warning.

Days after her tour of Brierfield, V kept trying to understand Jeff and Pemberton. And Benjamin Montgomery as well. She grew up a town girl and their beautiful rental home seldom required more than a cook and a couple of house servants and a man to take care of the lawn and their few horses. Her family never had individual servants around long enough to know them well. They came and went because of WB's theory—why take on the responsibilities of ownership when you can rent?

She knew true cotton plantations were meant to be horrific places, but Old Joe's strange version of Owenist social ideas confused her. She resolved to read up on the topic. And Jeff's friendship with Pemberton also confused her. She assumed that on Jeff's side of the pair, he had depended on Pemberton for all sorts of things over the years. At West Point, Pemberton would have taken care of laundry, cleaned the room, polished boots, emptied wastebaskets, carried letters to post, transported embargoed liquor in and out of the dormitory. All those student needs. Later, up in the forests of the north wilderness—way past so many furcations of the Mississippi that it cut a path through the land no wider than a common river—she imagined Pemberton's jobs would have been to chop wood, carry water, build fires, butcher deer, saddle horses, brush dirt off buckskin jackets at day's end. They had known each other before V was born, and they treated each other as friends. But even then, seventeen, she knew that could not be the full relationship.

A lifetime later—Jeff and Pemberton both dead and V living in New York City, much to the anger of the southern press—she tried to jot a thought about the two men, a memory, a brief note about them for her own memoir, having recently worn herself to the nub finishing Jeff's after he died in the middle of his opening chapters.

She wrote:

Don't think about the existence of an artifact representative of that time, the whipping post. It played no direct part in their decades together. One could be with them for days and forget that their fundamental relationship was anything but friendship and respect and mutual responsibility stretching back to youth. But then something would happen. A small shift in Jeff's tone of voice asking for the second time that some minor task be done, a moment of ignoring Pemberton as if he weren't there. Flashes of language and particular tones of rudeness revealed that the relationship between the two men was deeply complex. That the fundamental note of their long history together condensed to a simple fact—one member of the friendship was owner and the other was both labor and capital. And then the shadow of that post traced divisions clear and precise as the sweeping shadow of a sundial.

When V finally made it back to Natchez in March, sort of engaged to Jeff—but more on that later—she asked around about Pemberton's dollar worth, describing in general a bondman of his qualifications—his experience, his subtlety, his mannerly way of communicating, his skill in navigating the gulf between owners and workers. She omitted his literacy and his love of newspapers, which might have skewed the results. Estimates were, Pemberton would cost as much as the house a blacksmith or baker or milliner lived in, maybe even as much as Jeff's finest thoroughbred.

V has never made any claim of personal high ground. She grew up where and when she did. From earliest memory, owning other people was a given. But she began feeling the strangeness of it at about nine or ten—not the wrongness or the sin of it, the strangeness only. The sense that a strong line cut through all the people she knew and everybody who existed. And that she stood on one side and others stood across—free on her side, enslaved on the other. For the poorest southern whites or northern women and children working fourteen hours a day in the satanic mills of Yankee factories, the line between slave and free might have been only a foot across—but even then it cut deep, a bottomless chasm. Yet the only determinant of which side you occupied was a paper-thin layer of skin, a fraction of blood degree.

After a few months with Winchester as her tutor, she asked him who drew that line. He said some people believed God drew it. He had her read Luke 12:47—about how the slave that knoweth his master's will, and doeth it not, shall be beaten with many stripes. Winchester told her that many plantation owners kept that page turned down for quick reference. He told her she would find quite a few inconsistencies in that book and in the beliefs of Christians and suggested she think about the relationship between wealth and power and morality in regard to drawing lines.

As epiphanies go, her young recognition amounted to not much, except it seemed so for her then. Over the years with Winchester she came to know that people have enslaved each other from time immemorial. Spin the globe and point to a location and probably find slaves sometime in history. Study the golden enlightened Greeks and their marvelous language and history and mythology as she did for years, and you'll see Socrates and his comrades thinking lofty thoughts while pretty slave girls and boys pour their wine and less pretty ones pick and stomp the grapes. The Yankees' holy Puritan forefathers owned slaves almost from the moment they set foot on the continent. V's New Jersey governor grandfather owned slaves all through his eight terms. As a teacher, Winchester didn't advocate beyond adhering to facts as far as we can know them. The context of history ruled. He scoffed if she just talked about what she believed without supporting evidence. So even very young she saw slavery as an ancient practice arising because rich people would rather not do hard work, and also from the tendency of people to clench hard to advantageous passages in the Bible and dismiss the rest.

When she left Davis Bend for Natchez after an intense two months of daily courtship, she and Jeff had not become fully engaged, but they had put a hold on forming other entanglements. She was so young, and her parents needed to weigh in, though Jeff felt confident that her father would not offer an impediment.

Jeff accompanied her to the dock and leaned in for a full-on good-bye kiss. But distracted by memory—its habit of looping and echoing—V thought of Winchester at that same spot. She turned her head at the final second to take a glancing blow on her cheek. She said a confused good-bye and then rushed up the stage to the riverboat.

In a letter written a day afterward, Jeff asked,

When we parted at the river, how did you happen to call me by your Father's name? I've been so worried you are ill.

V wrote back.

My apologies for misspeaking. Take for granted a faint touch of blush on my cheeks. I'll try not to make that mistake again. From now forward, I'll simply call you Uncle Jeff, since Florida claims Cousin.

———

Jeff was right about her father, he was ready for a wedding and to wish the couple well and send them on their way. But V's mother put up a fight. Her judgment was to let the courtship proceed, but no wedding for at least a year—certainly not before V turned eighteen. So all that spring and summer, Jeff's love letters followed a formula. Each one started out rational and conversational in tone but then soon built to an emotional heft only the French language could bear. Most of them ended with *Mon amor, mon petit pomme.* He didn't seem to consider that V's understanding of the language was a great deal more complete than his and that she would not be impressed with his smatter of misspelled and ungrammatical West Point French. Though to be fair his limited vocabulary did contain more words for artillery pieces and the movements of troops than hers. He saw the French language as a tool, a weapon, rather than a portal into a culture and its history and literature. Eons of loss later, confronted with the reality of Paris—where some of their acquaintances from the war lived in exile—Jeff went twitchy as a squirrel looking at public statuary. V loved the city and was ready to start looking for a nice, cheap apartment with a sliver of river view, but Jeff declared that he could never live in a place where displays of human anatomy flushed themselves in his face every time he took a walk.

As for V's half of their courtship correspondence, her letters vanished during the war, stolen by the Federal raiders who looted Brierfield and destroyed The Hurricane. Jeff had tied the stack of them with a red ribbon as he had done with Knoxie's letters. Even the slight possibility that V's letters survive in a Connecticut or Michigan attic still makes her wish she'd burned them when she had the chance. Most of her correspondence to friends and acquaintances over the decades concluded with a line below the signature: *Private—Burn after reading.* Happily, she can't remember a word of her teen love letters to a man more than twice her age.

==

V tells James, I sometimes imagine meeting my seventeen-year-old self. She's still here inside me somewhere. Maybe one morning in the mirror, there she'll be. I look at her with affection and understanding and hope. She sees me and backs away in horror while I try to explain why I made the choices I made. Back then, a good marriage didn't require love. A good marriage meant security—money and position and a man who didn't knock you around. We all wanted both, of course—love and security—but mostly we settled for the second and manufactured an attraction to keep from acknowledging the arranged, contractual foundation of the relationship, the mercantile nature of it. All those years, I can't remember one girl from a good family who settled for only love.

—**I've thought** about something you said. That I should write a book.

—I believe I more noted how everybody's doing it, V says. If Virginia Clay can write a book, anybody can. The main qualification appears to be an ability to sit at a desk for many hours a day. When I wrote Jeff's memoir, it felt like solitary confinement inside his head. The last day's work seemed so much like a jailbreak that I set my little pistol on the desk in case I had to shoot my way out. After that, I thought I was going to write my own life, but I haven't. I've written all kinds of things to earn my living. For a while I even did a silly etiquette column for the *New York World*.

Pleasant days back then, she tells James. She had a pretty apartment with a big bay window in the Gerard Hotel—West Forty-Fourth between Sixth and Seventh. Winnie lived there too when she was in town, though she traveled a lot with the Pulitzers, who appreciated her command of several languages and knowledge of art and history. She came in once from spending the worst of winter in Naples and began immediately working every day on a romance set in the South Pacific that she had started on the ship back.

As for V's writing, giving advice on etiquette was easy. You opened envelopes and considered burning questions readers desperately needed answered—topics such as when and how to wear a high hat, dinner table manners, and how to deal with rude in-laws. V remembers one profound question in particular: How should one use one's handkerchief in public and not be vulgar? Her answer was: *Never—even under the greatest burden of curiosity—open it afterwards and inspect the contents.* Another young woman asked how she might respond to a gentleman friend's request for a lock of hair. V answered in print, *That is simply too disgusting for reply.* Brides especially required many wise words in regard to every phase of engagement and wedding planning—so much anxiety over correctness. V always tried to advise them to calm down, worry less about trivialities.

Writing of that kind was work, a job. You did it, and a check eventually came, and the rent got paid. That money and a scant income from a couple of inherited farming properties she leased out were her living. Census of 1900, when the man came knocking on her door asking questions, she gave her occupation as Writer and Landlord. In 1880, when Jeff answered the same question for her, he said, Keeps House.

Other pieces of writing, though, she would have done gratis. One such piece of free advice went to a friend whose daughter was about to jump into marriage with a wealthy older widower. The girl's name was Belle, and V had known her since childhood. In a letter to the mother, V spilled her heart—writing:

> I am not pleased with the widower prospect. It is offering a burnt out vessel to a fresh young girl like Belle. This suitor steps up long after a successful love he had identified as his eternal soul life, and then she was removed by death. I gave the best & all of my life to a girdled tree, it was live oak and good for any purpose except for blossom & fruit, and I am not willing for Belle to be content with anything less than the whole of a man's heart.

V would have offered her thoughts on the dedication of Grant's Tomb for free as well, but the *World* insisted on paying her, and she was in no position to turn down a check. She attended the ceremony at the invitation of her friend Julia, Grant's widow. The papers—north and south—found the friendship between V and Julia odd and exciting, and wrote about it as if the two women ought to have nothing in common when, in fact, they had a great deal. V and Julia took regular carriage rides in Central Park, and lunched at prominent restaurants. They wanted to be seen together, wanted their friendship to be noted and commented on in the papers, even if they both faced criticism by hard-shelled Confederates and Federals for it. They wanted to show that reconciliation was possible. For several summers before Julia's death, she and V spent vacations together—adjacent cottages at modest Adirondack lodges. So many evenings sitting in uncomfortable wooden chairs watching the sun set behind lakes and mountains, talking about everything except that horrible war.

—Write about that, V says to James. I'm rather proud of Julia and myself for our friendship.

—So if I decide to write a book, I have your blessing? James says. Your help?

—No. Let's keep calling it visiting and talking. Come again next Sunday. Then write what you want. Or not. Doesn't matter to me. For so long I thought everything I cared about was lost, never to be returned. Seeing one of my boys still in the world is plenty for me. Seeing you going and doing.

—The visits mean a lot to me too, and I want them to continue. But if I jotted notes now and then . . . ?

—No. Let's not get professional. Unreliable memory is all we have. You ask, and I'll try to answer the best I can remember, and then you patch my forty-year-old memories onto your photographic flashes and the blue book.

—All right, then. Your wedding and after?

=

Knoxie's death had been a deep and slowly killing wound and had weakened their marriage from the start. Her ghost haunted even their wedding. They'd had a big ceremony planned at Davis Bend, but that got canceled last-minute for reasons V has never discussed. They didn't much communicate for a while, and then all of a sudden the wedding was back on, at The Briers this time, with no Davis other than Jeff attending. Oddly, on the boat down to Natchez before the improvised wedding, Jeff ran into Knoxie's father, General Zachary Taylor—eventually to become President Taylor—for the first time since the elopement long ago. What a sweet moment for their reconciliation. About that same time Eliza thought it useful to write V a letter describing how Jeff had been going through an old trunk and found a pair of Knoxie's slippers and fainted from excess emotion. Then, after the wedding, on the way downriver to New Orleans for their honeymoon, Jeff insisted on stopping to visit Knoxie's grave.

That's when V should have realized that she could not miraculously heal a girdled tree—bark cut and peeled away past the living flesh in a wide belt around the trunk. The sap stops flowing, and you starve the tree to death. But it takes a long time. On a tree you cut the belt down into the white. On a person you'd cut into to the red.

As to the simple, rushed wedding at The Briers, V judged it elaborate enough for a farmer's wife. Since it happened spur-of-the-moment, she didn't wear a gown. She pulled an almost-white dress—Indian muslin—out of her wardrobe and on her way out into the yard for the vows, she picked a pink rose from the garden to wear in her hair because she had been doing that since she was a child. The rush to marry, of course, caused speculation at the time and down through the years. But that sort of curiosity V has never cared to satisfy.

She thought she had married an idiosyncratic widower with a raw plantation on the Mississippi between Natchez and Vicksburg. She expected they would spend their lives growing cotton and food crops and children. Maybe if he stayed interested in politics he would get elected to the state legislature and would spend a few weeks every year in Jackson, the capital city. Several times a year she would spend a few weeks in Natchez visiting her family, and maybe she and Jeff would make a tradition of spending two weeks in New Orleans together before Christmas. Whether she had married the dullard heir or the woodcutter remained unclear, but a quiet, ordered life seemed likely.

Except, while she was still eighteen—honeymoon barely over—Jeff spent a few weeks riding around the district enduring fish fries, hog barbecues, cockfights, and assaults of patriotic music blurted out of bugles and flügelhorns and French horns, and giving political speeches considered good but chilly, though everyone agreed he looked slim and elegant behind a podium. At one of the few rallies V attended, a woman whispered to her that she would be his greatest asset, said that previously he'd had everything he needed for high office except a hostess, but now he has you. And the woman was right—after the vote was counted Jeff became a member of the U.S. House of Representatives. V had lived in his strangely designed house only two seasons before they packed up and headed to Washington.

Before railroads, there were two choices for getting to the nation's capital. The southern route went down the river to New Orleans, and then by many rivers and stagecoaches to Charleston, and from there a ship up the coast to Norfolk, and finally a boat up the Potomac. So many connections to go wrong.

They chose the northern route, upriver past Memphis and onto the Ohio River, which V knew little about. The water was low after Cairo, and the Ohio was a crazy river, nothing but big meanders. But at least they didn't have to change conveyances every day. The farther up they went, the colder it got. At first the ice sparkling along the riverbanks seemed pretty, but then chunks of ice started floating in the river, and the chunks grew larger and larger until they bumped and scraped the hull, which was alarming at night. V hadn't experienced snow and ice since her partial school year at Madame X's in Philadelphia, and she hadn't missed those two expressions of weather one little bit. But she and Jeff snuggled tight in their cabin under piles of blankets reading books by candlelight. Then, at a narrows, the boat became iced-in by chunks big as johnboats. The paddle wheels wouldn't turn. After the second day, the situation quit being romantic.

They remained stuck for most of a week until a small boat, jangling its bells, took them to the riverbank where they sat on their trunks until a large farm sled with oak runners could be found. Partway to Wheeling the sled skidded down a twenty-foot bank and bashed into a tree and broke a runner. One of the mules was badly injured and had to be put down. Their one traveling companion—another Mississippi congressman, an old colonel—broke a rib, and V was bruised around the head and shoulders. Jeff—who'd spent many winters up in Wisconsin and Minnesota—knew how to manage ice and snow. He became heroic. He patched the runner together and mostly walked to spare the lone mule. He guided them, assured them, saved them. He was like Florida's Big Bear Theory made concrete.

They spent nights in farmhouses and inns. It was Dutch country, and every meal featured bratwurst drenched in maple syrup with maybe some mustard and a pickle. Maybe a boiled potato. V craved a bowl of shrimp gumbo with lots of okra, peppers and onions, hot sauce. And a big side of greens.

Eventually they fetched up at the edge of the Alleghenies in Wheeling. V had never seen mountains, so the snow-covered ridges seemed impossibly tall to a girl who'd hardly been out of Mississippi and Louisiana. At the hotel she looked in the mirror and her bruised face looked back in shades of blue and black and green. She felt like an adventurer.

From there it was east over the ridges in stagecoaches,

and then little boats on little rivers to Philadelphia. Then a mix of stages and railways to Washington. When they arrived at Brown's Indian Queen Hotel—days late for the opening of Congress—V met Mary Chesnut on her first pass through the busy lobby and couldn't have cared less how she looked that moment, which was disheveled, bruised, dirty, and excited at the sudden amplitude of her life.

=

James leaves The Retreat late, just before dinnertime. He reaches his hand to V in farewell, and she hugs him instead.

At the station, the 6:35 has already left. When the porter sees James on the platform, he comes over and says, I got worried when you missed your train.

—No need, James says. I'll be on the seven-twenty-nine.

The porter says, Must make it easier roaming the white world in those clothes.

James looks down at himself. He smiles, shakes his head, shrugs his shoulders.

On the way back to Albany, James hunches over his notebook. Trying to remember exact phrases, particular observations. Compounding her unreliable memory with his own.

Very fast, he scribbles a conversation—rehearsing for next week:

—*Was I born enslaved?*

—*I can't answer because I don't know. And why should it matter? That world's dead and gone.*

—*No, it's not. The answer won't change how I feel about myself, but it matters. It's a fact about my life I need to know.*

—*That's not your real question. Just voice it.*

—*All right, then. Did you ever own me?*

Third Sunday

Saratoga Springs

—A decade, that's the number, V says.

—Pardon?

—The past week I've estimated how much of my life since the age of twenty-five I spent wearing mourning. By the second half of the war so many had died that black silk disappeared. After little Joe fell, I had to wear cotton darkened with a muddy brew of walnut hulls and indigo. Those big black dresses wore you rather than the other way around. When we left Richmond, I had just shed the black from Joe.

—I thought about a lot of things last week too, James says. I keep trying to remember that journey, but all I come up with are those brief flashes. I'm not sure whether they're real or if I'm inventing them.

—For me, those fugitive months keep rolling back in great detail no matter how hard I try to push them behind me. I've accepted that they're the axle of my life. Everything turns around them.

—A place where a road splits in two is one thing I keep seeing. A Y with a big white house in the fork.

Abbeville

1865

Wet most days from Charlotte into South Carolina. This particular day had been every kind of weather from fog to fine showers to moments of sunshine to a brief thunderstorm in the early afternoon. So at camp that evening, firewood was damp and took time to light and then burned smoky and slow. Six miles at best from breaking one camp to setting up the next—bad time for sure. Except Delrey, a stoic philosopher of physical endurance, discouraged that kind of thinking. He had various sayings, doled out a sentence at a time as V needed them, each one a nugget of wisdom. She recorded examples in her notebook.

We're not by any means getting to Florida in one sprint, so don't start counting days or miles.

The end of every day has to leave all of us able to get up in the morning and do it all over again and then do it again day after tomorrow.

You have to get your mind right, and always look way down the road, not at your feet.

The slowest man sets the pace because we're not the kind of people to leave anybody behind.

In a collapse of such magnitude—a provisional country scoured to bare nubs—rules of behavior wash away. V knew the men accompanying her still suffered under the old rules, but the day they realized that everything had changed would be when they either slipped away in the dark feeling ashamed or told her to her face she deserved her fate and put spur to flank and rode toward home in broad daylight. And over the course of that April week—day and night—most of them did leave, taking horses and mules and what supplies they could carry and abandoning unnecessary wagons by the side of the road with the tongues angling to the dirt. V, though, believed Delrey would stay with her to the end of the road, and she knew Burton would.

Midafternoon, a rider came up from behind, pushing his horse at a trot hard enough to cover ground for hours but not enough to break the horse down. He wore farmer clothes—butterscotch canvas pants with dirty bagged-out knees, scuffed brogans, a worn-out straw hat. But V knew right off he was a cavalryman. He didn't announce it, but he posted smoothly and elegantly, and he wore interesting facial hair, as many in the cavalry tended to do. He had managed to leave the war with a fine sorrel gelding, its coat the color of copper in the sun. Battle wounds marked its hide, and it was weary and skinny from hard traveling—in need of grain and a month to rest and graze and become magnificent again. The saddle had once been as fine as the horse, but wear and weather left the flaps curling and leather peeling down to the tree at the pommel.

The man said his name was Biddle and that he was on the way home to a little town south of the Florida line where his family had a smallish plantation.

He said, If you'uns are who I think you are, I talked my way around a rough gang fifty miles back saying they were after the treasure caravan. Said a million in gold would make them all rich for life.

—And they think we have it? Burton said.

—Yes.

V held her hands out, palms up. Said, A million? We can barely feed the children.

—Yes, ma'am, Biddle said.

—Talked your way past them, how? Burton said.

—I claimed to be a dirt farmer.

—And that's your plow horse? V said.

—They didn't seem like the kind of men who attend to details. I'm just saying, they were questioning people. Asking had I seen a couple of ambulance wagons, a fancy woman and some children and a handful of men.

V looked at Delrey and under her breath said, Do I look fancy? I sure don't feel fancy.

Delrey said, Ma'am, we're in South Carolina. Who knows their standards?

—How fast are they traveling? Burton asked.

Biddle said, Not fast. They're branching off, talking to people, beating the bushes. They're searching, not riding hard. But they're coming faster than you're going. Maybe they'll get bored and head on home.

—Maybe, Burton said. Thank you for the information.

—If you're heading to Florida with the rest of us outlaws and you make it to Scrub Pine City down near the Suwannee River, the Biddle place is easy to find, assuming it's still there.

He tipped his hat and rode on.

That evening as they made camp Ellen sent the children to fetch deadfall for tinder from under a gathering of big oaks. Maggie, being oldest, supervised. Jeffy and Jimmie and Billy picked up sticks and tried to stomp bigger limbs into shorter pieces. Then they got bored and started having saber fights with long, curved pieces of limbs. Soon they were throwing sticks at each other and dashing around yelling and chasing and wrestling until Maggie joined in, whacking at the boys with a switch until they all laughed and screeched. They finally came back to camp with armloads of pencil-thin kindling to throw on the fire and watch flash up and instantly burn away.

The next day was brilliant spring weather, pastel blue sky and new green leaves on oak trees. The diminished fugitive band spaced out along a hundred yards of muddy South Carolina roadway. Mules and horses plodded heads-down, and the wagon wheels squeaked for grease. They camped out of sight in the woods by a creek. Burton and Delrey went opposite directions looking for food and came back later with little to show.

—Ma'am? Delrey said. Our foraging didn't turn up much. Or let's be straight and call it begging and bargaining and stealing.

—Yes?

—I bought a sack of biscuits and a jug of milk. There wasn't even a chicken to be had, never mind pig meat. And the people selling wanted a dollar each for a biscuit and a cup of milk, and even then they only sold them paired. Cup of milk and a biscuit, two dollars. But not two cups of milk and a biscuit. Or two biscuits and a cup of milk.

V interrupted and said, I understand the terms. Let's split what we have and eat around the fire.

—There's more to it, Delrey said. There's been smallpox aplenty all around here. So we need to know who's been inoculated. Or else already had smallpox and lived through it, but I guess we'd know that by the scars.

V said, Everybody but Jimmie and Winnie.

—I'll get on it, Burton said.

An hour later he returned to camp, a black boy riding behind him. Nine or ten, tall and skinny and hungry, his finger joints and elbows and knees rising like flower bulbs under the skin. He wore his hair cropped close, almost shaved. The boy stood before them neither scared nor comfortable. He watched all of them, wary and calm. Scattering all down his neck and arms and legs, a hundred fresh pox scars. Each one like the touch of a hot poker, a hundred healing burns, dimpled and silver with a starlike print at the center. Across both cheeks, patterns of scars the Greeks would have connected to make constellations.

He'd fought it off well. People who died had a thousand blisters and scabs wrapping their bodies, overlapped like reptile scales. Now, down around the boy's calves and ankles, only a few brown dry scabs remained.

V said, What is your name?

The boy looked off to the woods line, judging distance. He said, I don't have one.

—Yes, you do, Ellen said. Is it John? Benjamin? Samuel?

—No, ma'am. It's Bobcat.

Ellen shrugged and went back to the fire.

—Well, Bobcat, V said, I'll take your word on that. I see you've been sick.

He looked her in the eye and raised his chin and said, Better now.

—Yes, you are. You're going to be fine and live to be a hundred. You're strong. But those last scabs down your legs could help keep my children from dying. I'd pay you for a few of them.

The boy looked down at his scabby legs and bare feet and then looked up, more wary than before.

—They fall off in the dirt. Glad to get shut of them. But you want to buy them off me?

—It would be a favor, V said. I'll give you three biscuits or three dollars for three of them.

Bobcat thought a second and said, Both. Three biscuits for now and money for later. Hard money, not grayboy paper.

V said, Three big dry ones and we have a deal.

Bobcat squatted and picked around at his shins and ankles until he found loose scabs, domed and puckered and brown, gritty as sandpaper. They lifted from the pink scarred skin underneath with the first pull of a fingernail. He held them in his cupped palm.

V reached out her hand, but Bobcat stepped back.

—We trading or what? he said.

—Yes, we are trading.

Bobcat looked around at the white faces aimed his way.

—Then fill your hand too, ma'am, he said.

V stacked the biscuits in her hand and held them out to Bobcat.

He shoved them in his pockets but kept his fist clenched around the scabs.

—Yes? she asked.

—I gotta have my money, he said.

V said, Of course. I apologize for my forgetfulness.

She counted out the coins and reached them to him.

Bobcat grabbed the money and dumped the scabs into her hand and took off running fast for the woods.

Delrey watched him go and said, That child can mortally fly.

V took the brown scabs and crushed them to beige powder in a teacup with the back of a silver spoon, and then spilled the powder onto a saucer and pursed her lips and puffed the powder up the noses of Jimmie and Winnie, knowing they would get sick and might possibly die. Many people reacted to the inoculation with a slight fever and that was it—no smallpox for them. Some raised a few blisters and quickly got better. A scant few percent became very sick and passed to the next world. Like everyone inoculating, V was figuring odds, gambling. If Jimmie or Winnie took the actual pox full-on, they had less than fifty-fifty odds of living. With the inoculation, nine out of ten lived. When V finished, Winnie howled in outrage. Jimmie blinked watery eyes and stood with his fists clenched until V kissed him on the forehead and sent him back to Billy and Jeffy, squatting by the fire.

V bowed her head slightly to the north and then to the east. Praising Boston and Africa. Cotton Mather's slave Onesimus had taught him how to do it, how to powder the scabs and blow them up the nose. Or make a shallow cut in the skin and rub the powder in. Something they did back in Africa. Yankees put much stock in the famous Puritan witch-killer Mather, and V had read plenty of that crazy old man's thoughts, all the fear and dread he cursed America with down to the tenth generation. But Yankees loved to claim relation with him and all those other fanatics that came over here to establish their own flavor of dictatorship led by preacher tyrants. Winchester had made V read their writings, and even at fifteen she believed the English were right. Those people needed to be locked up. But instead, they ran to the wilderness and found the freedom to be as crazy as they wanted and to kill Indians and bothersome witch women and to drive a poison nail into the head of this country that still hasn't been pulled out.

The house in Abbeville stood in the Y where Main Street divides. A large, pretty house, its two-acre wedge of land filled with green lawn and foundation azaleas blooming scarlet and purple and white. The fugitives arrived an hour after dark, tired and dingy and hungry. Smelling like campfire and worse. The house rose before them like a white monument from a lost world. It belonged to Armistead Burt, and he didn't worry about Federal retaliation for offering hospitality to old friends on the run.

V held Winnie, who had taken a fever for half a day but seemed to be getting better. Jimmie had only one little pox welt under his chin. He and the other children peered out from the ambulance bed with aspects like the force of a great explosion had recently passed over them. Burton, his eyes dead in his face, sat hunched and braced with both hands on the pommel, his elbows locked to hold the weight of his torso.

V said, You're tingling from fatigue like the rest of us.

—No, Burton said. I'm fine. He sat up straight.

—Just claim it, V said. I know you'll ride till you fall out of the saddle, but at this point, denying is nothing but young-man pride.

—All right. I could use supper and a washcloth and a basin of warm water and a ten-hour nap.

Yellow lamplight behind the muntins and stiles of the windows projected geometric figures onto the dark lawn. The front door burst open and Mary Chesnut came flowing out. She hollered in her thin little-woman voice, Where the hell have you fools been? I'd have called for the home guard to go find you, except they've all run off to surrender and sign the loyalty oath. We wondered if the rounders and outliers had swarmed you. Good Lord, come here to me. We haven't hugged in months. We've got food and wine and hot water and clean beds. The men and children can all fall out when they want, but you can't sleep until at least one in the morning because I've so many questions that need answers. The Burts aren't due back for a few days. They went to see if their house in Columbia burned along with most of the town—and mine too. They left me in charge, since they're running the house like a refuge hotel until we all get home or get arrested or make a clean getaway.

—I'm so tired, V said.

—You never said that when we were nineteen in Washington City, Mary Chesnut said.

—I'll do my best, V said, rallying. In fact, I'll set my goal to put you to bed with a kiss on the forehead when the sun comes up, like I've done so many times before.

—You all clean up and we'll eat and then we'll put the weak ones to bed and meet in the parlor, she said. I'll have wine and suchlike.

Early on when she and Mary met in Washington—both teens married to congressmen, living and dining in Brown's Hotel and calling it their mess—they were famous enemies for the first month. Too much alike and neither used to sharing the attention that came with being young and smart and pretty. Every evening the sound of their crossfire over the dinner table was only partially muffled by laughter. Each of them made a dramatic public show of tolerating the other. Then they had a cup of tea—just the two of them, no audience—and it took about ten minutes to make peace, and before long they began getting together in their rooms before parties to comment on how their dresses hung.

Back then Mary's housemaid, Phoebe, said to V, Missus Mary won't ever get no babies.

—Why? V said.

—Too narrow across the hips.

Phoebe held her hands up, faced her palms about eight inches apart. Which was a slight exaggeration. But whether for that reason or some other, over the years of Mary's marriage, Phoebe's prophecy proved true. As far as V knew, Mary had never been even briefly pregnant, much less carried a child to term.

V too went long years without producing a child, but the reason was no mystery to her. Then for a few years she had babies one right after the other. So, she was different because of children, beaten up by having them and loving them and losing them.

Mary, though, had retained that frail girl shape, still looked slightly like a child who had raided her mother's closet to try on her best dress. If you looked hard, Mary's face had slightly broadened, maybe. Wrinkles no deeper than the light crescent press of a fingernail mark against the skin around her mouth and eyes. Under the powder, her color grayed some, but the backs of her hands remained smooth as a teen's. She still knew so much, having time every day to read as many books and periodicals as she wanted, and to sit around in parlors chatting with witty smart people keeping her on her toes. So to some degree Mary remained nineteen forever—bright and promising, her body intact and her mind free from the permanent grief of seeing your group of babies begin to dwindle away, leaving your wit hard to retrieve and permanently darkened.

Mary took out a plump wax paper packet and tore off the corner and tapped a pinch into her red wine and gave it a swirl.

She said, It's so nice not to have to make excuses. Would you care for some?

—All the rest, please, V said. She reached out her glass.

Mary ripped the packet wide open and shook until the last grains fell, and then she poured them both a splash more wine.

—That will give you some relief, she said. Though

I had an accident with it a while back. I sent Phoebe to the doctor to pick up my supplies, and he told her to mix the contents with a glass of red wine. The part Phoebe forgot was that he meant for her to divide the package into doses twice a day for a week, so she mixed it all at once. I remember thinking the wine tasted gritty. Three days and nights I slept uninterrupted, and on the fourth day I woke up much refreshed. The doctor said that killing me would take a lot of effort—which I've noted in my journal as an epitaph to be chiseled into my gravestone or an epigraph should I publish my book. But who has the time for that now?

They sat and sipped and talked. It was past midnight, silent outside until a rider went by at a canter, and they stopped to listen as he took the western branch of the road into deep country.

Mary said, It's all second- and thirdhand, but I hear the end times in Richmond fell pretty bad.

V sat awhile and finally said, Do you think the gods observe us?

—Lowercase plural, or big *G* singular?

—Either.

Mary said, If you mean watch over us all worried, making sure that everything happens for a reason, then I'll say hell no. But if you mean punish us whether we deserve a beating or not, I'll say maybe.

—I mean observe, V said. Form an audience. Judge us mostly on how amusing we are. How funny or sad or tragic or foolish. Or just to find us lacking in entertainment—a disappointment.

—More like a group of critics?

—Maybe. Because however bad we've all been—whether the gods jump on us with both feet or the Puritan God fries us in a red-hot skillet—all of us, we've made a story of our lives.

—Oh, Mary said, life is mostly just what happens. Choice or chance or fate, gods or not. Like it or not. Things happen, we do what we think is in our best interests or just convenient, and then we live with the consequences. When we finally start taking the long view back down the road we've traveled, maybe we repent. Or just dig in our heels and claim righteousness no matter how damning the evidence against us.

Mary stopped and said, But that's not what we're talking about, is it? You're thinking about him, yes? His ruin.

—Some. But also about myself and the children.

—And wherever Jeff is right now, he's probably worrying more about how he'll be judged by history.

—Yes.

Mary drank and thought and then raised her glass and professed, History reveals a person's deeds—their

outward character but not themselves. There is a secret self that has its own life rounded by a dream—
unpenetrated, unguessed.

V clapped two slow claps and said, Beyond the
Shakespeare, is any of that yours?

—The first part, a little.

V said, I'm fading. Coffee?

—Everyone's gone to bed. We could make some
fresh or drink the cold dregs left in the pot from dinner.

—I vote dregs. All I want is a jolt. I still aim to tuck
you in.

In that degree of late night transforming to early
morning—the oil lamp slightly haloed by the heavy,
wet April air gathering outside—Mary said, Young
Mister Burton Harrison? He looks worn out. But I
imagine when he's had a shave and not dead-on-his-
feet exhausted, he's probably handsome.

—Well, yes.

Mary studied V and then closed her eyes for two
breaths. She said, I'm sensing a story, and we're both
too tired to make me drag it out of you when we both
know you'll spill eventually.

Very dreamy, slow and with many pauses and diversions, V remembered aloud how in the Gray House,
Burton's office was upstairs, just across a narrow hall

from her little sitting and dressing room off the big master bedroom. Her room measured perhaps ten by ten. Burton's office was even smaller, with no exterior windows. But it was an intense space, dim even in daylight, books on shelves and standing in tottering stacks, papers everywhere, desktop covered with letters in his meticulous hand. In her room—whether she had the door open and sat in the chair reading a book or had the door closed drawing up a stocking—she could hear him clear his throat. Coming and going, they often brushed against each other in the narrow hall between their lairs.

Mary Chesnut sat with her eyes closed, the stem of her glass between the first and middle fingers of her upturned hand, her palm cupping the bowl. V paused, and Mary, without opening her eyes, said, Please proceed.

So, of course, V and Burton shared a lovely, brief flirtation. He had graduated from Yale before the war and frequently made calculated glancing mentions that he was a Bonesman, as if that shed more than a glimmer of golden light south of about Delaware. V grew up around Masons, whose magical tickling handshakes and dark secrets went back to King Solomon, so a recently formed boy club hardly registered. More interesting to her was she and Burton being several years

closer in age than she and Jeff. And that simple sum-
mation of years rested weightier on her mind than any
secret society, no matter how extra special.

Burton would have made a poor poker player. For two
weeks he moped about in love with her. He was a wise
young man who didn't hold her slight thickening in the
wake of children as an exclusionary fact. Besides, the
tallness that caused her to stoop self-consciously when
she was fifteen helped her carry a little weight regally
twenty years later. Though of course childless Mary
Chesnut still enjoyed the figure of a fourteen-year-old.

—Thank you for noticing, Mary said.

When V finally realized how twisted up she had him,
she enjoyed playing with Burton for a few weeks. Most
of those brushings-by in the narrow hallway were her
doing. Some days she laughed and flirted lightly, and
others she acted even more dark and brooding than
he did.

This was still early enough in the war that Richmond had not yet become flooded with beautiful young
widows. By the second year, town whelmed over with
them, all wearing flattering black dresses. A precious
few were broken beyond repair and would probably die
alone in a remote and unimaginable twentieth century
still holding tight to their identity as widows of sacred
Confederate dead. The rest told themselves—and any-

one else willing to listen—that they would devote their lives to the memory of their fallen heroes, while at the same time keeping one eye on the calendar for the earliest date to stop wearing mourning and be colorful again, and the other sharp eye out for new love, the likeliest chance to escape the land of helplessness and sorrow. Many could offer themselves as virtually virgin brides, having married their beaux just days before sending them off to fight and die. Burton eventually found a firecracker of a woman, smart and full of wit, pretty enough, but not too pretty, and V liked to think she had primed the pump and kept him from one of those predacious young widows.

But that was later. Early days of the war, Burton thought he loved V fully and hopelessly. Imagine the romantic pain of loving the wife of the most powerful man in the land. And for three weeks in May she enjoyed convincing Burton to give hope a try. She used any excuse to touch his hand or make a big-sisterly correction to his tie or to smooth his lapels. And then to tease him for blushing.

So it came as no surprise one day toward the end of the month when he kissed her. She stood in the dining room arranging a vase of flowers when he passed through. The summer slipcovers—bleached cotton duck—had just been fitted over the upholstery, protection against all the sweaty visitors during hot summer. Burton came in the side door. He carried his hat, his hair pressed flat to his head by the band.

V said, Burton, could you come here just a minute?

When he came she leaned in close and with both hands, fingertips against his scalp, fluffed his hair and then shaped it in place.

He stumbled forward and bumped against her, arms circling. He mashed his lips to hers and then backed away and squared up to take a stinging slap that she never delivered. His hat had fallen in the exchange, and it lay on the rug, crown down, an open hole at their feet that they needed to avoid plunging into.

V found it a stirring kiss, a minor key reminder of youthful love. She wanted so much to kiss back. Instead, she said, Burton, let's have coffee. Sit and compose yourself. I'll go make it, and then we'll talk. Do not even think of fleeing. Do not fail to be here when I get back.

He nodded.

She went down to the kitchen, and Ellen was there and saw a look on V's face.

—What in the world? Ellen said.

—Burton.

—He's been going around hangdog over you for a month. You didn't notice?

—He just kissed me, V said.

—That's different.

—Is there coffee? For two. I'll take it up.

—If I need to come upstairs, you want me to cough when I get to the top of the stairs?

—Ha, V said.

When she returned, carrying a silver tray of pretty china cups and cream and sugar, Burton looked miserable.

He stood and said, I'm as appalled by my behavior as you are. As soon as the president arrives, I'll hand in my resignation and confess to what I did.

He said it like a schoolboy reciting a bit of Shakespeare he did not at all understand.

—No, V said. You won't. And please don't ever assume you know what appalls me and what doesn't. At this moment, I'll claim my share of the blame, which is vastly the bigger slice of cake.

—Madame, he said.

A formulaic blurt. To be followed by some wearying assumption of behavior more appropriate to Lancelot and Guinevere than to the current world. He looked so earnest she almost laughed.

She sat next to him and held his twitchy hand. She said, When you're confused, don't talk. Listen. Yes?

He nodded assent.

—What we will do instead of your plan is become best of friends and allies. You will never again apologize to me. And no foolish confessions, ever. Not to anyone. We won't even speak of this to each other. At least not for twenty-five years. At which point, if we're both alive and lucid, this moment won't seem tragic or comic, only a cherished shared memory that binds us even tighter. We will drink a bottle of wine or two and look back with warm nostalgia. Yes?

Burton's face bunched around his nose, a painful contraction. So V went on talking, improvising. She said, Let's do our anniversary near water. At the beach or on a riverboat or at a mountain lake resort. Someplace where sunset is an event. Right now let's be quiet and drink our coffee and think our thoughts until you're able to say something not foolish.

They sipped until eventually he said, Yes?

His voice was speculative and searching, an explorer finding his way into unmapped territory.

She sipped and looked at him without offering directions.

He said, The two of us longtime friends. Decades on. A bottle of wine together. That will be a moment to anticipate.

—Forever friends, she said. But it won't just happen. It's up to us to make it so. And I'll do my share.

But just as important, from this moment forward, you will become more careful with women and not allow us to twist you up with so little effort and to your disadvantage. Not all of us will let you down easy. Some keep a tally of broken hearts, and they like to break them hard enough to stay broken. You'll be more careful. Yes? And don't fall for some little fool who'll become jealous of us for all the wrong reasons?

Burton nodded. Yes, he said. Absolutely yes.

—Now, V said, rising from her chair. Come kiss me again, this time on the cheek, and we'll both meet the afternoon fresh and free. Though if I were fresh and free as you, well I won't even begin imagining how this afternoon might have played.

He set his cup in its saucer and rose and gave her a very polite kiss, a soft trembly peck, his hands clasped behind his back to keep them out of trouble.

V said, Go and do, Burton. Go and do. The day still has legs.

Mary said, Oh my. I had no idea, and I was in and out of your house every day or two back then. That sort of thing led to so many stupid but thrilling duels back before the war. There were many who believed you and Judah had a long affair in Washington. Which I'm convinced you did not. I'd bet my house in Camden that it was no more than a brief few urgent encounters in carriages. He was so full of life and humor and of himself back then.

—That's another story, V said.

They talked all night, and in the silences, V thought how much she loved Mary Chesnut. Like everybody else's, Mary's life collapsed around her day by day, but she sparkled in the face of it, at least in her talk. V and Mary—or, to be exact, their husbands—were about to go broke spectacularly and apocalyptically. They would all soon find themselves where her father was when he bet all he had on the hope that a shooting match might be watched over by a benevolent god.

But a good dinner and better conversation, a bottle or two of Bordeaux dating back to the young days, some generous pinches of medicine, and for a few hours it became easy to pretend that the past few years had never happened, that the only thing wrong was that people hadn't had time recently to do as much reading as usual. Which of course didn't keep the real world from scything you off at the knees for having made a series of choices counter to good sense or common morality or even to the movement of history under whose cold gaze the pain of your existence factors less than chimney smoke in the wind.

It wasn't quite dawn, but close enough, when V

helped Mary to bed and kissed her on the forehead and blew out the candle.

Three mornings later they stood on the porch, wagons loaded and waiting. V carried a small musette bag tinkly with little brown bottles.

Mary said, I'm hoping this is not the last good-bye.

The corners of her big eyes welled and spilled.

V kissed her the polite way, pecks on the cheeks. And then she gripped Mary's tiny body, wrapped herself around the fine bones of Mary's frame so tight that she worried she would break her.

V said, Please no.

And yet, despite deepest feelings and best intentions, that was the last good-bye. Later, they wrote letters, and Mary sent V bits of the book she had started writing in the first days of the war. But in the chaos of life and years of complicated legal and personal trials and prison and exile, they never saw each other again.

=

Sun breaks through clouds and catches V's attention. She asks the time.

—Quarter to two.

—Still a few races to go. We could take the hotel surrey.

—Or walk on the grounds here if you'd rather, James suggests. Easier to talk. Quieter.

They take wide paths where the golf course will soon be, down toward the pond. Artfully rustic wooden benches appear every hundred yards or so, and they stop frequently for V to rest, catch her breath.

—If we go all the way around the pond, I can count this as physiotherapy, V says.

—Back to your arriving in Washington that first time—when you and Mrs. Chesnut were so young. Your husbands must have been busy in Congress. I'm wondering what you did to fill a day?

—Well, the days filled themselves. Brown's Hotel was packed with interesting and amusing and annoying people all during the session. You could sit in the lobby and entertain yourself for as long as you wanted. And there were dinner parties and gatherings most nights of the week. Everything from staid receptions at the White House to the hops Mary and I organized at the hotel for younger people.

V tells him about a dinner party, sitting with a secretary of the treasury, a vice president, and a few other old powerful men and talking about literature—Dante and Virgil, Byron and Wordsworth. They thought it was surprising and delightful that a girl had read so much and held strong opinions. They talked to her a little like fishing in shallow water, but they kept talking. She says, I wore a flower in my hair that night—that was the year of japonicas, whether they were heaped in table bouquets at the White House or pinned singly in the hair of young ladies.

She remembers that one of those important fishermen was an elderly scientist, and he invited her to his studio for a tour. A few days later she visited, and she recalls a roomful of telescopes and theodolites and microscopes, bent and corroded orreries, dusty geodes and staurolites, many framed maps on the wall, and an enormous faded brown globe in a corner, its geographic boundaries and names representing an obsolete world. She remembers telling the old scientist that she could hardly hold herself back from smacking a palm to the equator and giving it a spin. He said, Do it, dear girl—and she set the globe whirling.

=

Dull days, wandering the Capitol never failed to entertain. She could happily spend a morning in the steep seats above the House floor listening to speeches—the rube rhetoric, the various accents, the wisdom and fool-ishness of lawmakers. On the Senate side, Sam Hous-ton roamed the halls flirting with every young woman he met. He wore a cougar hide vest and left his coat open to display it, hoping to be asked what the material was. He introduced himself to V the same as to all the young ladies, with a set of moves like a fencing exer-cise. He lunged an aggressive step forward—pushing up much too close—then bowed low, and in a deep voice said, Lady, I salute you. Then he stood and took a snakeskin pouch from the pocket of his cougar vest and plucked out a little carved wooden heart. He spent his days on the Senate floor whittling dozens of them. He reached it out and said, Let me give you my heart.

Mostly during that first time in Washington, like any young person intent on charming everyone in earshot, V chattered on about books she had read or a piece of music currently stuck in her head. She and Mary Ches-nut vied to be considered Washington's most well-read ladies still in their teens. Mary once told grand old Senator Benton—a man they both revered—that V was particularly knowledgeable in regard to Icelandic literature and mythology. After which, for several days, she buried herself in the Library of Congress reading translations of Snorri Sturluson just in case Benton asked her about his work.

Other days, V drooped under the load of her strong dreams. Mostly they crowded with intense physical details that left her disoriented at dawn until she adjusted herself to the waking world. She had not yet become known for the frequent truth of her dreams, visited like some Cassandra by prophetic and terrifying night visions. She gave one of the most powerful of them a title—*The Execution of Jefferson Davis, Traitor and Assassin*. It began as an outdoor performance, a huge audience standing in a misty rain watching black-hat, frock-coat men climb stairs to the high stage. At the top they hesitate and mill about deciding where to stand. All of them—dignitaries, representatives of law and justice, deep believers in the paradigm of the passing moment—are intent on a simple performance of a simple role. Among them but not of them, Jeff climbs the risers imperially slim in black suit and white shirt. His eyes are sunken behind defiant cheekbones, equitation-perfect posture even though his hands have been tied behind his back in a fat wrap of fresh yellow hemp. He's hatless, since a hat would be inconvenient when it comes time to fit the noose, and his still-voluminous salt-and-pepper hair sweeps back dramatically like that of an aging hero leaning against the wind. He climbs like he's going somewhere he desperately wants to be, as if at the top of the stairs his true essence will finally reveal itself to the world and to himself.

The hangman waits onstage, occupying his mark. This is not a beheading needing a hulk in a black hood to slam a silver axe blade clean through a gristly neck into a wood block. He is a little man—brown suit, hair combed over a bald patch, narrow shoulders. His task at the moment is only the pulling of a lever a few degrees of arc against the light resistance of a simple mechanism—gears and pulleys—to trip the release of the deadly square of stage opening onto another world. Two fingers would do it. His real job is already done— solving a schoolboy arithmetic problem, a matter of acceleration per foot per second, a calculation of weight and force and the fragility of the human body. A foot of rope either way can make the difference between suc- cess and bright red faces for the dignitaries. Hard to remain dignified when a man hangs for long minutes bucking and choking ten feet below your boot soles while the audience gasps.

V woke from the dream feeling whispered to by snakes in her sleep, a taste of somebody else's spit in her mouth.

In all its muddy, smelly glory, Washington pulsed with endless excitement and entertainment until all of a sudden the party ended. War with Mexico had been brewing, sold to the public as a simple and stupid issue of border enforcement, though Texas had only been a state for a short while, and its southern boundary was still disputed and vaporous. The real issue involved a complicated, contentious grab of land that included Texas and the entire Pacific Coast up to Vancouver Island. And with it, an attempt to draw a line east to west across the continent, below which slavery would extend Atlantic to Pacific for ever and ever.

As war fever grew hot during the winter of 1846, V extracted a promise from Jeff that he would not volunteer to fight that utterly stupid fight. And she wasn't entirely being a new, young wife not wanting her new husband to leave her. The Whigs—party of her raising, party of Winchester—saw the war for what it was and opposed it, and decades later Ulysses S. Grant in his memoir said we intentionally provoked the war to grab territory.

A few weeks after Jeff's solemn promise, V discovered by accident—meaning one of his fellow politicians told her—that Jeff had lied to her and accepted an offer to lead the Mississippi militia with the rank of colonel.

So not a U.S. Army colonel, just a Mississippi colonel, which she thought established an uncomfortably low price for betraying her.

V and Jeff fought hard and bitter for two days in Brown's Hotel over the war and his decision and especially his deception. Then she packed a small leaving trunk and abandoned Washington, went westward by stagecoach to one of those little villages in the shadow of the Blue Ridge.

V spent a quiet spring month in a cottage with a sunset view. The ridges of old blue mountains rolled south to north in waves. The air remained dry and clear, sky crystalline blue rather than the humid summer color of shrimp shells. New, small leaves hazed the mountainsides.

She turned twenty and miscarried out there. It happened early days in a pregnancy she hadn't yet announced to Jeff. All he knew from her letters was that she had not been feeling her best. She saw a doctor in Culpeper who, of course, suggested strong doses of opium. Every few days—without actually apologizing for breaking his promise—Jeff wrote letters ending with his usual declarations of love in formulaic French.

Alone, V became peaceful. Clear nights she sat outside watching the sky until midnight, feeding a little twig fire for company. She followed moon phases for a month and watched bright planets set over the mountains. It focused her mind. Sometimes she breathed deep and let go all her resentments for as high as a day at a time. The thing that kept pulling at her the hardest was that Jeff had resigned from the army in order to marry Knoxie but rejoined it to leave V behind.

Eventually, what else? They left Washington together in early July, and again took the northern route, but the trip lacked all romance this time. A dreary, sweaty, mosquito-plagued float down the muddy river.

Jeff headed on to New Orleans and Mexico almost immediately after arriving at Davis Bend, and now all V remembers are the discussions between Jeff and Pemberton about whether he should go to Mexico with Jeff or stay at Brierfield. Pemberton finally decided to stay, arguing that V would need him.

Old Joseph liked to tell people what to do and to have them do it, and he strongly preferred that the white women of Davis Bend either praise him for his efforts or keep their mouths shut. Before Jeff even finished crossing the Gulf from New Orleans to Mexico, V learned she would have to deal face-to-face with Joseph by herself, without an ally.

Things quickly came to a head one night at The Hurricane when after supper Joe stabbed a long roll of paper across the table at her. When she spread it out, she recognized doodles depicting an ugly revision of the new house she and Jeff were about to build to replace Jeff's cat-and-clay experiment in architecture. Joe's vision grafted another house onto theirs—a lopsided wing with a sitting room and three large bedrooms. He said a cousin or niece or some other recently wid-owed in-law V didn't even know would be moving in with many children—too many to bother counting or differentiating—as soon as the construction concluded. They could all share the one kitchen and dining room.

V said, Mr. Davis, this won't be convenient at all. I don't think we're aiming for anything along the lines of a row house.

Old Joe looked off toward the windows and then looked straight at V and said, Not convenient? Let me be clear. This is going to happen whether you think it's convenient or not.

—We'll see, V said.

—No, *we* won't see. *I'll* see.

Joseph reached across the table for his plans and rolled them back into a tight cylinder and shook them in her face and said, You're evasive, elusive. I ask simple questions about the management of Brierfield, and you slide away into vagueness. I can't get a straight answer out of you to save me.

V said, Mr. Davis, What do you tell me about your business? Nothing. And I don't expect it, given that it's none of my business. But if a straight answer is what you want from me, then I'll say that I find the subjects of your curiosity to be essentially none of your concern. If I'm indirect, it's in an attempt to be mannerly. You call it elusive, but I call it etiquette. Brierfield is my husband's plantation, and I doubt we'll be building a wing for distant relatives. We don't intend to run a boardinghouse.

Joe reddened and glared like he wanted to slap her down. He shoved back his chair and stood up so abruptly his empty Champagne coupe tipped and broke against the edge of his plate. He came around the table and stood over her. He crowded close, twitching with anger. She pinched her lips shut and stood and faced him.

He said, You want to try me, little girl? I'll quickly become a master under whom you will be the first to learn obedience.

Eliza and Florida and the younger girls looked at their laps.

V's hands and voice shook. Very slowly she said, Mr. Davis, you may feel free to threaten me now. But I suggest we wait until Jeff returns from Mexico to sort this out.

—Oh, of course, Joseph said. My brother will sort this right out for you. Maybe he'll start by telling you things you apparently don't know. Like the fact that he doesn't own an acre of this land. It was a family handshake deal, an understanding with no legal foundation. On paper, Brierfield is still mine. I hold the deed, not Jeff. So whatever goes on anywhere here at the Bend is every bit my business and none whatsoever of yours.

V couldn't think what to say except, Even the house Jeff is paying to build?

—Strong argument to be made that it falls under the heading of improvements to the property conveying to the owner. Meaning me. Have you even looked at Jeff's will?

—No.

—I wrote it. Should make interesting reading. If Jeff dies—whether it's fighting in Mexico or whatnot—you don't inherit anything except the right to keep living here as a dependent of mine until you pass away or find some crazy old widower with a cornfield and a hog-lot out at Catahoula Lake willing to take you on.

—That sump? V said.

—Oh, you exaggerate. I'm sure there are a couple of fine weeks in spring. Anyhow, I'll have relevant passages of the will scribed so you can see your situation for yourself. You'll enjoy the Latin terms that crop up pretty often. And then you go on ahead and write Jeff to confirm. But meanwhile, considering your position, you need to amend your tone toward me.

—I will begin that effort tomorrow. Until then I'll think about what kind of low price you're establishing for selling out a sibling. By the way, has Jeff ever even seen the will you wrote for him?

—He signed it, you grubbing little bitch, Joseph said.

All the women sat quietly at their places. Florida wouldn't even look V in the eye.

V had planned to spend the night at The Hurricane staying up late with Florida. But she walked all the way back to Brierfield alone in the dark. She sat by one of the giant fireplaces with her mind whirling until eventually she stirred a full packet of medicine into a glass of wine and waited for the spin to slow.

—Catahoula Lake? she said aloud, her voice echoing down the long, dark room. That's what Old Joe wanted her to think was her best prospect in widowhood? In dry weather it was nothing but a great expanse of damp ground. Hogs running open range on the lake bottom. V thought of her aunt Jane, who inherited a fortune from her first old dead husband and then married a much younger man and soon decided to divorce him, during which procedure the young husband killed the judge in the case in a pistol duel. A scandal, yes. But more bearable, V imagined, than marrying a Catahoula hog farmer.

When she fell into bed at dawn, V had decided to run back to Natchez and never see Davis Bend or any Davis ever again. Two days later, on the next down-bound boat, she departed. Elusive V, she didn't announce her plans to anyone but Pemberton, swearing him to secrecy. She showed up, to much surprise, on her parents' doorstep with a trunk and three bags. She claimed the letter announcing her visit must have gone astray.

She stayed only a week. Her father hardly noticed she was there. He had yet another doomed business scheme simmering, and her mother fretted constantly about his lack of sense in regard to money and how desperately tight running the household constricted her, how heavy their lack of funds crushed. All the mouths to feed. V spent sunsets and evenings in a chair near the bluff looking down on the river, watching yellow lights flicker across the dark water from passing boats and barges and rafts.

A week later, she beat back against the Mississippi current to Brierfield, knowing that no matter which path she chose from then on—whether she flew away forever and changed her name and became a dowdy governess or went to New Orleans and became a fancy courtesan—dependency would doubtless follow. Might as well stay at the Bend and fight for her place.

Pemberton rallied the slaves around V, and she began a letter-writing campaign to Jeff in Mexico. Once or twice a week, Old Joe came out and harassed her about progress on the house construction, which with Pemberton's help she kept at a slow drag.

Joe would ride up and start complaining about the lack of progress before he even dismounted. V stood smiling and saying that if it were up to her they would be much further along. But what an unexpected amount of preparation would be needed before the laying of the foundation. If it were not for slow transport of materials to their remote outpost, faster progress might be made. She wished their efforts were more immediately successful, and if she were a builder herself and could lay brick and swing a hammer, they might be. Would that it were different.

What a friend she made of the subjunctive mood.

Eliza quit being polite and pretending to like V and stopped all communication with Brierfield. The other girls followed along, including Florida, the one V always considered the best of them, the only one worth caring about. Florida seemed to believe all their lies about V and only wrote a couple of brief notes expressing her concern for V's mental state and defending the others without knowing a pinch of truth about the shady deeds and wills that would determine V's future if she let them stand as the documents that bound her for life. All the women of The Hurricane lay under Old Joe's thumb just as he intended V to be. And maybe that's also what Jeff intended for her if he died—leave her roped tight to the Davis wealth, forever bound to him by money as tight as he held Knoxie in memory.

V wrote all the Davis women separate identical notes saying she perfectly understood Joseph's hatred, antipathy, and disrespect, but did any one of them understand hers toward them?

She held herself together to withstand Old Joe's outrage every time he rode to Brierfield for an inspection of construction progress. And, yes, sometimes at night she allowed herself room to express her full emotions in letters to Jeff. After all, marriage is not just a business partnership. Of course, as she suspected and confirmed later, Old Joe's letters to Jeff made her out to be a madwoman, hysterical and out of control despite his constant kind and gentle efforts. He argued that her youth and inexperience made her responsibilities at

Brierfield overwhelming. He suggested she might wish to move back to Natchez until the war ended and Jeff returned. That sort of self-serving thing. But V was where she was. She intended to fight her battles where she stood, with the boundary between the two properties as her front line.

Mornings, V and Pemberton sat under the big live oak in the yard and talked plans for the day as they drank coffee. Sometimes it would be plowing or planting or maintenance of buildings or roads or wagons and harness, the care of sick horses. Or that people needed pantaloons, dozens of pairs at a time, which V sewed herself. Or that someone's Auntie had died and it would be good to cook a pig for the funeral. Then in the evenings she and Pemberton would sit under the tree as the light dimmed and the air cooled to recapitulate the successes and failures of the day. This went on and on.

Pemberton very closely matched her father's age, but after a year of daily discussions, V realized she knew him better than her father, and vice versa. She was not so young that she didn't recognize the position he occupied—stuck in the center of a triangle between Jeff, Joe, V. And of course she knew she occupied the weak corner. But with careful calibration of power and distance and affection, Pemberton took care of her as if she mattered to him.

Sometimes in the evening after the daily business of running Brierfield had concluded, V would ask Pemberton about Jeff when he was young. Day after day she picked away, asking questions about West Point and the time afterward on the frontier, about Jeff's life as a young man and about his first wife.

Pemberton would have been forty-five or fifty during the Mexican War. Built solid and fairly tall, the gray in his hair mixed evenly, about 30 percent. Like several slaves on The Hurricane and Brierfield, he was literate, and he particularly liked newspapers, so V saved him the Memphis and New Orleans papers as they came up or down the river on steamboats several days after publication.

He started out wary of telling her anything about Knoxie to the point it was hard to glean from his comments that he ever knew her.

He'd say safe things like, After Mister Davis finished up school, we went to the north country and stayed an awful long time. We had cold winters at West Point, but up there toward the top of the river, winters kept on going until you worried the back of one and the front of the next might meet in the middle with no summer at all. He said, Winters, everything freezes up there. You could walk across the river. Play Jesus. It was awful weather.

But after he realized V knew a few things about Jeff's courtship of Knoxie—had visited her grave as a solemn honeymoon event and knew her death had wounded Jeff perhaps beyond healing—Pemberton talked more openly, though still only in snips and hints. She could tell Pemberton had liked Knoxie but didn't want to say it. And when V thought about it, his favorable opinion of Knoxie carried some weight. She had previously pictured Knoxie as a little half-pretty, sharp-eyed belle—decorated in every fluffy feature of that season's fashion—showing up in the middle of nowhere with her commanding-officer daddy and being as single-minded and witless in her search for a husband among the young officers as a hen pecking at cracked corn.

So V held back awhile on direct questions about Knoxie and went another direction. She made Pemberton awfully uncomfortable one sundown when she said, I've heard Jeff may have fathered an Indian baby up there. Some claim to know for sure it was a girl.

She told Pemberton that people in Washington gossiped about it, and that she needed to know how to help Jeff handle the gossip, and that how to do it best would be different, depending on whether the story was true or untrue. She reminded Pemberton that managing social matters wasn't where Jeff's light shined brightest—which everyone who ever spent thirty seconds with him knew for a fact.

Pemberton said, Ma'am, some things up the river back then's not for us to cover here between us.

V reminded him that when they sat under the tree at sunset, just the two of them talking, neither of them needed to worry about forms of salutation that slowed them down. Just talk the way he and Jeff usually talked. Not necessary to say sir or ma'am every other sentence. Just talk straight.

—I don't know anyone else to ask about this, V added. And besides, I was about one year old at the time, and he was a grown man on the wild frontier and very spirited.

Pemberton said, Mr. Davis ought to be the one answering your question.

V paused and then said, I'll take it that the rumors of a child are true. Otherwise, you'd deny them. And I appreciate that you're not going to lie to me.

—No, ma'am.

—Did you know the mother?

—She was . . . He trailed off, waved his hands in front of him.

—Let me guess. Pretty and seventeen? The way he likes us.

—Her daddy was supposed to be from England, Pemberton said, as deflection. Anyway, she was light brown color and could speak good English, but it sounded funny. A part-Sauk girl by her looks. Most folks up there were Sauk or Fox, and a few Dakota Sioux from on out West. I knew her half sister some. Real, real pretty woman. They had the same mama, but that sister sure had plenty of Sioux in her.

—Meaning what? V said.

—Hard to say. Sioux were real strong fighters.

Pemberton said it like a soft, happy memory.

—I forgot you were a young man too back then, V said.

Pemberton looked off toward the river. He stood and said, I believe I'll go down to the horse barn before it's too dark to see my hand in front of my face and make sure Jack is set for the night.

Jack was V's saddle horse and had been moving a little off in front the previous couple of days.

—Check his feet, V said.

—Been planning on it, ma'am, Pemberton said as he walked away.

V sat outside past full dark imagining thousands of half-blood children like Jeff's Sauk girl and Pemberton's Sioux girl, entering that strange liminal world of native villages and invader forts and tallgrass plains and dark fir forests under conditions ranging from rape to rapturous love. Maybe the Sauk girl's particular Brit father was a tallish blond fourth son, Cambridge educated but adventurous and looking to make his own fortune at a far and alien fringe of the New World. And he lingered almost a decade after the birth of his pretty daughter before fleeing onward toward the Pacific or backing away toward home. During those years he stayed, the girl became fluent in English. So Jeff arrives in the wilderness—winter, dark, cold—land cut in two by the Mississippi, which seemed not at all the same river that flowed wide and brown by Natchez. And he meets this girl and an old story only worth summarizing comes to pass. Two young people meet at that moment of accelerative emotion when nature floods our being with urgent demands. So, assume the usual plot elements—attractiveness, proximity, opportunity. She speaks a highly grammatical but oddly accented English, a matter of enunciation for the most part, a carefulness of the tongue in forming certain vowels that creates a music Jeff finds irresistible. Also assume variations on the usual narrative details, their differing clothes and social ranking and halting manners toward each other, the brief yearning and the quick consummation, including an oblique reference to the mechanics of reproduction. And then months later . . . what? No telling whether Jeff considered his next action as moving on or backing away.

V was tempted to spin her imagination on and on about the adventures and loves of Jefferson and Pemberton in the wilderness, but she resolved to pause her deductions and inventions and give all that north woods material a name and put it away for a while like a rough draft. Title it something like *Jefferson on the Wild Frontier,* or *Reckless Love,* or simply *Knoxie.*

A week later, though, she found a bundle of letters from Jeff's courtship with Knoxie in a desk drawer. They'd been tied with a red ribbon. V didn't read them, not that day nor thereafter. Their words to each other were not her business, but she assumed Jeff's letters followed his usual heart-throbbing pattern, plunging headlong into French at the end.

At seventeen V had been young and romantic enough to believe that, given time, she could occupy and eventually possess all the chambers of Jeff's heart—or at least a majority of them. But even during the Mexican War she had already started to wonder if Knoxie's spirit would hover between them, a beautiful ectoplasmic projection, throughout their marriage.

The Mexican War dragged on, and so did the war between Brierfield and The Hurricane. Politics and di-
plomacy between the two plantations became so bleak
that Jeff asked for leave to make an epic journey, a thousand miles, to forge peace at home. His commanding
officer was once again Knoxie's father, Zachary Taylor,
a general at the time. In Mexico, Jeff and the general
became friends, and Taylor allowed that between them
his daughter had been the better judge of young men.
He sent Jeff off with his blessings to do what needed to
be done in Mississippi.

Jeff traveled by horseback from Monterey to the
coast and then by ship across the northern Gulf to New
Orleans and then by steamboat up the river to the Bend.
He showed up with blood in his eyes, mad equally at V
and Brother Joe. During the three weeks Jeff stayed at
Brierfield, he and V fought nightly over the will—its
surprises and secrets, the unimagined complications
of property ownership, her lack of any inheritance or
protections against the future. He spent most of every
day huddled with Old Joe in his office conspiring about
how to deal with her.

When Jeff's leave ran out, Brierfield and The Hurricane had failed to reach a peace treaty, or even a cease-

fire. He left V with a chilly peck on her cheek on the porch, and V did not join him in the carriage to see him off at the dock. From Jeff's arrival until his departure, she slept in a separate bedroom. She told him that the crudest way to put it was that if he died in Mexico—leaving her to the predations of Joseph—she intended to save herself for her second husband. Whatever grim transaction a second marriage might involve, dragging a child into the negotiations would be an unwelcome impediment. Or, leaving future husbands out of it, imagine her bed and board entirely in the hands of Old Joe, and Jeff's child equally without inheritance so long as Joe kept the deed to Brierfield.

Just as he turned to leave, V said to him, How can I bring children into the world knowing the brutal, mercantile family they would fall into, holding money over all our heads to control us? Old Joe already controls so many destinies, his houseful of women and fields full of slaves.

All Jeff could say in response was, I think you're exaggerating.

After a stretch of weeks alone, V wrote to her mother, *I have become quite a savage, and I tear my food in silence.*

A few months before the end of the Mexican War, Jeff came home wounded and walking with a cane—the great hero of the Battle of Buena Vista, where his strategy and leadership and courage would enter the canon of military history. In Natchez, they rode together through town in an open carriage heaped to their armpits with flowers. All the way up from New Orleans, in every town, brass bands and dignitaries and barbecues and salutes of guns and cannons welcomed them.

Jeff hid his true pain to the extent that his limp seemed a theatrical affectation and the cane a fashion accessory. All along the way, he made speeches to the crowds. Stop by stop as they moved upriver he grew more confident and more powerful as a speaker. One newspaper said that if he ran for the Senate he would go through the state like a bolt of lightning. But settled back at Brierfield, it became clear how badly he had been injured. Pieces of bone kept working themselves out of his wounds, and the fight with Brother Joe weighed heavy on his mind. He wanted V to play along, leave everything for Joseph to sort out someday. Trust him. But there Jeff was, his foot and lower leg wounded to the marrow, and V picking bone shards out of the mess every morning with tweezers, knowing any day it could go septic and carry him away to the next world.

All the years later, living in the twentieth century, she's taken care of herself long enough to know how it's done. What she wanted at twenty-one was either to have the security promised as part of the deal when marrying an older man of property, or else to be left alone to live her life without some master like Old Joe lording over her.

Jeff, though, wanted peace at home and power out in the world. He got the latter almost immediately without even having to go through an election when one of Mississippi's old senators died in office, as they often do. War hero Jeff was immediately appointed to the position by the governor. As Jeff prepared to leave for Washington, he gave V a choice. Go along with Joe's system of management and accompany her husband to Washington, or carry on the fight and stay right there at the Bend by herself.

It was a mean ultimatum, knowing how much she loved Washington and that the wife of a senator would have even more access to the best parties and the most interesting people. They had mostly lived apart for the past two years, and if V didn't agree to Jeff's terms, they would spend most of another year separated. V

decided to dig in and fight on, besieged at Fort Brierfield.

Grim times after Jeff left. Letters passed between them
declaring love but ending in threats. He urged her to
become less bitter toward his family and declared that
if her behavior didn't change, it would be impossible
ever to live together again. She sent back letters suggesting maybe that would be for the best.

She thought for a while about getting a puppy for
company, a warm body to snuggle with when she
stayed up late reading. But eventually she decided that
at the Bend it would grow to be some vicious hunting
dog chasing deer to exhaustion and death.

At Jeff's insistence, Joseph's horrible patched-on
wing finally rose from the ground, and a very worn
and bleak woman with four insane children moved in.
Even the hour of supper became so full of running and
screaming and crying that V began taking her evening
meal alone in her room or out at the table under the big
tree. But she kept fighting Jeff and Brother Joe and the
damned will all along the way.

Jeff had a hard time alone in Washington, and it
wasn't just that he lacked social skills. He nearly got
into a duel with a mere congressman, and it took his

old father-in-law—now President Zachary Taylor—to calm the two men. Then shortly afterward, on Christmas Day, Jeff and his fellow senator from Mississippi, Henry Foote—both living at Brown's Hotel—fell into disagreement on either a political or a Constitutional issue. Jeff forever remained too embarrassed to talk about it, but V heard in letters from acquaintances and friends that he and Foote had been drinking pretty strongly from breakfast onward. Jeff, who still walked with a cane, began fistfighting Foote, a rolling-in-the-floor kind of fight. When they became winded and stood up, they threatened to kill one another for a while, and then on his way out of the room, Foote turned around and claimed he was the one who struck the first blow. Then Jeff got right in his face, and they threatened to kill one another all over again until Foote struck Jeff, and then Jeff knocked Foote to the floor and beat on him until the other members of the legislative branch dragged them apart. At which point Jeff, very cold-blooded, said he had two loaded pistols in his room and suggested they go up and lock the door from the inside and settle the matter for good. Foote declined. A few days later, when the event became public, both of them—politicians to the marrow—agreed to call their brawl a Christmas frolic, a regrettable celebration of the Savior's birth.

V didn't know what all was going on with Jeff at that time and didn't much care. But letters kept coming from friends sharing gossip—such as, that in the middle of the night, probably drunk, he had fallen off a bridge or down a bank into a ditch and limped around the Capitol for a week with his head and hands wrapped in white bandages. Their own letters to each other remained icy during that entire session, but it seemed clear Jeff needed a steadying hand.

At a long break in the congressional calendar, Jeff came to his senses and arrived back home with a draft of a new agreement among the three warring parties. A treaty wherein Joseph saved face and V got a true stake in Davis Bend should Jeff die ahead of her, with Joseph having a right to make the first offer to buy her share should she want to sell out. An entertaining negotiation to anticipate—V having something Joe wanted and the power to say no—which regrettably never came to pass, since she has far outlived both brothers.

When Jeff and V left together for the next session of Congress, V never again lived at Brierfield for more than a few weeks at a time. But the night after the signing of the peace papers, Jeff opened a couple of bottles of old Bordeaux and made a ceremony of burning the previous will in the bedroom fireplace, and V felt like the second half of an incomplete wedding had finally been performed, that for better or worse they were linked and committed and that she had become a full shareholder in her own future.

Gossips speculated as to why Jeff and V went years without her bearing a child and then suddenly she seemed to stay pregnant most of the time. It didn't seem mysterious to V, and that second will and second wedding ceremony by the fire had a great deal to do with it, a reconciliation of hearts and bodies that lasted for some years.

The return to Washington would have seemed triumphant to V, except that soon after they arrived news came from the Bend that Pemberton had died very unexpectedly. Jeff hardly spoke of Pemberton's death, but he brooded for a few days and then just said, I don't know which of us hated that north woods weather the most.

The news of Pemberton hit V hard—deeper than she would have thought. She couldn't stop feeling guilty that she hadn't been there for his burial, couldn't stop remembering how he had tried to divert Joseph's rage, couldn't stop feeling exposed and at risk knowing he was gone. But she kept her feelings tamped, since no one—especially Jeff—would understand her grief for

Pemberton. There wasn't a vocabulary to explain their relationship to other people.

=

—**There still** aren't words now, V says.

—But you could try. It sounds like Pemberton protected you the best he could when you didn't have anyone else on your side.

—That's exactly the way it was. And when he died it felt almost like Winchester had passed. Like a father had gone for good, but I couldn't say that.

She thinks a moment and then says, I don't know why, but I remember one evening Pemberton telling me he wouldn't be around for a day or two. That he was going to visit a man he knew—an old friend—on a plantation twenty miles away. He said he'd gotten word the man had been beaten badly because after he'd groomed a horse his master had wiped a white handkerchief down its neck and it came back dirty. I was so young. I mostly felt happy that he trusted me enough to tell me where he was going and why. I told him I'd never been around those horrors and always felt like they were mostly stories. He said, It's not one thing everywhere. People act their natures. Some plantations beat bloody every chance they get. Other places a man can go off two or three days to visit a girlfriend miles away, and when he gets back the master just says, I thought you'd fallen in the river and drowned.

—Yes, James says. I heard plenty of true stories from freed people when I first started teaching. A little kindness and a lot of horror. My first real job as a teacher—making my living at it—I was nineteen. A student of mine—she'd been enslaved in Maryland. She was about fifty, just learning to read. Her name was Martha.

James tells V that Martha was body servant to a young mistress who trusted her and chattered at length every day, telling every dirty secret about her disgusting older husband, every flirtation she had with handsome younger men at parties, her occasional adulterous flings, every thread of gossip in the county. Martha dressed her mistress every day from bare skin to composed belle—arranged her hair, applied powder and rouge, told her how beautiful she was. And yet the mistress sold Martha's ten-year-old daughter to traders for seven hundred dollars. She believed Martha would get over her crying and forget about the girl, and Martha did get over the crying because she had to. But she told James that not one day of her life passed without grieving for her daughter, and wondering which was worse, believing her child dead or imagining the fate that might have awaited her. And still every day having to touch with care the woman who inflicted such pain.

—*Inhuman,* V says. But that's an easy word. We've been doing that sort of thing to each other all through history, back past the Pyramids. Humans are inhuman, whether it's by direct action or by acceptance of a horrible action as normal.

—That godlike long view is fine. Sometimes we need it. But hearing a story like Martha's made me want to kill somebody right then. James pauses and then says, Anyway, let's circle back to what you call the axle of your life. Maybe the axle of mine too—when all that old order was in the middle of collapsing.

Writing on the Wall

1865

After their moment of luxury in Abbeville, the fugitives traveled west, crossed the Savannah River into Georgia. The town of Washington, Georgia, had once been pretty, but it had filled with refugees fleeing north from Sherman's wasteland. Garbage in the streets, stores looted. V's group kept right on going and spent the night in a little white country chapel, sleeping on the pews. Then through a stretch of beautiful broken country, slow going for a whole week. Wet weather and bad roads. Then they fell off the map for three days of greenwood country and tangles of curvy single-track, seven or eight miles a day at best, but pretty camp places. Not mountains, but low ridges, water running over big rocks in the streams. Little towns blurred together, but V remembers a place called Mayfield. She wanted to stop and buy a house and let the children grow up there.

Delrey and Burton and Jimmie Limber never owned their tiredness. Go twelve hours with little food and no rest, banging down the rutted roads dazed and numb, and then ask them if they were ready to stop for the night and they'd each say, I could keep going awhile. Like having a contest to see who could persist, who fell in his footsteps last.

—You tired, little man? Delrey said. Fading? Do we need to stop?

Jimmie said, Nope. I can go.

V said, Delrey, are you hinting you could use a nap? Jimmie can probably figure out how to drive this rig if he needs to.

Delrey said, I believe he could if he had a little teaching.

Jimmie looked far down the road and said nothing.

Delrey widened and lifted his arms, spreading the long drooping leather reins, and said, Come here and spell me, then.

Jimmie looked at V, and she nodded yes. He ducked

under and stood in front of Delrey and took hold of the reins. The backs of his hands were still childhood chubby to the extent that the knuckles at the base of his fingers were like four dimples in his plump handbacks. The reins were wide as his palms.

—Guide 'em easy, Delrey said. Don't pull, and don't flap. They have plenty of sense on their own. Use the reins to make suggestions. Don't go yanking and checking them unless they give you no other choice. Got it?

—Sure, Jimmie said.

—Well, I believe I'll take me a nap, then. Wake me up when we get to Florida. You'll know we're there when you start seeing alligators.

Delrey slouched down a little on the wagon bench and pretended to snore.

A night later at camp, almost bedtime, they heard horses trotting on the road and then heard them stop. As they had planned, Ellen eased the children off into the woods out of earshot, and Delrey hid outside the ring of campfire light with his shotgun and pistol ready in case of trouble.

At the campfire, V and Burton were joined by three bummers, raiders, deserters, or killers—whatever you want to call leftovers and scavengers from Sherman's army. Maybe they were just stray northern shop clerks conscripted against their wills a year before and had spent their few months of war trying to figure out which end of the gun you aimed at the enemy and now were lost on their way home. Except that's not at all how they looked and acted. They looked like they wanted what you had and would kill you to get it but would slightly prefer you just handed it over.

Burton sat on a log with his right hand loose by his side so he could reach his pistol. He talked polite. Had they come from the east? Were things bad there? Or from back toward Atlanta? He and V had agreed to be calm, friendly, not be angered by anything people said until they made their intentions clear. Not react to taunts or insults or rude words. If it went bad, hit the dirt fast and give Delrey room to fill the air with lead shot.

The man with the black beard and the red-haired man talked vague. The thin, pale man stayed silent. One thing rang clear in their voices. They did not come from around here.

V said, I can't place your accents exactly, but I'm going to guess north of Baltimore and south of Boston.

—Easy guess, the red-haired man said. Most of the world's somewhere between the two.

He stood up and walked about five steps from the fire and pulled his britches down on one side until it seemed like he intended to strip bare. But he stopped with just his hip exposed to the firelight, and on it a big pearly welted letter *D*. He patted it like a pet and said, Supposed to teach me a lesson. Down here you probably just shoot deserters in the head. We brand them.

The black beard man said, Good God, you can't piss right here.

The red-haired man turned his back and looked over his shoulder and said, I'm not aiming to piss right here. I'm aiming to piss way over yonder.

He made a graceful gesture with his left hand and arm, the smooth arc of a dolphin rising to take a breath of air. And then he let fly.

The black beard man smiled—a white flash of teeth, and then his mouth snapped shut and the lower half of his face became nothing but beard again.

He said, Doesn't really matter if you people know where we're from or not, but we're from Pennsylvania. Red and me got conscripted halfway through the war. It was us set fire to Atlanta and left on the Decatur Road with everything burning down. Blue sky ahead, black smoke behind. From there we angled southeast and left a black stripe nearly a hundred miles wide all the way across this shithole state to the ocean. We were a big machine. It took fifteen thousand horses and mules to haul our stuff. Just picture that. We had orders to seize everything we could eat, everything our horses and mules could eat, with a surplus of minimum two weeks. We took all their beeves and pigs and chickens, whatever crops still stood in the fields, whatever the farmers had put away, dried and canned and smoked. We had orders not to enter their houses and steal stuff unless we felt they'd worked against us—burnt bridges or hid food. Entirely up to our discretion, so that rule didn't mean much. At big plantations, no rules at all. Just wide open. We were free to bust in wherever we thought there might be something valuable—cash money, boxes of jewelry, cupboards full of silver forks and spoons. In smaller places, you quit bothering because all you'd find was just pitiful cigar boxes of low-number coins.

—And him? V said, looking at the pale man. He's from Pennsylvania too?

—I don't know. Somewhere. He's seen the whole show from the start. Name a bad fight and he was probably in it. He's about done now.

—Done with the war? Burton said.

Red said, With everything you could name. He's looking to venge himself against the world.

—I'm sure they'll welcome you heroes back home with brass bands, Burton said.

The bearded man said, How many have you killed

the past four years? We've shot so many men better than you it's sickening.

Burton didn't answer.

—What did you all do before the war? V said.

Red said, Shoe factory.

The bearded man tipped his head toward the pale man and said, Foundry. And for me, stockyard.

What is it you're wanting from us? Burton said.

The bearded man smiled his quick white smile.

Red said, What you got?

The pale man leaned into the firelight. He looked consumptive, blue around the eyes and fragile. He stood at least six feet but wouldn't have gone better than one-twenty. He had been hit bad in the face. Every piece of skin you could see had scars either gouged or burned. His mouth drew up on one side over his back teeth in a permanent wolfish grin. The eye on that side lay dead and milky in his face. About the only thing left normal about him was his nose and the other eye. And that good eye was the scariest thing about him. It looked out at the world like he was meeting God and didn't give a damn how he might be judged.

The pale man looked at V and said, We've met.

He talked whispery, from his throat, with a hiss of air from the part of his mouth that failed to close because his lips on that side were gone.

V looked at Burton, and then before she could catch herself, she glanced off to the woods where Ellen and the children and Delrey hid.

—Forgive me, V said, but I don't recall when that would have been.

—Richmond.

V said, Yes?

—Libby Prison Hospital. I'd been cut up by canister. Lost a deal of blood. And the first part of this happened then.

He raised a hand and patted it against the left side of his face, netted with scars like a sheet of caul fat.

He said, Richmond doctors told me I ought to get square with my Maker. You came in and acted like the smell of wounds didn't sicken you. Fed me cookies and tea and held my hand. You kissed me on the head and said you were sorry.

—What's your name? V said.

—Jens.

—Well, I'm still sorry, and I'm glad you made it, Jens.

He puffed out air from the broken side of his mouth. Made it? he said. I can't go home. I'd have to wear a mask to walk down the street.

—But you're still the same person inside.

—That right there is bullshit, Jens said. And you say

it to me knowing that I know it's bullshit. Good God, nothing's left of me.

—Go home and see. People might be better than you think.

—I always wondered why you were there, Jens said. One minute your people are ripping me apart. The next minute, kisses and cookies. Better for you if you went to the Rebel hospitals.

—I did that too.

—Boo-hoo, the bearded man said. A couple of months from now, after all this gets settled, maybe we'll start robbing banks and trains and we'll all be wearing masks.

Jens said to the bearded man, Let her be. We're done here.

He stood and looked at V and said, I'm calling us even.

He walked to his horse and mounted and rode off. The other two looked at each other and shrugged and walked to their horses.

Before they rode away, Red said, Must be your lucky day, folks.

One afternoon before supper, the boys had been hunkering on their knees, knuckled down at a marble ring they'd scratched in the dirt with a stick. But Jeffy's taw was a big, shiny steel ball bearing, and Jimmie and Billy had only glass shooters. Jeffy had run the table two or three times, and his jacket pockets bulged full of marbles he'd won. The younger boys claimed Jeffy was cheating, and all of a sudden they were wallowing in the red dirt, bashing at each other with their little soft fists.

—Do you want to handle this or let me? V said all irritable.

Ellen said, You sit. I'll go see whether a spanking's what they really need right now.

She stepped over beyond the campfire to the marble ring and broke up the fight and marched the boys to a fallen log. Ellen sat first and then thumped Jeffy down on one side, Billy and Jimmie on the other. She began asking questions, and they all answered at the same time, and soon their chins quivered and parallel tear tracks ran down their dusty cheeks. V watched close but couldn't hear much of what any of them said.

Before long, the boys stood, and Ellen nudged them underhanded on their way. They ran to the edge of the woods and started a new game that involved throwing big pinecones at tree trunks and then at one another.

When Ellen came back to the fire, V said, What's your secret?

—I'm not telling. But I will say, wading in slapping is not the only answer.

Georgia's a tall state when you aim to go top to bottom in wagons with a bunch of children. For a week the journey became a nightmare of repetition, every day the same routine, the same landscape—nothing changing but the weather. The fugitives probably hadn't advanced more than forty miles after meeting the marauders when two boys about fifteen or sixteen rode up from behind, one astride a mule and another on a halfway good dun gelding, its legs striped as a zebra and a black streak running from its forelock and mane down its back through its tail.

The mule rider was a tall black-headed goose of a boy and the other one middle-size and blondish. As they came alongside, they looked the fugitive group over good, and when they reached the ambulance and saw V sitting beside the driver, the tall one said, Afternoon, Mrs. Davis. He reached up and touched the brim of his hat about like greeting an acquaintance on the street.

Delrey immediately pulled up the mules and moved his right hand near the short double-barrel shotgun he kept by his leg. Burton rode between the boys and the ambulance. The canvas of the ambulance had been raised a foot above the sideboards for air, and four curious faces peeped out. Ellen held Winnie in one arm and eased the others back and rolled down the fabric.

—Where are you coming from? Burton said.

The tall boy, real caustic, said, Well greetings to you too. We're down from Richmond. Back in Washington, Georgia, Jeff Davis gave all us cadets back pay—or at least a fraction of what they owed us—and told us to go home.

—President Davis, Burton said.

—Not anymore he's not, the boy said.

—Did you come looking for us? Burton said.

—It's on our way home.

—You're navy cadets? Burton said.

—Yes, sir, the smaller boy said.

—Were you still there when Richmond fell? Burton said.

—Yes, sir.

—Y'all got names? Delrey said.

The tall one said he was Ryland and the smaller blond was Bristol.

Ryland said, We left town on the train the president escaped on. Like fleeing hell.

Bristol said, We've mostly been under General Duke since Greensboro, after the rail bridges got blown up and we had to travel by horse and wagon and afoot.

—Is Basil all right? V asked.

—Yes, ma'am, Bristol said. Last I saw of him, General Duke had a metal mirror tacked to a tree and was shaving and looked like he was going to a ball.

—And Judah?

—Mister Benjamin was telling jokes and smoking big Cuban cigars, Ryland said.

—And reciting poems, Bristol said. Especially "The Death of Wellington."

Ryland said, I heard him say that one so many times I remember a line that goes, *Hush, the Dead March wails in the people's ears.* And then something about sobs and tears and black earth yawning. The way Mr. Benjamin said that rhyme—*ears* and *tears*—was pretty funny.

—I expect it was, V said. And Mister Davis?

Ryland said, He didn't look good at all for a while. Then after Charlotte when things went really bad and it was clear the war was lost, he got sort of happy seeming and rode along talking about horse bits and bird dogs and books he read a long time ago. Except probably he wasn't figuring he'd soon have a fat bounty on his head.

—Bounty? V said.

—For conspiring to kill Lincoln. And—goes without saying—for treason.

—Lincoln's been killed?

—Yes, ma'am. And by a Southerner. The big money reward's on your husband, a hundred thousand. But they claimed pretty much anybody close to him or high in the government aided and abetted and conspired, so they've got a price on them too. Clay, Stephens, everybody big. You too, Mister Harrison. Twenty-five thousand apiece.

—That's nothing but rumors along the road, Delrey said.

—Not exactly, Bristol said. We read it for ourselves. General Duke showed us a newspaper before they paid us and cut us loose.

Burton stepped his horse over to the ambulance. He and Delrey and V mumbled about the boys, the requirements to get in the academy, and the training the cadets would have gotten. Not to mention the family connections they would have needed in the first place. And since the fugitive party had dwindled to such a small hard core, they could use help.

Burton circled his horse back to the boys and said, You wouldn't mind riding with us for a few days, would you? If what you say is true, we could travel faster if we had help making fires and washing pots and pans and dishes, taking care of the horses and that sort of thing? Doing whatever comes up? If you're willing, we'll be making camp in a couple of hours, and we'll put you right to work.

—Happy to be of service, Bristol said.

—We can't pay much at all, Burton said.

Ryland laughed and said, That also goes without saying.

V said, Maybe later you can tell us about that last day in Richmond. We haven't gotten reliable news for a long time. Third- or fourth-hand at best.

They stopped early to camp and cook supper and feed the horses and mules, and to let the children run around before dark. Also to plan how to deal with the latest threat, how to avoid people, how to become invisible. They made camp a good way off the road in pinewoods by an abandoned hayfield greening up after winter. Ellen cooked and the navy boys untacked and fed horses and mules and took them in pairs on lead lines to graze.

The children played in the new grass at the edge of the field, happy to be free from the wagon-bed. They chased each other, and Maggie spun with her arms out until she fell over dizzy and stared at the sky until the world stopped whirling. And then the boys all did it too. They cartwheeled and tried to walk on their hands and tumbled like circus acrobats. Jimmie showed them how to pluck a wide blade of fresh grass and hold it just right between the joints of their thumbs and blow across it and work their mouths to make high-pitched buzzing music.

V sat on the trunk of a big deadfall shortleaf pine and watched them and looked across the hayfield, its perspective flowing away in an hourglass shape, the borders and pinched waist delineated by dark tall incursions of pinewood. The sun fell low, and the light in the sky above the far end of the field stained upward from apricot to indigo. Tree shadows stretched across the new grass. How wonderful if that could be sufficient to our needs, a vision of static beauty without motion or change.

Burton and Delrey came and sat on either side of her, and she cupped their wrists with her hands and gripped them tight. Ellen came and stood with her arms crossed, holding her elbows

V said, That can't be true, what they said about Lincoln and the bounties?

—Exaggeration probably, Delrey said. But, smoke and fire. There'll be truth somewhere in it.

Tears welling in her eyes, she said, We're all lost now. They will punish us for the war, fair enough. But Lincoln would have let us up easy. Now, they'll hunt us all down. Even the friends who helped us in Abbeville will face charges. The Burts and Mary Chesnut arrested for aiding and abetting. Every preacher where we slept in a chapel to get out of the rain, that farm where the widow let us sleep in her dry barn.

Delrey said, Ma'am, we don't know what's coming behind us. Worry about staying in motion, going forward. They don't catch us, they can't hurt us. We make it to Florida and find a boat running south down the Gulf, nothing they can do. We'll be sailing blue water, eating fried grouper instead of moldy old bacon and musty grits. Skip down through the Keys and cross the Florida Straits to Havana. After that, Yankees can call us whatever brand of criminal they care to. We start over again without reference to their opinions. I ain't scared. I've lost everything I had two times already and built it back. I'm not so old I can't live through it one more time, and I'm the oldest one among us by at least ten years.

—It's not just me, V said. There's family to consider. Even if we make it out, reunion would be hard.

—Not harder than if we're all in prison.

Burton said, Delrey, no need to be alarming. Worst case, even if these stories are true and we're caught, the Federals won't charge either of you with treason or conspiracy. They'll try to make you think they will, but they won't. And I know I didn't conspire, and neither did Mr. Davis.

Delrey said, They'll sure charge you and try to hang you, no matter what the truth is.

V thought a minute and then said to Burton, So, Havana? You'll come with me?

—Yes, Burton said. Of course.

Ellen hadn't said anything. She'd mostly looked down the field. So when the men were gone, V stood beside her and asked what she was thinking.

—I'm trying to figure that out. When we left Richmond, Cuba never entered my mind.

—I don't know what to say. If we make it to Florida and find a boat, I want you to come. But only if you want to.

—I could get down there and not be able to get back, Ellen said.

—That's possible, V said.

—I'll have to study on it.

After supper—children settled in the wagon-bed for the night—the fugitives sat around a campfire burning low, and the navy boys started talking, and they mostly told their story over the top of each other. Bristol started by saying, That last day was terrible. No doubt about it. Everybody had to own that we were beat.

The boys went on to describe the fall of Richmond. How everybody in the city, to some degree, seemed blistered from the loss of a long war and the failure of a shaky made-up government created to represent the worst features of a culture. Leaders busy packing to run. Food scarce, money worthless. Roads clogged with scared refugees knowing the Federal army rode hard just hours away. And after nightfall, the city began to go up in flames. But, on the other hand, Bristol and Ryland were sixteen and armed. Chaos thrilled like a great adventure.

That night, eight cadets, four to a skiff, were given big casks of black powder and cans of coal oil and told to row out to the CSS *Patrick Henry* on the James River and blow her up and burn her down, preferably in such a way as to impede water traffic for the Federals. Sad, yes. She had been their training ship and mostly their home for over a year. But blowing things up—especially when they're large and important—thrills at any age, and especially at sixteen.

On board they gathered all the stray weapons and ammunition they could find quickly and heaped them into the skiffs and then lit the fuses and hustled to row away. They were almost to the riverbank when the powder blew. And then the oil cans caught with such a great sucking combustion and eruption of yellow flame that they stopped rowing and cheered in pure anarchic joy. Flames lit the water like sheets of crumpled gold leaf under sunlight, and then waves broke around them and bucked the skiffs until the boys gripped the gunnels to keep from being thrown into the river.

Ryland looked at the burning ship and said, We've sure hell done it now.

Soon as they reached dry ground, the eight heroes who sank the mighty *PH* stood at the riverbank and watched irreverently and in awe as their ship burned toward the waterline. Then they looked around for fellow cadets to praise them and for officers to tell them what to do next. But officers were not to be found. Important business elsewhere, no doubt. Back toward the city, undersides of clouds shone amber and red and yellow with buildings afire.

Ryland said, Appears like we'll call our own orders from here on.

Nobody agreed with him aloud. Some of those boys weren't more than fourteen and didn't know what to say. Ryland, though, had decided he never intended to trust rulers again. No bosses and generals and presidents no matter what government they came from. He felt entirely able to judge every man above him in the chain of command all the way to Wood and Lee and Davis.

Bristol said, Let's go see what's happening in town before we commit too far.

Ryland rattled through the weapons and ammunition they had claimed from the ship and came up with an ugly sawed-off twelve-gauge.

He held it up to the boys and said, See this scattergun? Soon as I get the material, I'm gonna pack me some shells with shot big as sweet peas. Nobody's gonna cross me then.

With nowhere else to go, they distributed the rest of the weaponry and walked toward the train station for lines running toward Danville and points south. The direction of home.

The city whirled all crazy. Little impromptu squads of people rushed around looting houses and stores and warehouses. People ran down the middle of the street carrying blanket bundles of clinking valuables slung over their shoulders—silverware and crystal and china. People cradled precious breakables in their arms like babies. One woman strode along with six or seven fancy hats stacked on her head, holding her arms straight out and palms up for balance. A man hauled an awkward purple velvet tête-à-tête love seat by himself with just the aid of a muslin tumpline running from the hind legs across his forehead. A man and woman dragged a great crystal chandelier the size of a cabriolet behind them, leaving a trail of broken faceted glass sparkling in the firelight.

City officials unwisely ordered bars and hotels to break open their barrels of whiskey and beer and pour them into the gutters. Therefore, many folks sat on curbstones dipping drinks with looted china cups and crystal goblets or just supping primitive from their two hands. Flames jumped gaps from building to building and the fire built minute by minute. Smoke and the crackle of burning wood and booms of exploded munitions filled the air.

Along the way the boys heard rumors spreading that the entire treasury—a million dollars in gold and silver bars from the several mints and also canvas bags packed heavy with floor sweepings, fingernail parings of silver and gold—waited on the platform to be loaded onto a railcar. And that the president and his cabinet were fleeing south with the treasure, leaving the capital looted and burned out so that the Yankees and also the inhabitants would be left with nothing. Other people claimed the president's wife had already left with most of the treasure days ago.

By the time the cadets rolled into the train station, they found a mob ruling the platform, dark-minded and globbing together in cohorts, talking loud and vicious. Two trunks sat by the rail lines and treasure hunters beat open the locks with their pistol butts and pulled out suits of men's clothes and some big underpants and socks. The cadets had been dipping from the gutters themselves and had just blown up a goddamn full-size side-wheel steamship, and they were heavily armed. So they had achieved a certain mood, under which the opinions of their elders factored small.

Firelight from burning buildings lit everything around the station lurid. Brick walls stood bloody red, washed over with black shadows and flashing yellow from explosions rising in the sky over toward Tredegar ironworks. The train waited at the platform. It stubbed off short—only a black locomotive and a wood car and two passenger cars and a stock car and one blue box-car at the end. Men loaded half a dozen horses into the stock car, and they clattered up the ramp with their ears back and yanking against their lead lines.

The train appeared to be waiting on something or somebody, either the treasure, if it wasn't already gone, or the officials of the government, or both. Pressure built up in the boiler and then periodically whooshed away in clouds of steam that broke white against all the hell colors lighting that particular instant in history.

Ryland said, I believe if I was hiding treasure, I'd put it in the stock car. Let robbers fight the horses to find it.

Bristol said, I'd put it at the bottom of the wood car.

About then, carriages pulled up. Four or five of them. All in a hurry, the president climbed out, looking sick and skinny, his face the color of ham fat. He went without a hat, and for a man his age, his hair flowed admirably back from his temples. He visored his bad eye with a hand and looked around at the fires and the torches. He lifted his nose and whiffed smoke in the air. He looked tragic and also like he might toss off an impromptu speech about sacrifice and the holy Constitutions—ours and theirs—both documents identical except for a paragraph or two having to do with slaves. Secretary of State Judah Benjamin, balding, plump, and almost jolly, followed him with a fat stub of cigar between his teeth. A few elder cabinet members hustled from carriage to car, looking stunned as fish just pulled out of water into sunshine and air. Davis looked at the mob and at the cadets in what appeared to be confusion.

Jeers broke out. Hecklers sang improvised songs with repetitious thumping rhythms suitable for drunks. Such as the tune to "Battle Hymn of the Republic," but chanting about how they'll hang Jeff Davis from a sour apple tree instead of the business about John Brown's mouldering body. Hard to say which version claimed worse lyrics.

The world fell apart. Fire blazed everywhere and

walls tumbled down. And yet, to a degree, the night felt a lot like a party. Ryland reached Bristol a full bottle of Cuban rum he had confiscated along the way, and they traded swigs.

Davis hurriedly climbed the stairs to the passenger car, and Bristol noticed as he lifted his foot to the first step what a pretty pair of low boots he wore.

A remnant delegation of slaves—three men and a woman lugging a baby on her hip—shifted bags from the carriage to the passenger car and then went to the boxcar and threw their own carpetbags inside and climbed in behind them.

Benjamin followed Davis onto the passenger car. He looked delighted by the chanting, yelling crowd—amused, as if he might break into applause at the unexpected entertainment. He doffed his hat, and then hustled up the steps.

After the big men disappeared through a door, the mob gathered strength and yelled death threats at Davis and called Benjamin every epithet for Jew in the English language, at least all such words known in the South. Moment by moment they built nerve to loot the train with support from gutter whiskey and the hortatory skills of angry drunks.

Lights in the passenger car stayed unlit, windows black. The train stood still. Some problem to do with the locomotive kept it from rolling away into the night. Steam built and released and rebuilt, and the train stayed still.

The cadets were a gang of boys unused to liquor in quantities greater than a raw taste of cheap rum on the tongue, all of them splinter-thin from a forced regimen of only two meals a day, mostly shreds of off-smelling salt pork and hardtack wetted with false coffee. Sailor food, the officers called it. The boys just called it shit. On the rare occasion they ate vegetables, their insides rebelled and they suffered the runs for days, their bowels working in the manner of a strong woman wringing water out of a dishrag. But, on the other hand, they were left calling their own orders. So they hung together arrogant on the rail platform, claiming a space between the mob and the train. They carried their newfound rifles and shotguns slung over their shoulders on straps, revolvers holstered on their slim hips or just shoved down their belts. They were not in a patient mood for outside opinions on how this next few minutes ought to play.

The mob roiled within itself until it found leaders.

A man in a plaid suit separated from the huddles and walked three steps their way.

—You better move along, he said.

A man in a greasy canvas coat stepped up beside

him and flippered out both handbacks loose-wristed, like shooing cattle. He said, Get on, young'uns.

The crowd focused and quit milling and aimed all in one direction, at the boys.

The cadets had not considered themselves guardians of the Confederate Treasure Train or of the old men who had led them to this point of collapse. They looked at each other in confusion.

Ryland, real flat and slow and disgusted, said, Well, shit fire.

The man in the plaid suit said, I mean it. Stand aside.

Somebody else shouted, Don't let Jeff Davis and his gang ruin us all and then get off with the money too. The Federals will be on us by dawn, and they'll steal everything not screwed to the floor.

Shouts went all through the crowd.

—Get what we can get.

—Get it while we can get it.

—Get it now.

Pushed from behind, the front line of the mob staggered forward a few feet toward the boys.

At that, Ryland and several other cadets unslung rifles and shotguns, and some filled their hands with pistols.

Ryland—rum bold—said, You bunch aim to try us? Really? Y'all?

He said it like there were certainly people who could try them and succeed, but not this particular bunch under any range of imagination.

The men paused.

—Oh hell yeah, Ryland said. Try us. Come on. Get some.

He didn't shout to the crowd but spoke only to that first row of mobsters. He said, Y'all old men just step up, front and center. See who gets cut down first.

He tipped his head toward Bristol and said, This one here? Best shot among us. Still a kid, but he sure hell can shoot. Not just the fastest, but the best. Bang, bang. Sound like one shot. And you'll have one neat hole in the middle of your forehead and two bullets blowing mess out the back.

That was a gross exaggeration. Bristol was better than average shooting paper targets with a rifle, but was no pistoleer and had not ever fired at a human being. But he played along. Bristol held his arms crossed in front so that his right forearm rested across his left forearm. His right hand holding the Colt's navy pistol drooped all relaxed and calm. He squint-eyed watched the mob for the first sign of bad intention.

A woman in the crowd hollered, You'ns sorry drunks gonna let those children face you down? Whoop 'em and run 'em back home to their mommas.

The mob surged again. Voices cursed God and Jefferson Davis equally for the pain they had rained down on the South.

Ryland raised his pistol and fired a single ceremonial shot into the air like the start of a horse race.

Five or six men on the front row of the mob broke to run, among them the man who had flipped his hands. He and two others stepped on each other's feet and then a half dozen fell in a pile, scrambling against each other like a trapful of blue crabs. Some of the cadets laughed, and then some of the mob laughed.

Loud enough for everyone to hear, Ryland said, Hey, do all us idiots need to be killing one another? We all bet on the same broke-down racehorse.

The steam engine came alive with a grind of metal. Long iron rods and pins and joints worked against the drive wheels until the whole train jolted forward a few inches. And then, shiny steel wheels spun two squealing turns against the rails until friction bound them together. The train began moving at a crawl and then accelerating.

Secretary Benjamin opened a window in the passenger car and stuck his head out. He yelled, You boys jump on. Be quick.

Quick was what Ryland and Bristol did best. They dashed toward the blue boxcar and tossed the long weapons before them into the open door and tumbled in laughing and whooping like they'd robbed a bank and gotten away with all the gold. Then they realized it was only the two of them. The other boys straggled slow and lost behind.

Bristol and Ryland let their eyes adjust. The slaves sat in a corner lit by the yellow glow of two candle lanterns. The woman held her baby close and her man reached his arm over her shoulders, and they looked only at the baby. The other two men looked only at Bristol and Ryland.

The train reached the pace of a strong canter, and then settled in for the ride south. One of the men looked less than thirty, very dark, wearing a gray suit and white shirt and with hands less beat from work than Ryland's and Bristol's—so housework. The other man was a little older. He had a large, round head and had gone bald halfway back. His skin was sort of russet color, and three pale, horizontal scars marked his forehead like old razor cuts. He kept rubbing and squeezing his temples with the thumb and middle finger of his left hand like he had a throbbing headache. The whites of his eyes had gone yellow. He was a big, strong man but looked like half the strength had been worn out of him.

Ry made a one-finger eyebrow salute toward the corner and said, Evening, folks. What's you'ns names?

The family paid no attention. The scarred man said, Cleon. The man in the suit just kept looking at the boys.

Ryland took a chug from his bottle and passed it to Bristol. After Bristol sipped, he reached the bottle toward the two men, but they declined with sliding level motions of both downturned hands.

Ry took the bottle back and swigged.

—Ah, he said. We're gonna need us a bunch more of this. They say all the smart people are heading to Havana, and I can see why. Swing in hammocks under palm trees, smoke cigars, and drink rum all day long.

—Cuba, Cleon said. Land of Paradise. Rum and cigars make their own selves down there.

—Not the night for scoffing, Ryland said. This is the time for hope. Everything's changed. We're all cut loose. Possibilities whichever way we look.

The two men looked at each other and then they looked out the wide door. The city stretched across its hill and along the river like burning red hell itself.

—Yeah, Cleon said. Keep talking. You know everything.

—I know I never owned anybody but my own self, Ryland said. And half the time, all I can do is half-ass manage me, much less make a bunch of other people do my bidding.

The couple with the baby were putting together sandwiches of pork belly and day-old corn bread.

—Wouldn't care to share that pone, would you? Ryland said. Belly too? A bite?

The man in the suit said, We've got little food.

—Break off a burnt edge, Ryland said. I won't complain. Remember, we offered to share our liquor with you.

Cleon looked at Bristol and then looked back at Ry. He said, If we're all cut loose and free to do as we please, then we might sell you some food.

Ryland and Bristol both laughed. Bristol said, We've not been paid in six months.

—White people all rich, Cleon said. But they sure go around poor-mouthing.

Ryland said, We're not rich. For a whole year, we been fed worse than a general's bird dog.

—Beefsteak and loaves of white bread, then? Cleon said. Great wedges of chocolate cake.

The man in the suit said, Pork tenderloin roasted over a wood fire and potatoes buttered yellow and then the whole plate covered with brown gravy.

Both men laughed.

—Not hardly, Bristol said.

—So no money at all? Cleon said.

Bristol said, I've got five dollars.

—Eight and pocket change, Ryland said.

—What I said, Cleon muttered. Rich.

—But which money? the other man said.

—Dixie paper, Ryland said.

—Hell, Cleon said. You boys nothing but truly broke. But I'd trade you some food for one of those pistols you've got stuck down your belts.

Ryland said, You've probably not had experience with firearms. They get you in trouble quicker than they get you out.

—Hey, Cleon said. Everybody else has got 'em. We want one too.

The other man said, Besides, they're simple. I used to care for the guns when the big man went hunting. Load, aim, pull the trigger. Unless you're drunk, and then you just pull the trigger. That's the way he did it.

—What's the worst pistol we've got? Ryland asked Bristol.

Bristol pulled a pepperbox with a broken grip out of his coat pocket. Ryland reached it to the men and they handled it and tested out the mechanism that turned the five barrels and then reached back corn bread sandwiches.

After they all finished eating, the man in the suit said, You boys expect this is truly the end?

—End of what? Ryland said.

—End of the war for you. For us, the Federals coming and setting us free.

—True fact, Bristol said. Sunrise tomorrow, new world coming for everybody. Day one.

—Y'all ever study the Testaments? the man said.

Ryland said, Naw. My momma and daddy was normally feeling so raw from Saturday-night drinking they couldn't bother with Sunday morning.

The man lifted his hand toward the open door and said, That city on fire, there's a story in the book of Daniel. About the night Babylon fell.

Bristol said, Please don't say you're a preacher?

The man said, No.

Ryland said, Proceed, Reverend.

—Well, the preacher said, what I was about to tell was about a big wild party in Babylon. A thousand of King Belshazzar's men and whores eating his food and drinking his liquor, all of it made by his slaves. Pretty barefoot slave girls walking around serving drinks and fancy food off of big silver trays. Round about midnight—when everybody reached the point of drunk where you drink a bunch more or else there's nowhere left to go but down—right in front of all these witnesses, a ghost hand appears in the air, clear as day. It's holding a piece of charcoal. A giant hand, charcoal the size of a singletree. It scribes strange words on that plaster wall where Belshazzar stood. Letter after letter lit by candle flames or maybe pine torches. Letters jagged and crossways as a bundle of spilled kindling. Everybody gets quiet and spooked, and they watch close. When the hand gets done with what it has to say, it turns into smoke. Poof, gone. King's men, they're all full drunk and his whores too. But they're all scared, and they start sobering up a little. They try to study the words, but nobody can read the writing on the wall. About then, Belshazzar's main wife shows up. She comes in cool-tempered, not a bit mad at all the drunks. She gives the wall a quick look and says she knows a man, the best of all the magicians and palm-readers and dream-readers. Mojo man named Daniel. Knows the invisible world like the back of his hand. If he can't read the writing, nobody can. Belshazzar sends out orders to get Daniel, and pretty soon big police haul him in. The king promises scarlet robes and gold chains and a job as foreman of all the king's lands and slaves if he can read the writing. Daniel says, No. Not interested in the king's fancy clothes and fancy job. But says he can read the writing clear as day. Words from a tongue ten thousand years old. Words for gold and silver, brass and iron. The names of the gods that the king and his men and whores praise above all. Things you can weigh on a scale or measure by a ruler or add and divide and count out piece by piece in order to sell. Daniel says that right that minute, the one instant they're all living in, it's the king getting weighed and measured and counted. And Belshazzar comes up short. He's been using the wrong scales, the wrong ruler, wrong numbers. Daniel says to Belshazzar, You're going to die before the night's done, your kingdom burned down and a new kingdom growing up to take its place.

The preacher paused to draw breath, and Ryland said, I never heard this one before. Does it just go on and on?

—Nope. What Daniel said happened. That night Babylon burned down, kingdom done and gone. Daybreak, Belshazzar woke up dead in hell.

Ryland said, Can you read the Bible for yourself?

The preacher paused and then said, Yes.

—Who taught you?

The two men glanced at each other. The preacher said, I'm not saying.

—Law, Cleon said.

Bristol said, Probably that law's not gonna apply after the sun comes up. A lot of others too.

They all sat quiet. Out the door, the burning city behind them had become nothing but a pretty amber glow in the sky. The train rolled toward Petersburg, and the night swept by in blurred gray shapes of houses and barns and cornfields and cow pastures. All they saw of Petersburg was the wrecked landscape of a lost war. The government train didn't stop at the station, just tooted the whistle. But crowds stood around in the lamplight of the platform watching it roll past, hope bleached out of their faces. Soon after that, nothing but black pinewoods on either side of the tracks.

Ten or fifteen miles south, the train slowed for a curve, taking it at a little above a trot. The preacher looked at Cleon and nodded. They didn't say a word to each other, but both stood and picked up their carpet-bags and underhanded them out the door. Then—like jumping down a well or taking a leap of faith—they ran three strides and disappeared into a future that looked nothing but dark and red at the moment.

Fourth Sunday

Saratoga Springs

After breakfast V sits by the window reading a new novel, *The House of Mirth*. She prefers books set in New York or Europe—anywhere except the South—because they don't bring unwelcome memories.

Laura wanders in, turns back the covers, and climbs into V's bed and immediately falls asleep.

When she wakes she asks, What time?

—Ten.

—Wake me at eleven? I need an ally. My mother's coming for lunch.

—Are you asking me to join you?

—Please, Laura says.

She turns her face to the wall and sleeps again.

V wakes her and says, Dear Girl, if we're going to meet your mother, you need to dress.

Laura swings her legs over the edge of the bed and looks at the floor.

—She'll be horrible. I've changed my mind. I don't want you to see it. She can be nice for half an hour, and then it's always horrible.

—Oh, I doubt she'll be too bad, and if she is, I've seen enough that I'm inoculated. If I can be a comfort to you, I'll come along.

—Really? You'd do that?

—I stood in the real White House arguing toe-to-toe with one of the more corrupt presidents of the United States, at least up to that point in time. So let's go back to your room and pick out a pretty dress.

They choose a summer frock, sky blue with tiny yellow flowers. V wipes Laura's face with a wet washcloth and powders her cheeks lightly and pats her hair into slight order, the way it looks best. As they walk to the lobby, Laura clutches V's hand.

Laura says, Please don't be frightened.

—That much I can promise, V says.

—My brother will be there too. He steals money from my inheritance and thinks I'm too dumb to know.

I come from a lineage of crooks dating back to the *May-flower*. I'm supposed to be proud, but I just imagine a very long card game down in the lower decks. Sharks all eating each other for months at a time.

—Long passage back then. Imagine all the different purses their coins fared through. The sleights of hand, dealing from the bottom.

—Exactly. But they were all so religious.

—Except about money.

—Mother claims they came for freedom, Laura says.

—Freedom to do exactly what they wanted without anybody getting in their way.

—I've had relatives so crooked they nearly went to prison, but if you have money you never actually go. They make you think it for a while, and that's your punishment.

—My husband was in prison for two years. They tried to make us think they were going to hang him, but they didn't.

In the lobby, V stops and asks Laura, When my friend arrives I'd like for him to join us.

Laura says, The bigger the group the better she behaves. And I'll make sure she gets the check.

V walks to the desk and writes a quick note and seals it in an envelope.

———————

Laura's mother looks late forties. She dresses expensively, and her eyes rest in her head hooded as a snapping turtle's. She rises from her seat at the table and kisses Laura on the cheek and then holds her by the shoulders and studies her at arm's length for an uncomfortably long time. Laura squirms.

When her mother finally lets her go, she says, Well, at least that's a pretty dress. Usually you look like a Gypsy in an opera. But your hair is still a mess. And you should get that boil looked at. We're paying the hotel enough that they can surely get the house doctor to treat an infection gratis.

The mother's every word leaves her mouth as a blaring pronouncement. The boil is a faint blemish below Laura's right cheekbone, slighter than an adolescent pimple.

The brother stands and shakes V's hand and says, Blount Scott. Head of our company's accounting.

Unlike Laura her brother is dark-haired, and it hangs lank and greasy. He talks in a sort of huffy barking voice rising from a chest constricted by phlegm and resentment.

After they sit, Laura scoots her chair closer to V, leans in, and—not quite whispering—says, A warning, we're all liars at heart.

Her mother says, Imagine living twenty years with someone who thinks that's ever an appropriate comment.

—My older sister isn't here, Laura says. We've never gotten along. She's angry all the time and holds it against me that I'm prettier.

Mrs. Scott says, You've never understood that when your sister was a girl, the Negro servants were so mean to her.

—Really? V says. Mean?

—Awful. It damaged her forever.

—Physical attacks?

—Verbal.

—This was when? V asks. During the great Negro revolt of 1885?

Laura stifles a laugh and then coughs.

—It's not funny, Mrs. Scott says. Laura's sister is very sensitive, and they were so sarcastic toward her.

—I see, V says. People can be so cruel.

Lunch arrives. Mrs. Scott talks while she eats, and the cavity of her mouth as she works her food makes sounds like a rubber plunger opening a sink drain. Chicken salad and lettuce at various stages of liquidation make repeat appearances between lips and teeth. She holds her fork as if her finger joints hardly articulate, a limp reluctance, as if other people's hands usually do that job for her. She talks without letup, complaining of Laura's expenses. The brother breaks in and goes over the figures exact to the dollar, to the extent that V worries she'll dream of nothing during the night but murmuring voices rising out of a dark fog saying numbers over and over. One thousand, five thousand, ten thousand, hundreds of thousands. Mumbles of millions rolling over and over like a rising tide until dawn.

Mrs. Scott obliquely suggests that Laura has derailed her life by developing inconveniently strong attractions to men she hardly knows.

—I suppose I should have been a harsher disciplinarian, Mrs. Scott says.

—You housebroke me by tying me to the potty and whipping me, Laura says.

—She's so dramatic, Blount says. I was seven or eight and remember how it was. Mother only striped her legs with a willow switch when she was willful. And if she'd just complied, Mother wouldn't have tied her.

The longer she stays among them, the more V believes Laura's family would gladly commission a hole to be drilled through her forehead and a long red-hot needle plunged into her brain if it would put her under their control.

—Are you taking care to see that she doesn't run off with some boy? Mrs. Scott asks V.

—Laura's a woman, so I'd advise her against a boy. I'd been married nearly three years at her age. Anyway, I'm her friend, not her caretaker. And I'm certainly not applying for the position of mother.

Mrs. Scott plows ahead and says, I worry about this little play you all are putting on. She'll fall in love with Hamlet if he's younger than sixty.

—He is, and maybe she will, V says. But I can guarantee he won't fall in love with her. His interests lie elsewhere.

—Another girl?

—He's a confirmed bachelor. Very resolute.

Mrs. Scott shakes her head all weary, like the world has gone too far wrong to comment.

Laura endures the conversation by pretending to occupy a whole other scene. She picks through her salad and eats the pecan halves and raisins and crescent moons of celery, leaving behind a plate of lettuce and tomatoes and croutons.

—At any rate, I plan to attend the rehearsal this afternoon, Mrs. Scott declares.

—Little to see today, V says. Only the boring parts—figuring out who stands where. And besides, the rehearsal isn't until late afternoon, almost dinner.

—I'll just say this, and you need to know it, Mrs. Scott says, leaning forward toward V. Laura never took blame for anything. That is the source of her difficulty. Failure of personal responsibility.

After delivering her mighty revelation, Mrs. Scott sits back justified and sanctified, stuffed sausage-tight inside her charcoal dress.

Laura says, Family trait.

The dishes have already been taken away and they're drinking coffee when James arrives. He carries the blue book under his arm and V's note in his hand like a traveler at a border crossing holding a passport ready to present.

—Oh, James, V says. I'd like to introduce my friend here at the hotel, Laura. And her mother, Mrs. Scott, and her brother, Mr. Scott.

To the table she says, This is Mr. Blake. We've recently reunited. Long ago he was a son to me.

James says all the correct formulas of words.

Laura says, So, the mysterious Mr. Blake I've heard V talk about so much.

She holds out her hand for a touch of greeting.

Mrs. Scott looks at James and then at V. She stays quiet. Blount doesn't stand to shake hands.

V looks at James with a slight eye roll, and says, Mrs. Scott and young Blount are shy folks and sometimes find themselves at a loss for words in polite society. But I'm sure they're pleased to meet you too.

Laura laughs aloud.

James looks a question at V and she nods toward the empty chair. He takes his seat and says to Laura, You were playing the piano a couple of Sundays ago. "Sunflower Slow Drag."

—I can't play Joplin fast enough.

—The title of the song has the word *slow* in it, but people always play it too fast, showing off. Your version was beautiful.

Mrs. Scott lifts her hand a couple of inches off the table and levels her forefinger at V. She whispers, You keep them away from each other. I mean it. One time, she ran off for a week with a middle-aged saxophone player.

V looks directly at the finger—not a trace of smile on her face—until Mrs. Scott withdraws it.

On the terrace, V and James regard the long blue and green view stretching hazy to the west. Between them on a low table, a silver tea tray, and a smaller tray with a dozen tiny triangular sandwiches, and the blue book.

—Was that awkward? James says.

—Not for me it wasn't. I like Laura very much, and

care about her well-being. I tried to distract her family, a feint at the flank to entice them to aim their artillery my direction, since I'm well fortified.

—And toward me too? James asks.

—A little. And only because I knew you could stand it because you're fortified too—even when you were tiny you were. Laura isn't at all, and her mother and brother are predators and will eat her alive if they can.

V drifts into talking about generations. How grand-parents and grandchildren so often get along very well. Remove one generation—twenty-five years at least—and the anger in both directions dissipates. All the failed expectations and betrayals become cleansed by an intervention of time. Resentment and bitter need for retribution fall away. Love becomes the operative emotion. On the old side, you're left with wrinkled age and whatever fractured, end-of-the-line knowl-edge might have accrued. Wisdom as exhaustion. And on the other side—which V still remembers with mo-lecular vividness—youth and yearning and urgency for something not yet fully defined. Undiluted hope and desire. But by fusing the best of both sides, a kind of intertwining consciousness arises—grandmother and granddaughter wisdom emerging from shared hope, relieved of emotions tainted by control and guilt and anger.

—I'll assume you're right, James says. But I wouldn't know much about long family relationships. When I was fifteen, I probably imagined they were all either perfectly happy or ended in gunfire.

V laughs and then sips tea. James takes two tiny sandwiches for his lunch. It is a warm day, and V pushes her three-quarter sleeves to the elbows and fans herself with one hand. She suggests James feel free to remove his jacket, but he declines.

James asks, What are you most afraid to lose?

—Now?

—Yes.

—Nothing, of course, V says.

James recasts his question.

He asks, What do you want to maintain?

—Memory, even if it's sometimes false.

—Well then, what I'm curious about right now is Washington.

=

In 1849 after the peace treaty between Brierfield and The Hurricane was signed, V finally returned to Washington. She was still in her early twenties and wife of a war hero, a senator, soon to be a U.S. secretary of war. Little did V know that for the next thirty years she would never live anyplace for more than a year or so at a time. A Gypsy fortune-teller with her caravan—red and yellow and blue—knew more definition of home than V would. Over those years she bought and sold several households of furniture. Some man in a brown suit, shiny at the elbows and knees—maybe a touch of lunch on his shirtfront—arrives. He goes room to room looking over your carefully chosen things like they're trash, makes an insulting offer, which you accept. Then you move on, leaving behind a ribbon of acquisitions like bright-colored snakeskin shed to turn pale as a fingernail and dissolve in the weather. You carry forward into the next future only a few trunks of clothes and extra-special books and paintings—a Gypsy caravan load at most.

That second time in Washington differed extremely from the first. They lived in a mansion a few blocks from the White House. It was beautiful, but she missed the vibrating energy of Brown's Hotel, which had been like living in a dormitory or attending a house party that stretched on for months.

However, the upper reaches of government existed on a grander scale than mere congressmen. At that time a memorable dinner party among senators and cabinet members and their wives sometimes involved slaves hunkering above the ceiling to drop fresh pink rose petals as if by magic through grates onto the diners to announce the first course—which she found showy and a bit crude. Those days, some people called her Queen Varina for her dinners—even without petals—and maybe sometimes for her manner. Dumbards usually selected out after one invitation, overwhelmed by the knowledge and wit around her table.

Uncle Jeff sat at the head, striking and graceful and stately behind his famous cheekbones and raptor-beak nose, looking out from ash-colored eyes that gave nothing away. Candle flame always flattered him, but even in broad daylight people walking down the street turned to stare at his handsomeness. Because of his health—recent battle wounds and lingering malaria—Jeff remained slim, even during the years when men thicken in the middle and their bellies declare themselves. He was especially slim if he had recently passed through one of his long sick twilights when malaria shivered him to the marrow or when his eyesight burned and ripped with pain at every beam of sunlight. This before the left eye clouded and he only allowed photographs in profile. Even healthy, his body coiled tight, gripped against itself, squeezing and quivering with a force some saw as nothing but raw, red anger and ambition. Most mornings, on his way out the door, V reminded him that every moment didn't need to be lived on a battlefield.

Mostly during V's famous dinners Jeff was not at all funny. He sat absorbing the wit of others for long stretches of conversation, and then he issued some piercing comment, dry and oblique, benefiting from long, silent reflection—sometimes just a half-dozen words, perfectly chosen. And everyone would erupt in laughter as he looked down at his place setting. Probably a lovely pattern of Wedgwood and Murano crystal that V would sell for pennies on the dollar when the next earthquake in their lives shook everything to the ground.

Those evenings were when they became close to Judah Benjamin, then a new senator from Louisiana who enjoyed boasting that he was the first Jew to honor that body. Judah was the only Confederate leader whose memoir V wanted to read, except he never got around to writing one—too busy after the war with success in London, eventually becoming a Queen's Counsel. In New Orleans, Judah had married a beautiful, wealthy French Creole girl named Natalie, and they very quickly—uncomfortably so—had a daughter. And then

Natalie took the little girl and moved to Paris. After he was elected to the Senate, Judah spent a fortune buying and furnishing a grand house in Washington, hoping to lure her back. She stayed a couple of months in that raw, young city and then fled back to France. Theirs became a marriage by post. V remembers Judah getting a big laugh at one of her dinners by sharing a note he had just received from Natalie. He held up the paper, her big looping hand. It read, *Speak not to me of economy. It is so fatiguing.*

V's mother—back during the conflict over the will—had said bluntly that V's marriage would be happier if she succeeded in becoming pregnant. Not the first mother to hold that opinion. But V and Jeff might also have been happier if they'd arranged something like Judah and Natalie, where they mostly corresponded and Judah visited her in Paris for a month every summer and then went away before they became tired of each other. It was a marriage that lasted decades upon decades. But V didn't move to Paris. By her middle twenties—after the treaty between Brierfield and The Hurricane—she began having babies, and that went on for more than ten years. She stopped calling her husband Uncle Jeff and started calling him Banny, a Celtic term of endearment. Husband.

=

A bellboy arrives and hands V the fat book she had asked him to bring down from the desk in her room.

She opens it and reaches out to James. A passage is marked in pencil.

Read this, she says. You're always shoving your Miss Botume at me.

He takes the book and turns it over to look at the spine. It's a volume of her own from twenty years ago—her completion of Jeff's memoir.

James begins reading to himself, but she stops him and says, Aloud, please. It's about famous people I knew back when I was young. Presidents and so on. Those times in Washington we're talking about.

James says, *When these august shades rise before me whose active lives had been lived before I grew to womanhood, the responsible, serious youth that fell to my lot is not a subject of regret. The history of their day has to me a very stirring interest, and as I read the chronicles of their deeds, they stand clothed in their well-remembered personality, struggling with united minds for the whole country, holding the interests and possessions of all equally sacred, and pledged to protect these with their lives.*

After a long pause he says, Lovely thoughts.

—No, V says. Words worth less than a pail of horse biscuits, which could at least fertilize a tomato plant.

—I went to New York City last week to visit Julie's family, and I spent two afternoons in libraries reading about you in histories and memoirs and newspapers.

—Interesting?

—Yes, it was.

—But why did you do it—go checking up on me?

—Not my intention. I want to understand as much as I can about what you're telling me. And I came away with a question. In some of the things I read—a couple—I was described as your pet.

—Who did?

—We don't have to get into personalities. I'm asking if there is any truth to that view.

—If you're leveling charges and concealing your witnesses, I refuse to defend myself.

They remain quiet for half a minute, and then V says, There were plenty in Richmond who needed to make up stories to explain why at the Gray House you lived upstairs in the nursery with my children rather than downstairs. They gossiped about my race from the day I arrived. My skin, my dark eyes and hair, the shape of my mouth and nose—every tiny bit of me used as evidence as to whether I was mulatto or squaw. Their words. And then after I found you, people came up with all sorts of conspiracies about your origin. Some said you were my son with Jeff, but that my percentage of black blood came out strong in you, and we sent you away at birth. But then I couldn't forget you and forced Jeff to bring you back and worked up a crazy story of finding you on the street to explain it. Others said you were Jeff's son with a slave mother from Brierfield. One of those many illegitimate children he was supposed to have. Indian babies up in the northern wilderness, black babies on Mississippi plantations. Both sides claimed your arrogant nose looked like his—more evidence for their conspiracies.

James reaches up and touches thumb and forefinger to the wings of his nose and then taps the tip three times.

—Arrogant? he says.

—I always thought of it as confident.

—Some of the things I read said I was Negro. Others needed to break it down into smaller fractions— mulatto, quadroon, octoroon. Those words don't matter to me. The word I can't get past is *pet*.

V—immediate and vehement—says, I cannot believe I'm sitting here having to listen to this. Having to explain. You're a teacher. What's a teacher's pet?

A favorite. Usually because they're alert and present, smart and teachable, the ones who repay your effort five times over.

—A favorite little animal. It means that too.

—I won't be responsible for your witnesses needing to apply skin color to every personal interaction. Strange to let that outer hundredth fraction of our bodies be so important. I'm guessing your Miss Botume was one of the people calling you my pet. Which way do you think those people meant the word?

—I'll repeat something you said two weeks ago— you don't need me to answer that question.

After a pause to regroup and redirect, James says, Hold out your arm, please.

V reaches it toward him.

James pulls back his sleeve and parallels his forearm to hers.

—See, V says, the difference is hardly more than which of us has been in the sun lately. Plus, I've faded with age.

—The difference is you're white and I'm not. I don't know what I am, and I'm never comfortable anywhere. I can't remember a time when people—white and black—weren't telling me how well I talk to white people. Both directions, they offer it as a compliment. But mostly it makes me feel separate.

—If you had been scooped off the streets of Richmond and taken straight to Paris at age four, you'd be good at talking to French people.

—That's nowhere near an accurate analogy.

—No, it's not.

Hog Fortress

1865

Down in the wasteland, crossing Sherman's wake, the world had shut down. Loose coon dogs and bear dogs, half wild already, had started forming packs as soon as their owners scattered, leaving them to discover their own manners without interference from human opinions. V saw them hanging at the edges of dark pinewoods as her gang of fugitives rolled slowly down the roads south—bunches of dogs, yellow and brown and mottled, with their ribs showing and almost countable even from a distance, pink tongues hanging from desperate grins. Only a little more time—three seasons, V speculated—until all sense of man's dominion over them would fade and they'd start taking down stray children and elder folks. Two or three dog generations after that, they'd go wholly wolf. Civilization balances always on a keen and precarious point, a showman spinning a fine Spode dinner plate on a long dowel slender as a stem of hay. A puff of breath, a moment's lost attention, and it's all gone, crashed to ruination, shards in the dirt. Then mankind retreats to the caves, leaving little behind but obelisks weathering to nubs like broken teeth, dissolving to beach sand.

It happened right after harvesttime—Sherman's raiders burned their way across Georgia. Corncribs full, fodder and forage stacked high in conical piles around eight-foot poles, apples all picked and stored fresh in root cellars for the fall or sun-dried in leathery rings for the winter. Onions and potatoes and turnips in root cellars, beans dried in the sun and ready for winter soup, cabbages still green in the fields almost ready for cutting. Fat hogs that you didn't want to have to feed for the cold months ready to slaughter and feast on fresh or salt and smoke for later. A winter's food wiped out and people left starving.

—Where did they all go? V asked as they passed a tiny ghost village surrounded by farms—only one house with light in the window, smoke coming from the chimney.

Delrey said, Somewhere else. Wandering refugee. Or off in the woods eating squirrels and grabbling trash fish out of creeks.

At a river ford, a blond child sat alone on the far bank and shouted directions to them as they began crossing. Gee and haw. She claimed there were holes in the river widely known to be bottomless and able to pull down entire wagons and their teams.

When they reached dry land, V reached her out a few coins, but the girl looked at them and said, Ain't nothing to buy around here. But if you've got clean water, I'll pester you for a swallow of it. That river's nasty. It's got dead people in it, just laying there spoiling.

She tipped her head upstream.

Midday, V wandered into the pinewoods for what all in their caravan delicately agreed to call a natural break. Men and women both scattered into the trees on opposite sides of the road, though the men only had to step casually behind a largish trunk a few feet from the roadbed and reappear a few seconds later looking at ease. V and Ellen trekked far beyond sight and had voluminous garments to deal with—awkward squatting and arising and so on.

Off in the woods in her moment of privacy, V thought about Winchester. He mostly taught mathematics by way of Euclid and Pythagoras. Winchester especially loved Pythagoras and his genius in understanding the ratios that order the universe, his declaration that number was God, and also his craziness otherwise, such as his rule that one should always answer the call of nature with back to sun, which was how V had aligned herself.

Walking back to the caravan, watching out for snakes, V plucked new growth from the center of a grassy plant, slid the innermost stalk of it free with a squeaky friction, a feel of suction. She put the white tip and the first pale green of the blade into her mouth like a farmer sucking on a wheat sprout. Her weed was an ugly nameless thing, except she believes that nothing is nameless. The weed's bitter green beautiful taste carried with it an essential question. Will this thing help or hurt? Be medicine or poison? Thusly, the earliest herb doctors sounded out the world in endless experiment. How many thousands of generations cascaded down through time just to find the healing power in goldenseal or ginseng or coneflower root? But surely only three or four to note the poison in pokeberries or green parasols or false morels. The urge to graze in spring abides, the need for something green after a winter of dried beans and potato. Country people called spring greens a tonic. Medicine.

Back at the caravan V said to Burton, We need a huge pot of greens, any kind you can find.

—Yes?

—And meat to flavor the pot. We all need it. We're starting to look pasty as corpses from traveling and living too much on white food. Biscuits and grits and flour gravy.

She multiplied people, counting children as half a person, figuring at least a quart per person for a good strong dose of greens and meat broth.

She said, We'll need about three bushels of greens. A couple of chickens or a pound of bacon or ham will do for the broth.

Three hours later, Delrey and Bristol and Ryland came back from foraging with comically big tow sacks paired behind their saddles. The bags bulged with various cresses and mustards and a great deal of dandelion and dock and plantain, even a few beautiful fiddleheads and wild leeks. But no meat, not even a skinny squirrel.

—I found a place with aplenty of hogs, Delrey said. This man's shaped his farm like a fort. Long pine logs axed to a point on either end and piled onto each other in a jagged circle with the hogs and the smokehouse and a pretty, white farmhouse in the middle of it. Like he's trying to live inside a brier-patch. He's got a pack of big dogs. The dogs and the hogs are all brown and black and some of them wear their colors in spots and some go striped, and all of them are so long-legged you have to get up close to tell the difference. I tried to buy some hog meat off him, but he wasn't selling. The man said he and his one boy and four daughters and wife have an arsenal of weapons and ammunition they've taken off of Sherman's raiders. Two Henry repeating rifles for the man and his son, and a bunch of Colt's pistols and shotguns for the women. Said they took the rifles off the first band of raiders and then used them afterward to pour down fire on every bunch that came to steal their food and burn them out. The boy looks about fifteen and very chilly. The man said the boy is God-almighty fast and can empty the Henry's magazine in twenty seconds and can hit anything he can see without really aiming. That's near a shot a second. Said all seven members of the family share one mind. They stand ready to fight anybody—North or South—coming to take what's theirs until one side or the other meets their fate right there in the hog yard.

—Is he just blowing? V said.

—He means it, ma'am, Delrey said. And two good

marksmen firing from cover with Henry rifles can take down a right smart of men fast, so I don't fully doubt the story he told. I said to him that we had no intention of robbing him or burning him out. Said we were traveling with a lady and children and they were hungry. The farmer said he didn't believe ladies existed in the world anymore. Or God either. But he said if we could produce one or the other of them at his fortress and prove him wrong he'd give us an entire smoked ham and send us on our way with his blessing.

—A ham? V said.

—Yes, and you could smell the smokehouse from where we stood talking. Like cooking bacon in a greasy skillet over a campfire. But that man's about crazy, and I don't believe we need a ham bad enough to deal with him.

V looked around at the children, at Ellen and the thin navy boys still traveling along. How sickly they looked. She said, Delrey, I believe you lack confidence in our evidence.

—Ma'am?

—Proof that ladies have not gone extinct.

—No, ma'am, not at all. But I will say that Richmond's a long way back and we've all been living rough for a while now. Of course, this is Georgia, and who knows what standards they go by.

—Delrey, is there a state with standards you know and approve?

—Not any I've been to.

—I do take your point, about rough traveling, though. Give me twenty minutes to clean up and change clothes, and trowel on a great deal of powder, and then you and I will take the ambulance and go out to this fortress and give it a try. The navy boys should follow along with us. An entire smoked ham and those beautiful greens you found would be a feast for all of us. And plenty of ham biscuits later.

Mottled coon hounds bawled at their approach with such force that V worried they would rupture a lung. But the nearer she got the more they backed away from the horses and hung near the porch, ready to retreat into the dark underneath.

She pushed the palm of her hand toward them and said, Bad dogs.

The dogs walked angling away, looking at her side-eyed.

She said, Good dogs.

They came forward with their tails wagging.

V said to Delrey, Just introduce me and then after that let me do all the talking. Do not use my real name.

Delrey nodded.

V looked at the boys.

—What? Ryland said.

—Simple, V said. Don't say my name. I'll do the talking. Yes?

—We've got it, Bristol said.

Ryland said, But what name should we call you?

—Just keep your mouths shut, Delrey said.

The man and his son—a boy even younger than the navy boys but looking completely dead-eyed—came out the door with their Henry rifles cocked and angled down over their forearms, ready to lift and fire, but being polite about it. Beyond the doorframe and through the front windows, V saw women passing behind the two men, their much-washed homespun dresses ghostly in the brown light of the house, their drained faces and dark eyes glancing outward toward a larger world full of threat.

The man said, What's all this, then?

—Sir, Delrey said, I would like to introduce Mrs. Anthony Thomas. The lady I mentioned earlier. However I don't know your name to make a proper introduction.

The boy took his eyes off V and Delrey and twitched his attention toward his father for half a second and then right back at them.

The father said, My name is Mister Wiggins.

Delrey said, Mrs. Thomas, permit me to introduce Mister Wiggins.

—Ma'am, Wiggins said.

He wore no hat to lift and sort of dipped his head toward her an inch. A vestigial bow.

V said, Mister Wiggins, I believe you know of our circumstances, and I didn't want you to trouble yourself with our difficulties. We all have more than enough responsibility in taking care of our own families.

—Amen, the boy said.

The father let his rifle down and stood its butt against the porch boards. The boy, though, kept alert. There was a good deal of killer about him, and it was why he still lived. The last four years had made a whole generation of young boys—who ought to have been going to school and learning a trade and thrilling deep in their bones just to dance with a girl and peck her on the cheek—into slit-eyed killers with no more tell of emotion than an old riverboat faro gambler.

V climbed down from the ambulance bench and walked toward the porch.

She said, Could I possibly speak a word or two with the lady of the house?

—With who? Wiggins said.

—Your wife? A word, please?

—What purpose?

—Politeness? What but manners do we have left?

Wiggins looked at the boy, but the boy just kept flicking his attention between V and Delrey and Bristol and Ryland. He held his rifle balanced scalelike in his hands, measuring its weight to be ready to lift it fast and fire.

Wiggins said, A minute, please, Missus Thomas.

He went to the door and spoke something inside, and a slim woman walked out and down the steps.

She wore a cotton dress laundered almost thin as gauze. The fabric might have been a sort of milky chocolate at one time, patterned with leaves or flowers. Now it looked like parchment marked with script too faint to read. She carried a heavy black pistol, and she looked young to be mother to five. Pretty in an exhausted way. Much as V imagined herself to look, having birthed one more than Mrs. Wiggins, and really the dead ones batter you even more than the living, pull more out of you in their leaving than their arriving.

When they were close enough to speak softly, V said, Missus Wiggins, are you and your daughters all right?

Missus Wiggins lifted her left hand and wiped the prominent second knuckle of the forefinger three swipes against the wings of her nose and then swept her loose and mostly brown hair back from her forehead with the inside angle of her elbow.

—All right? she said. If we're not, where could we go to be right? And what would we live on when we got there? Just breathe air and be fine? I'm not standing here to be judged by you or anybody else.

—I only meant . . .

—God hates lies, and I'm not going to tell one to you. We're not any of us all right. We're all about half crazy since the raiders started passing through. Wiggins and I didn't carry slaves. Didn't believe in them, and didn't want them. Believed there would be a bloody reckoning for them, and we were right. We hoed our own rows, emptied our own night jars, cooked our own meals, taught our children to read, and when we could spare the money, we bought them books too hard for us to read. Our goal was simple. If every generation helps the next take one step up, imagine where we might all be someday. But those boys from the Northern army came after us anyway. Six or a dozen at a time in waves for weeks. Trying to take what they could carry and burn the rest. If we had a choice but to let them kill us or to put them down, I can't see it. Every one of us killed at least a person, and two of the girls can't lift the blame off themselves. They dream about it no matter how I tell them the load's on those boy soldiers for their own dying. And on the old men who sent them here. You turn the other cheek too many times in this world, and before you can blink you're wiped away. We didn't go out to steal everything they had and burn their farms to ashes. They came here, and they stayed here. I'm sorry they believed whatever they believed about us that made it right to come try to kill us. They're thirty-one of them. They don't have markers, but we all went out in the pines to put them in the ground and say sad words over them about their delusions.

The pistol hung from her hand, pulling her down, a burden heavier than she could bear. The other women, all in their teens, hovered behind the front door and the flanking windows, watching. V pictured dark woods, a crescent moon riding across a deep indigo sky, a dark night procession of pretty girls and tall dogs lit by yellow pine-knot torches, tangled bodies of bloody young men heaped in a wagon-bed.

V said, Could I come inside and meet your girls?

They were indeed pretty and strange and might have fallen from Venus for all they knew of the current outside world. They lined up to meet V, a receiving line. They were all the same size, and V imagined a common pile of worn and faded dresses from before the war— every morning each girl just drawing something from the pile without thought of possession or personal style. They had names along the lines of flowering plants and tragic heroines. Names like Daisy and Daphne and Laurel and Hecuba, though V couldn't keep any of them straight. The girls flurried around preparing an afternoon tea, carrying their pistols and then setting them down on every horizontal surface in a percussive four-beat rhythm.

The tea was herbal, a sinus-clearing mixture that made a nice greenish-yellow cup. One of the girls set out a platter of cold breakfast biscuits cut into triangles and drizzled with honey and sprinkled with some brown spice similar to cinnamon but more piney.

By way of transition, V pulled her pistol out of her reticule. It rested in her hand so small and inconsequential compared to their heavy Colt's army revolvers. V's lay there unthreatening, prettier than it needed to be for its function. And too, at least while in her possession, it had killed no one. Hard to reconcile these lovely girls with Missus Wiggins's statement that everyone in the family had killed at least one human being.

—This is a gift from my husband, V said. He meant me to kill myself with it if I found myself on the brink of being dishonored.

They all looked at the little thing, and then one of the girls said, Did he understand how a gun works? Somebody comes at you, you point it at them, not yourself.

—Well, V said, I always planned on using it your way, no matter what his intentions were.

They sipped tea a moment, and then V said, I understand this has been a hard time.

The girl who looked oldest—meaning maybe seventeen—said, They didn't come marching across Georgia as one big army all together. They fanned out sixty or a hundred miles wide in little bunches of raiders. Sometimes only a few men, but one time more than a dozen. And then thieves and scavengers followed them. First bunch—four of them—it was clear you let them do what they wanted and take what they wanted or they would burn you out and leave you wandering the roads. Say one thing they didn't like, they might go wild and slaughter everybody. But Billy reached real fast and yanked away one of their Henry rifles and started working it. Six seconds later we were all standing around in a cloud of gun smoke trying to catch our breaths, watching those soldiers finish dying.

—After that, there wasn't any luck to it, one of the younger girls said. We had a plan. Of course if there had ever been thirty of them at one time or if just one got away to tell what happened to the rest, we wouldn't be sitting here talking.

—They made us choose, the older girl said. Them or us.

The youngest girl, very pale, her hair loose below her shoulders, said, Yes, that's the choice we made. Us.

One of the girls poured more of the herb tea and V looked around the dim parlor. Heart pine floors and pine wainscoting and pine plank ceilings. Yet it displayed flairs of decor. Many wide dark picture frames surrounded small watercolors, each one composed of three horizontal bands of color grading up from beige to green to blue, representing the only landscape they knew. Bits of needlework, antimacassars and tabletop doilies in patterns like overlapped leaves or explosions of flower petals or diagrams of mental geometry representing the physics of existence way into the depths of the night sky. Three dozen precious well-read leather books stood on a shelf over the fireplace. Milton and Shakespeare, Dickens and Trollope and Scott, and translations of random Greeks and Romans. And one volume which, when V pulled it off the shelf, turned out to be actual Greek, a collection of lyric poets.

By way of trying to prove the nonextinction of ladies she translated a few lines on the fly. The girls crowded around. Very slowly, pointing word by word, V read, *The moon sets. Then the Pleiades. Midnight. Time goes away. I am alone.*

When she closed the book they all applauded, as if she had just performed an amazing magic trick in reverse, starting with a sawed-in-half lady and putting her back together. They all talked at once asking how she knew the code to reading that strange book of runes. Their voices rose like a bird chorus floating lovely in V's mind without every note needing to carry a specific definition. She told them about Winchester, how much he taught her for no reason but his devotion to learning and for no compensation but her eternal love.

It would have been easy to dismiss their efforts toward culture as laughable, crude similitudes and dis-locations. Proximate at best. But where did the Greeks start? With fundamentals. Sheep and olives and grapes, white stones and dark blue sea. The moon and planets in the night sky and willing spirits—which these girls had aplenty. Smart, pretty girls with guns.

V was as touched as they were by such welcome company. Their yearning she recognized fully from that age, the need to become something at least within the vicinity of your dream of yourself. She looked at that quartet of lifted faces and wished each of them something better than the man they would most prob-ably find themselves bound to till death—even if that something better was solitude. She shaped a ragged philosophy to tide them through lonesome nights. It was simple, and not one she'd ever found the strength to follow. The idea was, the you you are with others is not you. To be lonesome is to be who you most fully are. And also maybe something about the great reluctance with which we let go of our belief in a just God.

When she finished talking she feared she had said too many of those things aloud. Or all of those things and more. The girls looked at her in some confusion, but excited and willing to consider and discuss the merits of her comments. V looked at Missus Wiggins to gauge her reaction, and Missus Wiggins reached and touched her hand very briefly in reassurance, so the girls and V talked on and on.

Despite being unable to keep their names straight, V fell in love with them all and wanted to take them with her, load them and their weapons into the wagons and have conversations around campfires every night until late as they made their way deep into the jungles of Terra Florida and through the horrors of its reptiles and outlaw inhabitants and across the Straits of Florida to safety in old civilized Havana.

But then came the immediate recognition that whatever V's best intentions, these girls were safer here smothered under dim pinewoods inside their hog fortress than coming along with her to talk about poetry and beauty while big-dollar bounties hovered like a vortex of buzzards overhead. V's contribution to their lives would likely be to drag them down darker than they already were. A sorry realization when you know the best you can offer is not your presence but your absence.

Eventually, V and the Wiggins girls all walked out of the house as a babbling group, talking over the top of each other about books they all intended to read and how much they loved each other. V promised that if she ever retrieved her library from Mississippi she would send them boxes and boxes of books.

They spent a great deal of time kissing cheeks and hugging and saying bye, including Missus Wiggins.

V pulled her aside and kissed her and said, You know these girls of yours are splendid?

Missus Wiggins said, I've been knowing it since they were old enough to stand up on their feet and talk for themselves.

Mister Wiggins had a bundle, a big awkward lump inside a greasy swaddling of hemp tow. A joint of yellowish bone stuck out the top in place of a handle.

He said, There's a ham and a couple slabs of bacon to boot.

—So you've reached a favorable judgment as to the existence of ladies? V said.

—Ladies maybe. I've been listening at the window. But God's still a great mystery.

—Yes, V said. Mystery is His primary attribute. But the pork is more than generous.

—Makes me happy to see my girls happy, Wiggins said.

Delrey gave V a hand into the ambulance and the navy boys mounted up and away they all went.

Still, the Wiggins boy stood on the porch watching intensely, his Henry balanced and ready to lift and fire.

At the first bend in the road Delrey said, So that's the way ladies do?

—Good Lord no, V said. Not in the least.

They rode back to camp in silence, and V thought about how the landscape would never be the same after this war even if the blasted battlegrounds healed with new green growth and burned farms were either rebuilt or allowed to rot into the dirt. The old land had become all overlain with new maps of failures and sins, troop movements, battles and skirmishes, places of victory and defeat and loss and despair. Slave quarters, whipping posts, and slave market platforms. Routes of attack and retreat. Monumental cemeteries of white crosses stretching in rows to the horizon, and also lonesome mountain burials with one name knife-cut into a pine board, weathering blank in ten years and rotted into the ground in twenty. The land itself defaced and haunted with countless places where blood—all red whoever it sprang from—would keep seeping up for generations to come. That place out in the pinewoods would haunt those girls to death and keep haunting. The last one, the youngest—at a hundred years old, tiny and translucent—might tell the story of the marauding army and the killings and the torchlight burials to a little girl in 1950 who would carry it with her into the twenty-first century.

==

—**Subtract everything** inessential from America and what's left?

—Geography and political philosophy, V says. The Declaration and Constitution. The Federalist Papers.

—I'd say geography and mythology, James says. Our legends.

He gives examples, talks about Columbus sailing past the edge of the world, John Smith at Jamestown and Puritans at Plymouth Rock, conquering the howling wilderness. Benjamin Franklin going from rags to riches with the help of a little slave trading, Frederick Douglass escaping to freedom, the assassination of Lincoln, annexing the West. All those stories that tell us who we are—stories of exploration, freedom, slavery, and always violence. We keep clutching those things, or at least worn-out images of them, like idols we can't quit worshipping.

—**Taking the** life of a nation is a serious task, V says. Few succeed, even if the cause is just. We didn't, and ours wasn't. But sometimes I can't help missing those days when we all just took care of each other.

—We? James asks.

—Everyone living together at Brierfield and The Hurricane.

—If you mean slaves, you only remember what they allowed you to remember. Even if Davis Bend was really as humane as you believe, they kept their misery to themselves, kept it a mystery to you. I promise that's true. Think of it as a great gift, a mark of affection. Their protection of your memory.

—Let's don't start getting ironic with each other.

—It's true.

V stands and says, A moment. Please don't go.

She walks down the steps from the terrace to a path leading into a flower garden. She is gone for fifteen minutes, and in that time an employee of The Retreat comes out from the lobby and asks how he might be of help. A certain tone to the question.

When V returns, she tells about the political fighting

in Washington during the whole decade of the fifties, how the struggle over slavery became more and more poisonous, even though a possible model stared the lawmakers on both sides square in the face. Some of the Northern states—Pennsylvania and Connecticut—had just recently finished the gradual abolition of slavery. Others—New Jersey and New Hampshire—were still in the process and remained so until the Emancipation Proclamation. But they all worked on similar plans, ending slavery bloodlessly over time. Of course all the Northern states, including those still holding slaves through the fifties and on into the sixties, claimed high ground. V says, Their moral position in converting from slaveholders to champions of freedom was about like a house cat on a cold night scooting through a closing door just before the latch clacks shut. But sometimes timing is all. A brief moment of history, less than a deep breath, becomes the difference between inside and outside.

=

In Richmond, people attacked V on the grounds that her greatest ambition had been to become First Lady of the United States of America—which she couldn't deny. She wanted to live at 1600 Pennsylvania Avenue for eight years and throw fine dinners for the smartest and most entertaining people in the world. And having that dream come real was right at the tips of her fingers. When your lowly congressman husband becomes a great, wounded American war hero in Mexico, widely known for his genius battlefield strategy and personal risk and sacrifice, and then he becomes a U.S. senator and secretary of war—well, living in the real White House someday is hardly a delusional aspiration.

Though, at the time Jeff became secretary of war for the United States, one of his old teachers at West Point wrote,

> *Neither Davis nor my opinion of him have changed since I knew him as a cadet. If I am not deceived, he intends to leave his mark in the Army & also at West Point & a black mark it will be I fear. He is a recreant and unnatural son, would have pleasure in giving his Alma Mater a kick & would disclaim her, if he could.*

Those days in Washington, she dreamed nothing but black doom. She saw the end from the beginning—all the loss and devastation, our beautiful country full of ghosts haunting cornfields and cow pastures and night woods for centuries to come. She told Mary Chesnut that the way it would all play out was that the Southern states would secede and cobble together a breakaway country and would make Jeff its president and it would all fail disastrously.

For a stretch of weeks in 1855, she dreamed in detail about being First Lady. But the White House was all wrong. She'd been all over it during the past fifteen years—not just the public rooms, but also every hallway and bedroom upstairs. In her dream, though, she wandered lost, looking for an exit. Whatever path she took—through hallways, up and down stairways—she always wound around to find herself in a dim downstairs kitchen with the servants. Eventually she did live as First Lady, but in a White House reflected in a grotesque carnival mirror, though downstairs she recognized the kitchen, that dead end her dream kept leading her toward.

Second half of the fifties—when government failed to do anything but shove the country into convulsion and apocalypse, Jeff's health declined. His malaria kept recurring and his bad eye dimmed slowly almost to blindness. V spent much of that time having children. Messages in bottles floated out into a terrifying future. Samuel was the first, a fat and happy baby. Everything struck him as funny. V's First Lady friend

Jane Pierce—the madwoman allegedly confined in the attic of the White House—loved taking Samuel on long carriage rides all around town and out in the country. She loved his company, his entertainment, his belly laugh that seemed far too big to come from such a small package.

Samuel fell ill and died when he was still three, and for months afterward V closed herself up in their big rented house. Jeff kept working, going to the Capitol every morning, but he couldn't sleep and sometimes wandered the streets of Washington late at night. Friends and family offered brief sympathy, but infant death rates stood so high that many people didn't really think of them as fully human those first few years. Case in point, V's father. Samuel had been gone only a month or six weeks when WB sent her a breezy note barely acknowledging her loss. He might have mentioned hearing she was under the weather. She tossed it in the fire and wrote back that she would let him know when she recovered from her grief, but until then his mercantile messages weren't welcome. She used the word a lot around that time—*mercantile*—to mean without emotion, businesslike. Jeff finally had to request that for the good of their marriage she stop using that word in regard to his family.

Maggie and Jeffy and Joe and Billy arrived at roughly two-year intervals, little bursts of life during dark days for the country when the arguments over slavery turned fatal for hundreds of thousands. She was pregnant with Billy when things fell apart completely, those frightening and chaotic days as state after state seceded and the Southern legislators resigned and packed up and went home to improvise a rebel country.

Toward the end, an English journalist reporting on the Senate described Jeff as having the face of a corpse, the form of a skeleton.

Jeff held on, the last of the last, hoping newly elected Lincoln and the Yankee Congress would take a deep breath and try to find a way to avoid war. But that didn't happen. Lincoln came to town refusing to talk to anybody who disagreed with him. Jeff stayed on, hoping to be imprisoned, since the North had vowed to arrest for treason any member of the House or Senate from secessionist states who tried to leave. All the others, even Judah, eased out of town. But Jeff always wanted a trial, to wrap himself in the Constitution and defend himself in front of the Supreme Court. Either win or go down a martyr. Wife and children be damned.

Except the Federals weren't really enthusiastic about charging anyone with treason, given that the Constitution wasn't clear about what to do if members of the club of states wanted to resign—whether to let them go or try to kill them. So Jeff and V went home to Brierfield, a dreary trip because V sensed the tidal wave rising to break over them. Jeff became more silent than usual, brooding over the unwelcome likelihood that he would become president, at least until an election could be organized. Neither of them felt surprised, therefore, when one afternoon a man came riding up at Brierfield, his horse in a lather, and gave Jeff the message—he had been appointed president of a country that didn't exist. Nevertheless, they both read the letter with faces grim, as if it were a death notice. Nor was V surprised when the attack on Sumter soon began brewing. Their friend Robert Toombs, until recently a U.S. senator from Washington, Georgia, sent Jeff a letter of warning against being pulled into battle. Toombs wrote,

It is suicide, murder, and will lose us every friend at the North. You will wantonly strike a hornet's nest which extends from mountain to ocean, and legions now quiet will swarm out and sting us to death. It is unnecessary; it puts us in the wrong; it is fatal.

Ultimately Jeff, who had read nearly as much history as V, refused to see that days of building and maintaining fortunes based on enslavement were passing quickly. Country after country had been finding various ways to end the ownership of people. Haiti, Bolivia, Chile, Mexico, Venezuela, and Peru saw the writing on the wall. Jeff and his wealthy and powerful friends couldn't.

Scaffold

February 1862

O ut the window a low sky and drizzle, everything gray. February cold radiated through the glass. Even in cobbled streets, mud swelled between stones and smeared into horse shit and the general everyday effluent to make a gray organic paste, slick and greasy and shoe-heel deep, shiny even in the absence of sunlight. V raised the window sash a few inches and reached her hand into the morning and found the day as raw to her palm as it appeared, the air fragrant as an outhouse.

She turned straight from the window to her medicine. Her new doctor had suggested—as if it were a brilliant discovery—that when she felt low, cored out, she should take a glass of wine and a pinch of morphine. Same prescription as when she'd miscarried and also when Samuel died. The current new baby, Billy, lived and existed as a real being in the world, sleeping and eating and crying and filling diapers to his armpits. But every moment her insides pulled at her, much like with the lost children, a feeling of absence, a suction. She unfolded the wax-paper packet and tapped some of its powder into a generously sized wineglass and then poured Bordeaux near the brim. Just enough room to stir with her finger until the lumps dissolved and then put her finger in her mouth so as not to lose a grain.

Fifteen minutes after, still feeling desperately empty, she poured another glass and the remainder of the packet. She put on a robe and walked downstairs to the kitchen, moving like fog from room to room, down two flights of stairs and along hallways. So drifting in her thoughts that she kept touching walls with fingertips to confirm reality.

In the kitchen Mary O'Melia and Ellen worked with their housemaids and under-cooks preparing for the party that evening. Mary ran the place as head housekeeper, and Ellen was the main cook. V was still fairly new to the house and to both of them.

—Coffee? V said, standing in the doorway, a hand on the casing.

Mary O'Melia was a broad-faced Irish widow of a ship captain—maybe a year or two younger than V, pretty and tough and weary. She'd been trapped in the South after borders shut down following Sumter. All her American family lived in Baltimore, and she let everyone know she couldn't wait for the war to end one way or the other so she could go home and be with her children. Mary said, Ma'am, I know you're new here. We all are. But the way it works is you pull the cord and ring the bell, and I send someone right up to see what you want done, and then we do it. So go back upstairs and let's practice.

V looked at Ellen, and Ellen smiled and shrugged her shoulders.

—Problem is, I'm here now, V said.

—Cup or mug? Ellen said.

—Mug, please.

Ellen poured and then walked V back to the third floor. Ellen was a slim, serious young woman who looked about an equal mixture of white and black and wore her hair pulled tight to her head, parted down the middle. She set V's mug down and said, I'd tell you Mrs. O'Melia's bark is worse than her bite, except pretty often she bites too.

———

Half an hour before showtime, V and Jeff emerged from the front door of the Gray House. With Jeff's up-turned hand cupping her elbow, they drifted with the rain across the sidewalk and into the carriage, a wave of perfect black and white fabric and a dark violet sheen in V's skirts. Jeff gripped his inaugural speech tight under his right arm inside a leather folder—written in V's blue hand, which Jeff read more easily than his own because she silently acknowledged his diminished eyesight and wrote extra large. Settled in the carriage, Jeff tapped her wrist, the intimate coin-size exposure of flesh where the glove hooked and blue veins pulsed, a touch of fingertip subtle and intimate as a Masonic handshake. He looked straight ahead. She turned her palm up and gripped his hand, feeling the bones beneath the skin, all knuckle and joint, a tiny bundle of kindling.

She said, You can make a bad speech sound good.

An escort of footmen, six black men meant to walk alongside the carriage, began forming up—two ahead of the front wheels, two behind the back wheels, two by the doors. They dressed as pallbearers. Mourning clothes. Black suits, black vests, black top hats banded with black satin. One man even wore a hank of limp black veil trailing like a horsetail from his hatband down past the collar of his coat. They might as well have fixed black-dyed ostrich plumes from the brow bands of the horse bridles.

V sat observing the scene through her side window. A few colors—highly saturated—dazzled in the gray morning. Teeth in the pallbearers' mouths, white and yellow, seemed exaggerated as colors of cake icing. Missing teeth deep black. One pallbearer's cravat a bluebird splash at his neck. Everything else rendered in shades of black and gray like a photograph. Mud wetted the backs of their pant cuffs. The black of the mourning bands around their hats blacker than a moonless night sky. Blacker than a hundred-year-old mojo hand, blacker than the bottom of a Welsh coal pit, blacker than the iris of the devil's right eye. A black with its own draw, a puckered suction pulling down.

V stepped out of the carriage and went to Jeff's new secretary, Burton Harrison, and said, Who would be responsible for the costumes?

—Ma'am?

—The men alongside. The choice of their attire.

—I'd have to ask, Burton said.

—Well if you don't know, who does?

—They would know, ma'am. The men. I could ask them.

—No, don't start troubling yourself.

V stepped to one of the men, the one who seemed like the leader. Dignified, proud, his posture perfect. A shiny black silk band clasped his outside upper arm.

V said, You are all dressed so handsomely. Who chose your wardrobe?

The man looked at her, his eyes sliding by her face, pausing only half a second, but seeing what he needed to see.

—Show respect. Same way we do a burying around here, ma'am.

V let that roll over her. And then she decided to ease back without interference. Let suitable equipage for living in a dying world pass without further critique.

She said, Thank you for your respect. And please pass my thoughts along to the others.

As their carriage moved through the streets, pedestrians all moved their same way, tending alike, a flow going where V and Jeff were going, birds in October shaping strange and beautiful patterns as they swirl against the sky finding a common direction. The men walking alongside the carriage—the swing of their arms, their step, sway of shoulders—moved like a dance to entirely different music from the brass band's march.

At the Capitol, V stood outside the carriage with an umbrella. The equestrian statue of Washington rose high above the proceedings. Very heraldic—rampant, dexter—all those conventions of honor. The bronze statue glowed wet and dark as obsidian above its pale, stone base. Behind Washington, clouds churned patterns of gray and black, ominous or meaningless. Trying to decide which of the two prevailed, V kept looking up toward Washington and his hat of ancient vintage. Knowing many eyes turned her way, making judgments against her slightest gesture, she collapsed her umbrella and stepped back into the carriage. She had been here before.

The band honked anthemic marching tunes from their bright horns—the flaring bells of trumpets and French horns, bright brass and at the center a black vortex. Most people stood under umbrellas—a field of tight black satin domes—and hunched shoulders against the cold and wet. From behind the crowd, V's perspective, the arching ribs and scalloped canopies of umbrellas lapped each other into a cloud of descending batwings.

The platform—the stage, the scaffold—had been hammered together suddenly and raggedly from raw yellow pine like a coffin at a July Mississippi funeral, but elevated in tone by bunting drooping lower moment by moment in the rain, the red and blue bands beginning to stain the white.

V rested in the morphine and watched. A play—something medieval and full of morality—began unfolding on the stage before her, a story that ended bad, a tragedy. Raindrops on umbrellas beat faint Celt clan rhythms.

Jeff climbed the steps to the stage, ascending to the scaffold, a willing victim throwing himself onto the wrong pyre. A volunteer. At the podium he looked ashen, skeletal in the depth of his eye sockets and the prominence of cheekbones and hollowness of flesh below.

But when he began talking, his voice swelled. He stood in the rain speaking strong and clear. Projecting. It was a learned skill, a vibration in the vowels sounding completely natural but impossibly loud, a frequency riding over the hum of the audience. A matter of breath, muscle, volume of air pumped from the gray sacks of lungs across the vocal cords. Operatic, and yet just a matter of physics. From times she had sat onstage looking sideways at him against the light, V knew that spittle spewed with his effort. All his thin body leaning forward, muscles clenched. A fighting stance, ready to clash.

Drops of spit and rain mixed and fell on the paper. V imagined the large words she had penned for him dissolving before his weak eyes, the blue ink on the exposed page becoming like a faint precious watercolor depicting the surface of a pond, a distant mountain range. Finally Burton Harrison thought to step forward and hold an umbrella over him.

V hardly noticed individual words, only the music of Jeff's speech. He believed in things—that much was clear from the rhythm and tone of his voice, the rise and fall of volume, the urgency. With those slight implements, he meant to shove a hot iron rod up the backbone of an entire collapsing culture.

He talked so much of God and the sanctity of property and the absolute rights of those who possess it this instant under a certain set of rules heretofore fluid but henceforth fixed. And no limitations allowed on the nature of property—land, gold, silver, houses, people, livestock. A deep belief that your moment in time is the pinnacle, the only standard of judgment extending from the creation of light until the black apocalypse, that what you believe right now is eternal truth because you believe it so fervently—those deep beliefs so crucial at the moment but none of them more permanent than a puff of air across a palmful of dry talcum.

As the speech trudged on, nearing its halfway point, V kept having to suppress a cough or a laugh or a yawn or a scream. Or an expression of mourning one degree short of weeping. Untoward remarks flooded into her mind. Funny and dreadful. Such as the feeling that if she were writing a review she would have to note that Jeff played his role with much less conviction than in her execution dream. She thought about how the flow of morphine through the human organism always carries with it so much clarity, so much objectivity.

Jeff stood up there minuscule and shouting, unreal in the distance, at the center of a parody of an inauguration. But not amusing, only terrifying. The wet black statue of Washington gleamed and expanded, a dark and indifferent god hiding behind his nose and strange hat, unwilling to pass judgment beyond his mere stern presence.

V felt a sort of vibration, a rattle, and wondered for a moment if this was what an earthquake felt like in its early seconds. She touched the window frame of the carriage and it felt still. She leaned out the window and saw the horses standing calm, resting and waiting, half asleep with their ears relaxed. So the vibration, the rattle, the unease rose from inside.

Still half out the window, she said to the driver, Home, please.

The driver twisted around, looked at her, and said, Right now?

V abided within herself a space of time until the driver grew uncomfortable and needed to say something.

—Ma'am, the mister's talk's not over. The president.

V said, Now, please. Now is the time to go home.

The reins snapped and the carriage lurched forward and rattled across the cobbles. Eyes closed, V took three breaths through her mouth and then three through her nose and then tried out an idea, a hypothesis. You've led an easy life. But everybody suffers. Judgment and punishment have hit with a light touch so far. The tap of a finger.

By evening—the inaugural reception at the Gray House—V's mood had lifted. A party usually had that effect. She moved from group to group of drinkers and eaters, being witty and gracious and sharp. She stood at a height that most women and quite a few men had to look up to meet her eyes and therefore resented her. Some in attendance found her too flirty with the men and tracked her progress through the rooms by clusters of their delighted laughter. Next morning, the papers noted her early departure from the inauguration ceremony but reported that as hostess for the reception, the First Lady performed with rare grace and unaffected dignity.

V woke, covers over her head. She reached her hand to Jeff's side of the bed, but it had already gone cold between the sheets. He'd long since dressed and walked to his office and probably skipped breakfast—which he knew he wasn't supposed to do. V thought drowsily how no one knows the inside of a marriage except the two people impounded together. Not family, not close friends, certainly not town gossips and the papers. Just the two bound in matrimony, and nobody can trust a word they say to anyone. Some are liars who claim that after forty years they've never had a cross word or that they've never gone to bed mad. And then there are those couples exhausted and baggy-eyed and not bothering to hide their misery, just struggling to keep their heads above water, trying not to drown in the long aftermath of a bad match. Or those happy and unequal marriages like that of Mary Chesnut where she emerged into her future husband's world at thirteen so unquestionably lovely and delightful and quick of mind that she swept over him—though he was twenty-one, son of a U.S. senator and later to become one himself—like an incoming full-moon tide, so powerful that he waited four long years to marry her and delight in her entertainment every day until death parted them. But if the marriage is at all between equals, the two will certainly disagree about many things at any moment of the day during their time together. Not just details and facts but the fundamental nature of the marriage, because the flow of power changes constantly, and the loser isn't always fully aware of defeat until much later.

A moment from the previous night pulsed into her memory. Late—the dregs of the party—she wilted, tired, and unwary and perhaps a little influenced by wine and leftover medication. A journalist, a new face among the press, stepped up and asked a question about her husband, something concerning the rash of harsh criticisms from Jeff's political enemies in Richmond, which landed vicious and endless with every morning's collection of newspapers. The journalist spoke with an English accent and seemed in his manner and appearance and clothing simultaneously polished and shabby, and very bemused by our bloody war. A tray of Champagne glasses eased by and V swapped her empty for a full.

What V ought to have done was ask what publication he represented, and then immediately say that his questions should be addressed to Burton Harrison or perhaps to Judah Benjamin. But without thought or filter, she actually said, What those miserable political animals are doing to that beautiful man—a man, let me be clear, I have wanted to kill many times for my own reasons—is disgusting and heartbreaking.

Those words were true—her truth—but also dangerous. The society ladies of Richmond went about like

beagles hunting rabbits, noses to the ground, yearning
for the least whiff of damning gossip against her. And
when they caught a scent they went barking and yelp-
ing, breaking down and examining every element of
her in order to come up with their own explanations
for her darkness, which they twined with musty stories
about Jeff's attraction to dark women.

So V groaned into her pillow, knowing that a passing thought or even a joke about killing her husband
could carry heavy consequences. How might the ladies fire that powerful ordnance once in control of it?
Some would have called her treasonous. However—be
honest—name a marriage of equals without murder-
ous thoughts now and then. Also, the damage from
her comment wouldn't have been only among the ladies. Their men—military and political and wealthy
and powerful—already thought V had too much influence, that Jeff's every action and decision bore her
thumbprint like a sloppily iced cake. As if his experience in Washington politics and especially his legend-
ary exploits in Mexico were all nothing. One rumor
constantly circulating was that V sat outside Jeff's
office during meetings, eavesdropping. Occasionally
true, of course, but only when Jeff knew he would
want her opinion later and asked her to sit near the
open door and listen. Goes without saying that her

sitting on the inner side of the door would have been impossible.

But reconstructing those blurted thoughts about killing Jeff, she pictured the shabby handsome writer. The instant the words fled her mouth, he lifted his pencil from his little notebook without jotting anything. He looked at her very seriously and for a length of time, and then said, My apologies for the question. I should speak to Mr. Benjamin. But thank you so much for chatting with me. I hope I shall always enjoy your trust.

He kissed her hand and walked away. At that dazed moment of the party, she thought she had failed to charm him. Now, covers still over her head, she realized the gift he had given her in that simple lifting of pencil from page. Also, his eyes rising from the notebook to meet hers had been so personal, human-to-human. Evaluative and curious, of course—that was his job—but also possibly some unmediated impulse related to sympathy. She wanted to go straight to the Spotswood Hotel and find that man and kiss the back of his writing fist in acknowledgment of a shining moment of honor.

Every day the several Richmond papers arrived at the Gray House, and V usually read most of them, trying to understand the city. She made note of interesting, strange, and awful stories in her journal.

5/11/1861: Letter to the Editor concerning "Dixie" as national anthem—I make no objections to the tune—it is bold and even pleasing. But the words, what are they? Mere doggerel stuff, from the brain of some natural poet, away down in Dixie—"that undiscovered country from whose bourne no traveler returns," because no one as yet has ever reached it.

7/5/1861: FOUND—A little Negro child, between 3 and 4 years old, calling herself BETSEY, yesterday evening at the new Fair Grounds. The mother or owner can get her by paying for this advertisement. Apply to GEO. WATT & CO., Plow makers, Franklin Street.

8/30/1861: Five Negroes, free and slaves, were apprehended Wednesday night by the watch while having a social gathering in the Lancastrian School House with dancing and other pleasing diversions. Being brought before the Mayor yesterday, they were ordered to be whipped.

10/25/1861: EXTRAORDINARY FREAK— Considerable excitement was occasioned on 12th

Street, below Main, yesterday afternoon, by the appearance of a man dressed in a woman's clothing. He soon made himself scarce, and the police did not succeed in tracing him to his hiding place.

11/13/1861: The Spotswood Hotel will begin selling genuine Clicquot and G.H. Mumm's by the case. Also this day: free Negro ordered whipped for smoking a cigar in the street.

So this was Richmond—a veneer of refinement over a deep core of brutality. And yet the women from the best families calling her too western, too frontier, too crude.

Burnt Plantation

1865

Sometimes the view from the ambulance included as high as a half-dozen black house fire circles with stubs of singed rock chimneys rising like great mildewed gravestones. Empty gray split-log corncribs and slat-ribbed lost dogs. Dark bloody smears in the dirt from the Union's hog and cattle butchering. Hardly any chickens to be seen, and those few gone wild and lank, little more meat to them than a hungry squirrel. Empty unplowed spring fields grew nothing but swaths of ragweed. Sometimes as the fugitives passed refugee camps, people raised their eyes, dim as if they were dead already, proof positive of Sherman's notion that unarmed farmers and their families were a great deal easier to conquer than armies. Mostly the colors of that land stuck to shades of red dirt and black cinders with a few dashes of sickly green. And yet look up, and the sun burned yellow and the sky rolled blue and deep like a strong argument that the world had not gone wrong at all.

Crossing the wide path of Sherman's army, flux ruled every moment even four months later. In that scoured territory, people divided into three categories—raiders, refugees, and fugitives.

The raiders moved fast, at a gallop, going from one easy target to the next, saddlebags heavy with plunder bouncing and flapping against their horses' rumps.

Refugees trudged the roads day and night, ravaged by history. People dragging their last spotted pig by a hemp rope around its neck, a precious black Dominican chicken riding bright-eyed under an arm. Packs of children, faces blank as empty pages, took turns pushing wheelbarrows heaped with quilts and cookware and canvas for pitching lean-tos. Hardly a horse or mule to be seen, since Sherman and the raiders took the ones they could use and killed the old and weak for target practice.

V's fugitives traveled slowly, stuck to the back roads, tried not to call attention their way.

On the road, the refugees all coughed. Sometimes V could hear the deep rattle in their lungs—their hawking and spitting—before she could see them. Sometimes refugees traveled mixed together, black and white, unclear what rules applied when elemental concepts like slave and free suddenly became uncertain.

Former slaves, whole plantations of them, followed after the Northern army, hoping to be fed and cared for. And then mostly they had their few possessions stripped from them before being told to move along. Some, lacking a better idea, returned to the plantations they came from. But V met others still wandering the roads looking for something hard to articulate beyond the vague but essential word *Freedom*. Bands of people as high as twenty-five or thirty members roamed with no money and no real sense of how money worked. For most of them, their only knowledge of the world was what little had been afforded them within the tight boundaries of a plantation.

One lone man—barefoot, wearing half-leg pants and a collarless linen shirt—carried four rifles by their leather slings and three pistols in overlapping holsters around his waist. He said now that he was free he aimed to be an American, and he knew you needed guns for that.

A black girl, maybe eight or nine, led an old white man, half blind and mostly deaf and holding a rusty ear trumpet. She carried what had been a smoked hog leg by its foot. They'd shaved the meat away to a few maroon petals clinging to the bone.

Heart of the wasteland. The day pressed deeply humid, air laden so heavy with moisture and pollen that the color of the sky was a matter open to argument. The edges of things—tree leaves, tree bark, the features of a loved one's face—from fifty feet away looked soft and blurred, barely identifiable.

They stopped in the remains of an empty one-street town. Houses and a few stores scattered on either side of the main road. Two of the buildings were painted white and the rest varied in color depending on how long the bare wood siding and shingles had faced the weather.

They walked into a half-burned hotel. A dark-headed girl played a dreamy nocturne at the lobby piano, notes spaced at careful intervals.

—Are rooms available for the night?

The girl looked around confused, her face the color

of cake flour and her eyes dark. She said, Nobody's
here. The piano still plays, so I thought I'd play it.

—Is there someone we could ask about rooms?

—Everybody's gone and nobody cares. Look on the
second floor. Go left at the top of the stairs. Some of
those rooms might still be dry.

V said, Please keep playing.

The girl stood up and closed the key-lid. She said, I
don't care for an audience.

Those strange days, a lot of people used up parts of
themselves they could never regenerate. Everyone in
the territory they passed through had lost so much and
were being offered many thousands in Federal gold—
money to last a lifetime—if they provided information leading to the capture of the fugitives. Who would
blame hungry people for claiming such a treasure?

They passed through rolling country for a few days,
and the towns seemed little more than collections of
sheds, but they took names from Greek and Roman
cities. V remembers an unexpected steep hill pitching
down to just a little creek, the way the horses squatted
on their hocks against the grade. It was sunset, but people stood by the side of the road and stared, and when
V said Good day, they looked away without a word.

Then a day where they didn't even break camp, hard rain from dawn to sunset, lightning and thunder making the children shriek. After the rains, they traveled three days through drowned pineland where mosquitoes flew so thick the fugitives couldn't sleep even when they dragged bedding directly into the smoke of the fire. More time went lost when everyone except Bristol and Ryland fell sick, a terrible purging. For three days, unrelenting fever and chills and raging bowels. The children were pitiful, and the adults alternated sleeping and rushing to the woods. Delrey tried to take care of the horses and mules, but stopped over and over to hump with his hands on his knees and heave. Same for V and Ellen when they tried to comfort the children.

The navy boys—so young they still grew pale down on their cheeks and shaved only out of vanity—worked dawn to dark doing the best they knew to nurse them all. Fetch water and clean children busy vomiting and having the flux. Whenever an adult could sit up to take liquids, they would steep herb tea or brew a bit of precious coffee.

The children suffered better than the rest. They fretted and cried, and their faces became gray with dark circles under their eyes, but they also slept a lot. Frantic and desperate one minute and then the next, without transition, dead to the world, unconscious yet still sucking a thumb, at least the youngest ones.

When they all recovered enough to travel, they only went two hours and then stopped for a day by a pretty river to wash and dry a pile of filthy linens.

Then for two clear days and nights they passed through country with few people and smooth roads. They went nearly twenty miles in one day—the first and only time.

Late afternoon, they took a side road to avoid passing through a town. For a moment V could see houses and stores distant across a cotton field growing up in weeds. No one in sight. Rain fell slow, and smoke from chimneys sank low to the ground. Then up ahead a group of people came around a bend in the road. They were wet and carried hoes and shovels and rakes over their shoulders the way men carry long rifles when they're walking a distance. These were farmers willing to plant fields without mules or slaves in a time of so much disaster and uncertainty that it took great faith and hope to gamble on a harvest months into a future that looked a shambles.

It was too late to do anything but keep moving toward them. The fugitives had agreed that in such circumstances, Delrey should do the talking. So V ducked under the canvas with the children and tried to keep them quiet, but they were in a talking mood. So the best she could do was make a game out of whispering and sign language. As they passed the farmers, V could hear their questions and Delrey's answers.

—Who is the lady?

—Mrs. Jones.

—Where you coming from?

—Up the road a ways.

—Where you heading?

—Down the road a piece.

—Pretty nice bunch of horses and mules.

—Because we've not allowed anybody to steal them from us.

—Who's these other people?

—Family members.

—Any news of the war?

—It's done's all I hear, Delrey said.

—Heard some fool shot Lincoln and killed him. That true?

—You know more than I do, Delrey said.

—If it is true, we'll all pay for it.

—Shit. Far as I know, Lincoln or not, we're all paying, every minute of every day, Delrey said.

He flapped the reins, and a hundred yards on he leaned around and said, If somebody comes up behind asking the right questions, I doubt they'll have forgotten us.

Twilight the next day, a storm began brewing far westward. Clouds lit up with pale blooms of distant lightning. Faint thunder. The wind blew the storm their way, and it looked like a bad night to be on the road.

An hour later, lightning flashed a couple of miles away, jagged bolts. Ryland walked toward a dark plantation house, one end burned to nothing but black, crazed timbers in a heap and tall Doric columns scorched halfway up. Empty fields, deserted rows of facing slave cabins off to the side. Thin wisps of human-shaped smoke rose from the burn pile and stood in the last beams of moonlight pinched off through a closing crack in the clouds.

Lightning struck nearby and then immediately a swelling sound like shredding metal. Rushing wind climbed the hill and whirled limbs of pecan trees. In the flashes, stacked parallel rows of sapsucker holes in the trunk bark—bands of black dots—appeared and vanished immediately like unreadable lines of ancient text, a false prophecy. Big greasy drops of rain, widely spaced, hissed as they fell, and off in the woods, a yap of distant dogs carried in the stirring air, faint and wavelike in rhythm.

Delrey said, That's the very way dogs sound when ghosts are roaming.

They stayed in the dark, watching, ready to flee while Ryland walked under the pecan trees and climbed the steps to the front porch. Horizontal jags of lightning silhouetted him. He knocked on the door, acting like a gentleman, and then tried the knob. The door swung open. He humped over against the wall to shield a match and lit a candle and went inside. One by one the windows of the front rooms lit up yellow as he scouted and then went black when he searched the back rooms. Soon the light grew brighter in increments as he pilfered around and found candle stubs and lit them. He came back onto the porch.

—Empty, he shouted.

The rain picked up and they all hurried unloading. Ellen carried Winnie under her shawl, and Burton led Maggie and Jeffy. Jimmie Limber and Billy walked fast across the weedy plot of lawn holding V's hands.

Bristol and Ryland ran back and forth in the flashes of storm carrying food and bedding while Delrey settled the mules and horses under the trees. Then all three of them collected downed limbs and broke them up the best they could, stomping them into firewood.

Inside, V and Ellen sat with the children and arranged their nest of quilts in front of the cold hearth.

The house was all chaos, gaumed up beyond belief. Everywhere scattered plunder, broken things. A wide drag-trail parted the clutter. All denominations of Georgia bills littered the floor, and Burton drew the worthless paper together to strike a fire. A few thousand dollars did the job. Twigs and spindles from dining chairs served as kindling.

Black windows flashed white, projecting images of pecan limbs like etchings against the glass, and then went black again. The fire caught and the chimney drew. Burton closed the curtains to keep firelight from showing down at the road.

The navy boys took candles and went exploring the back of the house, and returned shortly with a crock of strawberry jam and another of dark-colored honey, almost coffee black.

Ryland said, There's a case of wine sitting back there if anybody would care for some.

—Yes, please, V said.

She began digging around in her reticule, down past her pretty pistol, and came up with a corkscrew. Ryland set the case of Chablis down beside her, and she opened a bottle.

—Did you notice wineglasses? she said.

—Be right back, Ryland said. He and Bristol returned with Bristol carrying the candle and Ryland holding six stems upside down between spread fingers, and the bowls chimed against each other as he walked.

Burton and Delrey stood on either side of the fire. Delrey's clothes hung dark and nearly soaked on his frame, and as the fire heated up, he started steaming. Rain fell hard and drops sizzled in the hearth where they found a way down the chimney throat.

No milk for the children and everybody too weary for much cooking, V said, A good night for bacon and warmed-up biscuits.

Delrey said, Good Lord, a few more days like this and we'll be shoveling for terrapin eggs along the creek banks.

V said, Delrey, I count on you for optimism.

—Scrambled terrapin eggs—mighty good eating. Tastes like duck eggs but with a lot more tang.

—Thank you for the effort, V said.

Ellen fried two skillets of thick-cut bacon and then fried the old dry biscuits in the grease for a minute to freshen them up.

A sound carried from the second floor—a squeak of floorboards, a bump. Then silence.

Burton said, No worries. Just a possum or a bird that's gotten in and can't get out. But the boys and I'll go check. If you hear anything more than just the three of us walking around, get out and go to the wagon. We've left the teams fed and in the traces and ready to roll if there's trouble.

Burton and Bristol and Ryland went upstairs, searching for the source of the noise, and Delrey waited near the fire with his shotgun ready. Hardly sooner than they got up the steps, V heard many feet thumping on floorboards, raised voices, the sounds of things falling. Ellen and Delrey grabbed the younger children under their arms and V yanked Maggie by the hand. They fumbled out of the house and into the rain. Winnie cried, and then most of the other children started crying.

Before they reached the wagon, though, Burton came onto the gallery carrying an oil lantern in one hand and a pistol in the other. He said, Ease up. Safe to come back, I think.

Inside, a huddle of people crowded around the fire, remnants of two or three families formerly enslaved. A grown man and three grown women and some exhausted and frightened children and two crying babies. And also a greasy blond boy about sixteen.

Ryland held out a stubby pistol for V's inspection. It rested in his palm hardly weightier than her little suicide shooter.

Ryland said, Not even any live loads in it. I pulled it off that one.

He nodded toward the white boy, who grew less beard than the fuzz on a mullein leaf. Yellow strands of sticky-looking hair drooped across his forehead in front and hung limp to his shoulders in back. Everything about him glowed pallid and shiny. He wore what had once been a fine suit, now fraying at the collar and sleeves and cuffs, its carefully tailored structure wrinkled and broken down and bagged until it rode him like a spirit from the past.

V looked to the women and said, Are your people all right?

The white boy said, Address your questions to me.

Ryland looked around at Bristol and said, Good Lord, that little one features himself the leader.

V said, Ryland, step back, please.

The greasy boy lifted his two forefingers and abruptly hooked his hair behind his ears, as if he considered that a gesture of authority or at least defiance.

V looked him straight in the eye, and he glared back about two seconds and then looked down.

She said, Son, we're short on supplies, but would you like a biscuit with a little piece of bacon? Or a biscuit with some of your honey or jelly? One of those three choices, not all. We're sharing here and what we have has to go around.

You could see the gears engaging and the wheels beginning to grind with some effort.

—Bacon, he said.

—Bacon, please? V said.

The boy just glared.

—All right, V said. We'll try again when you
find yourself more composed. Meanwhile enjoy the
warmth of the fire we built. By the way, what's your
name?

—None of your damn business what my name is.

V looked back to the women, and one of them said,
He's Elgin.

V said, And what's your name?

—Belle.

They passed and shared food, including a bacon biscuit for Elgin, still sulled. He took a bite and stewed
awhile and finally spoke up with great pent emotion.
He swore that with the death of the Confederacy he
would pine down to nothing within a few months and
be the last of the Confederate dead.

V said, Elgin, if all you have to say is nonsense, stop
talking. While you've been here hiding, everything has
changed. It's not the same world out there. You need
real plans, not fantasies.

—I heard the government and army are moving to Texas. I might volunteer.

Ryland and Bristol both coughed a laugh.

—I've heard that same rumor about Texas, over and over, V said. Nobody sane believes it. The war's dead and done. Lost. Think of a real plan. Starting with, for example, who holds title to this place?

The boy looked puzzled. He said, How's that your business?

Belle said, Probably he owns it. His daddy went out on the porch to stop raider trash picking through the leftovers after Sherman's army. Carrying a shotgun against a half dozen. He didn't even get one barrel fired before they cut him down.

—And the mother? V said.

—Died first year of the fighting, Belle said.

—Brothers or sisters?

—Nope.

—Son, V said to Elgin, think hard about this place. It's a real thing, not some theory or philosophy or crazy dream. It could feed all of you.

—I ain't feeding every stray slave in Georgia. And I ain't feeding y'all neither.

Ryland—real sarcastic—said, Brother Elgin, correct me if I'm wrong, but ain't we mostly feeding you? You're offering us shelter in return. Calm down and consider something. In your position, what would Jesus do? He'd say something about inviting strangers in, about how he loves a cheerful giver.

Elgin stood up and all-fervent said, Probably Jesus would yank you by your neck and then beat you to the ground like a drunk foreman with a long tomato stob. Don't be talking Jesus to me. Just say Jesus one more time and see what happens. Come on. Say his name.

—You forget, Ryland said, rising to his feet, we're the ones with guns.

Since everybody else was doing it, Burton stood up too. He had his right hand in his coat pocket. Delrey stayed where he was, leaning against the wall with the shotgun angled half down, watching close.

Bristol kept his seat and regarded the moment.

He said, Ry, maybe sit your ass down and shut your mouth for a whole minute.

Ryland sat. And then the others did too.

Bristol said, Can we leave Jesus alone? He deserves a rest now and then.

When his minute ended Ryland said, I'm curious, Elgin. With all your strong feelings about the Confederacy, how come you weren't in on the fighting? You're old enough.

Elgin said, I paid a dirt farmer to take my place, like the law allows.

Ryland said, A study in courage. Mr. Elgin puts his money where his big stupid mouth is.

Bristol laughed, and so did Delrey and V.

Elgin's face blazed holly-berry red.

Belle said, You have to allow for him. He's lost so much. Ten years ago on this place, three hundred of us, nearly. Cotton growing to the sky every way you looked. Hog pens and pastures with cows. Lots of cotton, lots of corn and vegetables.

V said, After things settle, the land will still be worth something.

Elgin bristled and said, Who'd be buying? Nobody, that's who. Nobody's got money. And whatever happens, I ain't hoeing cotton. Or beans and corn and collards neither. Or milking cows. I don't plan to live in a world without slaves. Besides, we made more money breeding slaves to sell than growing cotton. So maybe I'll go to Brazil where the laws keep making sense. These people here want to think I'm responsible for them, but the truth is purely the other way around.

V looked at Belle, and Belle said, I wet-nursed him from the day he was born until he turned three. It's hard for me to believe he hates me, and hard to hate him.

—Not hard for me, Ryland said, in a whisper loud enough for everyone to hear.

Elgin said, Shut the hell up.

————

The children dozed in front of the fire, piled together in a nest of quilts. Except Jimmie Limber, who sat next to V, leaning a shoulder into her hip, a hand on her leg as she rubbed his back, cupped the side of his thin neck in her palm. He watched the freed children intently, and they looked back at him the same way, curious and confused.

Belle said what they were all thinking, Whose baby is he?

—Jimmie's mine, V said. He favors me a little.

—Hmm? Belle said.

Very quickly Ellen said, Nobody knows who his mother was. We found him taking a whipping on the street in Richmond. So Miss V moved him in with her children. Been living there for a couple of years.

—Polishing their shoes and fetching things? Elgin said. Or more like a pet?

—Not either one, Ellen said. They all slept in the nursery. Played and had classes. All the children together.

—Good Lord, Elgin said. You think you've heard every manner of shit there is to hear, and then some crazy bitch comes up with something new.

Ryland rose slowly, eased his pistol out of his belt, and held it down by his leg.

He said, Little man, that kind of talk ain't at all Christian.

V looked at Burton and Burton looked at Ryland and said very low, We can't afford to go around killing people for every stupid thing they say. We've all agreed on that. Stay calm.

Ryland put his pistol back in his belt and said, Now and then, though, it's the exception that proves the rule. He said it very bright, trying to hold the corners of his mouth level.

Burton announced to the room, We need some sleep, and all of us will sleep right here by the fire. One of us will be awake all the time. I'll take the first watch.

—You think you're going to put a watch over us? In my own house? Elgin said.

Delrey said, No judgment as to need. But we're going to do it the way we're going to do it.

He raised the angle of his shotgun barrel about an inch and said, I bet we all need to visit the outhouse now that the lightning's quit. I'll stand guard outside and make sure everybody's safe.

After they'd all gathered back around the fire, Elgin said, I'd been wondering how in hell y'all up in Richmond managed to lose the war. Then you show up on my doorstep and it's clear as day. Worthless people.

—Could have been they outnumbered us, Ryland said. But all the way down here, I've been thinking maybe we had it coming.

—Had what coming?

—Losing, Ryland said.

—Say that again, Elgin said.

—You heard me.

—I don't like to kill people unless I'm sure they need it. So say it one more time and I will lay you down.

Ry said, You've not ever worn a uniform or killed anybody, and you're not going to start now. Have you even had your first drink of liquor?

The boy reached to his waist and pulled out a little hidden Derringer. Silver-plated with pearl grips, three-inch over-under barrels.

Ryland and Bristol both laughed at him when he held it out.

V said, Boys, stop it right now. And you, Elgin, don't say another word.

—I don't let women run me, Elgin said.

He kept his little pistol leveled at Ryland.

Ry couldn't pass up a jab. He said, Except apparently that woman over there is not long since finished nursing you. Diapering too probably. He gestured toward Belle, hovering nearby.

She said, Mr. Elgin, don't pay attention to their rough talk.

Burton Harrison stood and spread his hands and said, Wait.

V stood too and said, Enough.

And then Elgin twitched a finger, almost a nervous impulse, and an awful instant of time later, Ryland was gone for good.

Bristol stood there, with a look of stunned recognition on his face at just the stupidity of it, just the damn overwhelming thoughtless ignorance and meanness and darkness of humans.

Ryland lay with a hole burned in the weave of his left jacket lapel, all the light gone out of him. Whatever fills the bloody mess inside our heads—the details that make us who we are, those threads of nerve and strange ugly tissues that make us different from each other—Ryland's had quit working, shut down all at once. He'd transformed in a matter of seconds from being so busy living—fired up and blazing and tiring people down to a nub most days—to being a dead pile of meat and bones and gristle without a spark. Three or four swings of a pendulum and he was all gone.

Elgin shifted his little pistol slightly toward Bristol and sort of smirked.

In the instant it took Ryland to die, Bristol didn't

have time to think or to choose, as if something in him beyond thought didn't wish to occupy the same world as Elgin.

Bristol drew his navy pistol and pulled two shots faster than the mind could register. One hole in the forehead and an ugly red mess blowing out the back onto the plaster wall. One heartbeat, and all that bragging falsehood Ryland made up on the rail platform in Richmond became prophecy.

Elgin wasn't surprised any more than a candle flame is surprised when you lick your fingers and pinch it out. Light, then dark. He fell as if he had just suddenly decided to lie down. But he was dead before he hit the floor.

And before Bristol even recognized what he'd done, V wheeled and slapped him hard. A roundhouse blow to the side of his head. He still held his smoking pistol aimed toward the space the dead boy had occupied before collapsing. Ryland lay peaceful ten feet away as if asleep, and Bristol looked too stunned to form tears in his eyes.

V looked at the two dead boys and back at Bristol and began to view that arrangement of bodies anew, as a feature of her current world needing to be understood.

She said, I'm sorry I did that.

She tried to hug Bristol, but he wouldn't stand still for it.

All the children, both groups, either cried and wailed or were too terrified to move. Belle's people hushed their children and put themselves, their bodies, between their children and V's people. Billy had burrowed up under the pile of quilts and lay sobbing. Maggie still had her eyes closed and held her hands over her ears, and Jeffy and Jimmie stared at the bodies in disbelief. V and Ellen and Burton got to their knees and hugged the children and patted heads and tried to turn the little boys away, but Jimmie and Jeffy kept looking back at the bodies and the blood. Delrey stayed where he was, with the shotgun ready and watching everybody closely.

When it seemed like the shooting was done, Belle went to Elgin and touched his neck where the pulse would have been, and then she took an indigo kerchief from her apron pocket and spread it over his face.

—What are we going to do now? Belle said.

—Sunrise, new world, Bristol said.

Dawn just a haze to the east, V and Ellen carried the sleeping children out to the ambulance in blankets while Delrey tacked and harnessed the horses.

Burton and Bristol dug two holes in the plantation cemetery. No boxes, just red rectangles cut deep in Georgia clay. Wide pine floor puncheons for markers, names and dates scratched by knifepoint. When they finished digging and had the bodies settled, Belle and her people came out of the house and stood over their little dead master before he got shoveled under. V came from the ambulance and stood with Bristol and Burton.

Belle looked down in the hole at Elgin, arms crossed and the kerchief over his face. She turned to Bristol and said, I think you ought to say some words.

—You knew him since he was a baby, Bristol said. You should say something in his favor.

—Not my place.

Bristol turned to Burton, and Burton lifted his shoulders a fraction. V looked Bristol in the eye and gripped his wrist a second and nodded yes.

Bristol stepped up to the hole and said, I didn't have one thing against you, Elgin. All we wanted was to get out of the rain. We didn't know this place was anything but a burnt plantation. We shared our food. I'd made it through my part of the war without killing or getting killed. And then you shot Ry for no reason but ignorant pride. I'll never forgive you, and I'll try every day to forget you. But I probably won't be able to. You don't deserve to be remembered one minute past right now. I'm done talking, and if anybody here wants to argue, this is the time.

Belle's people looked at each other, and then Belle said, I wish you'd finish by saying those words you said last night.

—New world coming? Burton said.

—Yes, Belle said. That'll do.

The freed slaves turned and walked back toward the burned plantation house.

Delrey left the horses and walked over to the graves and removed his hat. Ryland rested chalky in the bottom of his hole. Bristol climbed down and X-ed Ryland's forearms over his chest and heaped clean-smelling pine boughs to cover him.

When Bristol finished all the tasks except the shoveling, V said, Do you want to say something?

Bristol said, Ry's gone. And what he'd want would be for me to tell a joke. But I don't know anything funny enough right now.

Bristol patted palm to chest three times and started shoveling. When he had a mound of red Georgia clay he pitched the shovel away and walked to the horses and wagons. V walked with him. She said, Did you mean that? About worrying you'll remember that boy forever?

Bristol said, I won't even know whether I meant it for

a long time. But right now I'm more afraid your children will dream all their lives about the killings. Pictures of me with a gun in my hand triggering the last shot.

V touched his shoulder and said, They're so young. I'll shape their memories so last night won't be anything but thunder and lightning and a warm place in a nest of quilts by the fire.

The fugitives headed on down the road toward Terra Florida, escaping to its wildness and freedom. Ryland's mule trailed on a hemp line from the back of the wagon, trotting easy without a burden.

James watches the landscape flow across the railcar window, left to right. A sprinkle of rain beads on the glass and deepens the greens of grass and leaves.

He looks over his notes from the day, and at the end he writes,

I don't even know whether past feelings and memories deserve any respect at all. Maybe they're no more important than a pinch of pain from an injury decades old. Feelings and memories rise and pass every day, like the weather. Only important at the moment. Why not just notice them and let them go?

Fifth Sunday

Saratoga Springs

—I have questions too, V says. Such as, where did you go after Miss Botume? You were with her . . . what? A year? Two years? What happens after this?

She turns to the end of the chapter called "Jimmie" in the blue book and reads, *Finally the little boy drifted into Auntie Gwynne's Home. This noble woman placed him where he was well trained in all ways, having the advantage of school, as well as a good practical education, until he was old enough to support himself.*

—Drifted? V says. Like a tiny hobo carrying his bindle on a stick over his shoulder?

—I doubt it.

—So how was it? She dropped you off at an orphanage and said, So long? Or just found someone already going that direction to give you a ride? I don't imagine she was under arrest by the Federal government at the time she let you go. Or had a gun to her head.

James waits a moment for her to settle. He draws a couple of breaths and then tells V he hardly remembers Auntie Gwynne's orphanage, having been there only briefly. Before he found Miss Botume's book, he couldn't even recall the name of the place. For two years previous to arriving there, his world had changed radically month by month. Places and people blur. That orphanage rests in his mind as one picture—a room filled with lots of white children. That's all.

But he does remember that soon he went to Thompson Island Farm School, a mile out in Boston Harbor. Wealthy people—particularly Universalists and Unitarians—paid for it as a way of making the world a little better. Not all the boys were orphans, so some went home for holidays. The school aimed to help those who needed help, but the boys had to be smart and promising and willing. The main building, a big white house, sat on an open hill looking over the water. They could see the city from the third-floor windows, but it felt like looking at the moon through a telescope—interesting to observe, but not your world. His world was the island, and most of his memories begin there.

He took classes in literature, mathematics, geography, history, logic, and science. And along with studying, all the boys worked for the good of their little community. The younger boys had jobs around the big house, so James started out helping in the kitchen and in the garden. Even now, he still grows a small backyard garden with greens in the cool months, tomatoes and squash and beans in the summer. All the boys lived on the third floor in big rooms like he remembers in Richmond with V's children, except more beds and closer together. Lots of rules about laundry and personal cleanliness.

—Good, V says. Boys that age can never wash too often.

James tells her that the school had a big brass band. He played bugle. Sometimes they put on their uniforms and went out to the beach to greet passenger ships entering Boston Harbor, trumpeting marches to celebrate a successful crossing of the Atlantic. Passengers stood at the rails and waved handkerchiefs as they passed.

The island spanned enough land—good dirt—to grow orchards, hayfields, berry patches. The older boys each had a little flower garden to tend, and spring through fall, they kept the big house bright with reds and yellows and whites. Fat clams grew on the sand-bars, and boys sometimes went out with buckets and spades to bring back dinner. Older boys lived in a sort of village of tiny white cottages with green shutters. They elected their own mayor and held community meetings to decide how to deal with problems, how to punish boys who wouldn't work or who pilfered. One large room in the main building was the library, and James spent a lot of rainy Sundays in there. There were six long study tables, and the books were mostly donated, some quite old. He liked brown antiquated travel books describing trips that weren't possible anymore—explorations of the Western Hemisphere back when much of it was still unmapped. Pretty days of spring, summer, and fall, he spent all his free time outside, either walking the island or sitting under a tree with a book.

—The headmaster and staff searched out our aptitudes, James says. And when I reached thirteen, I began teaching reading and arithmetic and geography to the youngest boys. In some form, it's what I've done ever since.

Pretty days in late summer, though, he always volunteered for haying—forking the cut and dried hay onto an enormous wagon until the heap stood two shaggy stories tall, and then riding on top back to the barn, balancing on the shifting load, the fragrance of sun on cut grass swelling all around—itchy from the hay down your shirt, but feeling strong and tired and satisfied with the work.

He also tells her about winters when the wind blew in from the North Atlantic and the snow came sideways against the windows and the big house swayed and vibrated in the storms. How one winter the harbor froze solid and some of them walked over the ice to the shore, a mile away.

—So, not a bad place, V says.

—A very good place. A good school, plenty of teaching and learning, but also plenty of physical work. The boys learned how to take care of the buildings and the animals and the gardens and orchards. You were putting your food on the table. Literally. Not working to grow somebody else's food, growing your own. Your responsibility, your work, your enjoyment. We sold surplus from the gardens and orchards, and the money went back into the school for our benefit and for boys to come. You felt part of something. Out of a hundred boys, fewer than a dozen weren't white, but that rarely mattered. Teachers judged us by how much we learned and how much we contributed to the work, not on color. Boys who didn't follow that same practice came and went quickly. Of course the teachers who ran the school and the rich benefactors who paid for it were idealists, and if you said that all of us—white and black—may have finished school at eighteen with a distorted and naive sense of the world off the island, you'd be right.

When he finishes his story, James says, I know your feeling about taking notes as we talk. But I need to write something down. It's about me, not you.

—Please, V says. Scribble.

James opens his notebook and writes,

The island was a separate place, situated partway between America and the moon. Some clear nights out with the telescope—moon full or gibbous—I felt about equidistant between the sharp-edged craters and the sparkling lights of America across the harbor. I knew that off the island very particular rules and laws and customs about skin color and blood degree applied, that the entire stretch of country from ocean to ocean was a strange place with a very strict borderline, and that I didn't exactly fit on either side of it.

Then across the bottom of the page—in a larger, more swooping hand—he writes:

The island felt like home to a degree I've never ex-
perienced before or since.

After he caps his pen, V says, You're not even going
to read it to me?

—Revision first. It makes us all better than we are.
For now, tell me about our capture.

Place of Dreams

May 1865

They passed out of Sherman's path of punishment and went dragging down ordinary red Georgia roads, sloping south on their beaten way. Small towns and small farms lay wide-spaced among pinewoods. The horses and mules were as tired as the people, and they made fewer than their average ten miles a day. Florida still lay vague in the distance, and the only map forward might have been drawn in a crazy man's hand, speculating on a place V would never reach no matter how long she traveled.

Most days Bristol trailed off the back, riding by himself. Delrey kept reminding him he would need to hang a right at some point if he was heading for Alabama, but Bristol said maybe he'd go all the way until they hit the Gulf and then he'd peel off west and follow the coastline around the curve to Mobile. Take his time.

V sat with him one day at their lunch stop and said, I know you're hurting two directions. For Ryland and for having killed Elgin. I'll point out that better boys than that one—hundreds of thousands of them on both sides—have gone down in this mess.

—So you consider Elgin a war fatality? Bristol said.

—I don't consider him anything. He pulled the trigger first, over nothing but words and ideas. But you pulled the trigger over something real—a mean bloody act that took your friend's life. There's a difference. Don't let him weigh heavier on your mind than he merits.

—Yes, ma'am.

—Don't you *Yes, ma'am* me. This is too important to fall back on manners. A lot of boys would be strutting around, bragging like they'd killed their first buck. But that's not you, and that's why we're talking. I don't want what happened to ruin you for the rest of your life. I'm assuming your family had some money or else you'd have been in the infantry instead of the academy.

—Some. My father has a business, not a plantation.

—Then go home, and when colleges open back up, finish an education. Do something that helps people get through the chaos. For a long time, it's going to be like Noah after the flood—everybody, black and white, trying to understand what's left when the water drains away. Bad enough without having your mind overly darkened by that one instant.

—So we've all got a load of guilt to haul? That's my big lesson?

—Don't get sarcastic with me. I'm saying most of the load is not yours to bear. It's ours, the people who brought it on. When you get home, rest and start clearing your head from all this, and then go and do, Bristol.

As they trudged south, V kept Bristol close and watched his moods. She wanted him sitting at her campfire every night, not going off to spread his bedroll alone in the pines. She and the children and Ellen, Burton, and Delrey still usually sat an hour on low camp stools arranged around the fire no matter how tired they were. Some evenings they barely spoke and looked at the flames like they'd been dazed by a great blast of black powder. Cool nights, Jeffy and Jimmie and Billy sat sprawling against each other half asleep. Sometimes V would rouse up from such a moment of gloom and recite a poem. She would tell them all to attend, and then look off into the dregs of sunset and tell them the name of the poem and of the person who wrote it and then launch into something beautiful. V guessed Bristol and all the others were often too exhausted to listen close to the words, only the music of the poem, the tune of it. They could get all the meaning they needed right there in the rhythm without keeping up with grammar at all. That and the flow of light from the fire moving on their circle of faces as she recited.

At some point most nights she would decide her children looked or smelled dirty, which they all usually did. She'd take a pail of creekwater warmed over the fire, a washcloth, and a worn flat of fragrant pink soap and start scrubbing. And if Bristol was sitting there she'd scrub him too, forehead to collarbones. Push his hair back and scour his blemished teen forehead, run her finger covered with the soapy washcloth deep in his ears. When she was done he glowed red as firecoals, his neck and face chafed near to bleeding. He'd smell like roses and whatever fragrance that night's creek carried—pine needles or rotted leaves or minerals in the rocks.

Some nights V asked Bristol to tell a story—a tale from his time in the Naval Academy with Ryland or one of their adventures journeying south from Richmond with Jeff. One night he told about the remnants of the government in Greensboro, how some of the cabinet members and high officers had to sleep on pallets in boxcars.

From Greensboro on past Charlotte, nothing but confusion and bad weather, blown-up railroad bridges and muddy roads ahead, Sherman coming from the south and Grant coming from the north to rub out the remainders of the Confederacy. Before long, what was left of the Confederate government and army traveled by horseback and wagon train. Day by day, rank meant less, and even the officers lost interest in giving and taking orders. The powerful men became too consumed with the deluge sweeping over their own personal worlds to worry about controlling underlings like Ryland and Bristol, who floated on, rode the tidal wave.

They made themselves useful to Judah Benjamin and General Basil Duke, who had both so fully let go of rank that the boys weren't sure how to address either of them. Benjamin had occupied almost every position of power in the government short of president. Call him Mr. Attorney General, Mr. Secretary, Mr. Senator and he would laugh and say, Oh that's all gone. Call me by my first name. A band of outlaws should travel as equals. So that's what the boys called him. Mr. Judah. He traveled down the country roads the most cheerful outlaw since Robin Hood. His trunk must have been at least half full of fat Cuban cigars—big, dark coronas. From midday until bedtime he always had one fuming, and he gave them away like penny candy to keep the Yankees from taking them if he was captured. He said he was Havana bound and would restock there.

Similar attitude with Basil Duke. He looked like an actor playing the part of a young general. He was smart and handsome and knew it, but he didn't go around puffed up and stiff. He cracked jokes and shared tobacco and rum, and said outright that he thought it a good thing to abolish slavery. Said, Great God, imagine if we'd had the sense to abolish it fifty years ago. He shrugged off the title of general with the ease of a man who expects life to be unpredictable and defines himself anew almost daily.

When Bristol called him General Duke, he said, The country that issued my military rank is dead and gone. Call me mister or sir.

—Sir Duke? Ryland said.

—Damn, that does have a ring to it. But we're all near the same footing now. So I'll call you boys Bristol and Ryland, and you call me whatever you want.

—Yes, sir, Bristol said.

Every morning, sunshine or monsoon, Basil Duke would get up at gray dawn and exit his tent looking fresh, groomed, clean collar on his shirt. Everybody else wandered around bleary, disheveled, weary, and not wanting to keep doing what they'd been doing—which was break camp, load up, and slog down the road another day, clothes dirty and hair greased tight to their heads. The first miles of the day, Basil Duke talked about how well he had slept and how much he admired the landscape and enjoyed watching it unspool. He always said, A bad day on the road beats a good day sitting at home doing nothing.

Every night Basil Duke sat by the campfire like he was posing, finding the most flattering angle of light for a painting. He always had exactly three drinks no matter how late the night went. The younger officers—and anybody else who cared to listen, including Bristol and Ryland—gathered around, and Basil Duke led the discussion. Late, after the older men had bedded down, they laid odds that changed night by night as to which of the politicians would escape. Everybody bet that Judah Benjamin would be the first captured, and everybody but Basil Duke bet Davis would escape. But Duke didn't believe the president wanted to escape.

What Davis wanted most was justification, to defend himself in court and be hanged if he lost.

Odds on Judah Benjamin changed considerably when he took a disguise out of his big trunk—a beat-up brown suit and a gray felt hat with holes in the crown, and a dirty shirt without a collar. He took off alone with two half-dead mules and the most broken-down wagon they had. This happened around Washington, Georgia. He said he aimed for the Gulf, and if he met Federal troops, he planned to use his Louisiana French to act like a lost trader trying to get back to New Orleans—pretend he didn't know a word of English. When he left, he lifted his beat hat from his head, and around the fat, black cigar in his mouth, he said, So long, desperadoes. See you in Havana or Paris.

All that time President Davis seemed strange, aloof from reality. Some nights he lurked at the edge of the campfires, righteous and doomed, skeletal with the firelight on his face and deep shadows under his cheekbones. He muttered constantly about the Constitution, its precious phrases. Saying how he and the other hard men left over from Lee's and Johnson's surrenders would head west and become horseback guerrillas, fighting the Federals—not battles but running skirmishes, covering many miles and several days of desert and prairie. Light and fast. Or he might form an alliance with Maximilian, emperor of Mexico, and return with a vast army to sweep across the South and retake the homeland. Or wear the Federals down over time, make it a hundred-year war. Last resort, the true believers could go to South America and carve cotton fields out of jungle and create a new republic, where the original Constitution and full property rights would rule.

Basil Duke whispered among the dwindling remainders, said that they accompanied Davis only to help him escape, not out of delusion that the war would continue deep into the future.

By the time they reached Washington, Georgia, the remains of the treasury had fallen into Basil Duke's care. He acted as if it were slightly humorous, a burden. He made no secret that it had been represented to him as somewhere between five thousand and five hundred thousand dollars. Who'd lately had time to count? It took the form of gold and silver and other assets, including the Tennessee State School Fund and the old ladies of Richmond jewelry donation program, and it traveled in leather shot bags, green canvas bank money bags, little metal casks and big wooden casks, even money belts stuffed fat as an old gentleman's paunch with coins.

Bristol and Ryland helped transfer some of it from a

train broken down near the Savannah River into wagons. It was a dream night. They worked by light from a scant few tallow candles. By two in the morning they were so tired from lifting and carrying that all the gold and silver felt unreal.

Basil Duke supervised, but in a sort of bored, distracted way. As the loaded wagons rolled out, a man came running after Basil Duke shouting, Wait, wait, you forgot this. The man carried a small wood cask filled with gold coins. Basil Duke took it and said to the man, My God, you're an idiot.

As conclusion to his story, Bristol said that everybody except that idiot dipped a little from the pot that night. Said he and Ryland eased gold coins down the calves of their boots for traveling money and that Ry's gold was still down his boots.

—He's lying there making fun of me for not taking it, Bristol said.

The fugitives crossed the Ocmulgee River after a town called Rhine and then camped near the water. Bristol got down in the muddy river to his neck and grabbled two big catfish, which Ellen filleted and dredged in cornmeal and fried. After supper, Burton and Delrey studied their maps and decided an early start might get them near a settlement called Irwinville before dark.

Next day, afternoon, out of nowhere Jefferson and a last handful of die-hard officers came riding up from behind. V'd worked on the assumption he was halfway to Texas by now, but there he was, pale and wasted, trying to be her savior because he had heard marauders scoured south Georgia for the share of treasure she was rumored to have with her.

Among Jeff's small group was John Taylor Wood, the navy hero, who as a boy had lived in the White House during the brief term of his grandfather, President Taylor, Knoxie's father—so John was Jeff's nephew. Jeff and Wood had invented false identities—Texas legislators on the way home—since they still hadn't fully given up on heading west. Jeff hugged and kissed his family, though he looked so changed that Winnie didn't recognize him and wailed when he tried to hold her. He tied his horse to the wagon so he could ride with V and the children.

Her group and Jeff's traveled together for a while. Jeff said he didn't intend to camp with them, since Federal troops certainly followed him, not far behind. He and his little group would help settle them in for the night, eat supper, and then ride on to divert the marauders. Head for the Gulf and decide whether to catch a boat to Texas. But maybe he'd see her in Havana.

They made camp at the edge of pinewoods above a clear creek down in a swale. A cool breeze came out of the south, and John Wood said he caught a hint of Gulf to the nose, salt air, though they were still two weeks away.

V recognized the place immediately from a dream. It happened there, where the road dipped to a creek bordered with dark pinewoods and then a dry rise toward old open pasture. She begged Jeff to go, keep moving.

He said, Shortly we will. But remember, not all your dreams come true.

—But some do, V said.

Late afternoon, Jeff and V wandered up the creek and bathed alfresco.

They all ate supper right before dark and talked plans—where to go from here, the safest route. John Wood knew people in Florida. A man in Fernandina owned a boat capable of making a run down the Indian River and the coastal lagoons and skipping through the Keys and jumping across to Cuba. Or they could go the other way, hit the Gulf below Madison. Wood knew a reliable man with a boat there too. Except for a few forts, that western path was mostly wilderness, and Federals lay thin on the ground. In his little journal he wrote the names and towns of trustworthy people who owned boats big enough to make it safely across the Straits and tore the page out and gave it to V.

After supper, Jimmie and Jeffy went to the men's fire for a few minutes and then quickly backed away. That ring of faces lit red by firelight scared them. Gentlemen all, the men looked like a gang of bandits and killers and brigands, which some of them had become after four years of war. The Federals considered John Wood a pirate, and except for lacking a black eye patch he looked the part—long hair, face like a blade, and an exhausted level stare that examined the world with cool indifference. A useful man as long as you could keep him aimed away from you.

Long after dark, Jeff still hadn't left. His horse remained tacked and his pistols in their holsters over the saddle, hobbled to graze between the tent and the creek. Jeff and V took the tent on the far side of the road and the children with Ellen took the other. Bristol went across the creek and spread his bedroll somewhere out in the pines. The other men stayed by the fire, dozing but ready to ride.

V and Jeff lay on a pallet of quilts in the tent and he told her how much she would like Cuba. She would learn the language quickly, and with the sea breeze, summer weather was nice in comparison to Mississippi. He talked about his grieving and devastation in Havana after the loss of Knoxie and described the old city as a beautiful feast of loss and sad remembrances.

—That's fine for you, V said. But children need a future to imagine. They don't thrive on nothing but memories.

—Well, he said.

—You should go on. You can't travel at our pace if you plan to escape. Our best day this week was twelve miles. You can go double or triple that.

He said, Maybe I'll head out tomorrow or the next day.

—If you're waiting around to be captured, say so now.

—I'll go soon.

—Don't use us as an excuse. We've dealt with marauders, and we've made it this far. We can make it to Florida and on to Havana, but we can't outrun the men chasing you. You need to go.

—Soon. An hour of sleep and we'll ride the rest of the night and all day tomorrow.

He fell asleep almost immediately, and V lay awake trying to remember the details of her dream, trying to recall bits that didn't correspond—maybe the creek had been more like a river or the trees were oaks instead of pines or the swale had been deeper—hoping to convince herself this was not the place.

Sometime in the night she walked across the road to the men's fire and pulled Burton aside. She said, When they leave, you decide whether you go with them and travel fast or stay with us and go slow. Do what's best for you. I won't think less of you for going on.

—I'm seeing you all the way through, Burton said. No arguments on that point. Go sleep.

Before dawn, unaware of each other, two separate Federal cavalry units converged from north and south. Daybreak May 10, in a light rain, they burst upon the fugitives yelling and firing. Ellen had started cooking breakfast, and the first she knew of the attack was a ringing spang as a rifle ball struck the skillet from her hand. The confused Federals fired their weapons with such degree of enthusiasm and inaccuracy that the only casualties were self-inflicted—killing two of their own before they stopped firing at each other.

The next few minutes became a matter of contention and pride argued over in print for decades to follow. Jefferson's horse was down near the creek, and to escape capture he either disguised himself in articles of V's wardrobe, or else she tossed a waterproof raglan over his shoulders and a shawl over his hatless head as he left the tent. Ellen went along with him, carrying a bucket so they might be mistaken as two women going to fetch water. Northern newspaper cartoonists delighted in depicting the scene with Jeff in hoopskirt, ruffled pantaloon, and bonnet.

When a Federal officer held a gun on V and asked who that was walking toward the creek in the gray dawn, V said it was her mother. Then after they discovered it was the president and seemed eager to shoot him, V stood between them and said they would have to shoot her first, and the young officer said he'd be happy to oblige. Another soldier said that if there was any resistance, they had orders to fire into the tents with the children and make a bloody massacre of it.

After Jefferson surrendered, wild looting. In a frenzy all their baggage was broken open. One trunk had a fat padlock, and a soldier pulled his pistol and fired at it, and the bullet ricocheted off the lock and ripped through his boot and tore his foot apart. Soldiers cut V's dresses and undergarments into scraps for souvenirs, like knucklebones and hair of saints, and one man showed her his long knife and told her to hold real still as he cut a piece from the hem of the dress she wore. They stole or destroyed most of the children's clothes except what they had on, and the last few thousand dollars in hard money that V still had from selling their possessions in Richmond disappeared like smoke in the wind. Ellen held Winnie, and Maggie stood crying silently. A soldier had told the stunned boys to climb in the wagon and not come out.

In the confusion, John Wood eased into the trees and took a Federal horse and rode south toward the scent of salt air. From Terra Florida he went to Cuba and then to Nova Scotia, where he lived out his life. Bristol might have escaped similarly, though V never saw him or heard from him again. She still wonders whether he was killed in the attack and left dead in the woods or if he found his way home and shaped a life in the ruins and forgot all about her. She doesn't even know whether Bristol was his first, middle, or last name.

A young Yankee soldier drove the ambulance with V and Ellen and the children in the back, while Burton, Jeff, and Delrey were under guard farther to the front of the wagon train. When they reached Augusta, the Federals paraded Jeff and V through town to a dock at the Savannah River in an open barouche, ancient with the wheels wobbling. The crowds jeered and hooted. A Federal soldier shouted, We've got your president.

A hard-shell Rebel yelled back, The devil's got yours.

In the confusion of loading onto the shabby little river tug, all eyes fixed on the famous prisoners, Delrey slipped away. V saw him pretending to be working—hauling stuff, lifting and setting down, fooling with ropes—until he melted into the crowd, but she believed at the last moment he caught her eye and touched the brim of his hat with two fingers and then pressed his open hand to the center of his chest.

Late that first night on the river, Jimmie Limber waited until all the other children were asleep. He sat close against V and said, I don't know what's happening.

—You just rest, Jimmie.

—I can't sleep. I don't know what's going to be of me.

V hugged him tight. Said, Nobody knows that anymore. But remember how you and Delrey said you could keep going one more day and then one more day after that?

—Yes.

—That's what we've got in front of us. I'll take care of you the best I can tonight and tomorrow and as long as I can.

==

V pauses and says, A few weeks ago you asked why I picked you up off the street. Why I took you into the Gray House.

—Yes, but you didn't really answer.

—Because I didn't know the answer. But I've been thinking and remembering, and I've come up with a theory. It involves a story I've never told anyone. This happened very early in the war. My father had gone broke again, and I'd arranged a job for him in a government commissary in Alabama, and he died there.

==

V floated downstream through Montgomery streets inside a haze of opiates. She wore a startling mourning dress—fine threads of Mexican silver shaping and repeating a wave pattern all down the snug ebony bodice and flowing skirt. The waist, though, cinched not nearly waspish as before the dead child and the living children. Black veiling blurred her face and enlarged her dark eyes.

Her father had died three whole weeks before, so by now he was no longer leaving—he was gone. V hardly thought of him. The word *father* rested like a distant place-marker in her mind, like finding the cast list for a forgotten play in a bureau drawer, your eye striking the name of the actor in the role of second footman. And despite her lack of feeling toward him, his passing brought on another bout of morphine nearly as strong as after Samuel's death.

She bobbled traversing the slick cobbles. Red clay oozed between them like margins of recent wounds still weeping. Bubbles of medicine, though, levitated her, lightened her against the day, suds rising in a dirty washtub.

She felt the outside world must see her identical to the self she knew inside, unidentifiable and anonymous, disguised in a dim glow, an amber candle flame seen through seaside mist. Nevertheless, heads turned in recognition of the newish First Lady.

Fame. All it means is, people who don't know one true thing about you get to have opinions and feel entitled to aim their screeds your way.

The war was still fresh. Some rushed up asking urgent, impossible questions. When will it end? Will we whip them good and hard? Others needed help contacting a husband or son fighting in faraway Virginia. Help finding the lonesome field where their dead might be buried. Help getting a semi-illegal letter to a relative north of the Mason-Dixon conveying important facts about recent deaths and births in the family, pleading that surely V could help, since it was rumored that she broke the law all the time writing to her own Yankee family. And also, could she pen the message, since the petitioner remained weak in writing but could talk it out to her by heart?

An ancient gray man, Scot or Irish, rhythmic and oracular in his talk, called her Magdalene and cursed her to Hades where her husband would one day achieve his highest ambition and reign supreme. The man swayed and swept his hands in complicated gestures to make his dark dream come true. His long beard and his dingy black swallowtail coat moved with the rhythm of whatever dirge slogged inside his head.

V floated on to the market. A crowd gathered, bidders and window-shoppers. A young woman up on the sale platform saw her and screamed her name. Screamed Mistress V three times like a fairy spell until her breath gave out.

V settled in her walking, a leaf caught in an eddy. She stopped and turned toward the stage.

Everybody looked at the woman there in her loose muslin shift. A slight woman, perhaps seventeen, her dark hair wild and her skin coppery. She went barefoot, her ankles and calves wiry. Her face broke wide open at the eyes and mouth. She stood exposed at an extreme of existence not ever shared by the audience.

The woman called again, Mistress V.

Not a scream this time. Tired and pleading, her arms down, palms open to V alone, making an offering of herself.

The audience turned to V. An ominous swivel of necks and shoulders and backbones to aim hundreds of eyes through the veil into her two. She believed she heard the faint mechanical sound of those thousands of vertebrae shifting, clicking, grinding as the audience pivoted her way.

The woman onstage gathered herself. She drew a long breath and held her arms straight from her shoulders, hands open and fingers spread. She screamed again.

—I know who you are. I know you. You're a good woman. Buy me. You have a daughter. Little boys. I'll take care of them till I die. Buy me.

The sun broke a crack in the overcast, lighting the mute colors of red dirt and dirty cotton and muddy shoes, the black suits and dirty buff linen suits of the bidders. And V stood like a shard of midnight moonlight, ebony and silver, suddenly fixed in place and exposed to the day.

A mumble rippled the crowd. Who is she?

Some of them meant the woman on the platform and some meant V.

—She's a whore.

—She's the goddamn president's woman.

—They both are.

Behind the chatter of the crowd, the woman on the platform kept screaming. Her face torqued by the extremity of the moment and by a gleam of hope focused on a pretty woman in a startling black dress drifting by the stage where the enslaved woman's life reached a pinnacle of desperation.

A man in a Panama hat too new to be dirty even at the dimples where his thumb and forefingers pinched to lift it an inch in respect said, Mrs. Davis, please pay no attention. Her mind's not sound. Look away.

=

—**What I'm** beginning to believe, V says to James, is that when I first saw you, that girl was in my memory. Maybe I did what I did more for myself than for you.

—A second chance? Atonement?

—I had never thought of it that way, but it's possible. Those chances don't come around too often.

—Is that what the man in the Panama said, *look away?*

—I think so.

—The refrain from "Dixie"?

—I doubt that was in his mind.

—That line in the song, *Old times there are not forgotten.* I could argue that maybe they're not worth remembering.

—I've never forgotten that girl, and I wouldn't want to. Remembering doesn't change anything—it will always have happened. But forgetting won't erase it either.

Fortress Monroe

1865–1867

The *William P. Clyde* anchored off Old Point Comfort in that convolution of water and scraps of land where the Atlantic becomes the Chesapeake, and the Bay becomes Hampton Roads, where three rivers empty. Fortress Monroe squatted huge and bristling with black cannons just past the shoreline, among them the Lincoln gun, largest in the world. A fort had stood on that strategic spot since Pocahontas convinced her father not to bash John Smith's brains out with a big wooden mallet. The first fort would have been a small enclosure of earth berms and log palings, but the current one was an enormous, brutal piece of masonry architecture surrounded by a moat. Its final stages of construction had been supervised by Robert E. Lee when he was a young U.S. Army engineer. Also, Old Point Comfort was where the first Africans were set ashore from a Dutch ship in 1619. History loves irony, V thought.

She stood on the deck of the *Clyde,* studying the view and making an effort to believe that ten minutes of sunshine and salt air in fine spring weather might stop her trembling. She breathed and tried not to imagine how her life would go even a few hours into the future, not to wonder what the next loss might be. Directly in front of her, the brutal Fortress. Off to the side, across the mouth of the Bay, Cape Henry and Cape Charles, and beyond those two points of land, the Atlantic Ocean began and the whole world unfolded. She tried to picture a globe. A straight line across the Atlantic from where she stood would make landfall in France or Spain.

All the way up the coast and for a day after they arrived, the children hardly left their bunks, so terrorized that Jimmie had been taken and fearing they might be next. Small boats came and went exchanging messages with Washington. What to do with the prisoners?

Since Irwinville, their group had enlarged to include old friends Clement Clay and his wife, Virginia, and even the postmaster general, Reagan. Also former Vice President Stephens, who weighed even less than usual. His skin crinkled like dried corn husks, and he had spent most of the trip in his tiny cabin nursing his slave, Robert, who had been felled by seasickness.

Old Point Comfort, the Fortress, and history's love of irony drove V back into memory. During the war between Brierfield and The Hurricane, one evening under the big tree, Pemberton told her about the finale of the Black Hawk War, back when Jeff was a young lieutenant in the northern wilderness. Pemberton had been there by Jeff's side as always. Except the war was more a protest or an uprising over failures to honor treaties than a full-on war. The terrible enemy of the United States amounted to about five hundred people, all ages and sexes. The army quickly killed a bunch of men, women, and children and ended the matter. Jeff and Lincoln—both in their twenties—attended that conflict, and might have met briefly. After the army captured Chief Black Hawk, Jeff was put in charge of taking him down the river on his way to prison back east. Pemberton remembered Black Hawk as a man of sixty-four, beat and tired of living. Every river town they docked at, people crowded in, trying to see the famous conquered warrior. But Jeff refused to drag him out on deck for a show. The old chief, who spoke English, thanked him. Said the young chief—meaning Jeff—treated the old chief like he understood what it would be like to swap places. Pemberton remembered that along the way two of Black Hawk's men got sick, fixing to die. Jeff put them off the boat in heavy woods and told Black Hawk they should pass to the hunting grounds together. At Saint Louis, a huge crowd at the dock demanded to see Black Hawk, but Davis stood in front of them and shouted that he wasn't there to give them a show, a lion stuffed with straw, or some mummy king from Egypt. And the irony part was that at the end of his journey, the prison where Black Hawk ended up was right there—Fortress Monroe. And Black Hawk's vision of Jeff swapping places with him was about to become prophetic.

General Miles, the twenty-five-year-old officer in charge—he'd been a shop clerk before wartime brevet promotions elevated him—had made the announcement. Jeff and Clement were to go straight into Fortress Monroe. Burton to Old Capitol Prison in the shadow of the Capitol dome in Washington, where Mary Surratt and the other assassination conspirators awaited trial and hanging, and Stephens to Fort Warren on an island in Boston Harbor. Burton looked terrified, and Stephens seemed dazed, as if the announcement had been made in a foreign language. All V could do was look at Burton with tears in her eyes and touch her lips as he was taken away.

Jeff and Clement Clay were frog-marched down a narrow wood dock to a shoreline where crowds of on-lookers, jeerers, scofflaws, and journalists waited. A soldier walked by Jeffy and said, Oh, stop crying, baby. I doubt they'll kill your father. Jeffy wiped his eyes and said, When I grow up I'm killing every Yankee I see.

Next day the papers said Jeff's manner remained haughty throughout the public part of the ordeal. What did they expect? Contrition? Little General Miles took him not through the main gate to the Fortress but over the moat into a little side door through the thick walls and into the casemates. Jeff's cell was a sort of burial between wide-spaced stone walls and beneath twenty feet of soil growing grass, all supported by subterranean low brick arches seeping moisture and growing mold. A dim meditative space suitable for penance. That or digging deep into self-absolution and bloody-eyed self-righteousness.

All the servants—enslaved black, free black, white—were taken away, and Miles wouldn't say where they were going and wouldn't let her write a letter to General Saxton to ask about Jimmie. Wouldn't let her write to anyone. When they took Ellen away, she and V wept, and the children pleaded uselessly with Miles not to separate them from Ellen.

Then, before the *Clyde* turned around and headed back into the Atlantic for Savannah, Miles had V's last few articles of clothing confiscated as evidence that Jefferson had dressed as a woman in Irwinville to elude capture. Virginia Clay tossed pieces of her own wardrobe—petticoats and stockings and a hat with a plume—onto the pile to confuse the matter and lighten the moment. Then, as a parting gesture, Miles had V and Virginia Clay stripped and searched by two garish Norfolk whores hired for the job. Several soldiers and an aide to Miles stood and watched.

Through that summer she lived under house arrest in a fairly nice hotel in Savannah, which after months of flight and capture would have been a relief, except she could not communicate with her husband. All she knew about him was gossip reprinted in the papers—that he had been shackled and chained. Soldiers guarded against her escape, but they let the children outside to play. The guards taught them to sing the John Brown song with the words *We'll hang Jeff Davis from a sour apple tree.* They convinced the children that V would welcome a serenade with it. When the children finished, V kissed them one by one and then walked downstairs and through the lobby and out onto the street and told the soldiers they could shoot her if they wanted or beat her down with their rifle butts or throw her in prison, but she was laying a simple curse on them that could never be lifted. After they returned home—even into the next century when they would be old grandfathers—every time they wanted to tell their glorious tale of teaching Jeff Davis's children that silly cruel song, they would feel small and ashamed for what they had done to innocent children.

She couldn't communicate with Jeff, so she wrote letters to the old friends and acquaintances and dinner guests who still had influence in Washington. In letters to President Johnson, she begged for better treatment for her husband and to have her house arrest lifted. The president never responded directly but dismissed her to the press as an angry woman.

She read *Our Mutual Friend,* which she enjoyed, and then *Anatomy of Melancholy,* which she thought was scientifically filthy, but she copied a few words from it into her notebook—*a ruined world, a globe burnt out, a corpse upon the road of night.*

Around that time her mother took the children to Canada, hoping to find a safer place where they could go to school without being threatened. V wept when they left, of course, but for a while she wept whenever her body generated fresh tears. Every day offered its own calamity until she finally ran out of tears and became numb and then kept going.

Gradually, V's travel restrictions were eased. First she could walk in four of Savannah's beautiful squares closest to the hotel, and then eventually she could go anywhere in the city. Mostly she walked at night along the bluff over the river because it reminded her of childhood—moonlight on the water and lights from the boats and in the windows of houses on the far shore—except Federal detectives followed her and questioned anyone she spoke with beyond saying, Good evening.

Eventually the restrictions allowed travel within the borders of the United States. But the children in Montreal remained off-limits, and she still couldn't visit her husband, couldn't even write Jeff a letter without government censors striking out every word not related to family matters, wifely concerns. Her mother had left her some money, and a few generous friends sent what they could spare. When a Federal officer gave her a small box of things they'd confiscated, V found her little pistol and nothing of value. She said to the officer, I'd much rather have the gold and silver coins you took from me in Irwinville.

Burton Harrison, though, had just been released from his imprisonment, and he took the loyalty oath and came straight south to meet her in Savannah. Burton had not quite reached thirty, and V still lacked a little of being forty—though the war had aged them both in unspeakable ways. When they first saw each other V held him tight and said over and over, My beautiful boy. Burton still coughed from the damp prison, and his chalky face seldom looked anything but blank. They traveled together for nearly two months, viewing the vast wreckage of the South.

They first went to New Orleans and stayed a couple or three weeks resting in their new freedom, breathing deep breaths, visiting old broke friends like General Wheeler, who had found work in a hardware store selling nails and nuts and bolts—the opposite trajectory to vile little Miles at Fortress Monroe who had risen from shop clerk to general.

The city retained its shabby beauty—spared the destruction of Atlanta and Columbia because it had fallen to the Federals early in the war. Bureaucrats and army still swarmed in great numbers, intent on reshaping New Orleans in the image of their beloved northern cities. Some days—though still beautiful—New Orleans felt like a corpse and other days like a ghost.

Every morning they walked through the French Quarter, enjoying Deep South December weather, stopping to drink strong black coffee at a place with outdoor tables and bougainvillea blooming rich against a south-facing wall—every day telling each other chapters of their stories since being parted on the *Clyde* at Old Point Comfort. Burton said, That first part—a very bad time.

He told her how they'd taken him up the Potomac to Old Capital Prison and then Fort McNair within sight of the Capitol dome. The Lincoln assassination conspirators faced trial there, and the Federals attempted to bribe and coerce Burton into confessing to having a part in the conspiracy. They offered him total clemency if he would testify that Jeff had been in contact with Booth and the others. The Federals even marched him into the courtroom to watch some of the trial and conviction of Atzerodt, Powell, Herold, and Mary Surratt.

At one point Burton found himself in a room with Surratt's daughter, Anna. The Federals hoped the two might say something incriminating to each other. Burton described Anna as handsome and pitiful and terrified. She wore a white bandage around her forehead from having collapsed on the steps of the White House after President Johnson refused to listen even for a minute to her pleas not to hang her mother. Burton said Anna's face looked like it belonged on a Roman coin and that her eyes welled with tears the entire time he sat with her. An older woman, clearly meant to provoke information, asked them leading questions for hours as if they knew each other, but Anna was too stunned to speak and Burton was too smart.

Burton said he didn't see the simultaneous hangings, but he heard everything from his cell—the constant clatter of lumber and hammering for two or three days as the big four-person scaffold rose, and then on that hot day a murmuring crowd and solemn voices, a deep silence in the cells. Then a loud crack as all four traps opened at the same time. Next day, right in the middle of the path he usually walked in his few minutes of sunshine, a row of new graves spaced like beads on a string. He said the words twice—beads on a string.

Burton told how hard the Federals kept trying to hang him too before finally giving up—not so much convinced of his innocence as of the weakness of their evidence. They moved him to Fort Delaware, where he was the only prisoner in the big lopsided, star-shaped fort on Pea Patch Island that had once held ten thousand.

After fifteen days of rest and rich New Orleans food, Burton looked less gaunt and ghostly. They caught a steamboat upriver, stopping in Natchez with plans to stay awhile. But once settled into a modest hotel V realized no one she wanted to see in her hometown remained. She didn't want to go out to the graveyard and ponder Winchester's marker—he wasn't there. He was in her heart and her head every day. At The Briers she enjoyed the river view, but there was nothing else for her. So she and Burton rested and read for a few days, and then moved on toward Davis Bend to discover whether anything of value had been left after the Federal sacking.

In letters to friends posted during their journey, V settled on a formula to describe Burton, calling him *all in the world to me.* Why not? He had sacrificed so much for V and Jeff, and his loyalty had cost him his youth.

The big mansion at The Hurricane wasn't even a picturesque ruin of a plantation house. V walked the perimeter and found heaps of rubble, foundation bricks, a few burned stubs of great columns. The hole of the basement opened to the sky, and she looked down onto massive crazed timbers and dunes of gray ashes. She thought she saw a long, curved metal handle that might have worked the pump to raise water three stories high to flush Old Joe's amazing toilets.

Joseph was pathetic, diminished, ruined. He lived in a bedroom of the guesthouse and would have seemed pitiful to any humanitarian who hadn't suffered under his personality since seventeen as V had. She gave him a nice robe she had bought in New Orleans, and the old bastard looked so low and broken that she added four hundred dollars cash to the gift—money she didn't really have to spare. Men often age pathetic that way, even the meanest of them. Old toothless lions that once bit your hand off begin wanting a pat on the head.

Joseph wasn't even the owner anymore. He had sold Davis Bend—The Hurricane and Brierfield both—to Benjamin Montgomery, the man who'd picked V up at the dock on her first visit. Payments of $18,000 a year, a portion of which would go to Jeff. All V could think was that she hadn't been allowed to communicate much more to her husband than that she and the children missed him and loved him, but Jeff and Joseph had managed to negotiate the sale of an enormous ruined plantation to their former slaves.

———————

At dinner that first night, Joseph sat at one end of the table and Ben sat at the other. Ben still wore his goatee, now threaded with white, and his green eyes still gave nothing away, his face a perfect mask.

Ben's two daughters—very excited—told V all about going to Oberlin College the next year, asking for her advice on the classes they should take, their wardrobes. They treated Joseph like a beloved hoary grandfather and kept asking if he needed anything, kept checking to see if he was eating enough. More biscuits, Mr. Davis? Another spoonful of brown gravy on your potatoes? You're getting too skinny—eat another piece of cake. The girls were nearly the age V was when she first fell off the boat from Natchez naive as could be.

Strange as it seemed, it all made sense. Essentially, Benjamin had been running the whole place for years—keeping the books, writing most of the correspondence, managing Brierfield too after Pemberton died—so it wasn't a great stretch in terms of logic for him to become owner. It was a great stretch when it came to history, though.

End of the evening, Benjamin said to V, I hope this new arrangement isn't distressing to you.

—No, it isn't. Do you remember the first time we met?

—Yes, but I didn't expect you would.

—That day, riding in from the river, could either of us have imagined tonight?

—I could have. Or something like it.

V and Burton rode out to Brierfield very sedately in a two-wheeled gig. As soon as they came in sight of the house, Burton pulled back the horse. Across the horizontal white boards of the front gable, someone had swiped big red words with a paintbrush—THE HOUSE THAT JEFF BUILT. They'd been warned that the place was intact but had been looted to emptiness by Federal troops before being used as a school by the Bureau of Refugees, Freedmen, and Abandoned Lands. But V had to see for herself.

They sat and looked, and then Burton said, Do you have memories? Does this make you sad?

—I never want to see a picturesque plantation house again.

On the way back to The Hurricane, she told Burton how Benjamin had invented an effective shallow-water propeller for riverboats and had tried to patent it before the war, but the Federal government denied his claim because as a slave he was not legally a citizen of the

United States. So Joseph and Jeff tried to patent it for him in their names, but that didn't work because, obviously, they hadn't invented the device, since the patent office already had Ben's drawings and descriptions and whatever else a patent application required. She'd asked Ben about it after dinner, and he said that immediately following the war when he and all the other freed people had become citizens, he applied again to the federal patent office, and again the answer was nope—without even a reason given.

For old times' sake, maybe, Ben drove V and Burton to the dock himself. Before they boarded he said to V, My son, Isaiah, and I want to make a place for free black people here on Davis Bend. A community. Come back and see how we're doing sometime.

—If I ever pass this way again I certainly will. And please ask your girls to write and tell me about their college adventures.

V paused and then said, I'm reminded of a young man I knew not long ago—a phrase he used. New world coming.

—Yes it is, Ben said.

V and Burton headed upriver planning to make a big, leisurely northeast curve with plenty of stops along the way—Memphis and then Cairo and onto the Ohio River and eventually by railway to New York City. Between the Bend and Memphis, they enjoyed a stretch of perfect, warm winter weather—blue days, yellow sunsets, deep crisp nights of air so dry and clear that the bowl of sky filled with stars. V lacked optimism for a future, so one afternoon she suggested to Burton that since they were together on the wide Mississippi—no guarantees such a moment would ever happen again—they should go on and fulfill their promise to each other early. Wine, water, sunset.

Burton, surprised and a little embarrassed, said, I feel a century older than that boy.

—Let's call it a celebration. We've survived to see what happens next, even if it's grim.

So after an early dinner in the salon—sun setting over the water in colors of gold and silver, brass and iron—V and Burton found chairs on the hurricane deck above the bow. A lone kite glided over—scissoring its forked tail, banking and pitching as it swooped close by the pilothouse. A dense flight of swallows formed shapes against the sky like a child molding a dough ball, never quite creating a convincing box turtle or dog's head or teapot, but still moving from idea to idea with beautiful fluidity.

V and Burton sat long through the evening with

two bottles of fairly good Bordeaux dated before the war, scavenged by the captain from a private stock he'd stored cool below the waterline. They touched glasses in unspoken toasts to avoiding disaster that day and then they dinged spoken toasts to lifelong friendship.

Down toward the bottom of the second bottle—both of them laughing, shawled in blankets—V raised a glass proposing words she wanted Burton to say at her funeral. She said, I've been working on it, and I'll keep refining it over time, but write this down for now—*Had I been consulted about the cosmos, I should have criticized its parts with great vigor and complained about the result, in fact I—as at present informed—should have resisted imposing Adam's society upon Eve as an infliction of boredom not justified by a paternal government.*

—Really? Burton said. That's what you want at your funeral?

—Think of it as a closing argument. At least it will get a laugh from Mary Chesnut.

A couple of weeks later when they parted in New York, V hugged Burton close and then held him out at arm's length and said, Till death do us part, yes?

Eventually President Johnson's attention became distracted by his own impeachment trial, and his urgency to hang Jefferson subsided. V was given permission to visit her husband, who had been moved from his cell to a small aboveground room because the doctors thought he might die from the damp casemates. Then after a great deal of lobbying, she received permission to live at the fort, and she and Jeff were given quarters in a house with a narrow bridge from the top floor over to the ramparts, and they could walk the mile circuit of the fort with wide views of the bay and Hampton Roads. Jefferson's lawyers began to feel a little hope that the Federals lacked the nerve to try him, fearing they would lose their case and be forced to free a vindicated Jefferson Davis on the world.

Eased from dreading the worst by having it mostly happen, V tried out the idea that she was still theoretically youngish in body and mind. She started going out to the beach at Old Point Comfort at dawn and swimming with the young wife of an officer. When they made it a distance offshore and turned to start back, the huge black cannon barrels of the water battery loomed like a cresting wave. Sometimes when she wanted to swim or to walk beyond the walls and the shopkeeper General Miles tried to stop her, she'd remind him that she was not his prisoner. He agreed he couldn't legally make her stay inside the walls but suggested that if she needed total freedom she might find rooms with the whores in Norfolk, since she already knew a couple of them intimately. Otherwise, she should remember he had the power to have her stripped to the skin and searched again for any reason—including his own amusement—every time she came and went.

—The newspapers will love that story, she said.

Late afternoons she walked down the sand past shiny black devil's purses, beached jellyfish, sandpipers dashing at the waterline, black-headed gulls standing solemn as deacons, and brown pelicans skimming the water to fill their pouches with little fish. Before sunset, the sky domed soft and blue or flat and gray, and ospreys hovered high, bracing still as hummingbirds against the sea breeze and then plunging, wings tucked, into the water for menhaden and spot. She watched the ospreys so often and so long she realized they usually shifted the fish in their talons to carry them headfirst as they flew away. Always the hiss of low bay waves on sand and the shells of horseshoe crabs like empty helmets.

One particular sunset, a few folks from the town gathered on the beach to fry oysters dredged in cornmeal in a big iron skillet of bacon grease over a beach fire. Men shucked the oysters and threw the shells into a pile, and a woman patted the oysters into a trencher of cornmeal and slipped them into the grease. A few older people sat on three-legged stools and the rest on old patchwork quilts spread over the sand.

They invited V to sit and then continued their conversation. One man told how strong his garden had come in and how sad it was to watch the unpicked excess tomatoes fall from the vine.

A woman said, And yet you never give anybody produce other than squash as big as your arm and soft as a sponge. I'd welcome a basket of fresh tomatoes anytime.

The gardener said, Doesn't matter what you do, people complain.

One of the younger women eventually said to V, You're one of the women that has her man locked up in there?

—Yes, V said. A year now.

—Buried under those thick walls?

—He was by himself beneath the casemates for a long time and got sick. But they finally let me take care of him and now we have three rooms of a house.

—Not as bad, then?

—Much better.

An old man with salt-and-pepper hair gone far back at the temples shifted tone and told a story about courting a girl long ago, how he tried to impress her with his horse, which was really not much of a horse to impress a girl with. He said it was a five-gaited gelding—walk, trot, canter, fall down, get back up. But the girl married him anyway. Sadly they never got any children, but happily they lived like newly-weds for forty years, walking on the beach together every evening the weather allowed, except during the worst of the war.

People around the fire said things about how much he must still miss her and how often they remembered her.

After a pause one of the women said to V, You fish much, ma'am?

—Well, I've always enjoyed watching it done.

The man with the horse story said, We've been trying to be polite, but we know who you are.

—Yes?

—I don't know how to say it any way but one. We all hope they don't kill your husband.

—Thank you for that. I hope so too. Down in Savannah the soldiers taught my children to sing a cheerful song about hanging their father.

—They'll back down, the woman cooking the oysters said. If they wanted him dead they'd never have let him out from under the fort walls. The dirt is so deep over the casemates you can bury a body there. And besides, why make a rival for their own martyred president on purpose?

Everyone sat quietly for a long time. Gray twilight rose from the eastern shore like a morphine daze. And then the horse man said, I bet you have plenty of stories to tell.

—A few, V said.

But all she could remember at the moment related to seafood, a spring when she was twenty or so, the run of shad ascending the Potomac at Washington and men on the shore and out in boats setting seines. Lines of huge cork floats held the top ropes of the seines, and fat lead sinkers dragged the bottom to create a wall of netting. At night, oil lanterns fixed to the cork floats cast yellow light in long bands across the dark river. V told them about riding in an open carriage in the soft spring night, probably feeling all plush from some recent social success and a couple of glasses of wine. She watched the fishermen draw the nets and haul shad in by the thousands. The fish struggled, a roil of packed muscular life, their diamond scales flashing in lantern light.

That recollection did not prove completely satisfying to her audience, so she told the one about her father and the shooting match. She began by saying, Picture a muddle of wealthy ignorant Mississippi gentlemen, drunk and armed with muskets, in a raw patch of new-cleared ground, their horses and slaves shaded at the edge of the woods.

But now the story that seemed tragic when she was younger had become comic, and she successfully played it for laughs.

V sat among the storytellers until the colors of sky and sea balanced themselves alike into a single shade of slate, and she questioned if she were over or under the water, over or under the sky. Only the red coals of the cookfire broke the general blue-gray and fixed a point in space.

The cook spooned more oysters into the hot grease.

V said, Would you have a dozen of those to spare? I know he would like a few.

Moments later, V hurried back through the sally port with a napkin bundle of them, hot and greasy, eight to give to Jeff before they went completely cold and two each for the young guards at the gate who appreciated her treats of candy or pastries and welcomed her comings and goings. She always had something for them, even if only a hard peppermint.

The heavy cannons of the ramparts and the water

battery almost disappeared in the dark. The two boys at the gate—young enough to be her sons if she'd had children right after her marriage—ate their oysters in gulps and one of them slightly groaned at the pleasure of it. He raised his fingertips to his face and breathed in the salt sea of the oysters and the earth of bacon grease on his skin.

He reminded V of those thousands of young dying men in the hospitals of Richmond. Northern boys and Southerners, blown apart by war, lying swaddled in bloody bandages, their limbs and the features of their faces blasted away. How difficult on her daily visits not to tell them to go right ahead and die at that very moment of young life while still ruled by a rising tide of emotions, those same emotions old cynical politicians and businessmen and army officers used against them to convince them to fight and die. Hard not to hold their chilly hands with ragged dirty nails and push the long hair back and kiss their sweaty brows and say, Don't wait, do it now, not decades later when every throb of feeling ebbs, every action and choice becomes tinged with regret and harsh judgment, a sense of waste and loss and emptiness, life narrowing down to little more than an endless railway tunnel. Let go, son. It will be all right. Take one deep breath and then just rise from this bad place and from your broken body and keep going. I'll sit here with you and hold your hand until you've made it past the bend in the road and into the green woods.

And truthfully, one time she couldn't help but actually say it. She whispered into a boy's ear like a sweetheart, Walk into the big green woods. I'll wait here and watch until you're gone. She said it hardly louder than a sigh, and—like a magic spell—the boy died right then. Holding his hand, she could feel life go, the lifting of the spirit, a sudden lightness. And then that young man blown apart by the sorry war became young and whole forever.

Two years after his imprisonment, Jefferson and V left the Fortress and went up the James to federal court in Richmond. They stayed at the Spotswood Hotel only because few downtown hotels had been rebuilt after the fall and the fire. They agreed not to talk about staying there when they first arrived in Richmond.

Next day the court granted bail, and wealthy Yankees like Horace Greeley and Cornelius Vanderbilt put up the money, largely as a way to clear the last rubble from the war and help the country reunite and move forward. Jeff was free to go, though the treason charges hadn't yet been dropped.

They went straight back to their room in the

Spotswood. Jeff sat in a straight chair and looked out the window. V flopped onto the bed and lay staring at the ceiling blank as a corpse. Half an hour later, Jeff said, They lost their nerve. I didn't lose mine.

V, still staring at the ceiling, said, Yes. I never doubted you'd be willing to let pride dig your grave in that damp casemate. You already had dirt twenty feet deep over you.

=

On the way back to Albany that evening, James Blake writes:

Especially since I found the blue book, I've come to see Mr. Davis and his beliefs this way. He did as most politicians do—except more so—corrupt our language and symbols of freedom, pervert our heroes. Because, like so many of them, he held no beloved idea or philosophy as tightly as his money purse. Take a king or a president or anybody. Put a heavy sack of gold in one hand and a feather-light declaration about freedom in the other. And then an outlaw sticks a pistol in his face and says give me one or the other. Every time—ten out of ten—he'll hug the sack and throw away the ideals. Because the sack's what's behind the ideals, like the foundation under a building. And that's how freedom and chains and a whipping post can live alongside each other comfortably.

Sixth Sunday

Saratoga Springs

Race days, surreys from the hotel travel to the track every half hour. James and Laura and V ride three across—V in the middle, talking brightly about the horses and her strategies for betting, the latest gossip concerning owners and trainers and jockeys. She knows all the Kentucky thoroughbreds here now, shining like waxed walnut or coal or bronze in the sun, their strange names and individual personalities.

Laura says, I like to watch them eat their grain from their buckets. They're so serious about it. And I want to kiss their velvet noses, except racehorses are nervous and some of them bite.

—Do you bet? James asks Laura.

—I always bet everything I have with me on the

first race—the horse I think has the funniest name. I quit when I run out of money.

—Except she never does because she wins most of the time, V says. She refuses to tell me her real system. Mostly the horses she bets don't even have funny names.

—Funny to me, Laura says.

James says, I'm just going to observe for today.

Laura leans her head on V's shoulder and closes her eyes.

James asks, How did *Hamlet* go?

—Because it's a movie—no talking, all pictures, and film is expensive—the filmmaker went through the play with a red pencil and cut it to twelve minutes. Kept the ghost and the skull and all the killing and dying. Swordplay. And since our Ophelia is beautiful, they boiled her parts down to mostly embracing and kissing the prince. I played the aggrieved ghost. Flowing robes, white face, black around the eyes like a raccoon.

Laura barely opens her eyes and says, I couldn't even look at her.

They walk the rows of low stables and watch horses being groomed and tacked. The ones running later in the afternoon stand in their stalls and reach over the half-doors to pull hay from their nets. Laura holds V's hand much of the time, particularly when they approach knots of people.

Some of the grooms have known V for years and whisper tips as they pass by. They say, Missus V, Cairngorm's a little off today. Blue Girl's full of herself, about to jump out of her skin. Sir Visto looks good. Spindrift's ready to run. Ten Brooks and Asteroid about like always, like they know their jobs.

One groom says, This your family visiting, ma'am?

—Three generations, V says.

Just before V and Laura place bets on the first race, James says to Laura, I believe I know how you're betting.

—I never say.

—I'm sure of it. It's Cairngorm.

—How's that funny? Laura says.

—The sound of it?

—Not funny at all, Laura says.

—You'll know how she bet when her horse comes across the finish line first, V says.

—She makes it sound like I never lose, Laura says.

—Have we ever left at the end of the day and you have less money than you started with? V asks.

—Well, no. Because that's not the point of coming.

————

On the ride back, V talks about a book on Eastern religion she's reading. She says, Like most religions, they have something to say about the consequences of bad actions, of hubris, of sins against others. Karma.

Laura says, I know about that. It has to do with going around in circles, life after life, until you come to your senses and become less horrible and get to move on.

—That's reincarnation, dear. A different thing entirely, V says.

—But related, James says. Like together they're a gentler substitute for hell, with the possibility of an exit door.

—I'll loan you the book when I've finished, V says. We can talk about it.

Laura says, I've slowed it down so much I can take a deep breath between notes.

James says, "Sunflower Slow Drag"?

—When we get back, I'll play it while you two talk. But don't come stand over me to appreciate it.

V and James sit halfway across the lobby while Laura plays the piano. She leans forward so that her hair hides her face and plays notes that sound like wind chimes on a nearly still day.

James says, I keep struggling to remember Ellen, but the pictures in my mind are so vague I think I'm making them up.

Thief of Lives

1877

The crossing was perfect, beautiful and calm and dragging so slow that everyone except V complained. At the dinner table, passengers kept saying, You get what you pay for. Cheap tickets mean saving on coal by creeping across the ocean at a walking pace. But V traveled in a mood happy to foot-drag. She had never seen the North Atlantic so blue and glassy. The ship's library held quite a few good books, and every day she sat on deck and read and breathed long and slow, counting three Mississippi both in and out.

If she allowed her thoughts to move beyond the present moment, toward her destination, she clenched in the diaphragm and her breath pinched short. Her homeopathologist in London had recommended *Aconitum napellus* for vague fear and panic sweeping in strong waves, sleep disturbed by dreams of the dead. And *Kali arsenicosum* for the opposite, which V found confusing. Opposite of fear? Opposite of vague? Of strong? Of dead? One or the other potion was also supposed to help with fear of crowds and with sinus congestion, but the scrip didn't clarify which one. She took both, and nothing happened, so she took opium in her wine.

A few months before her voyage toward America, she had traveled all the way across France to visit a doctor in Karlsruhe, where Winnie was now in school. She'd imagined Karlsruhe differently. Jeff had settled Winnie into school there, and he had given V the inaccurate impression that the Rhine flowed right through town and snow-covered mountains towered just to the south. As it turned out, the town's main attraction was that it lay a day away from actual interesting places without being one itself. She found a room in a guesthouse with a partial view of a tall church steeple.

V had not written to Jeff in a while—months, in fact. Before long, a note came, forwarded from her London apartment: *How are you and where are you?*

In Karlsruhe Winnie was busy with school, so they mostly saw each other on Sundays, leaving V free to visit Doctor Richter three times a week. He was a few years younger than V and had become renowned for his ability to diagnose mystery illnesses. One of her doctors in London had said her poor health was no mystery—when she felt so washed over with panic and terror that she couldn't breathe, she was having a heart attack. Richter, though, began seeing her with no preconceptions. He checked her reflexes with a rubber hammer and looked into her eyes and listened to her internal sounds. With various large and small calipers, he measured every dimension of her head. But mostly he was awfully interested in her personal life and emotions and history. They talked for an hour or so each visit.

He asked, When was the bottom? The worst?

—Impossible to say.

—Try, please.

She told Richter that most people would probably say it was when she and the children lived fugitive on the road like escaped convicts. But the truth was, the shape of her life wasn't a deep U or a sharp V that you went down into and came up out of. It was a saw blade, jagged and dangerous from end to end.

Doctor Richter had a big upholstered chair in his

consulting room, and V sank into it very comfortably. His voice was quiet and even, so soothing that most days she dozed off for a few seconds as they talked. The children interested him—the dead ones and the live ones equally.

V told him she had always tried not to define Maggie as a Davis and Winnie as a Howell, but that's how it was—a correspondence of personalities. V loved Maggie, but at heart she was smart, chilly, serious, mercantile, single-minded. Maggie and Jeff were always very close, so much alike. Winnie, though, was a Howell—smart, funny, emotional, impulsive, open-minded. She and V were alike in most ways, except that Winnie loved everything about boarding school—the girls, the teachers, the classes, the dormitory and dining hall. V, on the other hand, couldn't name one redeeming moment of her months at Madame X's.

She told Richter about Samuel and Joe, their very different personalities. She guessed Samuel would have been a Howell had he lived. After Joe was born, she fell into a deep depression because he looked like a Davis, and as if that hadn't been bad enough, Jeff wanted to name him after his brother Joseph, who had been cruel to V from the time she was seventeen until middle age. They argued and Jeff would not relent about the name. All V could do was pray little Joe would not share all the Davis traits and might outgrow looking like one, though whether her prayers were answered remained unclear at the time he fell off the balcony.

Jeffy was the most Howell of all, probably too much so. Nothing interested him more than jokes and having a good time. If he couldn't find trouble to get into, he created some. He was still finding his way in life after trying out a number of schools and colleges. Billy, though, had a personality totally his own, and Jefferson thought he would be their great success, except he died at ten of diphtheria. Those hopeful messages in bottles she had sent out during the dark times before the war—so many washed back.

Some days Richter wanted to talk about Jeff. The sources of their attraction, the sources of their disaffection. V told him about Florida's Big Bear Theory, about her own romantic sense of marriage at seventeen—the woodcutter and the plump heir. She said, Jeff seemed like all of those things back then. And it wasn't his fault she saw her choices so simply.

One day Richter floated fourteen syllables out to her during one of their sessions.

Mania = Fury
Melancholy = Fear

He recited the words, his voice rising in pitch, tentative and with a hint of a question mark at the end.

—It's like a poem, V said.

—What I'd like is for you to think about the equations, and if seeing them as a poem helps, then fine.

At the end of her time in Karlsruhe, Doctor Richter announced his diagnosis like he was Newton under the apple tree.

—You suffer from misplaced malaise, he said.

V said, Well, malaise of course.

But even leaving the war out of it—looking back at the loss of children, marital challenges, lack of a home for a decade, financial ruin, recognition of fundamental moral failure—how exactly was her malaise misplaced? Which horror had she emphasized too much or too little? She certainly hadn't lost track of it like a house cat that wandered off.

Richter got fussy and prideful at her question, her challenge. He didn't want to debate. He prescribed walks in fresh air, a diet heavy on bread made from Graham flour, doses of valerian and laudanum alternating every eight hours.

She told him that since the age of thirteen, under doctors' orders, she had taken every amount of opiates from feather-light to locomotive-heavy, sourced from dirty traveling-show tinctures to white pharmaceutical purity. And yet malaise persisted, impervious, and right in its usual place. With two fingers she tapped the center of her chest three times.

V never wanted to see the South again. But she had run her string near its frayed end. She and Jeff always got along best apart, even back when she was young and he was middle-aged. When geography separated them, their letters became sweet. Months passed, a year, and time bleached them clean of resentment. He sometimes sent her pressed flowers from special places. Harebell growing near Sir Walter Scott's grave, jewelweed blossoms growing along a path at The Greenbrier, accompanied also by Mary Chesnut's love and the good wishes from so many old friends summering at that beautiful Virginia resort, all of them suffering together in the depths of their poverty. On her side of the correspondence, V mostly documented her worry about his eyes and his diet. One time, when she was in London, he came across the Atlantic to see her, but when he got to Liverpool he decided on a spur-of-the-moment tour of Scotland and some of the northern European countries alone. Another time, she agreed to join him on a ship back to America but changed her mind after a rough crossing of the Irish Sea and kissed him good-bye in Dublin and went back to London for her health. All that time of wandering, he traveled Europe as a man with no country, no papers, just his own recognizance to get him across borders. V mostly enjoyed his letters and believed she and Jeff could live happily married for decades caring deeply for each other by post, eventually receiving death notices by telegram. But the surviving children didn't work that way. At some point it was go back or be forgotten.

Baltimore. Hotel Barnum. Dickens's favorite American hotel and V's too. Also meeting place for Harpers Ferry conspirators and Booth's gang of assassination plotters. V stayed as long as she could afford, which amounted to only a week.

As soon as she registered, V learned what a mess she had sailed into. Waiting for her were numerous letters from friends welcoming her back to America and informing her that Jeff currently lived in Biloxi with a woman, Sara Dorsey. The widow Mrs. Dorsey. Great glee in sharing the news.

V had been in school with Sara for those few months at Madame X's in Philadelphia. All she remembered of Sara was her membership in a huddle of malicious thirteen-year-old girls who entertained themselves by commenting on V's shade of skin, her unnecessary height, her pride and precision in translating Greek and Latin.

Halfway through the stack of letters, V opened one from Jeff informing her of what she already knew, that he no longer called the Peabody Hotel home and had also changed plans on renting a house in Memphis. He was enjoying the hospitality of their mutual friend Mrs. Dorsey. V should plan on joining him at her home, Beauvoir, on the Gulf near Biloxi. He reminded her that she had once loved Biloxi's beaches. As she was surely aware, Mrs. Dorsey was a novelist of some reputation and offered considerable help to Jeff in composing his memoir.

V ripped open all the rest of her letters hoping to find a cache of money, a forgotten bank account, or an inheritance from her New Jersey people allowing her to turn right back across the Atlantic to London and see if 18 Upper Gloucester Place, Marylebone, was still available. Had she been a man she would have walked out the front door of the Barnum and spent the night in dives drinking, losing her last dollar in card games trying to win a stake, a bundle of getaway money.

Dreams troubled her in the Barnum, which never happened in previous visits. Her sleep swirled with details of her old life. Dark rooms swelled with furnishings long since sold or given away or abandoned in flight. Bookshelves crowded with spines of lost books, lapping dense as reptile scales. She could read titles and authors stamped in gold, and sometimes her vision could penetrate the binding to read penciled notes in the margins. Small sculptures and ceramic figures rendered precise down to fingernails of tiny long-fingered hands too delicate to touch. Intricate patterns of Turkish rugs and the warp and weft of upholstery and drapery fabric. Three hundred sixty degrees around the walls of the room, her lost artworks shone in brushstroke detail.

But the last thing she wanted was to revisit all the physical matter of her previous life. She resented it shouldering into her dreams, disliked the way being in America made her mind turn back to regrets and losses. In London, most days, she could almost forget the past. Even on the worst days, details of her old life seemed like a museum exhibition, artifacts to study and understand in historical context.

To fight Barnum dreams, every morning V wrote three lists on separate pages of hotel stationery. A page for things in the dreams she resented and didn't wish to see or think of ever again—things consigned to the burn pile. Another page for things she still liked but had no room for in her mind or her life. And last, a short list of precious things she missed and hoped existed somewhere in the world whether she saw them again or not. Each night before bed she burned all three pages in the fireplace.

Day by day the lists grew shorter and the dreams less detailed until V began to hope that soon all she would have to burn would be blank pages.

But the things she couldn't stop missing and dreaming about were a few lost paintings and a half-dozen books she'd had since the days of Winchester. One tiny watercolor—a few watery brushstrokes suggesting a view across the Potomac to the raw new capital—appeared in her dreams night after night. The last time she saw it was the day she and the children fled Richmond. In the Gray House she had placed it carefully, at seated eye level, over the desk in her dressing room. She had framed it deep and thick and dark with a band of gold leaf around the opening, leaving the watercolor a bright beauty, precious inside its large box.

For three nights of dreams she passed through rooms and saw her little watercolor from before the war. In some of them it grew large enough to cover a wall. In other dreams it appeared over and over in endless replication like a wallpaper pattern.

When money ran too low to keep staying at Barnum's, she moved to the boardinghouse Mary O'Melia had opened when she made it back to Baltimore after the war. They hadn't always gotten along perfectly back in the Gray House, but now, on more equal footing, they loved each other for remembrances that nobody else had, strange and noble and stupid things done or said by important people within the Gray House. And tiny moments with the children, such as Mary recalling how nervous Joe became when General Lee—at his most graybeard imposing—asked, What's your name? Instead of Joseph Davis, Joe quickly said the first two consecutive words that rose into his mind, Eight Nine. Lee congratulated him on his unique name, shook his tiny hand.

Mary's place was five bedrooms, and she ran her establishment as if a horde of inconvenient distant family had descended on her unannounced. Anyone showing up more than twenty minutes late for breakfast went hungry. The fact that they were paying guests didn't excessively influence her behavior toward them. Mornings, V sat by the fireplace while Mary directed a pair of young housekeepers, just as she had done in Richmond. She looked so much the same except her pretty, broad face was broader, and gray threads scattered evenly in her dark hair, and she no longer even tried to moderate her judgmental direct gaze.

V sewed, mended Mary's bed linens so as not to be idle.

—Do you remember a little watercolor in my dressing room? V said. Mostly taupe and green and blue? Very small with a large dark frame? Nearly this big?

She held up her hands and touched her forefingers and thumbs to make a rectangle.

—Not in particular, Mary O'Melia said. You kept the walls so cluttered I couldn't say.

—I hoped you might remember that one over my desk and might know what happened to it after I left. I loved it and would never sell it, but it might be valuable now. The artist has become famous.

—I kept my eye on Lincoln when he came, so I don't think he took it.

—He might have had too much on his mind to pilfer.

Mary said, He walked about sitting on all the furniture. Like marking his territory. Every damn chair and chaise he needed to plant his ass for a minute. Gloomy-looking fellow. Like winning the war made him sad. But also like breakfast made him sad, if you see my point.

—I never knew him, V said.

—But the Custers . . . Dear God, the way they carried on. I wouldn't put a little looting past those two.

—Carried on?

—She barged in straight from Washington—parts of Richmond still smoking—and went straight up to your big bedroom and set up camp. Made sure I knew what an adventurer she thought she was, coming into war territory. Messengers came and went all in a rush. She told me to have a hot bath drawn. But there wasn't anybody left. Just me and that little thin kitchen girl Edith, and she couldn't do much but cry. So I carried up a basin of warm water and a used sliver of yellow kitchen soap and a washcloth and towel. Missus Custer looked at it like I'd opened the lid on a full chamber pot. She said, What do you expect me to do with that? I told her that it was the best I could manage under the circumstances and that many a grand lady throughout the history of the civilized world had been forced to take a whore's bath now and then.

—No, you didn't say that to Lizzie Custer, V said.

—I damn well did. She wasn't paying my wages. The only reason I hadn't packed my valise and walked out the door was that the house needed caring for and because I hadn't quite figured where else to go, since the trains to Baltimore weren't running yet. So to get back to the point in my tale where I was interrupted, come about midnight, young Mister Custer gallops up straight from the battlefield, throws open the front door without knocking, long saber rattling in a scabbard at his side, red faced and greasy blond hair hanging down from his hatband past his collar. Had been riding for hours, and he more than sort of smelled. Didn't say a word to me other than, Where is she? I lifted my thumb straight up, and he climbed the steps two at a time with his scabbard clashing against every baluster. He stopped at the top and shouted down to send up a few bottles of the best wine or whiskey you've got, immediately. The headboard banged the wall half the night. Next morning at breakfast, he looked half drunk still and his face the color of flour paste. But she came down bright-eyed and rosy, barefooted and still wearing a silk shift so thin that when she walked by a window you knew everything there was to know about her.

—Sounds like they found fun in that sad old place.

—I couldn't take much of it. As soon as the trains started running north, I packed and left.

One morning Mary mentioned that Ellen was to be married in a week, out between Harpers Ferry and Shepherdstown. Mary said, It's not so far. We might go together? Out on the train early and back late after the wedding. A long day, but the schedule works. I wrote her you were here.

—I haven't been invited, V said.

—I'm doing that. She's afraid to ask directly, worries you're angry with her because of what she said after the war to a New York paper.

—What?

—The reporter asked her how you were, Mary said. You know, as a master or owner or whatever you people called it back then. He was looking for dirt, I guess. Ellen said you were fine. Nice enough. But that she much preferred not having an owner.

—Why would that make me mad? It's generous of her. And who wouldn't rather be free? Write her back and tell her I'll happily come. I'll even sew her a pretty summer dress for a wedding present.

And yet, V kept thinking, Just all right? Nice enough? We were friends.

V took a guess at Ellen's current size based on the fact that everybody seemed to have swollen some with the passage of time. Except probably Mary Chesnut. And of course Jeff, whose flesh drew year by year closer to his bones. So for Ellen's dress, V left plenty of fabric behind the seams in the parts where it might need to be let out.

=

—**Wait, James** says.

—What?

—Even years after the war, you thought of Ellen simply as your friend?

—It felt that way.

James opens his notebook, turns pages looking for something he wrote on the train three or four weeks ago.

—Here, he says. Pemberton. You talked about the complexity of his relationship with Mr. Davis. You found it dark and ominous, a relationship twisted and falsified by ownership. Always a vast imbalance of power with the threat of violence. How did your husband and his brother put it? That the solution to the fundamental problem of capitalism was slavery, making labor and capital one and the same? He didn't address the methods necessary to keep human beings under control to make his system work.

—Their ideology, not mine. He and Joseph were of one mind on that. Ellen and I were women raising children and keeping a complicated household going during a difficult time. Not men with power. It didn't feel nearly as ominous as Jeff and Pemberton.

—Ominous to Ellen, though, I would think. Look at what she said very politely to the newspaper reporter about freedom. Think about it. Remember that back in the Gray House, every hold she had on her own life, any sense of security, ran straight through you.

===

Ellen's wedding was a quiet, middle-aged sort of ceremony. V and Mary were the only white people. All the others were farm families making a living off of twenty acres, or else people with jobs in the nearby towns, men who worked for the railroad, women who managed households for wealthier people. Ellen's husband was named Gabriel, a slim, balding widower with hazel eyes. They had a green farm with a big vegetable garden and cornfields and potato fields. An orchard of apple trees, a few hogs and a milk cow and a plow mule, and a yard full of chickens and ducks and turkeys and guineas. A small white house with a green roof and a big porch with red rocking chairs and a brown hound dog and Gabriel's two young girls named Rhina and Tay that Ellen kept hugging and kissing before and after the ceremony until they squirmed and laughed and ran away and then ran right back for more.

Gabriel came to V and said, Missus Davis, welcome and thank you for coming. It means a lot to Ellen to have you here. I hope you're comfortable.

V said, It means a lot to me to be here. Ellen and I went through difficult times together, and I'm happy to see her new life.

—Things are different now.

—Yes they are. And I'm very glad these are better times.

The weather that day was fine, so the ceremony happened at the bottom of the porch steps. Guests spread across the front yard, some standing and some sitting on quilts. For afterward, people brought ham biscuits and fried chicken and bowls of vegetables and pies. After lunch, V hugged Ellen tight, and said the first stupid thing that came to mind, Be happy.

Ellen laughed and said, Oh, I've been being happy almost all the time lately.

V laughed too and kissed her cheeks.

Ellen said, The thing seeing you has got me wondering about most is Jimmie. We split his mothering between us.

—The truth is, you were with all of them more than I was those years in Richmond. I can't tell you much. I wrote to General Saxton while Jefferson was still in prison, but the general already passed Jimmie on to someone else, a teacher so he could continue getting an education. Not knowing his real name, that's as far as I could get.

—I didn't know it either. But he was a smart little boy, and I like to think he's still out there in the world somewhere.

—I do too, V said. My boys keep fading away.

—Jeffy the last one left? Ellen said.

—Yes.

Ellen just shook her head.

Later, as V and Mary were leaving to catch their train, a man walked by and said something as he passed. He didn't look at V, just spoke and kept walking. She wasn't sure what he said, but she was *pretty* sure. Thief of lives.

In the railcar V sat quiet trying to think of other words—three syllables—that would sound similar. But nothing matched.

Halfway back to Baltimore she said to Mary, I'm glad to see you both settled. To have a place in the world.

Mary turned her head and looked closely at V. She said, You're not becoming the kind of woman who weeps at weddings, are you?

—I'm just glad.

—Question arises, though, do you have a place in the world?

She kept finding ways to drag her feet on the way from Baltimore to her reunion with Jeff in Mississippi. She had written two letters to him saying she had no intention of crowding in on his cozy situation at Sara Dorsey's beach house. Maybe she would find a room in Gulfport or Pass Christian and he could stop by for visits now and then. Talk about the children, try to remember past happy moments, swap favorite current books.

She counted her money and calculated the time it would last. For lack of other destination, she decided to go to Richmond and spend a few days looking in the used shops for the lovely things she had not been able to eliminate from her dream lists. On the way down, she reckoned anyone from the war years she cared to see again had either died or fled. The remainders were people she wished to avoid. At the hotel desk she signed the register as Mrs. Howell.

V told herself she would not do it, but she did. The first morning, she walked by the Gray House to stand at the place on the sidewalk where Joe fell from the balcony and died. Nothing remained. No bloodstains, of course, but not even a feeling. No faint trace of that bright little boy hovering nearby waiting for her to reappear and apologize for letting him slip away.

Same thing out at Hollywood Cemetery standing by his marker in the green grass, nothing but absence, a hole in her life that would never fill. Her dead boys lay all scattered—Sam in Washington, Joe there in Richmond, Billy in Memphis.

V opened the door and a spring-loaded bell jangled its warning. One more in a string of shops she had visited looking for remnants of her past. Not exactly an antique shop, just a dim used furniture and dinnerware and decorations shop on a back street. Brown light fell through the storefront window, and the ancient melancholy smell of dust and lost lives breathed out through the open door. Once inside V looked back as if to identify her route of escape. The name of the store's proprietor lettered backward on the glass, black against the light—SAMOHT MW.

At the front desk a skinny man read a book without looking up. Black suit with great notched lapels spreading to the bony points of his narrow shoulders, the collar of the jacket standing three inches out from his shirt collar. When he finished displaying his superior ennui and apparently reached a good stopping point, he marked his page and looked up and studied the newcomer.

V could see the change in him when he recognized

her. That quick bright spark, and then the immediate suppression of it.

—Yes? he said.

Finally, a long deep breath later, he added, Ma'am.

V knew it would be the carefully measured pause and the irony in his tone that would represent a point scored and would comfort him all through his days, proof of his precious individuality and refusal to bow to past fame and present notoriety.

—Just looking, V said.

—For what?

—I'll know if I see. Don't let me interrupt your reading.

But he climbed down off his stool and followed her through the store, either afraid she might slip something up a sleeve or probably just wanting to observe her for recounting details of her visit later—how she scavenged for bargains on secondhand crystal and once-fine tablecloths.

V found a few shards of her old life. Scraps, nothing more. Random pieces of Limoges, Sèvres, Spode. A favorite gravy boat with its lid broken and poorly glued, two dinner plates, six teacups and two saucers, three place settings of her silver pattern engraved with the swirling *D* of their monogram, five Murano wineglasses—beautiful with slight variations from stem to stem—that came from nine or ten dozen she once owned. She didn't touch anything, hardly looked.

She walked all the way through the store to a back window with a vista down toward Shockoe Bottom and the railroad and river. A large crow or small raven passed across the scene, a black presence coasting on spread wings. But not really oracular, just nature commenting on recent history in a pretty obvious manner. A swelling black thundercloud full of lightning would have served equally well.

The skinny man hovered behind her until she moved along toward the front door. But along the way she noticed a familiar frame on the wall and walked to it. Her tiny Whistler.

A small tag hanging from twine showed a penciled price, just a number without a crass dollar sign—5.

V turned to the man and said, I'll give you three dollars.

—The frame itself is worth at least five.

—I see scratches. And I'll have to find something to fit it. It's an odd size.

—If three's all you have . . .

—*Have* is not the point. Three dollars is what I'm *willing* to pay.

—I'll wrap it, and it will be ready tomorrow afternoon.

—Wrap it, and I'll take it with me, V said.

That night she propped the Whistler on a table and looked at it a long time—a little faded but still so beautiful.

She had bought it—just the little rectangle of thick paper—one day while Jeff was secretary of war. He walked her through the offices and workplaces of the department. In a large room with tall windows, young men worked at drafting tables drawing maps. As Jeff explained what they were doing—the process and the importance of mapmaking for the nation's defense—V noticed a slim almost-boy with long curly hair hunched over a large paper. He would have been pretty but for the nose. She walked over and said, Excuse me.

He looked up at her and then saw Jeff standing across the room and quickly stood and nodded his head and said, Ma'am.

V admired his map in progress and then noticed on his table a rectangle hardly larger than a postcard, fewer than two dozen wet watercolor brushstrokes muted and pale. Nevertheless, V recognized the view from Arlington across the Potomac after sunset with

the raw capital city hazy and hopeful in the distance.
She bought so many paintings then.

She said, I like that very much and would like to
have it.

He said, Please take it. It would be my pleasure for
you to enjoy it.

V said, No, this is too beautiful not to pay.

She gave him twenty dollars—a flashing double
eagle fresh from the mint—and wrapped the thick
paper in her handkerchief and eased it into her beaded
reticule.

As they walked away, Jeff said, What was that about?

—A watercolor.

—Yes?

—I gave him twenty dollars.

—My God. He's recently been booted from West
Point. You could have gotten it for fifty cents.

—He wanted to give it to me, V said.

—Why didn't you accept?

—Because I wanted to pay.

She had met Whistler again at an exhibition in
London. He had become famous. The press variously
made him out to be either a grand fop, a fraud, or a
genius, as if those were mutually exclusive. Either way,
prices on his paintings had become mind-numbing.

He didn't remember V until she mentioned the little watercolor and the shiny twenty-dollar gold piece, at which he rushed to kiss her cheeks and said, loud enough for the whole room to hear, You never forget your first sale.

V said to him, I've always wondered about something—probably because my husband barely escaped it himself—why did you have to leave West Point?

—Misbehaviors and misdemeanors, Whistler said. But it was the last and worst in a series of unsuccessful chemistry exams that finished me off. I was asked to discuss the subject of silicon. My essay was so lovely. The first sentence was brilliant. It read *Silicon is a gas.* And if silicon had been a gas, I'd be a general today.

From Richmond V zagged over to The Greenbrier hoping to find Mary Chesnut or at least a few other people who might welcome seeing her, but the guests were nothing but rank strangers. After a week she moved on to Lexington—the one in Kentucky—and then down to Nashville. All along the way she and Jeff traded letters, always very politely exchanging suspicion, jealousy, resentment, blame, shared history, love of the children.

In one exchange he wrote that all he had left to plead

was poverty. If she objected to him accepting Mrs. Dorsey's hospitality, where else would she have him go? He was writing his eyes blind every day trying to dig them out of their hole. She wrote back reminding him of an old saying about being in a hole. Quit digging and start building a ladder. She told him she had drawn her money down low, and then Jeff's return letter claimed he had almost none left to send her. So she asked, where would he have her go?

She spent six weeks of dwindling dollars in a shabby boardinghouse near the river in Memphis. Every evening supper was the same colorless mess—bowl of boiled potatoes and another of stewed chicken. She bought carrots at the market and gnawed them raw in her room just for the color.

She wrote Jeff a birthday letter:

This is your birthday, and I write, not to remind you, but to show that I have not entirely forgotten the day. How very sad anniversaries become. They are for the young and hopeful and for the very old and hopeless. A spark of expectation reveals the gloomy, weary waste.

A few days later she counted her dollars and then gave up and bought a ticket to the Gulf.

Before the last leg of her journey V kept thinking about schedules. Jeff had sent a note saying Sara Dorsey planned a dinner for the three of them, about seven or seven-thirty the evening of her arrival. V's train was to reach Biloxi at five. A carriage would pick her up at the station and deliver her to Beauvoir.

Leaving an hour or so at the cottage to, what? V wondered. Unpack? Greet? How do husband and wife behave after a year or so apart? She imagined a couple in their twenties, their first evening after only a few weeks. Oh, my. Then imagine this couple. V in the latter days of her forties and Jeff sailing headlong against the shoals of seventy. What then? Complaints of aching joints? Grudging liniment rubs? Attempts to renegotiate grievances three decades old? Refight every battle long since lost?

V decided to arrive twenty-four hours earlier than Jeff's and Mrs. Dorsey's careful plans, just to be able to take a breath and collect her thoughts. Reconnoiter. She had her trunks held at the station and stayed at a two-dollar hotel in Biloxi, a town she knew from before the war. It had been nice enough then, broad beaches, tourists in the warm months. Now the town huddled barren at the edge of the Gulf, ragged and brown as a scab. The railroad station, three hotels, three general stores, and a few dozen houses—some grand before the war—stood unpainted and in poor repair because now you had to pay people actual money to get such jobs done rather than just buying the people and owning their labor forever. Lumberyards and docks for fishing boats mostly appeared idle. She read a local paper and found that Biloxi had become the kind of town that gets awfully excited about prospects for a new fish cannery. On the streets, so many men were broken apart from the war. A crutch in place of a leg, a pinned-up empty sleeve, scarred faces lacking noses, eyes, ears they tried to hide in the shade of a low hat brim. The worst of them wore bandannas or frightening leather masks across half their faces, leaving the horror underneath to the imagination. All the way from Baltimore to Memphis she had seen the same.

Taking the grand scheme—leaving the *mal* works of humanity out—Biloxi was only a wee ugly interruption of luminous Gulf and dense pine and palmetto scrub forest, a place scoured periodically by hurricanes, plagued by malarial mosquitoes, fat snakes, and thick bull alligators submerged to the nostrils in black swamp water, dreaming of an epoch before man. Nighttime, the air ripped with their bellowing.

She walked along the beach remembering long ago, when the children were tiny, spending five beautiful months in a rented beach house west of town. Give the children buckets and spades and they could occupy themselves for hours at the shoreline while V sat in a sling chair under an umbrella and read. Jeff came once or twice to visit for a few days when he had politics or business in New Orleans. She had been so happy she stayed past the summer and halfway through November. All the tourists went away and the days drew short and almost cool. Humidity drained from the air, leaving the sky pure deep blue. Most days, after supper, she and the children went back to the beach and stayed until the moon and stars appeared. She had wanted to own a house there. Nothing elaborate—a place where little sandy feet and smears of jam sandwiches on the furniture would be welcome. So Jeff bought a dozen acres stretching from the water back into alligator marsh. But they never built the house. Events got in the way. Now, all the children she planned to build it for had died or grown up.

At five the next afternoon, pretending she'd just arrived, V met the carriage at the station and was carried down the sand road from Biloxi to Beauvoir. When they turned off the road to the house, the broad beach and Gulf stretched on one side and lawn on the other. Beauvoir was not grand, but it was pretty, with big windows and deep galleries. The main floor sat at the top of tall steps so that hurricane tides might surge underneath with minimum damage. Jeff's cottage was a miniature of the main house, a small square with porches around three sides, a parlor across the front half with tall windows on three sides, and two tiny bedrooms across the back.

Quarter past seven, V and Jeff walked across the lawn from the cottage to the house. No flirting, no holding of hands. They walked as if wearing armor. Inside the front door, Sara and V hugged, kissed cheeks. It went as intended, polished and utterly empty. V had done it a thousand times in Washington and Richmond with people she loved and people she hated. She could hardly remember what Sara looked like decades before at Madame X's. A short blondish girl, maybe. Now Sara looked very middle-aged and graying and very comfortable in her home.

They sat in the parlor for half an hour and drank Sazeracs heavy on the absinthe. V set it aside, too much like sucking a licorice stick.

—How was your trip from Baltimore? Sara said.

—It was travel. Annoyances and delights. I took my time getting from London to here. How many months has it been?

—Well, whatever. I'm so happy you've finally arrived. Jeff's work is moving forward at a steady pace and I'm sure your presence will only speed it along.

V sat and looked at them both, watching for a flicker. A particular gradation of intimacy.

Sara said, It is a difficult story he's trying to tell. Just the truth of it is hard enough, much less making sense of it. Never mind all that business of interpretation and reinvention.

V said, I read things now about the South back when we were young, and it's like they're describing Arcadia and believe it really existed.

Jeff sat with his eyes away from the light. Five tall triple-hung windows looked out to the Gulf, and he aimed his head just to the side, like trying to see a faint star. With his dim eyes, his view might have been nothing but beautiful rectangles—horizontal bands of gray water and blue sky—set in a cream-colored wall. He tipped his head as if listening to the rhythm of low waves breaking and drawing back against sand, over and over, a black mesmeric hiss.

—Jefferson makes daily progress on his book, Sara said. Some days good and others less so. But pages accumulate.

—Don't look at your feet. Look far down the road, V said.

Jeff entered the conversation, saying, By that you mean, what?

—Where you want to be rather than where you are. A wagon driver said it to me somewhere in the northern part of Georgia.

—Well, Sara said, you're right about the long view. Poets can burn themselves in the sun for a single poem, a page. A book, though, calls for shade and time. That applies even to the entertainments I've written, and much more so to the history of a nation, its rise and fall.

V barely suppressed her laughter, a stage gesture meant to be readable from the upper balcony. Meant to provoke. She said, The Confederacy was not the Roman Empire—just four apocalyptic years. A blink of the eye with a horrible cost. Walk around Richmond or Lexington or Biloxi and count empty sleeves and pant legs and face masks.

Jefferson seemed not to hear, maybe listening exclusively to the tide.

Supper ready, they moved to the dining room. Sara said, I hope our simple food here on the Gulf suits you. The boats didn't come in with good fish today, so we're having oysters and shrimp, potatoes browned in bacon grease, and greens from the garden sautéed in the same pan. For a salad, sliced red and yellow tomatoes with oil and vinegar. And for dessert, fruit. We're casual here. Fanny does the cooking and puts it on the table family-style and we serve ourselves.

Afterward they sat together on the gallery and watched the light fade over the water, shades of blue and yellow and gray. A breeze sometimes rattled the palmetto fronds. Sara and Jeff had tiny glasses of Chartreuse, which she said they habitually took as a digestif, a ritual of the evening—an abstemious, medicinal, astringent toast to strength for the coming day's work.

V had glasses of white wine with dinner and a few more on the gallery instead of the Chartreuse. She began talking about Karlsruhe, her trip across France to visit Winnie in school and consult with a doctor, a specialist in her sorts of distress. She described how well the dry air had agreed with her. Or she with it.

Jeff said, The soft, damp air here is delicious.

At that point V rose and without a word walked carefully down the long stairs to the lawn and then dashed, or sort of bustled, around the side of the house and then stopped to decide which direction to flee. Jeff walked to the end of the gallery and looked down at her, but with his eyes so dim he would have seen little but a darker shape against the grass. He said, Oh my.

Sara said, Please stay here. Do not follow.

—Yes? he said.

V rushed toward the dark woodline of big live oaks and palmettos and pines.

Sara followed down the steps and across the lawn as V struggled through the trees toward the alligator swamp. A trail of footprints and broken twigs.

V stopped a hundred yards in, at the muddy edge of black water. She sat on a log, her skirt wet at the hem and winding around her legs, shoes and stockings muddy past the ankles. She cried out of anger and fear and shame and exhaustion. Weariness of wandering.

She looked up at Sara and said, You?

—This isn't the kind of thing he does well, Sara said.

V raised her hands in surrender. Said, How the mighty have fallen, yes?

And then she began laughing.

Sara laughed too and said, Carpe diem? Remember our Latin tutor?

—No. That's not what it means, V said. Never your best subject.

—Wait. I do remember something. Where be the roses gone, which sweetened so our eyes?

—Yes, V said. Back then a line like that meant nothing, but it's what we're searching for now. The snows of yesteryear.

Sara sat down beside her on the log.

—I don't know what you imagine or pretend to think, she said. And to a degree, I don't care, except when you try to use it to gain an upper hand. I'm not hiding anything.

Sara told how Jeff arrived in Biloxi—sick and worn down and out of money. She had help to give, and she gave it—a refuge free of encumbrances, whether money or anything else. A refuge to write his story.

—You've always been welcome here, Sara said. God knows this is no elderly love nest, and if you stop and think for even a minute you'll know it as well. Unlike you, I've never had a taste for old men. He lives in the cottage, and I live in the house. I send over a tray with breakfast and lunch so that he can work on his book undisturbed. He takes dinner with me. I ask how the great work has gone today, and he always gives the same answer—Incremental advancements. Which I tell him is the most any writer ought to expect.

—I love objectivity, V said. It's so entertaining to hear others try it.

—Correct me if I am wrong, but we didn't much like each other in school, did we?

—Not in the least.

—I had been there two years when you arrived, tall and slim with huge dark judgmental eyes. Strangely so, since we veterans thought we did all the judging. Your skin so smooth and without blemish across those high cheekbones.

—But also a shade darker than everybody else, which you all used to your advantage, V said.

—Of course we did, and I'm sorry. But think about it, throw out all the stupid little belles and even stupider banking and railroad princesses, and who would have been left except the two of us? We're too old to keep acting like girls.

Sara went on to tell how Jeff arrived at Beauvoir beaten down, near broken, slim as a crane. Looking to see what had become of that little piece of land on the Gulf he bought twenty years before for V and the children but got too busy and rich and powerful and responsible to worry about. Twelve acres of beach and scrub, the last thing he held clear title to in the world. Past the tideline and the sand burrs and sea grass, nothing but woods so thick he had to thrash his way to the back property line at the swamp. He sat at her table that night pretty beaten, claiming he'd hardly spent a month sleeping in the same bed for most of a decade except for two years of Yankee prison where they kept him awake with light in his cell all night, guards shouting at him periodically, loud chanting of "Yankee

Doodle Dandy" at three in the morning. He said he'd traveled all over England and Scotland and Ireland and most of Europe job hunting with no success.

—He told me you were still over there, sick, Sara said. Or maybe just sick of the South and of him and wanting to live anywhere but here. He is poison up north. You know that. Couldn't get a job blacking boots without wearing a disguise.

—Not long after the war, V said, he declined an offer to be president of a college high on a mountaintop in Tennessee, gave itself the grand name University of the South, like Virginia and North Carolina hadn't already had colleges for nearly a century. It didn't seem like enough money, but thinking about it now, I can imagine living up on a green mountain in a pretty white president's house, rebuilding a life.

Sara said, In Virginia, at the college where Lee presided, they made a shrine of his horse's grave, so imagine what they're doing now that Lee himself has passed.

—Constructing a three-quarter-scale replica of the Great Pyramid of Giza?

—Even Stonewall's amputated arm has its own gravestone. And yet Jeff shows up here looking like a scarecrow if you snatched all the straw out and draped the weathered suit over a cross of old gray tomato stakes. He looks out at the world like an archer peeping above a parapet to see what new enemy lays siege now.

V sat and stared into the dark woods, the gray moss swagging from the trees, the flat black water.

She said, I understand there are snakes down here nine feet long, indigo colored with the undersides of their necks yellow.

—You don't often see them that long, Sara said. Six feet or seven mostly. They're beautiful in the sun, and they run from you and hide in the bushes and eat rattlesnakes for breakfast.

—I worry a great deal about his book, V said. He was good at writing speeches. Bursts of opinion and belief and knowledge shaped to entertain a crowd for an hour. A book is different. Longer, but not just longer. In a speech, you say something foolish, you can deny it later. Fog in the wind. You can claim faulty remembrance on the part of audience and press, then recast your thoughts in a better direction. If you happen to say something brilliant, all you have to do is keep saying it, and it sticks. But a book binds you to it forever, every damn word, from the moment of publication. All those permanent black marks on paper. You think you own it, but over time it owns you.

—He's doing fine, Sara said. Learning as he goes. And since I've written a few books, I try to help.

—Yes, I keep intending to read one of yours. But as for Jeff, so far I've always been the one helping him write.

—He enjoys help, doesn't he? He was a man of action when he was younger, so now I try to encourage him in the day-by-day sitting still at a table draining memory dry to fill blank pages with strong words. The lore of the job. The necessity of taking small pleasures where they come—the acidic smell of the inkpot, the texture of paper passing under the nib, cool wet air in the afternoon when a thunderstorm passes. And we haven't even gotten to the joy of revising yet, which unlike life allows you to go back and rethink and make yourself better than you really are. I'm trying to help him see his days at the desk as honorable work, forward motion, effort toward some effect other than wandering two continents blind and aimless. Even if the work comes to nothing, he will have these days to shape the past, make sense of how the runes fell against him.

V laughed and said, You make it sound like chance, roll of the dice. But that's not the case.

She talked awhile, developing an argument that they—she and Jeff and the culture at large—had made bad choices one by one, spaced out over time so that they felt individual. But actually they accumulated. Choices of convenience and conviction, choices coincident with the people they lived among, following the general culture and the overriding matter of economics, money and its distribution, fair or not. Never acknowledging that the general culture is often stupid or evil and would vote out God in favor of the devil if he fed them back their hate and fear in a way that made them feel righteous. After years of loss and reflection, your old deluded decisions click together like the works of a watch packed tight within its case—many tiny, turning, interlocking wheels, each one bristling sharp-toothed with machine-cut gears. The force of every decision transferring gear to gear, wheel to wheel, each one motivating a larger energy going in no direction but steep downward to darkness at an increasing pitch. And then one morning the world resembles the wake of Noah's flood, stretching unrecognizable to the horizon, and you wonder how you got there. One thing for sure, it wasn't from a bad throw of dice or runes or an unfavorable turn of cards. Not luck or chance. Blame falls hard and can't be dodged by the guilty.

V and Sara stood and gathered themselves.

Sara said, We don't have to be enemies.

V leaned into Sara and kissed both her cheeks and said, Thank you so much for coming.

She performed it like saying good night at the front

door after one of her famous soirées in Washington long ago. Frogs croaked nearby, and in the distance, the mighty belch of a bull alligator.

—Let's walk back together, Sara said.

—Shall we? V asked. Why not? With the moon rising so big and bright.

They climbed the steps to the gallery arm in arm. Jeff rose to meet them, a thin pale presence, his face and hands exactly the color of moonlight and his linen suit perfect.

—Wonderful that you've both returned, he said.

He kissed V's damp cheek and then kissed Sara's.

The Gulf lay flat, almost a mirror, only a breathy hiss of tide. Sea grass, sand, water, sky—everything a shade of slate.

They all three sat up until after midnight talking, laughing, drinking more wine. Sara and V remembered schoolmates in Philadelphia and how explosive and frightening Madame X could be when angry. Jeff told a story about the northern wilderness when he was a young officer—a hairy, raging monster people called the Windigo.

When they grew sleepy and began aiming toward bed, V said, I wonder what people talk about who've destroyed their lives with addictions other than books and politics and money and war?

After the Deluge

1879–1893

S ara Dorsey died of cancer—sort of willing Beauvoir to Jeff and sort of selling it to him. Afterward
V and Jeff lived in Sara's beautiful haunted house on
the Gulf for their longest stretch of years together. Add
up the time in Washington before the war, four years
in Richmond during the war, and their decade or so at
Beauvoir after the deluge, and they were together little
more than half of a forty-five-year marriage.

At Beauvoir they gardened, read, walked on the
beach in good weather, corresponded with wide-cast
acquaintances. With increasing frequency they received
telegrams announcing deaths of friends and important

figures from Washington or the war. She helped Jeff write and revise his articles for the *North American Review* and other journals. Winnie, off in school as usual, dropped by for a month or two now and then. Maggie married and went west with her husband, and Jeffy—last of the boys—died of yellow fever in Memphis. He was twenty-one and had been the least Davis of her children—never responsible enough to suit his father, prone to impulsiveness, easily bored. He shared some of V's gift or curse of dreams that presaged the future. She and Jeff had gotten word he was sick, and yet neither of them went up to see him and to take care of him. She still can't explain why. It was a long trip, and they were old. Though to be precise, she was not even fifty-five at the time. Maybe it was certainty that he would recover or overwhelming dread that he would not. Either way it was a weakness, a bad decision for which she would always carry guilt.

For years, mostly a quiet life on the beach after decades of clash, disaster, loss, failure. As Jeff neared his eightieth birthday, V often had to remind herself how much younger she was. Some days felt like a competition to determine who had become more attenuated. Like many old men who had been always ready to fight, to plunge into rage, Jeff eased down in his eighties. He became dependent on V and almost sweet.

Long afternoons he sat on the porch looking at the water or on a bench in the garden when flowers bloomed. She asked him what he thought about for those silent stretches of time, and he said, The longer I'm here, the more I seem to remember. Every day, the past flowing in.

She still considered time with smart people to be the honing steel to her dull blade, but life on the Gulf passed mostly solitary. Now and then, friends from long ago livened a few days and then went away leaving a lonely, quiet void. All of them graying, time-draggled, still recognizable but looking as if they wore costumes and makeup for playing a role. Burton Harrison, ever faithful, came by a couple of times a year when business brought him down from New York to New Orleans. He and his wife, Connie, had succeeded among the Yankees. Burton was busy and wealthy with many clients in the railway business, and Connie had begun publishing novels and having her plays produced.

A few times a year Mary Chesnut sent brilliant, scattershot letters, often on scraps of mismatched paper like war shortages still applied. She always said her book was almost done—except it needed to be overhauled one more time—and that so many of her old acquaintances—but not V—would hate her after it was published. And then, without warning, Mary Chesnut died after only two days of illness and distress in breathing alleviated by heavy morphine. The letter V received from one of Mary's nieces said she was buried in a cold November rain. You don't get to choose who you outlive, so V ripped the letter to shreds and shaped in her mind an alternate funeral for her friend, a bluebird spring day and Mary a hundred and ten years old instead of sixty-three, the last bright repository of all their dead memories.

During her days of mourning for Mary, V kept remembering one of the dark times in the middle of the war, having regular breakfasts, receptions, and matinee musicales at the Gray House for a small group of friends like Mary and Buck Preston, who made her laugh. Society ladies not invited kept asking Mary Chesnut what they did at their gatherings. Mary grew weary of the questions—the constant pumping for gossip—and said they danced on tightropes. V said, Better not tell them that. And Mary said, They swallow everything whole. This time next year they'll all claim to know the lengths of our petticoats and the patterns of spangles sprinkled on them.

On one of his famous book tours, Oscar Wilde came for dinner. He had been in New Orleans being scandalous and lionized and wanted to come meet the great Rebel, Jefferson Davis. Afterward, an editorialist for the *Boonville Pleader*, a paper from up the river, wrote that the evening must have been like a butterfly making a formal visit to an eagle.

V thought the simile ought to be an old weary badger ruminating in his den uninterested in the value of fluttering quickness and flashing color.

Wilde arrived bearing flowers, several bottles of wine, and a signed photograph of himself. V greeted him in the foyer, holding out her hand, but he leaned and kissed her on one cheek and then the other. He called her My Dear throughout the evening.

He towered above Jeff by half a foot or so, which may account for a little of Jeff's attitude that evening. Every angle of Wilde expressed itself awkwardly. Long feet, long shanks, long nose, and long hair, dark and swooping. As he talked he waved his hands and fluttered tapered fingers with dingy nails. They seemed only partly under his control. His shoes needed polishing, and the stockings he affected below his half-trousers were laddered with runs. His long face was highly asymmetrical, one side serene and earnest, the other smirking and snide, a simple matter of the angle of his mouth, the slant of his eyes, the apertures of his nostrils. He wanted so much to be famous. Such an attractive and repellent quality.

At some point in the evening V said, Dear boy, please draw a slow deep breath. Now count three and release it. Now another. Rest easy in the fact that since I was seventeen, I've known few unknowns.

Dinner was simple stuff out of the garden and off the daily boat. It started with half-shell oysters, a sprinkle of minced country ham and cornmeal on top, browned for a few minutes in a very hot woodstove—three precise drops of Tabasco on top. And then a clear soup of little pink shrimp and yellow corn and the beautiful green-and-white geometry of sliced okra, beads of butter around the circumference of the small, white bowls. Then fish of some kind with a sauce, and vegetables, green and yellow and red. Probably just fresh fruit afterward. V lost interest in food if the talk around the table burned bright, and that evening it did. At least the talk across the table, since Jeff sat at the head and hardly spoke.

It reminded her of the past—decades deep when she was barely twenty—holding her own several nights a week against the smartest and wittiest and most powerful people in the country. Now, in exile with just this lanky boy at the table, tired from his endless lecture tour but doing his best to entertain—even though it meant dredging up every witty remark he had made since his college years—she felt like an old fire-horse hearing the jangling bell and surging forward against the traces.

Even before dessert and coffee, Jeff arose from his chair and gave a slight head-nod and retired without a word.

Wilde looked at V.

She smiled and said, You'll find that as you grow old, you stop bothering to hide the self you've been all along.

—I aspire to that every day.

—Let's schedule a conversation on the topic thirty years from now. I'd like to hear your thoughts.

Jeff abed, they moved to the porch rockers to enjoy the light of a three-quarter moon on the water, the Gulf a metallic silver-green sheen extending to the limits of sight in the thick air, and to continue the evening with Champagne and opiates.

Wilde said, I sometimes begin the day with Champagne. I'm somewhat less experienced with opium.

—It's a fascinating substance, V said. Doctors have been shoving it at me since I was thirteen for everything from monthly melancholy to childbirth. Also fatigue and excitement, sore throat, heartbreak, and boredom. They see it as the cure-all for excitable women. But I've learned the real key to opium is never allowing yourself to cross the line from amateur to professional. A bit tonight because it is pleasurable and because we're having a lovely evening is amateur. Taking it tomorrow because I'm sad you've gone borders on professional. And if you move to the professional category you give up the simple amateur pleasures, which I never want to do.

—I'll make a note of it.

—And remember, cheap laudanum is mostly grain spirits. Avoid it.

—That sounds like a professional judgment.

—No. It's discriminating. Taking whatever waste matter comes to hand because you can't do without it is professional.

Wilde said, I hoped he could offer advice on ways Ireland might free itself. He has been the greatest revolutionary of the past century.

—He was never a rebel. He was a businessman and a politician who believed the Constitution protected the capital of his class and culture above everything else. And he may have been right on the legal front, given that the federal government held him in prison for years under the charge of treason and then lacked confidence to try him. What a disaster if they had lost the case on Constitutional grounds. They would have won a disastrous war for nothing. All the dead and all the living with empty sleeves and eye sockets, all the widows. Half a generation wiped away. Still, a part of Jeff deflated when the government dropped the treason charge and set him free. He very much looked forward to a trial, the chance to argue his case. And if he lost, he welcomed climbing the stairway to the scaffold that would make him a martyr. All that was much more important than how his wife and children would survive, how we would go through life shadowed by his execution.

—You said capital?

—Yes. The most cold-blooded view is that the war was a violent argument over the forms it could take. One form was people. My husband argued that the slave economy was more humane than the child labor mills of Yankee capitalism. His argument was that with slavery, labor and capital were one and the same. The owner had a strong stake in the welfare of his workers because they were a great portion of his capital. Whereas the mill owner up north can work his people to death and it costs him nothing. Another boatload from Ireland or Italy will solve his problem.

—But the differences between gold and a person?

—His theory recognized none at all. And his ideas on war were equally abstract. He said, War is an affair of lines—a problem of geometry.

—Except pencil marks drawn on paper with a straightedge and a protractor don't bleed.

—Exactly, V said.

The driver returned and waited at a discreet distance. Eventually Wilde rose to go. He said, I'm not sure where I'm going next. Is it far to Colorado?

He was a young man still in his twenties—an age when most of us feel we know more than anyone else, an age of pronouncements. And he was better at it than anyone. Wilde stood awkwardly, his frame angled every which way. His soft cheeks caught the moon and mirrored its roundness, and his hair drooped in the humidity. He looked sad to be leaving.

V said, Try to find time to rest on your travels. The key to wandering around constantly speaking to the public is simple. Take naps.

He said, Dear, if you prescribe it, I will doze at the slightest opportunity.

—And take time to eat breakfast every day. Preferably including pork. A firm foundation for the day ahead. And on toward dinnertime, Champagne and opiates provide much assistance.

Wilde laughed and kissed her again and said, If we lived in the same city, imagine the trouble we might cause for others and for ourselves.

—Don't tempt me. I might pack up and move back to Marylebone.

The carriage driver fussed with the reins and Wilde wandered off into the night.

The next morning V asked Jeff why he had been so rude to their guest, and Jeff said, Because I did not like him.

Years later, reading the sad conclusion of Wilde's life—trial and imprisonment with hard labor, and death shortly after he served his term—V was sure had Jeff lived to see those events played out luridly in the papers he would have been genuinely shocked that such vectors of desire existed in the world and that he had been exposed to them even for the brief duration of a dinner. V was not so shocked. She fell into depression at each new report where that brilliant, exhausted young man she had instantly liked was shoved deeper into the dark.

One morning, halfway into writing a letter to Mary Chesnut, V remembered with fresh shock and loss that the postal service could no longer connect them. The first bit of the letter read,

> *It is a frightful thing to drop out of one's place in the world and never find it again. I try very hard to keep my memory green and thus by sympathy live anew, or if not anew, aright, which is more to the point, much more.*

After Jeff died, V wrote his memoir. Or at least completed it based on his fractional manuscript with the help of his pile of notes and old speeches and congressional records and memory. Every day she wanted to pack and leave Biloxi. She didn't inherit Beauvoir—Winnie did. But Winnie had no more interest in living in that little gem on the beach than V. What would either of them do there in a dead town, no matter how pretty the house and view?

V worked in the cottage Jeff had used as his study. All his books and papers were already there, and walking across the lawn to write every afternoon between lunch and supper created a separation, a time and place for work. She moved the writing table near one of the tall side windows looking toward the water, and the least Gulf breeze riffled through her pages. In June, when the afternoon thunderstorms became regular, she looked forward to them. The palmetto fronds rattling in the wind, the air suddenly fresh and cool, the entire Gulf disappearing behind a wall of rain streaking down at the rate of an inch in a half hour. And then the clouds breaking, light rising into a soft evening, clouds touched with yellow and rose and the water settling to a bronze mirror in the low angle of sun. And yet, awake in the middle of the night, she wrote in a letter,

> *The testimonies of my youth are hidden in death. I feel like an executed person swinging in chains on a lonely road.*

One night during that long job of writing, V woke with a clear thought immediately in her head, a belief that if there is an afterlife, the morning Jeff woke to the sunshine of the next world, he did not wonder how to fill his time waiting for V's arrival. He spruced up, tied a puffy silk cravat around his skinny neck, and went out searching for Knoxie.

When she finished Jeff's book, exhausted and depressed, she considered her work done, a debt paid in full. She packed her leaving trunks and walked away from another houseful of furniture and moved to New York City, mainly because she could not afford London or Paris. One of those first weeks in the city, she had heart attacks every day—or at least that's what her doctor told her. Newspapers all across the South ranted how traitorous she was. V back-talked, saying she was free, brown, and sixty-five and could live wherever she wanted. She bounced around residential hotels awhile and then found a pretty apartment near Longacre Square—West Forty-Fourth between Sixth and Seventh. What she wanted was a new life. Reconnection with people. Galleries and libraries and museums and theaters. The *New York World* had offered her work, and so she intended to write for part of her living.

She did, though, keep having to deal with her husband's remains—before, after, and long after he died. As with many things in those last years, Jeff was indifferent to where he would be buried. He asked V to deal with it. The tentative entombment took place in New Orleans, a big funeral. And then a year or two later V accepted the offer from Virginia, so they hauled him out and moved him to Richmond.

Jeff made a leisurely journey through the South, lying in state in various places along the way. As the train passed, church bells tolled, people threw flowers on the tracks. She attended the second funeral, another grand ceremony. The new grave looked over the river, and the dead children had been moved from their scattered graves to surround him there in Hollywood Cemetery.

Winnie died in 1898, and V considered her the last casualty of the Civil War because she had gone down to Atlanta to appear at a reunion of Confederate veterans and fell sick after being drenched during a parade. She joined V at Narragansett Pier where they had spent the summer. Winnie became worse day by day through August, and by mid-September she joined the others in Richmond and was buried with full military honors on the hill above the James River. For V nothing remained, and no new revelations concerning grief were delivered. She wanted to die but had learned long ago—all the way back to Samuel—great loss wasn't that simple. You couldn't just wish yourself out of it. You had to go through it all the way, had to let grief roll over you like Mississippi River floodwater until it decided to let you rise to the surface and keep going, more beaten and broken than before.

The next spring, when V reentered the world, she realized that though she'd never wanted to own Beauvoir, Winnie's death meant she had inherited it. When she went down to Mississippi to deal with the last of her things there, she couldn't even cry over Winnie's guitar and a baby doll. And then she remembered the doll was hollow and had been used for smuggling morphine. She moved the left arm just right and the secret compartment opened—empty. She wondered, though, when she might have found it necessary to smuggle morphine. Maybe it was during the war. Everything happened during the war. She kept almost nothing from the house and sold Beauvoir for much less than its value so that it could become an old soldiers home and so that she would never have to go there again.

===

A cool September afternoon—days already shorter and the lobby emptier after the end of the racing season. A man walks through the room turning switches, and large glowing filaments loop petal-shaped inside the clear bulbs. Three big checked logs glow red in the hearth.

Laura is leaving in two days and sits close by V on the settle. She's bundled to the chin in a blue-and-gold brocade wrap, and she says, I'm so anxious about going home that I start trembling every time I try to pack. But I'm sure I'll be back next year, because my mother has gotten interested in that thing they do back in the basement with the helmets. She thinks it might be the cure for me.

V says, Well, I'll be here next summer too—I'm already booked—and you will not be doing that thing with the helmets. You're an adult woman, and I will stand beside you when you say no. And if we have to, we'll pull out my little suicide pistol and shoot our way out of here.

Laura kisses her cheek and says, I'd be so scared of you if you were aimed in my direction.

—And you remember, V says, anytime this winter your mother causes trouble, you pack a bag and come to New York and stay with me as long as you want. I'll arrange for a piano in my apartment, and the city will give you energy. It has for me.

James says, Laura, maybe I'll see you there. You can play me your latest version of "Sunflower Slow Drag."

—I keep count of the times I play it. I think when I get to a thousand I'll have it.

—Where are you now? James asks.

—Seven hundred and three.

Laura stands and wanders out into the late afternoon, trailing her pretty wrap on the ground.

V turns to James and asks, When will you be coming to see me in New York?

—I certainly will come, but with the greater distance

and school having started for the year I won't make it so often.

—Goes without saying. But come at least once a month instead of once a week, yes? And we need to have a plan because if we don't, other things will get in the way. So two or three weeks after I'm settled in the new place—Hotel Majestic—I'll write and we will set a date. You'll like it—Central Park is the front lawn, and the view from my apartment is across the treetops. Carriage rides right from the door, and they've promised me unlimited use of the library for interviews with writers and meetings with visiting dignitaries.

—I wonder which category I fall into, James says, smiling.

—Both and neither. We'll have so much fun this winter on our days together—talking and going to museums and concerts and matinees. All of that. Bookstores, I have a half-dozen favorites I want to show you.

Then V hands James a book—Mary Chesnut's journals, finally in print.

—Read it and we'll talk in New York, she says. You'll see why I loved her. It's been chopped to pieces, abbreviated and smoothed out. There's no plot and her mind flits from thing to thing, but Mary shines through on every page—a true record of consciousness.

Seventh Sunday

New York City

October 1906

James Blake walks through Central Park until the Dakota's gables rise over the trees and the square towers of Hotel Majestic stand alongside. Leaves have turned colors, reds and yellows rich in the angled light before sunset. Hollow sounds of horses' hooves—almost pastoral. V moved to the Majestic partly because her previously near-worthless land in Louisiana and Mississippi had started producing more income, and partly because the din and glare from the new theaters on West Forty-Fourth drove her away. She'd complained that her bay window buzzed with light and sound into early morning.

———

It's true—that thing she said about biographies all ending the same.

She wrote James a note three weeks ago, inviting him to visit at the end of October. Said Maggie had offered to come from Colorado and help supervise her move, but V had answered that she was perfectly capable of handling things herself.

But then, according to the papers, V came down with a bad cold during the move, and within ten days pneumonia took her away. She died in her new apartment, and Maggie had made it from Colorado in time to be with her at the end.

Tonight a cortege will pass through the city to the Pennsylvania ferry, and then—feetfirst in a box—she will return to Richmond for a military funeral. James tries to find the word for the feeling he has—a *truncation, compression, concussion.* She was in and out of his life so fast. Again.

James sits on a bench, waiting to follow the cortege. He thumbs through Mary Chesnut's newly published journals. Torn scraps of newspaper mark passages related to V.

She wrote or said to Mary during the war—*I live in a kind of maze. Disaster follows disaster. How I wish my husband were a dry goods clerk. Then we could dine in peace on a mutton scrag and take an airing on Sunday in a little buggy with no back, drawn by a one-eyed horse at fifty cents an hour. This dreadful living day to day depresses me more than I can say.*

Then an incisive question—*Is it self-government or self-immolation that we are testing?*

Then a personal declaration—*I am not one of those whose righteousness makes their prayer available.*

And then at the end of the war—*My name is a heritage of woe.*

James has stayed the weekend with Julie's family in Harlem, and they've all gotten to the place in grieving for Julie where they can laugh and find joy in her life but still tear up telling stories about her. They remind James they will always want him in their family, and they hold a place for him in their business if he ever gets tired of teaching.

On the park bench, a string of words rises uncalled in his mind. The landscape architect of this big beautiful green rectangle once wrote that slavery was an economic mistake, or something to that effect. James opens his notebook and makes a note to self. *Olmsted's exact words? Was economic the only mistake he identified?* And then he writes, *Every beautiful thing in the country darkens to one degree or another by theft of lives.*

Then he jots a thought about V.

Her last years, she was in many ways a very modern woman—unanchored and unmoored, unconstrained by family, poverty, friends, or love of place. Making a major portion of her living from her own work and talent. So why such sense of crisis in her life near its end? Yearning for a reconciliation with the past—the country's and her own. Her need to shape memory into history.

After dark the cortege leaves from the Majestic, the casket draped in black, two white horses pulling. There was a small, private memorial service late in the afternoon, and everything has been scheduled according to when the ferry leaves Manhattan to connect with southbound trains in New Jersey. James follows through the streets to the station. General Frederick Grant—son of V's friend Julia and General Ulysses S.—leads a military escort of bluecoats and some old gray Confederate veterans living in the North. A brass band plays funeral dirges and "Battle Hymn of the Republic" and "Dixie," confusing people passing on the streets.

Afterward, James walks all the way back to Harlem,

and when he gets to the point where electric streetlights change to gas, it feels like traveling in time as much as space.

He fully intended to take the train back to Albany, but instead James buys a ticket on a limited to Washington, where he changes trains. As he boards for Richmond, a conductor tells him to go three cars back and look for a white sign with black letters saying COLORED.

—Nobody mentioned this when I bought my ticket.

—Virginia law, the conductor says.

—What happens if I take a seat in whatever car I want?

—The railroad company enforces the law. You don't sit where the law says and want to pitch a fit about it, they'll stop the train and leave you in the middle of no-where.

—I need to be in Richmond by tomorrow.

—Well, the conductor says, there's one way to make that happen.

Until Fredericksburg James sits in the colored car alone, feeling separate as usual. Then an old man in a brown suit boards and takes a seat as far from James as possible and opens a newspaper. James writes in his notebook, *What railcar would be specific enough?*

It's late when James reaches Richmond. He finds a

room in Jackson Ward. It's a town within a town, like you'd find in every city in America, whether north, south, east, or west. Black hotels, black stores, black theaters and restaurants and nightclubs, black banks. The hotel is a short walk from the Gray House, and not too far to the cemetery down by the river.

Next morning James stands on the cobbles where Joe died. He remembers the spot clearly but not much else. The house is a little familiar—also a sort of dreamlike recognition of the neighborhood, the slope of the hill, the streets and alleyways. Joe had been his double. Same age, same size. They'd worn the same clothes. Both the same except the final layer of skin—so not the same at all, even now. Forty years on, James survives and Joe doesn't, though James's life keeps circling back to its beginnings. He thinks of karma, Laura's mistaken definition of it—going round and round until you come to your senses and make yourself better and get to move on.

He remembers saying to V, Someday you'll be forgiven for all this, yes?

—No, she said.

James stands up the hill to watch the ceremony from a distance—green grass stretching downslope to the gravesite and the brown river. Clouds build to the west. A brass band honks and a preacher repeats platitudes from a dead culture. Toward the end, volleys of rifle fire pop and then echo from across the river. He believes she would have hated that noise while enjoying the attention.

The whole thing is sad. Funerals are supposed to be, but this is particularly sad. To see the circle of graves, all the dead children huddled around the statue of their father—a very ordinary statue, a lazy or unskillful effort by the sculptor. Jeff the president of an imaginary country stands with generic determination, facing a future that no longer exists.

James wonders if the preacher doing the talking is named Minnigerode. He remembers a story—V called it a moment in time, a cupped handful of the million clock ticks she never fully understood. A soft morning in May, early in the war. The tall windows of the Gray House open wide and the sheer curtains ghosting in the slight breeze. Jeff, all solemn, knelt on a cushion. And Minnigerode, the Episcopal rector of the most important church in town, sprinkled him in baptism, no more water than the tap of a damp blossom against his brow. Jeff had suddenly become religious after years of indifference as to whether he'd been baptized as an infant or not. At the end of the ceremony, the divine

Minnigerode said, I look upon you as God's chosen instrument.

James wonders if that endorsement more than fulfilled all Jeff wanted out of the ceremony, given that the most powerful and political families in town went to St. Paul's every Sunday. Or maybe all the Bible Jeff and the preacher needed was the one passage from Luke, the slave beaten with many stripes.

Maybe even that early in the war Jeff knew he was betting everything on a losing idea. And all it was was an idea—airy, theoretical, abstract—backed up by human souls equally airy. But somewhere down below all the thinking, the digging into the entrails of the Holy Constitution for prophecy and justification, very real human bodies suffered the pain of theory gone bad.

After the service ends and most people leave, James walks down the hill to the graves. V doesn't have her own marker, just a plaque on the side of Jeff's monument. Maggie, the only surviving Davis, chose a dreadful compliant-wife passage from the Bible to be V's last testament. James starts to write it in his notebook but stops after three words because it doesn't apply to the person he's known.

He wonders how it is possible to love someone and still want to throw down every remnant of the order they lived by. He thinks, I don't want to be a mirror too perfect in imaging flaws—gratitude and resentment, that's what I have.

Next morning on the train north, James reads a newspaper claiming that V's last words to Maggie were, *Don't you wear black. It is bad for your health, and will depress your husband.* But what he wants to remember and writes in his notebook is something she said to him one Sunday:

When the time is remote enough nobody amounts to much.

Acknowledgments

I 'd like to express my appreciation and thanks to Katherine Frazier, Kyle Crandell, and Annie Crandell for their patience, advice, support, and daily effort to maintain a clear space for me to work. Annie Crandell provided more kinds of astute and meticulous assistance, insight, and advice than I have room to enumerate. Also, my thanks to Betty Frazier and Dora Beal, both avid readers, for their encouragement over the years.

I wish to thank K. B. Carle for her insightful reading and perceptive comments.

My gratitude to Amanda Urban and Dan Halpern and everyone at Ecco.

Thanks to Kit Swaggert for many years of friendship and support and for the mandala of this book's world, drawn from the lid of Varina's inkpot. And to Chan Gordon for finding Varina's pen and inkpot and James Blake's blue book.

Varina is a novel. For those interested in the history behind the fiction, I would point first toward the following:

Cashin, Joan E. *First Lady of the Confederacy: Varina Davis's Civil War.* Cambridge, MA: Belknap/Harvard University Press, 2006.

Cooper, William J., Jr. *Jefferson Davis, American.* New York: Vintage, 2001.

Ross, Ishbel. *First Lady of the South: The Life of Mrs. Jefferson Davis.* New York: Harper, 1958.

Strode, Hudson. *Jefferson Davis, Private Letters.* New York: Harcourt, Brace & World, 1966.

Woodward, C. Vann. *Mary Chesnut's Civil War.* New Haven, CT: Yale University Press, 1981.

HARPER LUXE

THE NEW LUXURY IN READING

We hope you enjoyed reading
our new, comfortable print size and found it
an experience you would like to repeat.

Well – you're in luck!

HarperLuxe offers the finest in fiction and
nonfiction books in this same larger print size and
paperback format. Light and easy to read, HarperLuxe
paperbacks are for book lovers who want to see
what they are reading without the strain.

For a full listing of titles and
new releases to come, please visit our website:

www.HarperLuxe.com